"I WANT YOU TO REMEMBER WHO'S BEDDING YOU, MRS. STEELE."

His clipped words, an icy contrast to the warmth of his body touching hers, echoed against her ears like a blow to the head. He didn't want <u>her</u>; he only desired revenge. His hands might reduce her to liquid hunger, but that didn't make his actions any less an assault.

Rachel twisted away. "Don't touch me."

He raised one eyebrow. "A little late to play the innocent maid, don't you think?"

She clutched her robe closer to her chest. "That's not why I pulled back and you know it. I thought . . ." She shook her head. "Never mind. I made a mistake."

He stood and towered over her. "See that you don't make it again, or I might not be such a gentleman. Next time there'll be no stopping."

"There won't be a next time, Luke Hawkins. I'm leaving in the morning."

Praise for
Frontier Flame
by Susan Macias

Diamond Books by Susan Macias

FRONTIER FLAME
TENDER VICTORY

TENDER VICTORY

SUSAN MACIAS

DIAMOND BOOKS, NEW YORK

This book is a Diamond original edition, and has never been previously published.

TENDER VICTORY

A Diamond Book / published by arrangement with the author

PRINTING HISTORY
Diamond edition / February 1993

ISBN: 1-55773-862-9

Diamond Books are published by The Berkley Publishing Group, 200 Madison Avenue, New York, New York 10016. The name "DIAMOND" and its logo are trademarks belonging to Charter Communications, Inc.

PRINTED IN THE UNITED STATES OF AMERICA

10   9   8   7   6   5   4   3   2   1

To Tony, with warmest personal regards

TENDER VICTORY

Chapter One

Wyoming, 1883

He wanted a drink and he wanted a woman. He didn't much care which came first—as long as by morning the ghosts in his head had been banished and the ache in his loins had been relieved.

Luke Hawkins shifted on his horse and settled his worn felt hat more firmly on his head, then glared into the darkening afternoon. Heavy gray clouds, like mounds of unwashed wool, hung close to the horizon. There'd be no trip into town today, or anytime soon.

The last watering hole came into view. Luke dismounted, then untied the ax from its sheath behind the saddle. After chipping a good-sized hole in the ice, he stepped back and let the cattle drink their fill. Several of the cows were heavy and awkward with the calves that would be born, blizzard or not. He only hoped they'd hold off until he and his men were able to ride out and help.

He brushed the ice off the metal blade and retied the ax to his pack. There was nothing to do but wait. Luke settled back into the saddle, turned his horse in the direction of the barn, and gave the animal its head.

The storm was almost upon him. He could taste it in the wind, feel it in the cold that seeped through his lined greatcoat like water through a sieve. He sighed. There'd be no relief tonight. No friendly bottle to ease his mind . . . no friendly woman to ease his ache. And the hell of it was, he was almost too tired to care.

Most of his men were already back at the bunkhouse, settled in to wait out the storm. A dozen or so were in town, taking advantage of their last free days until calving was over. He could have had someone else ride out to check the watering holes, but that wasn't his way. This was his ranch and those were his cows. Still, with the temperature dropping as fast as the sun, he questioned his dedication.

By the time the big barn came into view, his body was stiff with cold. As the horse moved next to the door, Luke pried himself from the saddle and half fell to the ground. Wind howled around the building, pushing him against the door and causing his lungs to throb with each breath. His fingers wouldn't straighten; they curled tight, as though still holding on to the reins.

He clawed at the latch, but it was frozen shut. God, he hated the winter. Raising his fist, he pounded on the door. There was the sound of footsteps, then a familiar voice.

"Hold on to yer hat, Luke. I'm a-comin'."

The barn door swung open slowly. He stepped aside to let his horse go first, then staggered into the warm darkness.

"Dang fool. That's what you are." The old man closing the door spit tobacco into a corner of the barn to punctuate his sentence. Wisps of white hair drifted back and forth with each motion; the scalp showing through was tanned and looked as tough as leather. "You know better than to ride out alone in weather like this. You want to git yerself killed?"

Potter's words washed over him, but Luke ignored them. "See to Red," he said as he slowly untied the wide woolen scarf around his neck.

The barn was twice as long as it was wide. Hay was stored in the loft up above. Twenty stalls lined the walls. Four milk cows and several cow ponies shared the enclosure. To the left were the tack room and a small office; to the right, Potter's quarters. This was his domain. Luke might own the ranch, but Potter ruled the barn.

A small stove stood in the far corner. The heat of the animals kept the temperature comfortable, even in the worst weather. Already Luke could feel the tingling in his hands. The sensation would deepen to pain, but he welcomed it. He'd seen too many cowboys who had lost fingers and toes to the cold.

Potter unstrapped Red's saddle and bridle, then led him into the last stall. The old man's mutterings accompanied his every action. "Some people ain't got the sense the good Lord gave a turnip, but don't ask me about it. No, sir. I'm an old fool who knows when t' keep his mouth shut. Yup. That's me. Old Potter. I jes' work in the bark. I don't know nothin'. . . ."

Luke chuckled as he started to pull off his gloves. The laugh turned into a wince when he straightened his fingers. "You got any coffee going, Potter? I sure could use something hot right about now."

"I'll get it."

Luke spun at the sound of a child's voice. "What the hell?"

"Here."

A tin cup was being offered by a boy. He couldn't have been more than five or six. In the dimness of the barn, Luke couldn't see his features, but he had an impression of sandy hair and a slight build.

"Who are you?" he asked.

"Mark." The boy grinned engagingly.

"What're you doing in my barn?"

"My ma and me are running away."

As he spoke, Luke noticed the heavy wagon at the far end of the building. Two unfamiliar horses were tethered in the stalls next to Red's.

"What do you know about this, Potter?" he asked as he sipped the steaming liquid.

"Nothin'. Sarah done brought me this bundle of bones to mind while she talks with his ma." The old man's words were harsh, but the boy didn't seem to mind. He stepped closer, and Potter ruffled his hair. "He's been helpin' me mend the tack. Calving's bound to start soon, and you'll be needin' every able-bodied cowboy you got."

"And I'm helpin'." Mark's brown eyes grew wide. "I had me a pony back home. Blackie used to . . ."

Luke sat on the split-log bench by the door. As the boy chattered on, Luke wondered what had brought him to the ranch. Running away, Mark had said. That could mean anything. Sarah, his housekeeper, was forever taking in strays. He wondered who she was taking in now.

". . . over the creek. But Mama said it was fine with her." Mark finished his story with a look of triumph.

Luke blinked a couple of times, but he didn't have a clue to what the boy had been talking about. Nor did he care. Aching tiredness weighed him down. He wanted the boy to disappear, along with his runaway mother. Between the pregnant cows and the miserable weather, Luke didn't have the time or patience to deal with visitors. He leaned back against the barn wall and sipped his drink. "Well, good for you, son. I guess you've—"

Something cold and wet pushed against his hand. He glanced down, then sat up straight, sending his coffee spilling over his arm and leg. "Potter?" His voice was even, but ominously cold. Even the boy took two steps back.

"I, ah, see you've, ah, become acquainted with Dawg,

there.'' Potter pulled a dirty calico handkerchief out of his back pocket and wiped his face. ''He ain't no bother, Luke, and I didn't think you'd want me to leave him out in the cold to die.''

''Dawg?'' Luke continued to glare at the old man. ''This mutt is a sheepherding dog. Are you telling me you rescued it? Are you going to start raising sheep next?''

''No, Luke. You know I hate them smelly things, same as you. They ought to be outlawed. But I found Dawg by the stream. I think some nesters was tryin' to drown 'im.''

A whine accompanied the old man's speech. Luke looked back at the dog. It was a pup, really. Probably only about four months old, with a thick black and white coat. It seemed to know its fate was on the line, because the dog licked Luke's hand. When he snatched it away, the animal rested its head on his outstretched leg and gazed soulfully into his eyes. Luke turned away and saw both Potter and the boy staring at him with the same hopeful expression.

''That animal will start a stampede,'' Luke said grimly. ''You want to be responsible for that?''

Potter shifted his weight and tried to smile. ''He's just a pup.''

''Pup or no, he'll want to herd the cattle. Next thing you know—''

''You ain't gonna hurt Dawg, are you?'' The boy stared up at Luke, his eyes wide with disbelief.

Luke swore under his breath. He'd never objected to Sarah's willingness to offer hospitality before, but this was going to far. He took a deep breath and thought that he'd be willing to sell his soul for a bottle of whiskey and a soft feather bed. He wanted to be away from all this.

The barn was silent except for the sound of the cows chewing their cuds and the stirring of the horses. He didn't want any damn farmer's or shepherd's dog on his property. It looked like he wasn't getting a say in the matter.

He stood up quickly and downed the last drop of the coffee. "I don't want to see it or hear it. Do I make myself clear?"

Potter and Mark nodded. The boy dropped to his knees and hugged the dog. The animal wiggled and tried to lick his face. They rolled over and over on the hay-covered floor.

"Is his name really Dawg?" Luke asked.

Potter scratched his head. "Yup. Unless you can think of something better."

"Not a chance." Luke walked toward Red's stall. "I'm not getting involved with that mutt. And Potter?"

"Yeah?"

"I mean it. Keep Dawg out of my way."

Rachel Thompson Steele sat quietly at the large pine table. The varnished surface was pitted and burned, as though previous owners had served and then eaten their meals in a hurry.

Heat from the stove against the far wall swirled around the kitchen. Rachel raised her woolen skirt a few inches to trap the warmth against her frozen legs. Would the chill ever leave her? She watched Sarah move across the wooden floor and add fuel to the fire.

"This is the best stove I've ever had," Sarah said as she closed the door to the oven. "It bakes the bread so nice and even, it's fit for the governor himself."

Rachel smiled slightly and met the older woman's eyes. It had been over six years, but Luke's plump housekeeper hadn't changed all that much. Perhaps there was a bit more gray blended with the rich chestnut hair coiled neatly at the nape of her neck. Pale blue eyes still looked the world straight on; only a few new lines at the corners marked the passing of time. The smells in the kitchen—baking bread, simmering stew, and a hint of cinnamon—were as familiar as Sarah's ready smile.

"I made this yesterday and put extra away just in case I had some company." Sarah set a plate of shortbread on the table. "Go on, child. Unless you've grown up too much to still like my cooking?"

Rachel laughed softly. "Never. You always made the best sweets." She took a bite and let the buttery confection melt on her tongue. "I've missed your cakes and pies. I was never able to match them."

Sarah dismissed the praise with a shake of her head, but a light blush stole up her smooth cheeks. "Get on with you." She reached across the table and patted one of Rachel's hands. "Six years. Seems like only yesterday you and Luke and Matthew were stealing pies off my kitchen windowsill. And now you've got a fine boy of your own."

"He's just as wild as we ever were."

Sarah sat down and studied the younger woman intently for a moment. Rachel wondered if she'd changed that much. The last time they'd seen each other, she'd been barely seventeen. Now she was a mother . . . and a widow. Sarah hadn't said anything about Matthew's death, and Rachel didn't want to open old wounds. But she hadn't traveled hundreds of miles simply to drink a cup of tea. Surely her old friend had questions.

"Mama asked to be remembered," she offered, hoping to give Sarah an opening.

"I'm so pleased. How is she?"

"She's well. We've had several good years. Land prices are booming all through Kansas. There was talk of adding on a few more acres, but I decided against it. I, um . . ."

Rachel stared at her lap and folded the wool of her navy skirt into even pleats, then smoothed it flat. She'd been in the house for almost an hour. There were pasts to explain, sorrows to be shared, yet all of that faded into the shadows; she couldn't wait any longer. "Tell me about Luke."

Sarah used her cup to trace a random pattern on the pine table. "There isn't much to say. He's healthy as a horse. Works harder than any two men I know. Still quiet, but he's been known to howl at the moon from time to time."

That told her he had survived, but left out what she really wanted to know. "Did he marry?"

The older woman met her eyes. "No, Rachel. I've been keeping house for him ever since we came up here. Oh, there were a few ladies sniffing around him, if you know what I mean, but he never paid them any mind."

Rachel sipped her tea. Relief relaxed the fear that had knotted her stomach. For six years she'd been waiting to see Luke Hawkins again. Not a day had gone by without her remembering, hoping, dreaming, wishing. Every detail of what their life together might have been like was as deeply etched in her mind as the old scars on the kitchen table. And finally, the time for imagining was past. She'd been worried when he hadn't answered her letters. She had written only four, maybe they'd never arrived. She shook her head. Whatever had happened in the past was unimportant; they would be together now. Luke had never married. Perhaps he'd waited for her.

"Can I help?"

Luke glanced down at the child standing just outside the big gelding's stall. "What do you know about horses, boy?"

Mark puffed out his chest importantly. "My grandpa taught me to take care of my pony, Blackie. I can brush 'em and feed 'em, only I can't carry the hay yet."

The glow from the overhead lantern danced off his sandy

hair. His brown eyes were filled with an eagerness Luke couldn't ignore. "All right. Grab a brush. Just stay clear of his back hooves. We don't want you flying through the wall there. Your ma would be mighty angry with me."

Mark ran the bristles across the powerful flank of the gelding. "You're right. She's always tellin' me to stay outta trouble."

Luke groomed the horse's neck and back, then lifted each of its legs to check his mount's shoes. His little assistant brushed what he could reach. Red stood patiently, enduring the boy's short, uneven strokes, but snorted in irritation when Mark ducked under the horse's belly and began grooming the opposite side. Luke added an extra measure of oats to the feed trough.

"Are you a real cowboy?" Mark asked.

Luke nodded.

Mark pushed his hair out of his eyes. "We used to live on a farm. Once Grandpa took me on a train and showed me where the cattle came up from Texas. There was this one man. He had a black hat and coat and the biggest rifle I ever seen. Do you have a rifle? Mama don't shoot much, but Grandpa used to run people off with his gun."

Luke ushered the boy out of the stall and closed it behind him. He found himself liking the boy. "You always talk so much?" he asked.

Mark grinned. "Yup. Mama says her ears get tired just havin' me around."

Luke made a great show of tugging on the lobes of his ears. "I know what she means," he said with a straight face. "Mine are plumb tuckered out." He started buttoning up his coat. "Time to get back to the house, Mark. There's a storm coming. You don't want to get caught out here in the barn."

The child put the brushes away. "Can Dawg come with us?"

Before Luke could do more than frown, Potter had cleared his throat and moved next to the animal in question. "Dawg stays here with me, boy. He wouldn't cotton to bein' indoors 'n' all."

"Can't I stay and play with him for a little while?"

The refusal hovered on Luke's lips. It was getting late and cold. He didn't know where the kid was from, but nothing in his young life could have prepared him for the fury of a Wyoming storm. And the last thing Luke needed was some greenhorn mother whining about her child.

"I'll bring 'im back to the house in an hour or so, boss," Potter offered.

They made quite a picture—the old man with his arm draped around the boy's shoulders, Mark with his hand resting protectively on Dawg's head. If word got out that Luke was getting soft, every cowboy in the territory would come looking for a fast buck and a feather bed.

"You got food, Potter? Once the snow starts, you'll be inside here for about three days."

"Yup. Got me enough smoked beef and hot rocks to last a week. And Sarah brung me a new can of Arbuckles' this mornin'."

Luke shook his head. Beef, biscuits, and coffee? "Don't you want a couple of tins of vegetables? I think there's some tomatoes left."

"Nope. I'll be jes' fine."

Luke wrapped the scarf around his neck, then glanced at the boy. "It's not my place to give you permission to stay in the barn."

"Ma won't mind none," Mark promised.

Potter shrugged. "And I'll bring him back safe and sound."

"It's your hide, old man."

"I ain't scared of no woman."

Luke smiled. "That's not how Sarah tells it."

"He'll be all right with me, Luke. I'll see that he gets in safe and sound."

"Yippee!"

The child and dog tumbled together on the floor, a rolling mass of black and white fur and brown coveralls.

Luke turned toward the barn door. He was getting old and soft. There was no other explanation. When the spring thaw came, he'd have to ride himself hard day and night. He'd thought every trace of gentleness had been exorcised by six years of anger and bitterness. He'd been wrong.

For, the third time in as many minutes, Rachel glanced out the kitchen window. The path from the barn to the house was a well-worn trail of mud and ice between two banks of snow. Any second, Luke Hawkins would walk toward the kitchen. Her stomach twisted nervously at the prospect of seeing him again.

As though someone had read her mind, the barn door opened slowly. A tall man in a coat and hat pushed his way outside, then let the wind slam the door back in place. His breath came out in wispy clouds; his long stride was unhurried.

He was taller than she remembered, and broader. With a scarf around his neck and lower face, it was impossible to see his features, but her heart recognized him. A glow, brighter and warmer than that of a bonfire, began in the center of her chest and worked its way out.

"S-Sarah?"

"What is it, child? Oh, my." The older woman looked outside, then back at Rachel. "Sit tight. I better go tell Luke you're here."

"I . . ." She tried to stand, but her legs felt unsteady, unable to support her weight. "All right." Don't be nervous, she told herself. She was finally going to see Luke. Everything would be fine once they were together.

Luke hung his coat and hat on the hook by the door. After scraping his boots on the wood mat, he moved toward the kitchen. Sarah met him in the pantry.

"Luke, there's something I have to tell you."

"I already know about your latest stray," he teased. But she didn't respond. Her pale eyes were wide, and the corners of her mouth trembled with an emotion he couldn't quite define. Sarah Green had practically raised him single-handedly; he'd never seen her so upset.

"Sarah, are you ill?" he asked, reaching for her arm.

"No. I'm fine." But the hand that clutched his was as cold as the wind whistling through the walls. "You met Mark?"

"Yes. Why? What's wrong?"

"He's . . . It's his mother . . . You'll be surprised."

He started to move toward the kitchen. She held him back again. "Luke, give her a chance."

"Who?"

"Go see for yourself."

Luke stepped into the kitchen. To his left, a pot bubbled on the stove. The pine table stood in front of the window, as it always had. But there was something unreal about the picture.

In the back of his mind a warning sounded. He looked at the rocker in the corner of the room. Seated in the hand-carved chair he'd made himself three winters ago was a woman.

Part of him registered that her hair was still the color of corn silk. The white-blond curls were pinned back, leaving her face open to his gaze. He drank in the deep blue of her eyes, the hopeful expression that made him feel as if he'd been swept back in time. Her lips were still full and soft-looking. He wondered if they tasted the same.

But the most overwhelming sensation that came over him was a slow-building rage. He stood there trembling until a dark cloud of hatred, colder than ice, colder than death, had dulled his vision. He felt it shrivel his very soul.

Six years too late—six years after the fact—Rachel had decided to come find him.

Chapter Two

"What the hell are you doing here?"

The smile froze on Rachel's lips, then began to falter as his harsh words hovered in the air. The hope and promise of their meeting melted away, leaving her numb. Anger radiated out from the man in front of her. Slowly, stiffly, she pushed herself up from the seat. He stood only a few feet away, yet the distance seemed uncrossable.

"L-Luke?" One hand reached out toward him; the other clutched the collar of her dress.

"I asked you a question. What the hell are you doing here?"

She winced, but didn't step back. Maybe he didn't understand why she'd been forced to stay away. If he knew how she'd been waiting, hoping. "I came to see you. And Sarah." She glanced at the housekeeper and found comfort in the other woman's encouraging nod. "It's been a long time."

"Not long enough."

He continued to ignore her outstretched fingers and she was finally forced to clench them and lower her fist to her side. Gathering clouds lumbered in front of the sun. The fading light caused her to shiver.

Her mind screamed at her to run and hide from this silent stranger, but she remained in place. Her muscles grew numb

14

with shock. She leaned forward and stared into his face. Shaggy hair, as brown as freshly turned earth, tumbled onto his forehead and curled over the collar of his faded red flannel shirt. Thick eyebrows were drawn together forbiddingly. She worried the top button of her dress.

His features were much as she remembered, harsher perhaps, with hollows and grooves etched by the passing years. Yet he was a stranger. No humor or gentleness softened his expression, and his eyes—they frightened her the most. They were a dark shade of gray. Cold . . . empty . . . unwelcoming.

She dropped her gaze, unable to face his censure. His mouth straightened into a line, the deep brackets at either side a mute testament to his pain. A log crackled in the stove. The familiar sound gave her courage.

"Luke, I want to explain."

He cut her off with a quick shake of his head. "There's nothing you can say that I want to hear. As I recall, the last time *I* came calling, you and your husband were too busy to see me. Hospitality's a mite better up here, *Mrs.* Steele, so I won't ask you to leave tonight. But don't plan on an extended visit."

Rachel's breath caught in her throat. He couldn't mean that; he was their only hope. If he turned them out, they had nowhere else to go.

She didn't allow herself to consider that possibility. She'd traveled hundreds of miles to find sanctuary, but the promise of safety was nothing more substantial than the memories of the man she had once known.

"Luke Hawkins!" Sarah stepped forward and glared up at him. The housekeeper barely came to the middle of his chest, yet she faced him with all the fearlessness of a mother bear defending her cubs. "I won't have that kind of talk in this house. Rachel and her boy need a place to stay, and we're going to provide it. You hear me?''

Rachel saw Luke physically flinch, then felt the ice of his gaze on her. The unspoken accusation destroyed her last shred of hope. She swallowed, knowing the coldness she'd seen before had multiplied tenfold.

"A son?" His voice seemed to come from a long way off.

"Yes."

"Matthew's son?"

She had wronged Luke with her actions, but he couldn't make her betray her own child. Mark was innocent of any sins she might have committed. She loved her boy with all her heart, just as she'd come to love his father. Raising her chin, she answered calmly. "Yes. Mark is his son. My son."

"I see."

The reproach in his tone pricked against her skin. She tilted her chin up slightly and hid the trembling of her hands by tucking them into the fullness of her skirt. "You see nothing but what you want to see. I know this is unexpected. I even understand your anger. Rage at me all you want, but Mark's never done anything to hurt you."

Luke folded his arms across his chest. "You've become quite a fighter."

"Maybe I had to." Picking up her skirts, she marched out of the room.

Sarah stared after her, longing to run and comfort the girl. "Luke!"

He shifted his weight, then moved to the table. "Is my supper ready?"

Sarah glanced at him. He'd already seated himself and was patiently waiting for his meal. His face was carefully blank. To a stranger he'd have seemed calm and unaffected by his encounter with his past, but she knew better. The too stiff set of his back and the proud angle of his head spoke clearly of his pain. When he was a boy, she'd been able to comfort his hurts with an embrace and a few gentle words of encouragement. He was a man now, with a man's pride. He would brush off any such attempts at comfort as unwelcome and unnecessary.

She moved to the stove and began ladling the rich-smelling stew into a bowl. After removing the biscuits from the oven, she placed them on a plate and carried his meal to him. Part of her wanted to dump the steaming food onto his lap. He'd always been stubborn, but the years had made him hard and unforgiving. He'd rather raise a flock of sheep than admit he'd spent the last six years waiting for Rachel.

"Are you just going to stand there glaring at me or are you going to join me?" He asked the question between mouthfuls of food. Not even the slightest flicker of an eyelash hinted that anything had just happened.

Sarah sat down across from him and clutched her now cold cup of tea. "I won't have you turning her away."

"Why is she here? Shouldn't she be with her husband?"

"I don't know." Sarah glanced out the window and sighed as she recognized the coming storm. "She'll tell us in her own time."

"She's leaving as soon as it's safe."

"No. I won't allow it."

He never looked up from his meal. "It's my ranch, Sarah."

"Oh, and I'm just the housekeeper?" She didn't bother to keep the hurt out of her voice.

"No, of course not." He shifted uneasily on the chair, then looked up at her. There was a haunted emptiness in his eyes. "You don't know what you're asking me."

"I do. I know that six years ago you and me left the

Steele farm. Between us, we didn't have enough saved to keep body and soul together for more than a month or so. Rachel's father loaned us enough money to get by. Have you forgotten already?''

''No.'' He tore open one of the rolls and spread it with sweet butter. ''I paid him back, with interest. The debt's gone.''

She shook her head. ''The least you can do is to take in Paul's daughter and grandson for a few weeks.''

''Let it go, Sarah. She's leaving. I've made up my mind.''

She wanted to shout at his stubbornness, but saw the tremor in his hand as he took up the spoon. He'd no more made up his mind than he'd forgotten the past. Sarah stood up and walked around to Luke's side. Laying her hand on his shoulder, she said a prayer for them all.

Luke added the column of figures for the third time. Wind whistled around the house, finding its way up through the double layer of floorboards. He ignored the sound and the cold, much as he ignored the cramping in his wrist from an hour of continuous ciphering.

When the third tally matched the previous two, he leaned back in his chair and tossed down the pen. Maybe, just maybe, this would be the year he'd finally make it.

The lantern cast uneven shadows on the plain wood walls. Sarah had insisted on papering the other rooms in the large house, but this office was his. The stone fireplace in the corner and the wall of bookshelves were his only concessions to comfort, the hand-carved mahogany desk his only indulgence.

He rubbed his palm along the sleek, strong line of the flat desk top. The huge piece had been ordered from New York and had taken almost a year to arrive. The shipping alone had cost an even three dozen head of cattle, but it had been worth every cow. He pulled out one of the perfectly fitted drawers and removed a ledger. Brass fixtures gleamed from Sarah's polishing. This was the sort of desk a man would be proud to leave to his son. He'd earned every square inch of wood, forcing a living out of the harsh land.

The wind circled the house, howling as if in frustration when the foundation remained strong and unyielding. Luke pushed back his chair and moved to the window. Darkness and his own reflection stared back at him. He saw the silhouette of a tall man, a hard man as uncompromising as the storm itself. Snow swirled and danced, beating against the window, then falling silently onto the growing drifts.

Despite the blanket hiding the world from view, he knew every acre of his ranch. Each knoll, each stream, was as familiar as his office. After spending his first twenty-two years trapped as a virtual indentured servant, he couldn't seem to ride his own land often enough. No one told him where to go, what chores to do first. Never again would the fists of an angry drunken man pound at his flesh for not doing a task quickly enough.

He pushed away the memory and returned to his desk. The thick parchment resting on top contained the culmination of six years of planning and hard work. When he'd first arrived on the ranch, the house and outbuildings had been in good shape, but the herd had been wild, consisting mostly of scrawny mavericks. He'd branded those he found and started learning everything he could about cattle. Within a year he'd begun a breeding program and was saving for a blooded Hereford bull. The effort was finally paying off. If only . . .

If only the spring came early enough and he didn't lose too many calves. If only the price of beef stayed high. If only the next winter was mild. With a little luck and a lot of hard work, he would have made enough to see him through ten bad seasons. Then he could finally stop looking over his shoulder and feel secure. Although the land had been an inheritance, he'd put his mark on every blade of grass.

A muffled voice followed by uneven clicking caught his attention. Luke dropped the paper on the desk and walked to the open office door. His brows drew together as he watched the boy trying to guide that damn dog down the hall of the house. The animal danced around in excited circles, sniffing wildly at the walls and furniture.

"Shh," the child said and grabbed the dog's neck. "No one can know you're here, Dawg. Now, walk soft, like me." He demonstrated the proper stealth, but Dawg simply trotted alongside, his long nails scratching against the polished floor.

"Going somewhere?" Luke asked as he stepped in front of the twosome.

Mark raised his head; the light in his brown eyes flickered, then died. "M-my room." He puffed out his lips as if he were going to say more, then tucked his chin into his chest.

"I told you Dawg stays in the barn."

"Yes, sir."

"Did you forget?"

"No, sir."

Luke sighed and shifted his gaze to the puppy. Dawg had collapsed to the floor and was using one of his boots as a pillow. "Why'd you disobey me, son?"

Mark shrugged. "I wanted . . ." He looked up, his eyes wide and dark. "I thought Dawg could stay with me, just fer tonight I mean. He can't do any work, with the storm and all, and Potter's got all them other animals to keep him company. I don't got nothin'."

Without warning, Luke remembered being twelve years

old. He and Matthew had stood before Matthew's father much as Mark now stood before Luke. His friend had pleaded to be allowed to keep one of the barn kittens. John Steele had pulled the furry animal from his son's arms and had, with one swift motion, wrung its neck. "No boy of mine's going to keep a cat as a pet," he'd shouted, then cuffed his son on the side of the head.

Matthew had stood unmoving until his father returned to the house. Then he'd picked up the dead kitten and cradled it in his arms. Four years older and wiser, Luke had helped his friend bury the animal. Together the two boys had stood over the small grave. That was the last time he ever saw Matthew cry. It was the first time Luke vowed to kill John Steele.

The memory of that kitten was the only reason he hadn't told Potter to shoot the dog in the first place. The smelly mutt would no doubt get into trouble and start a stampede. He couldn't kill it, but there was no way he'd have it sleeping inside the house.

"Dawg stays in the barn," he said hoarsely.

Mark nodded and turned back toward the kitchen. He took two steps and stopped. "Am I gonna get a whippin'?"

The light from the lantern slanted across the hall. Luke saw echoes of Matthew and Rachel mingling in the boy's face. His nose was small and turned up, like his mother's, his eyes wide-set and dark, like his father's. A hint of John Steele lingered in the stiff set of the child's shoulders. The walking, breathing reminder of all Luke had suffered, all he had lost, exploded like a gunshot to the belly. He drew in a deep breath, knowing that his affliction would not allow the relief of a quick death; he'd go on for years bearing invisible but forever open wounds.

"No whipping," Luke said quietly. "Get on to your room. I'll take Dawg back to the barn."

The boy nodded and gave the animal a last pat. As he walked past, Luke ignored the tears trailing down the child's face. Only when he reached the kitchen did he risk turning back. As silent and unexpected as a ghost, Rachel appeared and bent down to comfort Mark. Her eyes, when they met Luke's, told him she'd heard the conversation, that she knew what he'd been thinking and why he'd spared the dog at all. When she opened her mouth to speak, he turned away. He didn't want or need her compassion. Luke whistled for the dog and walked into the kitchen.

Rachel held her son in her arms and let him cry. When the last sob had turned into a hiccup, she gathered him up and carried him into the bedroom.

The small room backed up on the kitchen; the heat from the cookstove radiated through the common wall.

"You're practically asleep on your feet, little man," she told him as she helped him out of his flannel shirt. Underneath, his long underwear was as threadbare as everything else they owned. She made a note of the most recent hole in the sleeve. More darning come morning.

As Mark settled in the bed, she smoothed the blanket under his chin and lowered the wick on the lantern.

"You all right?" she asked.

"Yes, Mama." Mark sniffed and rubbed his nose. "You mad at me?"

When he'd acted so strong and brave during their hurried journey from Kansas, Rachel had allowed herself to believe her boy was growing up. But now, in the darkness of night, with the tracks of his recent tears crisscrossing his smooth cheeks, she knew he was still very much a child.

"It was wrong to bring the dog into the house," she said finally.

"I know."

"You must promise to obey Luke and Sarah."

He nodded vigorously, causing sandy hair to flop into his eyes. She smoothed back the lock. "I'm not mad."

Mark smiled then. As always, the faint dimple appearing on his right cheek reminded her of Matthew. At first, the memory had angered her, but she'd since made peace with her past—except for Luke.

"Go to sleep," she murmured, leaning forward to kiss his forehead.

"Night."

He rolled onto his side and pulled the covers up around his ears. By the time she reached the door, the sound of his steady breathing filled the room.

"Is he asleep?"

Rachel saw Sarah standing in the doorway. "Yes. Just this minute."

The older woman tiptoed across the floor and gazed at the child. "It's been a long time since Luke let me tuck him in."

Rachel bit back a smile. "I can imagine." She followed her friend to the kitchen, but hesitated at the threshold. "Is he here?"

"He's back from the barn and has gone to his room. Sit down. I know you didn't get any supper."

"I'm not really hungry." She didn't want to mention that her lack of appetite had to do with the conversation she'd overheard earlier. After she'd fled from her initial meeting with Luke, she'd lingered in the hall and then had returned, intending to confront him. But his words had halted her as effectively as a stone wall. Even now they continued to echo over and over in her mind: "She's leaving. I've made up my mind. . . . She's leaving. . . ."

". . . with your stew?"

Rachel jumped. "What? I'm sorry, I was woolgathering."

Sarah planted her hands on her hips. "You're worse than Potter. I said for you to sit down at that table and eat what I put in front of you."

"Yes, ma'am." Rachel pulled out the chair she'd used earlier and collapsed onto the seat. It felt glorious to have someone else in charge for a change.

"Biscuits?" Sarah unwrapped a plate of perfectly baked rolls.

"Please." Rachel's stomach tightened at the thought of food and sent out a loud growl of anticipation.

Sarah placed a bowl on the table. "Hope this meets with your expectations."

Rachel dipped her spoon into the rich gravy. "I'm sure it's perfect, but I wouldn't care if it tasted like paste. I can't remember the last time someone else fixed me supper."

She smiled her thanks, but Sarah ducked her head in embarrassment. "Get on with you, child. I'm just being neighborly. We do things differently out here."

"I imagine everyone does things differently than John Steele."

Luke's housekeeper brushed crumbs off the stove, then poured a cup of coffee and sat down at the table. "Is he still scaring off would-be visitors?"

"Of course. I rarely saw a new face. He took Mark to Abilene once, but in the last few years I haven't been farther than Natty's general store."

Sarah's pale eyes softened with compassion, but Rachel didn't dare accept the silent comfort. If she gave in to the heaviness clawing at her heart, she might slip into a blackness from which there was no escape. She wasn't safe yet; there was still a long way to go.

"And now you've come all the way to Wyoming. Did you have trouble finding the ranch?"

Rachel chewed the last piece of beef and sipped her tea.

"No. I took the stage from Cheyenne and rented a wagon in Horse Creek. I didn't expect you to be so far from town. If the man at the livery stable hadn't warned me it was over three hours away, I might have turned back too soon." She was silent for a moment, listening to the sound of the wind rattling at the door. "How do you like it out here, Sarah?"

"I like it fine. The winters are hard and long, but we get by. Luke loves the land. Those first few months he worked so hard, I was afraid . . ."

The older woman's voice trailed off, and she glanced away. Rachel heard her sigh softly. They both knew the reason Luke had worked so hard—it had been for a bride who, instead of waiting, had married another.

Rachel questioned the wisdom of her visit. When she'd left Kansas a short time before, her only thought had been to get to Luke. It had never occurred to her that things wouldn't be right between them.

"I get lonely for a woman to talk to," Sarah said, breaking the silence. "But we get people passing through. And the neighbors are only a few miles away."

"It's very different from Kansas." Rachel smiled. "I didn't see a single bean field."

Sarah grimaced. "And you won't. I swear, John had a passion for his green beans. If I'd known I was expected to water and hoe and harvest those endless fields, I wouldn't have taken that job with him in the first place. Don't tell me he still plants them."

"Yes. Every year." Rachel frowned. "I won't miss that at all." There were many other things she wouldn't miss. It didn't matter if Luke turned her out; she wasn't going back. At least not while John Steele could still draw a breath. She shifted on her seat and changed the subject. "I was a little concerned you might not still be here, especially when I didn't get an answer to my letter. That's why I wrote to Luke instead of to you after that.''

"I never was much good at learning. Luke read me that first letter you sent, right after we arrived. I always meant to get him to write back for me, but there never seemed to be the time.''

"I thought maybe you'd gone and gotten married.''

A blush rose on Sarah's cheeks. Rachel was surprised when she stood quickly from the table and began adding wood to the stove. "What an idea! Who'd want an old woman like me?''

"Any man would be proud to have you for a wife. Are you telling me there isn't even one who has caught your eye?'' She raised one brow and smiled.

Sarah patted her chestnut hair and adjusted the waistband of her red calico apron. "I have no time for such nonsense. Married! Why, I never.''

"Seems to me you might be protesting just a little too much, Auntie.'' Rachel slipped back into the familiar form of address. The Steele farm adjoined her father's. John's housekeeper had been as much a part of Rachel's youth as Luke and Matthew. Sarah had arrived on the farm shortly after Matthew was born and had stayed until Luke took her with him to Wyoming.

Sarah shook her head. "You're just imagining things because you're tired. Now leave those dishes for me to clean up and get yourself off to bed. We may not have bean fields out here, but we still rise with the sun.''

Rachel stood and brushed her hands over her patched wool skirt. She was tired clear through to the bone, but that was no guarantee of sleep. She had spent too many nights waiting for the sound of a drunken step on the porch, too many nights wondering what would happen if her father-in-law didn't make it home—and what would happen if he did.

She walked over to her friend. "Thank you for everything."

Sarah opened her arms, and Rachel stepped into her embrace. Plump hands held her in place while a soothing murmur quieted her rapid pulse. The familiar scent of violet water and baking bread caused a burning sensation behind her eyes. If only she could stay like this forever—a comforted child with no memory of the past, no fear for the future.

The grandfather clock in the hall chimed the hour. Luke rolled over and pounded his pillow in frustration. It was two in the morning. He needed to be sleeping, not lying awake fighting off ghosts from his past.

Throwing back the covers, he rolled up into a sitting position and rubbed his eyes. The frigid night air pressed against him and stole the heat from his naked body. He welcomed the discomfort and sat shivering until the last trace of throbbing warmth had dissipated. Damn the blizzard that had kept him from finding comfort in town, and damn the woman who'd caused the ache in the first place.

Luke got up and tugged on his trousers. Pulling on a shirt, he stuffed his feet into moccasins and started down the hall. Since he couldn't sleep, he might as well get more paperwork done. With the calves ready to start dropping any day, he'd fall behind fast enough.

The sounds of the wind and the storm were as familiar as the creaking of the floorboards. He hesitated for a moment, like a wolf sniffing out his prey, then moved in the direction opposite to his office. A faint glow guided him toward the parlor.

He saw the lantern before he saw the woman. Set on the

low table in front of the horsehair sofa, it cast a pool of light that reached the window and the blanket-clad figure standing there. She stood beside the chiffonier, a motionless statue carved out of snow and ice. Long hair cascaded to her waist; it was the color of molten silver. If he stepped forward and gathered the curling locks into his hands, would they burn him? Would he then carry a physical scar to match those he held inside?

The slow rise and fall of her chest was the only indication that she was alive and not one of his many dreams. While daylight and hard work could banish her from his waking hours, nightfall signaled the unlocking of the door to his past. It didn't seem to matter that his passion had been replaced by rage and his love by hate; she haunted him as much this minute as she had the day he'd ridden north. He'd left behind a vow to return and had carried away her promise to wait. That promise had sustained him through the long lonely months of winter. In the end, it had turned out to be as worthless as fool's gold.

"I didn't mean to wake you."

The sound of her voice called him back to the present. He looked up and saw her watching him. Half her face was in shadow, half illuminated by the lantern. The early hour stole all color from her skin, leaving behind only shades of cream and gray. Eyes, dark and mysterious, probed his soul.

"I wasn't asleep."

"I'm sorry," she said softly.

"For my not sleeping?"

"No. Of course not." She glanced down, then gazed back at him. "For everything. For what happened between us. For hurting you."

She paused as if waiting for absolution. He had none to give. His own soul was already in hell; he'd welcome the company.

The gentle curve of her cheek caused his hands to clench into fists as he fought the urge to step closer and touch her. Would she disappear as she had so many times in his dreams, or would she be warm and alive and real?

She shivered under the force of his gaze and drew the blanket tighter around her shoulders. The bulky length of wool hid her body from view, but he remembered how she'd looked standing before him in the kitchen. Time had added fullness to her breasts and hips but had left her waist small and her face unlined.

Hunger long denied made his blood rise while resentment gnawed at his insides. The feelings churned until every muscle tensed in anticipation. One or the other would be satisfied.

"I-I shouldn't have come here," she murmured.

He took a step forward. "It's a little late to be having second thoughts."

She continued to watch him. Slowly, one measured footfall at a time, he approached her. When he was close enough to see the dark lashes framing her eyes, he stopped.

The wind died. The hiss of the lantern and the sound of their breathing filled the room. If he took her, he would be released from the past. He didn't give a damn whether she wanted him or not. It wasn't about love or caring anymore. It was about power and punishment and release.

When he was done, he'd return her to her husband. Matthew had always wanted everything to be perfect. Taking back a wife soiled by another man would stick in his craw. Give him a sleepless night or two. Let Matthew be the one to worry that another man had pleased his wife more or longer or better than he ever had. Let him wonder.

Luke reached up to touch her face. When she started to pull away, he knew she'd understood. But she stood trapped by the wall and chiffonier. There was no escape.

Her lips parted, and he waited for her to beg. She began to tremble, then raised her chin and stared him full in the face. His hand closed on her long hair, and he pulled her head back. The motion exposed her pale throat to his view.

"Go ahead, Rachel. Fight me."

"I don't have to. You'd never hurt me."

The conviction in her voice made him hesitate, but only for a second. "Then you're a fool as well as a liar."

"I never lied to you." In the half-light, her blue eyes darkened to black and flashed defiantly.

"The hell you didn't."

Moving his fingers against her hair, he felt the warm satiny strands slipping against his palm. The silver didn't burn; it tickled and enticed and smelled sweeter than a summer morning. He lifted a lock and rubbed it against his cheek. She bit her lip and closed her eyes. A groan started somewhere deep in his core, but he held it back. This wasn't about pleasure, it was about . . .

Placing his other hand on her chin, he drew her face closer to his. His thumb traced the full curve of her lower lip. She continued to tremble. He felt a moistness and pulled his hand away. Blood covered the pad of his thumb.

"What the hell?" He dug around in his trouser pocket and pulled out a ragged handkerchief, then pressed it to her mouth. When he pulled it away, a line of red stained the fabric.

She opened her eyes. A wave of horror washed over him. He released her hair as if it had suddenly become the molten silver he'd so feared.

"Rachel." Luke handed her the handkerchief, then stuffed his hands in his back pockets and turned away. His rage and desire were swept away by a flood of shame. All the years of swearing to himself he'd never use force to bully anyone, all the times he'd watched John Steele beat or kick those less powerful than he, Luke had vowed *he'd* never act like that. His promises meant nothing. The realization left a metallic taste on his tongue.

"I'm sorry," he said hoarsely.

She continued to blot her lip and check the cloth. Her silence was the worst accusation of all.

"I don't . . ." He raised his hand to touch her, but she flinched away from him. Swearing under his breath, he held both palms up in a gesture of surrender and backed away. When his calves bumped against the sofa, he slowly sat down. "I'm sorry."

She turned to face the window. The curtain had been tucked behind the chiffonier and he could see her reflection in the glass. The murky outline made her seem more ghostlike, rippling lines of light and dark mingling, separating, never quite forming a complete image.

"This has all been a mistake," she said. "I know you don't want me here. I'll leave first thing in the morning."

"No one's going anywhere. That snow isn't going to let up for about four days."

"I see." Relief and regret threaded together to form a sigh. "So I'm safe for the moment."

Safe? He questioned her choice of word. "What do you mean?"

She shrugged. He saw her shoulder's rise and fall and the faint reflection in the window. "If I can't get out, no one can get in. But eventually he'll come for me. No matter what it takes, he'll find me." She spoke with a certainty that sent a chill down his spine.

"Look. If you and Matthew had some sort of fight, I don't want to be in the middle."

She turned and stared at him. "Matthew? What are you talking about? I mean John."

"John Steele?"

She nodded.

Luke shook his head. "I don't understand. Why would John care if you left? Matthew's your husband."

She moved closer to the lantern. Her eyebrows drew together in confusion. "Didn't you get my letters? Matthew is dead."

Chapter
Three

"Dead?" Luke repeated the word as if he didn't quite understand its meaning. "He can't be." He glanced up at her. Shock erased any other emotion. "What happened?"

Rachel carefully lowered herself onto the far end of the sofa. After adjusting the blanket more firmly around her body, she drew in a shaky breath. "He caught a chill. It was right after Christmas. For a long time he seemed to be getting better, but . . ." She sighed, remembering the horror of finding her handsome young husband unconscious on the floor of their bedroom. "He took a turn for the worse. His fever was so high. It lasted for days. John wouldn't let me send for the doctor until it was too late."

"When did he die?"

"Three years ago."

"What?" He glared at her. In the dim room, his eyes were twin pools of anger and hurt. Once she had thought she could drown in his gaze and welcome the sensation, but now there was only the cold accusing stare of a dark stranger.

"Luke, I sent you letters, before and after Matthew died. You never wrote me back."

He glanced away. "I had nothing to say to you."

"I tried to explain why—"

"I wasn't interested in explanations." He cut her off. "I burned the letters without reading them."

Earlier, when he'd told her she wasn't welcome in his house, she'd felt sure nothing could make her feel worse. She'd been wrong. All this time she'd been deceiving herself with foolish dreams. Luke hadn't understood what she'd done; he hadn't forgiven her. He'd never even cared enough to read what she'd written to him.

He stood up and walked to the window. The proud set of his shoulders and head made her heart ache. She'd seen the same posture in her husband. For years she'd assumed that Luke had perfected the stance and that Matthew had learned it from him. But when her small boy faced his grandfather with that exact unyielding pose, she knew it had been the other way around.

How tangled together their lives were. John to Matthew to Mark—three generations of Steele men. And Luke. Separate from the line, yet influencing each of them.

It shouldn't have turned out this way, she thought. She, Luke, and Matthew should have stayed friends forever. Instead, her husband was dead and Luke was lost to her as well. And John had . . .

She shivered in the night air. Don't think about him now, she told herself. As long as the storm lasted, she'd be safe.

"So all these years I've been hating a ghost," he said.

"You don't hate Matthew."

"How would you know? I'm not the idealistic young man who used to court you on those long summer nights." She could see his anger reflected in the glass. "Working here has taught me to be hard. Your marriage taught me never to trust anyone. I learned both lessons well."

His hurt reached inside her, tearing at her heart, clawing at her soul. "Luke, please." She hesitated, searching for the right words.

"Go to bed."

Luke's command shattered the silence of the room. Her

heart wept for him. The urge to cross the floor and offer comfort was tempered by fear. She could still remember moments ago when his unholy desire had almost pushed him to take her in anger.

After rising from the sofa, she moved toward the door. "Why?"

His question halted her in her tracks. She sensed he spoke without turning toward her, and she did the same. "Why what?"

"Why did you marry Matthew? Was it the money? Were you afraid that a ranch in Wyoming wouldn't be enough to keep you in style?"

She clutched the door frame for support. "No, it wasn't the money. It was my father. He was dying and concerned about my mother and the farm." She drew in a deep breath. "John Steele agreed to take care of our land and split the profits with us—if I married Matthew."

"You were promised to *me*."

She blinked against the tears that formed behind her eyelids. "I waited for you as long as I could, but after six months with no word, I married him. I told you everything in the letters."

Luke turned to look at her. Her head was bowed; the long silvery hair hung like a curtain, hiding her face from view. "It's late," he said hoarsely. "Go to bed. We'll talk more in the morning."

"Yes. Good night." She walked down the hall and disappeared into the darkness.

Luke waited until he heard the bedroom door close; then he picked up the lantern and went into his office. After setting the light on the desk, he pulled out the top left drawer. There was a notch in the back. He pressed it, and a wooden panel sprang open, revealing a secret compartment.

Inside were the deed to the ranch and a small bundle of

letters. Rachel's letters. He set them on top of the desk and
studied the carefully addressed envelopes. There were four
in all. The oldest had arrived about a year after he left
Kansas. The second and third, he now knew, told of
Matthew's death. The most recent was about six months
old. Each was unopened. Each was singed at one corner.
The burned edges provided proof that he had indeed tried to
burn the messages.

Turning the small bundle over and over in his hands, he
sat in the chair. Should he read them now? Would these
slips of paper provide answers to the questions that had
haunted him for so long? He ran a finger along the seam of
the top envelope.

No.

He pushed them back into the secret compartment and
set the wooden panel in place. He didn't want to read her
lies. She'd made her decision and by God, she'd live with
the consequences.

"Golly, look at that snow. I betcha I couldn't even get all
the way to the barn without gettin' lost." Mark pressed his
nose against the kitchen window. His warm breath fogged a
ragged circle.

Rachel shook her head and tugged on her son's foot until
he turned in his chair. "I'm sure you're right. Now finish
your breakfast."

The boy ate another spoonful of oatmeal, then frowned.
"Who's gonna take care of Dawg? Maybe I should go and
make sure he's all right."

Sarah set a plate of cinnamon rolls on the table and
smoothed Mark's hair. "Don't you fret yourself about that
mangy animal. Potter lives in the barn and looks after the
horses and the milk cows. He's got enough food and coffee
to keep body and soul alive for at least a week. Last night

I made sure there was enough to keep your dog fed as well.''

Mark grinned his appreciation and reached for one of the gooey treats. Rachel swatted his hand. ''Don't even think about it until you've eaten all your oatmeal.''

''Yes, ma'am.'' He hunched over the bowl and began shoveling the porridge into his mouth.

Rachel shook her head and glanced up at Sarah. The older woman tried to smile, but the humor didn't reach her red-rimmed eyes. Luke had told his housekeeper about Matthew's death, and she was obviously still grieving.

''All done.'' Mark pushed the bowl away and looked at his mother.

''Go ahead. But only one.''

He picked up a roll and carried it over to the pantry. ''I'm gonna build me a fort in here today.''

''There's some canvas and wood planks on the bottom shelf,'' Sarah told him. ''Use what you'd like, child, but keep away from my jars of preserves.''

''Yes'm.'' He sent them both a grin over his shoulder, then ducked into the small room. The door banged shut behind him.

Sarah picked up the dirty dishes and carried them to the metal sink. ''That boy's got more energy than a colt on the first day of spring. Tires me out just to watch him.'' After pouring hot water from the stove into the sink, she added soap flakes and began to wash.

''Let me help.'' Rachel joined her. She took a clean plate, dried it with a cloth, and put it in the proper cupboard. ''I'm sorry I didn't tell you about Matthew.''

''How were you to know that Luke hadn't read your letters?'' She sighed. ''It's funny. All these years I've been imagining you with Matthew and wondering what your lives were like. I practically raised him, you know.''

"Yes."

The older woman continued as if telling the story would ease the hurt. "John Steele hired me six months after Matthew was born. The boy's mama wasn't long for this world. He was a good boy. Always wanting to fit in and make his daddy proud of him. I just can't believe he's been gone and I didn't know. I miss him so much."

Tears slipped down Sarah's cheeks, and Rachel felt her own eyes burn. "He missed you too. He wanted to write, but . . ."

"I know. His daddy wouldn't have liked it, and pleasing John was always important to Matthew."

"I tried to tell him that no matter what he did, John would never be satisfied, but he wouldn't believe me." Rachel closed her eyes against the memories. "Matthew never did any job fast enough or well enough to suit his father. John considered Matthew's opinions childish. His hard work went unappreciated."

"That old man is mean clear through to the bone," Sarah said. "I don't know how Matthew and Luke ever survived living with him."

Rachel took the last cup and dried it. "At least Luke isn't related to John."

"All the same, he had to live in that house for twenty-two years. There's something evil about John Steele."

Rachel held down the shudder that raced through her. "I know."

Sarah added wood to the stove, then brushed her hands across her apron. "Were you happy with Matthew? You know, after you were married?"

Happy as in carefree? Rachel wondered. Happy as in at peace? Happy as in safe? No, she hadn't been happy. She'd adjusted to what life had offered, but that wasn't what Sarah meant.

She looked at Luke's housekeeper. The news about Matthew had left Sarah pale. For the first time, Rachel realized her friend wasn't a young woman anymore. Her chestnut hair was streaked with gray. Lines fanned out beside her eyes and bracketed her trembling mouth. The plump womanly curves that she had carried so proudly now weighed her down.

"Matthew and I understood each other," Rachel said at last, trying to ignore the sound of footsteps moving closer to the kitchen.

"Did you grow to love him?"

Luke stood just outside the doorway. Rachel saw the hope in Sarah's face. She couldn't withhold the truth from her friend; she couldn't deny what Matthew had come to mean to her. Closing her eyes so she wouldn't have to see Luke's face, she spoke. "Yes, I loved him. He was the father of my child."

Only silence greeted her declaration. When she opened her eyes, Luke was gone.

Luke transferred his column of figures to the green ledger and tried to ignore the loud war whoops coming from the hall. Feet clattered on the polished wood. They sounded more like a herd of horses than the excited play of one five-year-old boy.

Mark galloped to the open doorway, then skidded to a halt and stuck his head inside the room. "Whatcha doin'?" he asked.

"Working."

The curt reply wasn't enough to discourage the child from entering. An oversized coat was tied around his neck like a cape, and an old cowboy hat rested behind his ears. "I'm playin' calvary. Chasing Injuns."

Luke frowned. "Do you mean cavalry?"

The boy nodded. "Tomorrow I'll be the Injuns. You got any feathers?"

"You'll have to ask Sarah about that."

"I will."

Mark leaned against a bookshelf and studied the titles, eyes narrowed in concentration. "Br . . . Br . . . Breading Cat-tle."

Luke bit back a chuckle. "That's '*Breeding* Cattle.'"

"What's breeding?"

"It's, ah . . ." Luke cleared his throat. "It's when big cows make little cows."

Mark looked skeptical. "How'd they do that?"

"Well, they . . . That is, the bull and the cow . . ." He exhaled and swore under his breath. "Maybe you should ask your mother."

Mark looked as if he meant to pursue the topic, then turned back to the bookshelf.

"Aren't you a little young to be reading?" Luke asked.

"I don't know. Grandpa didn't want me goin' to the town school, so Mama's been teaching me at home. I can say all my letters and count near to a hundred."

The boy's proud smile was so much like Matthew's that Luke felt a clenching in his gut. The pain of his best friend's betrayal fed the pain of his best friend's death; the ache grew until it was white-hot.

Mark shuffled across the floor and leaned his arms on the desk. Luke saw the pale skin of the child's elbows poking through the holes in his shirt and underwear. "You think Dawg's all right?"

"Dawg's fine. Come here, boy." Luke motioned for him to walk around the desk.

Mark moved slowly, eyeing him suspiciously as if he feared punishment. When he finally stood next to the chair, Luke looked at his clothes. Suspenders hung limp over a patched flannel shirt. The once blue fabric had faded with time and washings to a nondescript gray. Brown trousers, let out at least twice, stopped three inches short of worn boots.

"Who dressed you this morning?" he asked.

"No one. I did it myself." Mark tilted up his chin. "Why?"

"You're a disgrace. Just look at you. Don't you have anything that fits and isn't patched?"

The boy shrugged. "I dunno."

It didn't make sense, Luke thought. The Steele farm was the largest and most productive in the area. Even if they'd had several failed crops in a row, there was enough money to keep the family going for years. Concern gnawed at the edges of his mind, but he pushed it away. What Matthew's son wore wasn't his business. If Rachel wanted to dress him like a poorhouse waif, then let her.

Luke smiled stiffly and nodded at Mark. "You can go back to your game now. I've got work to do."

The boy didn't move. "Did you know my pa?" he asked finally.

Luke closed the ledger and set his pen in the stand. Turning in his chair, he faced Mark. The child meant no harm, he told himself. "Yes, I knew him."

"Really?" Mark's dark eyes lit up. He untied the coat from around his shoulders and let it fall to the floor, then inched closer to Luke. "I was still a baby when he died, and I don't 'member much. I heard—" He glanced toward the door and lowered his voice. "Mama and Sarah was talkin' about him this morning. Sarah was cryin'. Did she know my pa too?"

"Yes." He swallowed. "Sarah and I didn't know that your father had passed on. We were both sad when we found out."

"Me too." The boy stepped forward a few more inches.

Luke's knees were sprawled open. Mark moved in between his legs and put a hand on Luke's thigh.

There was a smudge of dirt on the child's right cheek, and icing from his cinnamon roll clung to his chin, but his smile was full of trust. Luke remembered Matthew as a small boy always asking to be held.

He reached down and pulled Mark up. The boy's hat fell as he shifted on Luke's leg and leaned against his chest.

The slight weight felt awkward at first. Luke held his arm stiffly, then slowly let it rest across the child's back. The scent of cinnamon and little boy clung to Mark's tattered clothes. Everything about him seemed small and helpless. Even his breathing seemed short, shallow. He was so damn trusting.

Luke closed his eyes and felt the hurt and anger ease away, leaving behind only regret and a god-awful lump in his throat.

"I don't 'member my pa much," Mark said again. His statement was an invitation and a plea.

"We grew up together. Matthew is . . . was four years younger than me. I remember . . ." Luke sighed. What one story could he tell? There were hundreds to choose from. "Your pa and I used to go to the creek and fish every summer. Your ma came with us more often than not."

Mark twisted around to stare at him. "You knew Mama, too?"

"Yes. She used to tag along and get into trouble all the time."

The boy shook his head. "Mama didn't catch fish, did she?"

"Sure. She once caught a four-pounder all by herself." Luke smiled as he remembered Rachel's elation. Her excited squeals had brought him and Matthew running to help. "She was so proud that she insisted on removing the hook herself. Only the fish wasn't quite dead yet and she ripped open her finger on the hook. I think she still has a scar to prove it.''

''Golly! Mama never fishes now. Grandpa don't like her to go any farther than the barn. Except to the bean field, o' course.'' He wrinkled his nose. ''Mama said that if we came to live with you, we wouldn't have to hoe beans ever again.'' He smiled. ''I'm sure glad we're here. Did you used to live in town?''

''No. I lived on the Steele farm.''

''What about your ma and pa? Did they live there too?''

Mark's innocent question brought back a familiar feeling of isolation. Damn it, Luke thought. He was almost thirty years old. So what if he had no family? He was a grown man. It didn't matter anymore. He'd found a place to belong the day he'd ridden onto this ranch. ''My mother used to work for John. She was the housekeeper. She died, and he kept me on.''

''What about your pa?''

''I never knew him.'' He grabbed the boy's waist and lifted him to the floor. ''I've got a lot of work to do, so go on and play somewhere else. You hear?''

Mark picked up his coat and hat and walked to the door. When he reached the hall, he stopped and turned back. His brown eyes were filled with sympathy. The expression was so like Matthew's that Luke wondered if he was being haunted.

''I was just a baby when my pa died,'' Mark said. ''But I 'member being sad for a long time. If you want to go fishin', I like to fish.''

Luke had to cough before speaking. ''I appreciate that, son. Now, go on.''

Mark hesitated a second, then quietly pulled the door shut behind him.

*   *   *

Rachel lifted the heavy black flatiron off the stove and
tested it on a small piece of damp cloth on the end of the
table. The material hissed slightly but didn't burn, so she
smoothed out the ruffle of the petticoat she was working on
and continued to iron.

"I can't thank you enough for helping," Sarah said as
she worked next to her. "I've been putting this off for
weeks now. I was running out of clean clothes."

"I'm enjoying myself. I can't remember the last time I
was able to chat with someone while I was ironing." The
two women smiled at each other.

"It does get lonely," Sarah said. "Once Luke was gone
so long I finally had Potter come up and sit in the kitchen
while I baked bread. That old man hates being away from
his animals, though. He fretted so much I had to let him go
back to the barn."

"I know what you mean. When the weather was fine I
sometimes had to go for weeks without seeing another face
except during mealtime. I used to save all the table linens
and special clothes for a rainy day. When Matthew stayed in
I'd work in front of the parlor window. He had made a grate
for over the fire so I could heat three irons at a time." She
smiled, remembering the quiet moments. "Mark would play
in the center of the room, and Matthew and I would talk
about the crops and who was marrying whom."

"Sounds like you still miss him."

Rachel glanced at her friend, but Sarah was busy ironing
a pale cotton blouse. "Sometimes I do. The marriage was
arranged, but I'd known Matthew all my life. It wasn't
difficult to live with him."

"I'm glad. I often wondered how it worked out for the
two of you. Matthew loved you from the time he was a

young boy, but you . . .'' She frowned. ''What I meant to say was that you and Luke were much more . . .''

''I know what you mean,'' Rachel said. ''Luke and I were in love.''

She spoke the words without any emotion, but that didn't stop the knot from forming in her chest. After six years it was easy to pretend she hadn't minded giving up her dreams. They'd continued to live in her heart, fed daily by the promise she'd one day find Luke.

Now she had, and he didn't want her anymore.

''I often wondered what would have happened if Luke hadn't inherited this ranch,'' she said.

''You would have married him,'' Sarah said.

''Probably.'' Rachel smiled with a casualness she didn't feel. ''Between my temper and his stubbornness, we would have made each other miserable within a year.''

She finished the petticoat and hung it over a chair. The next garment in the pile was a white shirt—a man's shirt. The cloth was still stiff and new. The broadness of the shoulders and the length of sleeve spoke the name of the owner as clearly as an announcement from the heavens. After flattening the collar, she picked up the iron and began to work.

The heat erased the wrinkles and softened the fabric. She closed her eyes for a moment and allowed herself to imagine that the lingering warmth had been caused by the man and not by the flatiron. Her fingers trailed past the placket and brushed against the iron.

''Ow.'' She jerked her hand away and opened her eyes.

''Are you all right?'' Sarah asked.

''Yes. I wasn't paying attention to what I was doing.'' Rachel stuck her fingers in her mouth and nursed the burn. ''I'll be fine.''

''This must belong to Mark.'' Sarah held up a small shirt and a pair of trousers. ''Do you want me to iron these?''

''No. I'll take care of them.'' Rachel reached out to grab the clothes away, but her friend had already started folding them.

Sarah smoothed out the pants and stared at the worn seams. Turning them over in her hands, she looked at the patches as well as a new hole in the seat. Rachel said a quick prayer that the shirt was in better shape, but God apparently had other things on his mind. The scrap of flannel was so thin that light shone through in uneven waves. One sleeve was made from a different fabric.

She waited for the other woman to say something, but Sarah simply folded the clothes and set them on the counter. ''As soon as the snow lets up, I'm going to ask Luke to slaughter a cow for us. I'm getting tired of smoked beef. I think I still have a couple of cans of tomatoes left. Do you remember how I used to bake them with a little . . .''

The words washed over her. Rachel continued with her task, breathing out a sigh of relief. No doubt Sarah had questions about the state of Mark's wardrobe, but she was too polite to ask them. What was there to say? The truth? That would only lead to more inquiries. First one, then another, until she was forced to reveal the reason she'd fled Kansas and John Steele.

''This is the last one,'' Sarah said, pressing a tablecloth. She motioned toward the pile of shirts. ''Would you mind taking those into Luke's room? They go in the armoire, third shelf on the right.''

Rachel nodded, picked up the stack, and walked down the hall. In the three days she'd been in the house, she'd managed to avoid exploring any more than she had to. There was no reason to become attached to the spacious well-designed home when she'd only have to leave it as soon as the storm was over. But by the process of elimination she knew which room was Luke's.

For the last three nights she'd lain awake and listened for the sound of his boots on the wooden floor. His room was two doors down from her own. Since their midnight meeting, they'd been polite, even cautious, in each other's presence. Not by a word or the flicker of a glance had they let on that anything had passed between them.

The sound of Mark playing one of his games came from the dining room. Earlier that morning Luke had disappeared into his office and hadn't been heard from since. Even so, she knocked softly on the bedroom door before entering.

Her heart pounded against her ribs as she stepped inside. Drapes were pulled back from the window and revealed the white world beyond. Snow fell from heavy gray clouds; wind pushed the flakes into tall drifts that rose halfway up the house. But the fury of the storm had been spent. By morning the sun would shine; within a week the roads would be passable. She'd take her rented wagon, return to Horse Creek or Cheyenne, and find a job.

Turning away from the window, Rachel allowed her gaze to move around the room. The ceiling sloped at one end. A four-poster bed took up more than half the floor. An armoire stood opposite, and a low dresser nestled under the eaves.

Tears burned in her eyes as she stepped closer to the bed. A thick quilt hung almost to the floor. The familiar patterns matched the faded circles and lines on the one that had covered her bed back in Kansas. It was Sarah's handiwork, the housekeeper's favorite pattern.

She remembered a winter's day, much like this one, seven years before. She and Luke had cuddled together in the hayloft, their closeness generating enough heat to defy the storm that raged around them.

"I want Sarah to make our quilt," she'd said. "In pink and rose and trimmed with lace."

Luke had scoffed. "Lace? No, Rachel. It'll be blue."

"But I like pink."

"But I'm going to be sleeping in the bed, too."

Her eyes had met his, then skittered away, like a shy colt. His reminder that they would share a bed when they were finally man and wife had sent a shiver of anticipation coursing through her. When he'd turned toward her and pressed his lips to hers, she'd met him with an urgency that left them both breathless and ready and wanting.

After setting the pile of shirts down on the dresser, Rachel walked over to the bed. The blue and white pattern was edged in pink ribbon and trimmed with lace—the perfect compromise. She knelt on the floor and clutched the quilt in her hands.

He'd had the quilt made for her, for both of them. And when he'd returned to claim her as his bride, she'd refused to meet with him, refused to offer a single word of explanation. She'd vowed to love him forever, and had married his best friend instead.

Sarah picked up Mark's clothes and carried them to the boy's room. After putting them in the drawer next to his other things, she started to stand up. But the memory of the worn shirt and trousers made her glance over her shoulder, then pick up another item.

She carefully looked at all the other garments. Each one was as worn as the first. What had happened, she wondered, that Rachel would let her son go around dressed like this? Even as a little girl, Rachel had liked to dress in pretty things. She didn't mind getting dirty playing with Luke and Matthew, but she always knew how to look like a lady.

Sarah rose slowly and moved back toward the kitchen. She remembered noticing Rachel's clothes when she had arrived. Her coat had been old and ill fitting. The lining had worn away, leaving only the outer layer of wool to keep out the wind. At the time, she had thought it was just an old coat that Rachel wore when traveling, but now she wasn't so sure. Even her day dresses were patched and out of style.

Sarah stopped in the middle of the hall. If Matthew had been dead for three years, why had Rachel waited so long to visit? There was a hunted look in the girl's eyes, a cold expression of fear that never quite left her. What had caused her to leave the town she'd grown up in and race hundreds of miles to a place she didn't know?

A slight sound caught her attention. Sarah tiptoed down to Luke's room and glanced inside. Rachel was kneeling on the floor beside the bed; tears trickled down her cheeks. She held a corner of the quilt in one hand.

Sarah had made that covering square by square the first winter she and Luke were in Wyoming. He'd picked out the colors and the fabric. It was to have been a wedding gift for his bride. When he returned from Kansas alone, she tried to put the present away. But he insisted on using it every day. She often wondered if it was a reminder of what he'd had or what he'd lost.

Matthew and Luke had been like brothers. Both had loved Rachel, but she'd had eyes only for Luke. John had sworn his only son wouldn't be denied what he wanted, but Sarah hadn't paid attention to him at the time and neither had Luke. Maybe they'd been wrong to ignore him. Maybe if Luke had stayed in Kansas instead of traveling all this way to claim the ranch, Rachel would have married him instead of Matthew.

Shaking her head, Sarah backed slowly out of the room

and walked to Luke's office. After knocking on the door, she entered and sat across from his desk.

"You've been here all day. Don't you want something to eat?"

He glanced up and smiled. "No. I can wait until supper. Are we having stew again?"

"Yes. What else? With this snow, I can't get to the smokehouse or the chicken coop."

One lock of brown hair fell across his forehead. The rest hung down onto his collar. Green-flecked gray eyes met hers; the crinkling at the corners only added to his charm. He was a good-looking boy who had grown into a handsome man.

She felt a rush of pride. He was her son. That she hadn't delivered him from her body was unimportant. From the first day she'd arrived on John Steele's farm, she and Luke had belonged to each other. She'd tended him in sickness, cooked for him, sewed his clothes. That first winter, after they came north with only a few dollars and a trunkful of dreams, she'd knelt beside him and joined in the prayers that the cattle would survive the snow. When the last speck of his gentleness had been worn away by land and time, she'd continued to love him and worry about him.

"You need a haircut," she said at last.

"Fine. You busy right now?"

"No. Let me get my shears."

Luke walked into the kitchen and pulled one of the chairs into the middle of the room. He sat down and folded his arms over his chest.

Mark slid in from the hall and stopped in front of the stove. "Whatcha doin'?"

"Sarah's going to cut my hair."

"Can I watch?"

"Of course you can watch," Sarah said as she walked in carrying the scissors and a flour-sack towel. She wrapped the cloth around Luke's neck, then pulled a comb out of her pocket. "In fact, I'll cut your hair next."

Mark tucked his hands behind his back and shook his head. "I don't need a haircut, Sarah."

Luke spread his legs out in front of the chair. "You're not scared, are you?"

"Me? Naw. I just don't want Mama gettin' upset with me or anything."

Sarah tilted Luke's head forward and began to cut. "I sure like having your ma here, Mark. She's been a big help with the chores, and so have you."

The boy puffed up his chest and grinned. "I have chores at home, too." He sank to the floor at Luke's feet and compared the size of their boots. "Am I gonna get big like you?"

"Could be. But growing up means doing things you don't want to do."

"Like lettin' Sarah cut my hair?"

Luke grinned. "Yup."

Mark considered the advice, then sighed. "I guess it would be all right, just this once."

Sarah combed the right side of Luke's hair and gave Mark a pat on the shoulder. "After I'm done, I'm going to make a pie. You want to help with the crust? We can make tarts from the extra dough."

"Sure."

The woman and the boy continued to chatter. Luke closed his eyes and half listened to their talk. Something Sarah had said echoed in his mind, something about having help with the chores.

He'd never thought about Sarah wanting anything of her

own. Whatever he had, he shared with her. But was it enough? He remembered all the laughter he'd heard between Rachel and Sarah these last few days. When he'd inherited the ranch, he'd just assumed Sarah would come with him. It had never occurred to him that she might not want to.

She moved in front of him and combed his hair over his forehead. Opening his eyes slightly, he studied her from under his lashes. She was short and plump, with pleasing womanly curves. Despite the gray woven through her rich chestnut hair, she wasn't that old. He did some quick figuring. If she was fifteen when she went to work for John Steele and Luke was three, then today she was about forty. Her quick smile and ready wit had charmed many of their neighbors, and she was a skilled cook and housekeeper. That combination, he realized, would make her quite a catch for a lonely rancher.

She untied the towel and brushed the hair off his neck. "All done," she said. "Next."

Mark bounced to his feet and braced his shoulders. "I ain't scared."

"Good for you."

Luke stood watching Sarah work on the boy's hair. Her hands moved swiftly, exhibiting love and skill in equal measure. After several minutes she stopped working and looked at him. "What are you staring at?"

He drew his brows together. "You. I'd forgotten how pretty you are."

A blush crept up her cheeks. "What brought that on? Now get back to work, Luke Hawkins. I have a mind to order some new wallpaper for the parlor, so go figure how much money I can spend."

He left without commenting. If Sarah wanted to make a life of her own, he wouldn't stand in her way. She'd never come out and tell him she was lonely, so he'd have to keep an eye on her and find out for himself. For twenty-five years she'd been his whole family, but it looked as if it might be time to let her go.

Chapter Four

Luke shut the back door behind him and plowed his way through the drifts of snow. The pre-dawn sky was clear. The stars were just beginning to fade into the light of morning as he reached the barn. An arc of cleared ground showed that Potter was already up and at work.

"Been wonderin' if you was fixin' to spend the whole day lazin' about in bed." Potter's statement was accompanied by a snort of laughter.

Luke stepped inside the building and shook his head. "Don't push me, old man. I came to tell you that Sarah's making your favorite pancakes and you should get your mangy old hide up to the house."

Potter licked his lips in appreciation. "That woman always knows the way to take care of a man. If I weren't so set in my ways, I might jes' give a thought to marryin' her."

Luke walked to Red's stall and greeted his horse. "Whoa, boy. Ready to go out?" He stroked the animal's nose. "Been cooped up in here long enough, haven't you?"

After leading him out of the stall, Luke tied the horse to the wall and began to saddle him.

"Storm didn't last as long as I thought," Potter said. "But it's been near a week since you last rode out. You gonna go check for calves?"

"Yeah. I hope there aren't too many. It's still early in the year, but there's nothing like a good blizzard to get the mothers to start dropping. After you eat, you'd better get prepared for a couple of sickly calves.''

The old man stuck a wad of tobacco in his mouth and grinned. ''Already done. Me and Dawg's been makin' quick work of our chores.''

At the mention of his name, the gangly puppy stood up from his bed in the corner and ambled over to the men. Luke ignored the animal, but Potter leaned down to scratch his ears.

After cinching the saddle, Luke led Red outside, then mounted the horse. He shifted his weight and pulled on his gloves. ''We'll have the first calves back here around noon. Tell Sarah I don't know if I'll be back for dinner or not. She wants a cow slaughtered. Have one of the boys in the bunkhouse see to it.'' He kneed Red and they started moving off. About twenty yards away, he reined him in and looked back. ''And keep that damned dog out of the house.''

Three hours later, Luke knelt beside the cold, still body in the snow. Nearby, the anxious mother blew air and snuffled over her young, but it was too late. This was one baby that would never again hear the maternal sounds of concern.

''That one too?''

Luke looked up at his foreman and nodded. ''It's been dead at least a day. How many is that so far?''

Jake Evans tightened the scarf around his neck and shook his head. ''Five. Not too bad.''

''It's early in the day yet. Send a crew to the east eighty. Times like this they tend to crowd down by the stream.''

''Right away, boss. You want to keep checking around here?''

''Yes.''

"Be right back."

Jake strolled over to a handful of cowboys still sitting on their horses. He was a tall man, barely thirty, with long dark hair and the permanent tan of someone who'd spent his life in the saddle. The pleasant set of his features made him popular with the ladies, though he hadn't yet settled on just one.

The two men had met in Cheyenne. Some con artists had mistaken Luke for a patsy and had tried to cheat him at cards. When that didn't work, they ambushed him behind the saloon. Jake happened to be passing by and joined in the fray. After finding out they fought well together, the two men shared a drink and supper. Later, over a couple of cigars, Luke discovered that Jake had spent ten years herding cattle north from Texas. He was tired of being on the move and was looking for a permanent place. Within the month, the tall Texan had signed on as a foreman of the Flying H Ranch.

"Olsen says there's a few dozen cows about two miles west," Jake said as he walked back. "You want to take a look?"

Luke nodded and swung onto his horse. "If we don't have another snowstorm, we've got a chance at a good year."

"If we don't have another snowstorm, I'm gonna take a couple days off and go into town."

The foreman's edge of frustration made Luke smile. "Nights getting a little long, Jake?"

"Hell, they're getting unbearable. Long, lonely, cold— you name it. Do you know how long it's been since I had a woman?"

Luke thought of his own wants and desires. "Yeah, I know."

"Heard tell you had a little lady visiting up at the house."

He wondered how long it would take his friend to mention Rachel. There weren't any secrets on the ranch. "She's just someone Sarah and I used to know."

"She here for a long visit?"

His foreman's voice sounded merely curious, but Luke glared at him. "Hands off, Evans. Rachel Steele isn't one of your saloon girls in town. She's a widow and a lady."

"Sorry, boss. Didn't mean to intrude on your territory." Jake's apologetic smile was two parts sincere, one part amused.

"She's not my territory. I'm just looking out for a guest. Nothing else. You got that?"

"Yeah, got that. Just tell me one thing?"

"What?"

"Who are you trying to convince, me or you?"

Rachel watched Luke lower the calf from his saddle into Potter's waiting arms. Mark stood to one side, dancing impatiently from foot to foot. Dawg's excited barks added to the confusion and caused the calf to struggle in terror.

"Luke's back," she said, smoothing the curtain into place and turning to smile at Sarah. "And he looks hungry."

"Finding calves is hard work." Sarah dropped several thick steaks into the frying pan and peeked into the oven to check the biscuits. "Go ahead and pour the coffee, will you?"

Rachel had barely finished adding a spoonful of sugar to the mug when Luke burst through the back door.

"By God, it's cold enough to freeze the . . ." He looked up and smiled sheepishly. "Afternoon, ladies. Is that my dinner you're cooking, because I could eat a whole side of beef.''

"It'll be ready in a minute, so wash up and grab a seat.'' Sarah picked up a towel and pulled the pan of biscuits out of the oven. After putting half a dozen on a plate, she draped a shawl around her shoulders. "I'll take this to Potter and bring Mark inside. Rachel, watch the steaks for me. I think they're about ready to turn.''

Rachel held open the back door, then returned to the stove. Luke had removed his flannel shirt and pulled up the sleeves of his undershirt. The basin of warm water was next to the soap. He scrubbed his face and hands with an economy of movement.

Rachel tried not to stare as he washed, then rinsed, but there was something so intimate about the moment. He smelled of leather and hard work and man. The fragrance of his skin was different than she remembered, stronger, more enticing. The flutter in her stomach became a stampede when he looked up and caught her watching him.

He picked up the towel and wiped the moisture from his face and neck. There'd been no time for a shave that morning. Stubble darkened his chin and jaw and accentuated the hollows of his cheeks. The firm set of his lips and the steady gaze of his eyes told her nothing, except maybe that she was a fool for still wanting him.

"I think you'd better see to the meat.''

"What? Oh!'' She spun back to the stove and flipped the steaks. After completing that task, she made a great show of checking the baked beans and corn. When there was nothing else to occupy her, she allowed herself to glance at him once more.

Luke had already slipped on his shirt and buttoned the front. The sight of those long, lean fingers adjusting the cuffs reminded her of all the other tasks at which he excelled. There'd been the time she'd gotten a splinter in her leg from playing in the barn. He'd removed the sliver of wood so easily that she hadn't had time to cry. And there was the spring morning she'd found a baby bird. He'd quieted the creature, then put it back in its nest. Then there were the nights his hands had played tender, tickling games across her body, teasing them both to the top of the precipice without letting either of them take the last plunge over the edge.

She looked at him now. He was older . . . a stranger really. Once warm eyes had cooled, transforming the windows to his emotions into barriers. Even his smile seemed empty and distant. They were to have spent a lifetime together; instead, they'd never shared a single day.

She sighed and stirred the vegetables. As soon as the snow melted, she'd be gone. No doubt he'd be relieved to see the last of her and Mark. The boy reminded him of all he had lost, of all that had been stolen from him.

"Do you know—"

"Sarah was telling me—"

They spoke at the same time.

"Sorry," she murmured. "Go ahead."

Luke sipped his coffee and walked to the table. "Sarah was mentioning that she enjoyed having you here. I appreciate all you've done to help."

"You don't have to thank me. I *like* Sarah. Besides, it's the least I could do after showing up unannounced."

He pulled out a chair and sat down. "Do you think . . ." He looked up at her and then away. Rachel tried to read the expression on his face, but the mask was firmly in place. "Does Sarah seem happy to you?"

"What do you mean?"

Luke shrugged. "She's been working as somebody's housekeeper her whole life. I was just wondering if maybe there was something else she'd rather be doing. I worry that all this"—he motioned to the room—"is too much for her."

Rachel set down her spoon and wiped her hands on her apron. "Sarah loves it here. She told me so herself."

"I'm starved." Mark flew into the room and made a beeline for his mother. From head to foot he was covered with coats and scarves. The only visible part of him was his eyes. "When do we eat?"

Rachel laughed. "After you wash, little man. Is that really you under all these layers or has Sarah brought in someone else's child?"

"It's me." He unwound the length of wool from around his face and grinned. "See?"

Sarah came in behind him and hung up her shawl. For the next several minutes confusion reigned. By the time everyone was seated and the meal served, Rachel had almost forgotten to be nervous around Luke. The relaxed atmosphere lasted until she sat across from him at the narrow table and accidentally brushed against his knee. She jumped in her seat, but didn't dare glance up.

"Potter's helpin' me teach Dawg to sit and lay down," Mark announced. "This afternoon I'm gonna feed the calf Luke brung in."

"Brought," Sarah and Rachel said in unison. She looked up at the housekeeper and smiled.

"Are there gonna be more calves?" he asked.

"Probably." Luke cut into his steak. "Looks like most of the herd is going to hold off for a week or so before giving birth, so we may be in for a good year."

"How many are lost so far?" Sarah asked.

"About six. A couple of the boys have ridden to the east eighty. I'll hear back from them tonight."

"Mama, what's 'breeding'?"

Rachel turned to look at her son, but out of the corner of her eye she saw Luke start to choke on his meal. "Are you all right?" she asked.

He coughed and nodded weakly. "F-fine."

"Why do you want to know?" She directed her question to Mark.

He wrinkled his nose. "I saw me a book in Luke's office. I asked him what it was, but he said I should ask you."

Sarah covered her mouth with her napkin, but Rachel saw the humor dancing in her eyes. Luke wouldn't even meet her gaze.

She poured more coffee into her cup. "Do you remember when we watched the two dogs mating last year?"

Mark thought for a moment. "Yeah."

"That's breeding."

"Oh." He took a forkful of beans and chewed thoughtfully for a moment. "But aren't bulls awful big? I mean how do they get on top of each other?"

Sarah rose quickly with a muffled burst of laughter. Rachel felt her own lips twitch in amusement. Luke stared at his plate as if its contents were the most fascinating discovery since the steam engine. Only Mark continued to wait for her answer.

"I've never observed it personally," she said at last. "But they seem to work it out."

The boy shrugged and went on with his meal. Sarah walked back to the table and held out a pot. "More beans anyone?"

After the plates had been cleared and Mark had returned to the barn, Rachel started pumping water into the sink. Sarah poured the last of the coffee into Luke's cup.

"Are you going back out?" she asked.

"Yes. About twenty cows are missing. I have a good

idea where they went to during the storm, but I want to check to make sure they have water.''

''Did you happen to speak with any of our neighbors?''

Sarah asked the question casually, but something in her tone caused Rachel to glance over her shoulder. The other woman was carefully scrubbing the pine table.

''No. I sent boys to speak with both Ian and Henri to find out if any of our cows are over there. Did you have a message you wanted me to send?''

A slight flush crept up Sarah's face. ''No. I was just wondering.'' She placed the cloth on the counter by the sink and ducked out of the room.

''What was that about?'' Rachel asked.

''I don't know.'' Luke stood up and walked to the back door. ''But I mean to find out.''

Twins. Luke stared down at the newborn calves and grimaced. They were both small, their spindly legs barely able to support their matted, skinny bodies. Usually one calf was much bigger than its sibling, but this time the awkward infants were almost identical.

''You want me to kill one, boss?'' Jake asked.

Luke hesitated. Practicality dictated that a cow could care for only one calf at a time. If the runt seemed too small to hand-raise, it was often sacrificed for the good of its mother and its twin.

A gust of wind swept through the valley, sending the two youngsters stumbling to the only warmth and security they had. Tremors shook them, and the little female went down in the snow.

Luke stared out over the land. It was late. A full moon was rising out of the east, illuminating the frozen acres. He was tired and sore. His right foot throbbed from being trampled in an earlier encounter with a concerned mother.

Muscles across his shoulders and back ached from overuse. It was cold, and he was hungry. The last thing he needed was to carry a calf back to the barn.

He swung down from his horse. "We'll take them both in, and the mother will follow. Potter can keep an eye on the family and hand-raise one of them if necessary."

Capturing the calves wasn't easy. Despite their youth and exhaustion, the animals darted away from the unfamiliar scents and figures. The mother, sensing her children were in danger, charged and tried to stay between the cowboys and the calves.

Luke finally captured the larger of the two. She protested being raised to his saddle and showed her displeasure with two sharp kicks to his thigh.

"You all right, boss?" Jake asked as he tied the back hooves of his calf.

"Take care of your own bundle, cowboy. I can handle this little girl just fine."

His foreman grinned. "I've heard that from the ladies in town, Hawkins. You take care of them mighty nice."

Luke ignored him, and they turned their horses toward the barn. As expected, the mother trotted anxiously behind them. Her maternal calls were answered by her babies' bleats.

As the moon rose higher in the sky, the temperature dropped. He pulled the blanket from behind his saddle and draped it over his passenger. "We'll be there in another hour or so, little girl. Potter'll have a warm stall and plenty of milk. And in the morning you and your mama can move into the corral out back. Your brother will be with you, along with the territory's stupidest dog. Not a bad start, eh?"

The calf raised her head for a moment, then relaxed

under the blanket and blew out air in time with the horse's trot.

By the time the animals were fed and settled and the horses put up, it was after midnight. Luke limped into the kitchen and stopped at the sight of the large wooden tub standing in the center of the room. Clean clothes hung over one of the chairs, and a plate of biscuits rested next to a pot of coffee.

Saying a mental thank-you to Sarah, he stripped down and stepped into the steaming water. The heat was painful at first—his arms and legs were stiff with cold—but he simply sank deeper and closed his eyes.

After a few minutes he risked glancing at his right foot. Hoof-shaped bruises covered his skin. Gritting his teeth, he tried to bend his toes. The motion was agony, but nothing felt broken. Matching circles marred the skin on his thigh. "Ungrateful vulture bait," he muttered under his breath as he stepped out of the tub.

He dried off and pulled on a clean pair of trousers, then dumped the water outside. In the morning the cycle would start over again. There wouldn't be a moment's peace until summer.

He checked the stove, then picked up the lantern and made his way out of the kitchen. From the hall, he sensed more than saw the light in the parlor. His gut, twisting and turning in agitation, told him who was in there. She seemed happy and calm during the day, but he heard her restless stirrings each evening as she paced the house. Apparently he wasn't the only one haunted by ghosts.

Moving cautiously so he wouldn't step on any squeaky floorboards, he made his way into the front room. A fire flickered in the grate. She sat on the floor, her back to the door, a blanket tucked around her legs and waist. A thick robe hid her body from his view, but not from his imagination. Slowly, sensuously, she brushed her silver-blond hair.

The long wavy strands shimmered and glowed in the firelight. The ritual she performed was private. Only a husband would be allowed to view the dance. Or a lover.

He walked closer. A board creaked in protest. Her hand stilled, then fell to her lap.

"It's late," he said. His voice was husky, giving away the conflict raging within him.

"I—I washed my hair and was just waiting for it to dry. Did you find the cows you were looking for?"

"Yes."

He was drawn forward by a force more powerful than his hate and anger. As unerringly as a bee seeking out the sweetest bloom, he sank on the blanket behind her.

Her breathing was low and shallow. The wind rattled at the windows, then slunk away in silence. He reached around and pulled the brush from her hand. When his knuckles grazed her thigh, he felt as if the flames from the grate had leapt up and singed his groin.

He pulled the bristles through the wavy satin. With each stroke, her head fell back and the ends of her hair tickled his thighs. Although he couldn't feel the sensation through his trousers, he imagined the wisps caressing his bare skin. The fragrance of the soap rose up to surround him, as sweet as wildflowers, as heady as wine.

When the last hint of moisture had been smoothed away, he dropped the brush and buried his hands against her scalp. Raising the long tresses behind her head, he let them fall against his chest. The low moan could have come from either of them.

Rachel closed her eyes as she felt his fingers massage her neck and shoulders. It didn't matter how many times she told herself that Luke was dangerous, that he couldn't be trusted, that he no longer loved her. It didn't matter that he had nearly attacked her in anger just six days before. It didn't matter that she was lost and alone with no money, no job, no home.

The only point of focus in her mind was the sensation of his touch. He was strong and capable. He was alive. There had been too many nights of loneliness and fear. Too many nights of dreaming of this man and his magic. She'd spent the last six years being strong. Surely God could forgive one night of weakness.

When he turned her and lowered her onto her back, she opened her eyes to gaze at him. He lay next to her, one arm bearing his weight, the other resting against his side. He wasn't holding her down; in fact, his posture almost begged her to escape.

Firelight created shadows across his face, sketching tenderness where she knew there was only anger. His mouth straightened into a thin line. The battle still raged within him. Tentatively she raised her hand to his cheek, hoping to tip the scales in her favor.

He flinched away from her touch as though her skin had burned him. Carefully she brushed one finger across the line of his jaw. The stubble scratched and enticed. She swallowed thickly.

He leaned forward. Sweet breath fanned her face. Tilting up her chin, she let her eyelids drift closed. Anticipation stilled her heartbeat. The count of one . . . two . . .

He kissed her. Lips, firm yet soft, pressed against hers. At the first contact a band of fear tightened around her chest. But there wasn't any punishment in the pressure, and her anxiety faded away.

As he deepened the kiss, she moved her hands to his back. Tight, hot skin covered hard cords of muscles that bunched and relaxed when he moved closer. His tongue traced the curve of her bottom lip; she parted her lips to admit him. He fleetingly licked the inside of her lower lip, then slipped away.

Trails of short, nibbling kisses defined her jaw. Moist, slow kisses paid homage to her throat. She arched her head back and gasped at the liquid warmth pouring over and through her body. Desire, long asleep, woke slowly, almost painfully. Her breasts swelled against his chest, the sensation only faintly familiar. Dear God, it had been so many years since a man had touched her this way.

One leg slipped between hers. The movement tightened her nightgown and held her still. Her hands traced random patterns on his back, silently begging his mouth to return to hers. She hadn't tasted him in six years—she would surely die from hunger if she couldn't sup on him this night.

"Oh, Luke," she whispered. This was the sanctuary she'd sought. At last they would finish what they'd started a lifetime ago.

He read her mind. "Yes," he murmured. "It's been too long." Drawing himself up on his elbows, he grasped her head in his hands. "Look at me."

She complied. His gray eyes burned through to her soul and unlocked the last of the feelings she'd kept buried. The morning would bring judgment, but tonight she would give herself to the man who had always possessed her heart.

"I want you to remember who's bedding you, Mrs. Steele."

His clipped words, an icy contrast to the warmth of his body touching hers, echoed against her ears like a blow to the head. Her eyes closed. The need evaporated, leaving behind only shame and the desire to escape. He didn't want *her;* he didn't care at all. He only desired revenge. His hands might reduce her to liquid hunger, but that didn't make his actions any less an assault.

She twisted away and pushed up to her knees. Her breath came in rapid pants. "Don't touch me."

He raised one eyebrow. "A little late to play the innocent maid, don't you think?"

She clutched her robe closer to her chest. "That's not why I pulled back and you know it. I thought . . ." She shook her head. "Never mind. I made a mistake."

He stood and towered over her. "See that you don't make it again. I'm not a patient man, and I don't take kindly to being aroused but left unsatisfied. Attend to your hair in the privacy of your own room, or next time I might not be such a gentleman."

"Gentleman?" She stared up at him, then rose to her feet. It didn't help; he was still much taller. "You started this simply to settle an old score. You call that acting like a gentleman?"

"In one night I couldn't begin to settle the score with you. And no, that wasn't the only reason I wanted to bed you. You lived with a man. Surely you remember the needs, the pleasure? Or wasn't Matthew able to keep his wife content?"

"Leave him out of this." She planted her hands on her hips. "He was a fine man and a good father. And yes, he *did* satisfy me in bed."

Luke folded his arms over his chest. "Do tell."

"I . . . You . . . Never mind. I'm going to bed." She walked to the door, frustration adding emphasis to her steps.

"Don't forget what I told you. Next time there'll be no stopping."

"There won't be a next time, Luke Hawkins. Mark and I are leaving in the morning."

She hadn't walked two feet when he grabbed her arm and spun her around. "What do you mean?"

All the passion and hostility faded from his face, leaving behind the mask she was growing to hate.

"Just what I said. You've made it very clear you don't want me here. I need to find a job and support my son."

"Doing what? Working as a saloon girl?"

She jerked her arm free. "If I have to. What does it matter to you?"

"I won't have it."

"You won't have it? And when did you give a damn about me?"

He glared at her. "While you're under my roof, you're my responsibility."

"Fine. As of tomorrow I won't be under your roof. End of problem." The floor was icy under her bare feet, and she shivered. The last flicker of anger was swept away by a wave of exhaustion.

His expression softened. "Get on to bed, Rachel. We'll talk in the morning. I don't want you rushing off to do anything foolish. Agreed?"

She stared at his chest. A mat of hair clung to his skin; the broad pattern narrowed at his waist, then faded into the waistband of his trousers. A lump formed in her throat. Despite everything he'd done, everything he'd said, she still . . .

"I won't do anything foolish," she said and turned away. As she opened her bedroom door, she looked up and saw him standing in the hall.

Leaving wasn't foolish, she told herself. It was the only course of action that made sense. When Luke had a chance to think about it, he'd realize that she was right. There wasn't anything left between them. Their love had grown as cold and unwelcoming as the night.

Chapter Five

"Are you sure you must go?" Sarah asked.

Rachel didn't look up from her packing. "Yes. It was a mistake for Mark and me to come here. I should have written first, or sent a telegram to find out if it was all right."

The older woman stepped closer to the bed and placed a restraining hand on her arm. "It *is* all right for you to be here. Luke needs you; I need you. It's been so lonely and now . . ."

Rachel closed and buckled the carpetbag and sat on the quilt. Pulling her friend down beside her, she gave her a hug. "I'm sorry to leave like this, but it's for the best. I should have realized we couldn't ignore the past. Too much has happened."

"Nonsense." Sarah's pale blue eyes flashed with determination. "You set your heart on that boy when you were twelve years old, and as far as I can see, nothing's changed."

"Everything's changed. I married Matthew and bore him a son."

"All the more reason not to go running off like some buckshot coyote. How are you going to take care of that boy in town?"

"I'll get a job."

70

"Doing what?"

Rachel sighed and pleated the skirt of her navy wool dress. The heavy fabric had worn thin with time, leaving the weave hanging open like half-shuttered windows in a storm. "I can cook and clean and sew. There must be work for me somewhere—the general store, a laundry, it doesn't matter. Mark and I will be fine."

"Assuming you can find a job—which I seriously doubt—who's going to look after Mark while you're working?"

"He's not a baby anymore. He'll take care of himself."

"Please, Rachel. Don't go. I know you still love Luke. Don't deny it," she said when Rachel started to shake her head. "I see it in the way you watch him. And I know he has feelings for you."

"You're right. He does. He hates me. He's never forgiven me for marrying Matthew. I'm sorry, but I can't stay." She rose and pulled on her coat. "Potter should have the wagon hitched by now."

Sarah stood up and folded her arms across her chest. "There's nothing else I can say?"

"No."

"You got any money?"

Rachel thought of the meticulously folded bills and coins in her reticule. It had taken her six years of careful hoarding from the household account to save the precious little she had. She nodded, afraid to reveal the amount.

"How much?" Sarah asked sternly.

"Enough."

"How much?"

"Twenty-six dollars and thirty-one cents."

"That's it? The bunkhouse cook makes more than that in a month, and he gets room and board besides. You won't last a week. At least let me—"

"No." Rachel picked up her carpetbag and headed for the door. When she could no longer see her friend and the affection in her eyes, she continued. "I can't. But thank you for offering."

After the tattered bags had been loaded into the rented wagon, she turned to Sarah, who had followed her outdoors. "Thank you for everything."

Sarah pulled her close. "Promise me you'll write. As soon as you get settled in town, I want to come for a visit."

Rachel returned the embrace. "I promise." She stepped back and called for her son.

Mark shuffled out of the barn, Dawg trailing at his heels. "Can't we take him?" the boy asked for the fourth time.

"No. I told you I'm not sure where we'll be staying. They might not allow animals. Now say good-bye to Sarah."

Mark flung himself at the housekeeper with all the honest emotion of a five-year-old boy. Harsh sobs shook his shoulders, but when he stepped back, he brushed away the tears.

Rachel lifted him up to the seat, then climbed on beside him. The reins were thick and rough; her kid gloves provided little protection. Wincing at the memory of the blisters she had earned on the trip out, she clucked at the horses and the wagon moved forward. Everything within her cried out for her to stay. Only pride added steel to her backbone and allowed her to deny the sudden moisture on her face.

Luke swung down from the saddle and pulled open the barn door. "No calves tonight, Potter," he called.

The old man moved forward, his slow pace accentuated by his unsmiling face. After stuffing a pinch of tobacco under his lip, he took Red's reins and led the horse to his stall.

"I'll git him fed and watered," he said finally.

"Thanks. I'm tired and sore. We had to help with three birthings today."

Potter continued with his work and didn't say a word.

"You feeling poorly, old man?"

"Nope."

"Something wrong?"

"Nope."

A vague feeling of unease slipped over Luke. He glanced around the barn, but everything seemed in place. The tack was cleaned and hanging on the wall, and several bales of hay were stacked in the corner. Even that damned dog was curled up on his blanket.

He started to go, then stopped. For the first time in a week the animal hadn't jumped up to greet him.

"Is something ailing him?" Luke asked, pointing at the black and white mutt.

"He ain't sick, if that's what you mean."

Luke shook his head. "I'll see you in the morning."

"I guess Dawg and I'll be here. *Boss.*"

The last word came out with force and something else Luke couldn't name. It must be the late hour, he decided as he walked up to the house. Or they were all exhausted from the grueling work. Hand-raising half a dozen calves wasn't easy.

In the kitchen his supper sat on the table. The covered bowl contained stew with a side of canned green beans. Luke poked his fork at the serving of greens, then pushed them aside. What was Sarah doing giving him green beans? She knew he hated them. After hoeing John Steele's fields for years, he and Sarah had promised one another to never eat another green bean unless they were starving.

He wolfed down the stew and biscuits, then carried his plate to the sink. As he poured a cup of coffee, he heard footsteps in the corridor. Anticipation slammed into his gut.

But the woman hovering in the doorway wasn't Rachel.

"You're up late," he said.

"I couldn't sleep."

Sarah's voice was flat, almost accusing. The heavy plaid robe parted slightly, revealing the length of her chestnut braid and the lace collar of her flannel gown. His eyes moved upward. There was no smile on her lips, no light in her eyes.

"Is something wrong?" he asked.

"She's gone."

"What?"

Sarah stepped into the room and glared at him. "Rachel left this morning. Took the boy with her."

"No." He set his cup on the counter. "We talked last night. She said she wouldn't do anything foolish."

"Well, she's gone now, and as near as I can tell, it's your fault."

"Mine! What did I do?"

"Acted like a jackass, for one thing. Did it ever occur to you she might have come here for a reason? Folks don't just pack up and travel halfway across the country without being invited unless something is wrong. Did you ever look past your own feelings to think about hers?"

"That's easy for you to say, Sarah, but you aren't the one she betrayed. You seem to be forgetting that she married my best friend and didn't even have the decency to tell me. Then when I went back to Kansas, both she and Matthew refused to see me. So don't talk to me about other people's feelings."

"Don't you even care that she's gone?" she asked.

"No."

He grabbed his cup and walked past her and into his office. But the familiar room with its heavy desk and large stone fireplace failed to work its usual magic. There was no peace tonight, no respite from the ghosts that rose up about him.

He remembered the day Sarah had arrived on the farm. He'd been about three and already used to being shut out by the Steele family. A storm had blown in, sending lightning bolts crashing across the sky. As he'd trembled alone in his bed, he'd fought back screams of terror. His door had opened and there Sarah stood in her nightgown. Without saying a word, she'd crawled in next to him and held him until his tears were dry and he fell asleep. From that moment on, she'd been his mother and father, all the family he'd ever needed and wanted. Until Rachel loved and then betrayed him.

The next morning Sarah fixed his breakfast as usual. Only the silence filling the room reminded him of what had happened. He hated admitting he missed Mark's bright chatter. When he'd finished his oatmeal, he rose from the table and shrugged into his jacket.

"I'll be gone all day," he said. "Probably won't make it back until close to ten. Don't bother to wait up."

Sarah nervously touched the white collar of her dress. "Bring her back, Luke. If not for your sake, then for mine. I liked having another woman here to talk to and help me with the chores."

Her quiet voice made him feel lower than a rattler in a mudhole. "I've never meant to keep you tied down here. If you want to leave, Sarah, I won't keep you. I know I owe you a lot."

She sighed in frustration. "I'm not trying to make you

feel guilty or tell you I want to leave. I thought it might be nice to have some help around the house.''

Luke picked up his hat and spun it in his hand. Sarah rarely asked him for anything. ''I'll get you some help. I'll ask around and see if anyone needs a job.''

''I already know someone. Rachel. She's in town right now looking for work. If you don't want her to stay here as a guest, then let her earn her keep.''

''No.''

''Luke Hawkins, I swear.'' She planted her hands on her hips. ''Do you know how much money she has?''

He shook his head.

''About twenty-six dollars. That's all there is between her and starvation. And what about the boy? He's Matthew's son. Doesn't that mean anything to you?''

He jammed his hat on his head and stomped to the door. ''Yeah, it means something. It means she should go home and ask John Steele to look after his grandchild.''

On the morning of the fourth day, Luke didn't even bother speaking with Sarah. Her red eyes and accusing glances said enough. She didn't shirk her duties. His clothes were washed, his house was clean, his food served on time. With the exception of a serving of green beans with each meal, he had no cause for complaint.

After eating his breakfast, he picked up his coat and walked to the back door. He met Potter halfway to the barn. The old man was also giving him the silent treatment. Luke would have fired him, but he couldn't fault his work or blame him for missing the boy. God knew he'd listened for Mark's childish shouts of laughter often enough himself.

He reminded himself that he was well rid of Rachel. She was trouble he didn't need. He was only being considerate last night when he crept into her room to see if she might have left something behind. But the drawers were empty. Sarah had already washed the linens, so her scent had been erased from the pillows.

"I gotta talk to you," Potter said without preamble.

"After four days? What do you want?"

"I need to borrow a gun."

Luke stuffed his hands in his pockets. "You going to shoot me, old man?"

Potter shuffled his feet. "Dawg ain't been eatin' these last few days. I mean to put him out of his misery. Can't do that with a rifle."

Luke glared into his wrinkled old face. "You're pushing me too far."

"I don't know what you're talkin' about. I jes' asked for a pistol. If you ain't gonna help me, then I guess I'll make my way to the bunkhouse."

Luke stared up at the sky. The sun was peeking over the horizon, casting golden light across the house and yard. About fifty cows had yet to drop their calves. He had cowboys due to arrive within a couple of weeks. The spring roundup would be starting, and a hundred other details required his attention. So why the hell did he care if Potter shot that damned dog?

"You win," he said finally. "Tell Sarah to get her supply list ready, then hitch up the spring wagon."

Potter's mouth dropped open, then spread into a grin. "You won't regret this, boss. Fine thing you're doin'. We gotta catch that boy early, afore his mama turns him into a nester."

Luke pulled his collar up around his neck and walked to his foreman's house. "I already regret it."

"Are you sure you don't need someone to stock the shelves or clean the windows?" Rachel asked desperately.

The pregnant woman behind the counter offered a sympathetic smile. "Sorry, honey. My husband and I barely make enough to feed our family. We can't afford no help. Have you tried the other dry goods stores?"

"Yes, thank you, I have." Rachel offered one last smile, then walked out of the store. When she reached the wooden sidewalk, she resisted the urge to plop down and cry her eyes out. She knew it wouldn't accomplish anything, but it might make her feel better.

"Try the dry goods store," she mumbled as she made her way back to the boardinghouse where she'd been staying. She'd tried *all* the dry goods stores, along with the laundry, the hotel, three boardinghouses, six restaurants, the newspaper office, the dressmaker, and the butcher. Horse Creek was a good-sized town, but no one wanted to hire a young widow.

Walking carefully across the muddy street, she tried to ignore the gnawing hunger in her stomach. To save money, she was eating as little as possible. Mark was growing and had to have more food, but she could get by with a roll and some coffee.

The growling in her midsection reminded her that she hadn't even had time to eat a roll this morning and it was already noon. She sat down on the bench in front of the boardinghouse and pulled a chunk of hard bread out of her reticule.

It wasn't supposed to be this difficult, she thought. She was strong and able-bodied. Why couldn't she get a job? There had to be one somewhere; but there wasn't. The only places she hadn't tried were the saloons. Just the thought of serving drinks or dealing cards or whatever it was that women did in those places sent a shudder of fear rippling down her back.

Maybe she should check the newspaper to see if a local

rancher was advertising for a housekeeper. If he didn't mind Mark, that would be her best option. Yet, how could she live in the middle of nowhere, and with a strange man to boot?

A burst of laughter from the building next door caught her attention. It was called the Silver Spur, according to the peeling paint on the sign. The wide windows in front were opaque from dirt and smoke. As she watched, a cowboy stumbled out of the door and fell face first into the street. An oncoming carriage swerved around him, the rear wheels barely missing his head.

Bile rose at the back of Rachel's throat. She couldn't work in a place like that. Besides, what would she do about Mark? They had been in town only a few days, but he was already getting restless in the room. Yesterday she'd come back and he'd been gone. She'd found him talking with the owner of the boardinghouse, but she couldn't always depend on the kindness of strangers. Even if she put him in school, he'd still have to spend several hours alone every day. And paying someone to watch him would cost most of whatever wages she could earn.

The asthmatic wheeze of a pump organ drifted onto the street. The cowboy lying there rose to his knees and promptly threw up. When he was finished, he climbed to his feet and stumbled back into the saloon.

Rachel closed her eyes. As far as she could tell, she had three options: First, find a rancher who'd hire her as a cook or housekeeper; second, work in a saloon; third, move on to Cheyenne. The thought of returning to Kansas passed through her mind so briefly that she barely acknowledged it.

Years ago life had been simple. She'd loved Luke and he'd loved her. It was supposed to have been . . .

She remembered one terrible afternoon with a clarity that made her ache. The smell of baking bread, the sunlight filtering through freshly washed windows and curtains, her hands moving swiftly as she sat in the kitchen and folded the linens she'd carefully sewn in preparation for her new home. How eagerly she'd counted the days until Luke would return to claim her.

And then, with a few words, everything changed.

Her father, his blond hair as light as her own and not yet streaked with gray, had crouched next to her and admired the small, even stitches in the linens.

"Matthew has asked permission to marry you," he said, never meeting her eyes.

For a second she'd felt cold, as if an icy hand had reached inside and squeezed her heart. Then she'd laughed. "Daddy, don't tease me like that. Marry Matthew indeed! I know he's always had feelings for me, but he knows I love Luke."

"Rachel." Her father sat down in a chair next to her and pulled the linens from her hands. His long fingers held hers. "I gave him my blessing."

"What? No! You can't! Daddy?" Panic clawed at her chest, making it hard to breathe. "No!"

"Rachel, please." Their eyes met. She saw his pain, the pallor of his skin, the lines that had deepened over the last year. "Child, I'm dying."

"What?"

"Doc says only a few more months. John has agreed to run both farms and give half the profits to your mother. She won't want for anything. And if you marry Matthew, neither will you."

How easily her world was destroyed. Her head ached from his words. Her father couldn't die. He was still a young man. Then she remembered the cough that never went away, the sharp pains in his chest that stole his breath.

"Oh, Daddy." She flung herself in his arms and cried.

"Hush." The familiar embrace comforted her. He

murmured soothing words. Gradually she calmed, her tears slowed. There was silence for a few moments, then, "John wants you to marry Matthew."

She stiffened and sat up. "Or he won't help us with the farm?"

He nodded. "I wouldn't ask for myself, but I have to think of you and your mother. She can't manage the farm, but with John's help, you can. That's why I'm leaving it to you. You'll own it free and clear. Whatever happens, you'll have the land."

"Does Matthew know about your bargain?" She was unable to keep the bitterness from her voice.

Her father winced. "No. He thinks that with Luke gone, he has a chance to win you."

"I love Luke, Daddy."

He kissed her cheek and rose to his feet. "I know. I wish there was another way."

"I could refuse Matthew. You can't make me marry him."

Sad eyes, dark with pain, studied her. "I've never asked you for anything before. You are my child, and this is my dying wish. I want to go to my grave knowing you and your mother are cared for."

Over the next several days she considered his words, her conscience wrestling with her heart. Love versus duty. She knew what she wanted. That was easy. But what was right?

The following Sunday Matthew took her for a walk after church. When he proposed, there was only one answer she could give him.

"Yes, Matthew, I'll marry you."

As he held her close, she felt her eyes burn. There were no more tears left. Silently she swore she'd never forget Luke. He was the only man she'd ever love.

They'd set the wedding for the next month, six weeks

before her eighteenth birthday. In the end it had come down to a question of duty and loyalty to her family.

Another wagon rumbled down the street and recalled Rachel to the present. Shading her eyes against the sun, she watched the tall driver pull the team of horses to a stop, then set the brake and jump out. Her heart froze when it recognized what her eyes could not believe.

"L-Luke?"

"I thought I'd have to spend a whole day looking for you. And here you are, sitting outside just waiting for your ride." As he walked closer, he adjusted the brim of his hat so it shadowed his eyes. "I guess you expected to be rescued sooner than this."

The anger in his voice matched the fierce expression on his face. He looked like a cornered wolf—dangerous, resentful, ready to attack.

"I don't know what you're talking about," she said finally. "I left to get away from you."

He rested one foot on the bench and placed his forearm on his thigh. "And here I thought I was being a real gentleman by offering you a place to stay."

"I didn't mean to imply that—"

"I know what you meant. You were too much of a coward to face the consequences of what you'd done. You ran away from me six years ago, and you're running away now." His scorn cut through her brittle facade of control, shattering her mask and releasing raw emotion.

"I never ran," she said. "You're the one who left."

"I came back for you. I rode into town ready to claim my bride. You can imagine my surprise when I found out you'd married Matthew."

His self-righteous attitude was beginning to wear on her. "I had responsibilities. It's too late to go back and change the past," she snapped. "I've already said I was sorry."

"Sorry?" He laughed harshly. "You hid it well. As I recall, I sent a message asking to see you and your husband. I guess it was inconvenient for you to show up."

"I *couldn't* see you."

She stared at the ground and wished he would leave her alone. Two women walked past them and stared, but Luke simply tipped his hat as though nothing out of the ordinary were occurring.

"Why?" he asked.

Irritation filled her. If he wanted the truth, then he would have it. She glared at him. "I didn't see you because of Mark. I was several months along."

The color fled from Luke's face, leaving a thin layer of tan covering the gray. His hands clenched tightly as he straightened. "What was Matthew's excuse? I asked to see him as well."

If she hadn't been so exhausted and hungry, she wouldn't have answered him at all. But she didn't have enough strength to do battle anymore. "He wanted to, but John found out and forbade him to see you. We both felt bad about what happened." Pulling herself to her feet, she looked at him. "If you came into town to punish me some more, you'll just have to find another victim. I'm done letting you treat me this way."

She had almost reached the door of the boardinghouse when his voice stopped her.

"I came to take you back to the ranch."

The mat on the sidewalk needed sweeping, she thought calmly. And the front windows were dirty. She'd mention it to the owner when she paid for her room later today.

He moved next to her. "Did you hear me?"

"Why do you want to take me back?" she asked.

"Sarah needs help with the house. I want to hire you to work for her."

"No."

He tugged on her arm, then led her back to the bench. "I'll pay you very well."

"I'm not interested in your job, Mr. Hawkins. Now leave me alone."

He gritted his teeth. "I can't tell you how much that would please me, *Mrs. Steele*, but it's too late. Members of my household have been taken in by your charm. They'll make my life hell if I don't take you back."

So it was about the others. *He* didn't care at all. "I know you don't want me around."

Luke glanced away. "That's not important. I have a responsibility to you and the boy."

She stamped her foot. "I'm not your responsibility. I don't need you or your job."

"You haven't found anything yet. What are you going to do?"

"I have several prospects."

"Oh?" He arched one eyebrow, pushed her onto the bench, and sat next to her. "Such as?"

"That's none of your affair. Now if you'll kindly leave me alone."

She made to rise, but he held her with an unrelenting pressure on her arm. "What about Mark?" he asked.

"He's fine."

"What will you do with him while you deal with your 'prospects'?"

"That isn't your concern."

"Perhaps not, but surely it's yours? Will he be going to work with you?"

Before she could answer, a young woman dressed in a low-cut red and black ruffled dress flowed out of the saloon. When she saw Luke, she smiled widely, revealing perfect white teeth and a dimple in one cheek. "Afternoon, cowboy. You look mighty familiar. Have we met?"

Her sultry voice lingered on the last word. Rachel felt a blush creep up her face as she realized what sort of woman this was.

Luke slowly rose to his feet and looked the saloon girl over from head to toe and then back. "I believe we have."

"I thought so." The young woman flicked an imaginary piece of lint from the bodice of her dress and succeeded in pushing the fabric even lower. "If I recall correctly, it was a long and pleasurable evening."

Rachel stood up and tried to slip past Luke. Despite his attention to the cheap floozy in front of him, he grabbed her arm and prevented her from moving away.

"I wouldn't do that if I were you," he warned.

"I'm concerned about my son. Mark's been alone in the room all morning, and I want to check on him."

The brunette saloon girl swung her gaze from Luke to Rachel. "Did you say Mark? Is he about five?"

A bad feeling knotted in Rachel's chest. "Yes. Why?"

"Oh, he's been visiting us. In fact, I was just leaving to go find his mama. And here you are."

Without bothering to look, she could sense Luke's amusement. "If you would be so kind as to bring him outside, I'll take him off your hands."

The brunette leaned forward, exposing her ample bosom. "He's been no trouble at all. Such pretty manners for a little boy. You've done a fine job with him."

Indignation competed with outrage. How dare this . . . this strumpet compliment her on her mothering skills! The woman had no sense of decency. A curt reply began forming, but a warning glance from Luke cut it off.

"Thank you," Rachel said between clenched teeth. "If you could get him?"

"Sure thing."

The other woman smiled at Luke, then swayed back into the saloon. A few seconds later Mark ran through the doors, a bundle in a dirty cloth clutched against his chest.

"Mama, guess what them ladies gave me." He skidded to a stop when he saw Luke, then flew to the tall cowboy. "Luke! I thought I'd never see you again." He wrapped one arm around Luke's thigh.

Luke crouched down and pulled the boy closer to him. "What were you doing in a saloon?"

The boy shrugged. "I got tired of stayin' in the room, so I crawled out the window."

He pointed up to the second floor of the boardinghouse. A balcony jutted out from the upstairs portion of the saloon, but there was a gap of about two feet between the boardinghouse and the balcony railing. Rachel shuddered to think of Mark risking such a fall. Fear, anger, and hopelessness braided together and twisted in her chest.

"I met this nice lady who gave me cookies and milk and this." He proudly displayed his gift.

Nestled in the crook of his arm was a calico kitten. Orange, black, and white fur had matted together in a random pattern. The animal's eyes were bright green, and its nose was pink.

"But, Mark, we can't have a cat," she said.

"The lady said she don't go outside none, so she can play with me in the room."

Just then the kitten blinked sleepily and yawned. The movement exposed tiny white teeth and a pink tongue that sneaked out to lick Mark's chin. The boy laughed and stroked the animal's head. "Can I keep her?"

Rachel closed her eyes and thought of their rapidly dwindling funds. She'd have to find a job soon or move on.

"If you're worried about the other night," Luke said quietly. "It won't happen again."

She risked a glance. The set of his shoulders confirmed his statement. She wasn't sure if she felt regret or relief. "Luke, I don't . . ."

"Fifty dollars."

"What?"

"I'll provide room and board for you and the boy, plus pay you fifty dollars a month."

"Take it, honey. Offers like that don't come along every day." The brunette had rejoined them. "Of course, if you're not interested . . ." She trailed her fingers over Luke's arm.

Rachel looked at Mark. His dark eyes pleaded with her. She could fight the entire world, but not her son. "What about the cat?" she asked.

Luke stared at the animal as though seeing it for the first time. "What about it?"

"Can Mark bring her?"

He shrugged. "Sure."

"Fifteen dollars."

"What?"

She touched her son's hair and smiled at him, then turned to Luke. "Fifteen dollars a month, plus room and board for the three of us."

"Thirty."

"Twenty."

"Twenty-five."

Her mind told her to refuse and move on to Cheyenne. Her eyes traced the strong lines of his handsome face as her heart begged her to stay. She glanced at Mark. Her son was more important than her fears or her pride. No matter what happened to her, Luke would protect the boy. After all that had happened, she owed both of them that.

"If you don't want to take his job, honey, we've got us an opening for a girl right here in the saloon," the brunette said.

Rachel drew in a deep breath. Laughter floated out of the bar. "Twenty-five," she agreed.

John Steele turned onto his back and groaned. He felt as if the plow had taken a wrong turn in the east field and run over his head. Squinting against the bright morning sun, he reached for the bottle beside the bed and swallowed the last inch of whiskey. Fire burned down his throat, then flamed into his stomach, but the pounding in his temples quieted to a steady thumping.

The clock on the opposite wall had stopped again, but he judged it to be close to noon. The faint memory that he had to be somewhere pushed him out of bed and onto his feet. The room lurched a couple of times, then stood still.

John staggered over to the dresser. After pulling off his woolen shirt, he tossed it onto the growing pile on the floor. The basin was empty again. He cursed out loud.

He opened the top drawer and pulled out the last clean shirt. Tonight, when he rode into town, he'd ask about getting someone to take care of the house. It didn't seem right that a man should have to pay for such services when there was a perfectly good woman available to cook and clean. But the scheming bitch had run off, and until he brought her back, he'd have to make do.

In the kitchen he picked up a match and scraped it against the side of the stove. The stick hissed and flared, but his trembling fingers couldn't maintain their hold. He swore and lit another, then another. On the fourth try, the kindling caught fire. He nursed the tiny flame, blowing and feeding it until the logs began to burn.

By the time the wood was crackling, he was steady

enough to fill the pot with water and add the coffee. A mirror over the steel sink showed an aging dark-haired man with bloodshot eyes and three days' growth of beard.

John scratched his chin. He'd have to shave before he went . . . Where the hell was it he was supposed to be? He moistened the soap and spread lather on the lower half of his face. The blade cut into the skin a couple of times, but he washed away the blood. A meeting, he remembered. But why?

A pile of papers on the table provided the clue. Three notices from the bank informed him that the mortgage payment was overdue. Mr. Gridley had told him to come by today.

Stupid little city boy in his fancy-pants suit, John thought. He ought to be out earning a real living. It took a man to wrestle his wages from the soil.

By the time the coffee had boiled, he'd worked himself into a frenzy over Mr. Gridley and the bank. Pouring the steaming liquid into the cup, he practiced exactly what he was going to tell the banker. No one threatened John Steele with foreclosure.

He gulped the coffee and jerked the cup away when it burned his tongue. Dark patches stained the front of his shirt. Damn. This was all *her* fault. If she hadn't run off, he wouldn't be in this mess.

After mopping up the spill, he pulled on his coat. There was a card game tonight. He'd win enough to pay Gridley off; then he'd go bring her back. She wouldn't be hard to find. There was only one place that little tramp would have run to. Only one man.

Despite all he'd done, she'd never shown him a moment's gratitude. He'd given her to his son, then let her mourn his passing. But now it was *his* turn to have her.

In the parlor he stopped at the portrait of his late wife.

The sight of the familiar face brought him up short. "Why, Mary?" he asked hoarsely. "Why'd you care about him more than me? Why'd you leave me?"

The hazel eyes and unsmiling lips offered no response. John looked away and counted his money. The dull ache in his belly matched the pain in his head. He needed another drink and fast.

This was all Rachel's doing, he reminded himself as he turned away from the portrait. When he found her, he'd take her. She owed him, but her debt wasn't half as much as Luke Hawkins's. And by God, they'd both pay.

Chapter Six

The wagon moved quickly up the dirt path. They'd left Horse Creek behind almost an hour ago. Rachel secured her hat against the cold gusts of wind, then pulled her coat tighter across her chest. Despite the bright blue sky, snow still covered the ground around them. The calendar might say April, but spring weather was a long way off.

"You all right back there?" she asked, twisting around in her seat. "Are you warm enough, Mark?"

"Yup." Her son was tucked in the rear of the wagon, protected from the cold by sacks of flour and boxes of foodstuffs. He grinned up at her. The scarf had fallen away from his face, exposing pink cheeks and a red nose. "I'm gonna have to think her a name." He nodded at the bundle on his lap. He held the kitten protectively, both arms supporting the slight weight. "She purrs loud. Maybe I'll call her Thunder."

"That's a nice name, but she's only going to be a little cat. What about something more her size?"

"I don't know. What do you think, Luke?"

Worship radiated from Mark's eyes and echoed in the excited pitch of his voice. Rachel sighed softly. No doubt the boy had seen Luke's unexpected appearance as a rescue of the grandest sort. Bad enough that he loved Luke being a real cowboy; now he would remember how he'd taken

them back to the ranch and to all the people Mark had
grown to care about. It was history repeating itself.

How many times had Matthew looked up at Luke with
that exact expression lighting his dark eyes? How many
times had she? Hot pressure tightened her throat. The
exhaustion of looking for work had made her vulnerable,
she told herself as the memories collected together, offering
an assortment of tableaux from the past.

Luke had always been the one who said which game
they'd play, who would be the Yankee, who the defeated
General Lee. He was the one who had decided when
Matthew was old enough to shoot a rifle, when Rachel was
old enough to ride the big farm horse. He was the one
who—that last night before he'd left for Wyoming—had
determined they wouldn't take the final step into adulthood.
He'd been the one to pull back, the one to button up her
dress and tell her they'd wait until they were married.

Rachel felt herself smile at the memory, the tugging at
her lips more poignant than happy. It seemed so many
lifetimes ago. They'd both been innocent, young, and now
everything had changed. Luke had become a successful
rancher and a stranger. She was alone in the world and
responsible for a small boy. She was also now Luke
Hawkins's employee. No matter what sort of past they'd
shared, she could not forget her current place in his life.

"I don't care what you call the cat," Luke said, never
taking his eyes off the path in front of them. "As long as it
has a real name. Not like that damned dog Potter kept."

"Do you think Dawg missed me?" Mark asked, shifting
his legs so that his feet were propped up on a sack of flour.

Luke made a noise that could have been an affirmation or
a growl.

Rachel glanced at him out of the corner of her eye. His
strong profile seemed harsh in the daylight. Under the shade

of his hat, the shape of his brow spoke of strength, the set of his jaw, stubbornness. He sat easily on the bench seat, his posture erect but not stiff. It was as though they were in the parlor instead of on a moving wagon. While she occasionally had to grab the side to stay upright, he seemed to absorb every bounce.

There was a power about him. He was a danger to her; her heart hadn't forgotten what was supposed to have been. And yet she felt secure. If there was anyone in the world who could keep her and her son safe from John Steele, it was Luke.

"If you don't like Thunder, I could think up another name," Mark said hopefully.

She recognized the appeal for attention. Before she could tell Mark to be quiet, Luke tossed the boy a grin.

"I like Thunder just fine. But how do you know it's a her?"

"The lady that gave her to me said so. She showed me how to check to see if—"

"That's enough," Rachel said, careful to hide her smile. "You've named your kitten. Why don't you try to rest till we get back. It's been a long day for you."

"But, Ma . . ." Mark rose to his knees, the kitten held precariously in one hand. "I'm not tired. It's not even near dark."

"It will be by the time we get back," she said.

"Listen to your mother." Once again Luke kept his gaze up front as he spoke.

She fought down a flush of annoyance when her son scrambled to obey.

They continued the journey. Rachel stared out at the vast land. This was the same road she'd taken on her way to the ranch. Had it been only eleven days ago? The first time she'd traveled with equal parts of fear and hope; the fear had been for the past, the hope for what lay ahead. Now she felt that Luke's sense of betrayal was stronger than the love they had shared. They could never recapture what had been. But even without his love, she would survive.

The clopping of the horses' hooves echoed in the still winter afternoon. There was a peace in the moment. For now it didn't matter that Luke would never love her; she didn't dwell on John Steele or the past. She thought of nothing but the melting snow and the promise of spring.

The silence lasted only five minutes.

"I'm hungry," Mark said. "And Thunder is, too."

"There's a basket under the seat," Luke said. "Sarah packed some chicken and biscuits."

Rachel reached down and felt a blanket-covered basket. The sudden rumble of her stomach reminded her she hadn't eaten anything but a hard roll the whole day. After she and Luke had worked out their financial agreement, he'd taken her and Mark to the general store to stock up on supplies. The shopping had been rushed; they'd needed to leave Horse Creek by two-thirty to get back to the ranch before dark.

After pushing aside the covering, she set the basket between them on the bench. An inventory of the contents showed that Sarah had also included jars of water, half a cake, and a cup filled with honey.

"There's a lot of food here," she said, handing Luke a napkin. "More than enough for the three of us. You must have been pretty confident that I'd be willing to come back with you." She knew he could hear the bitterness in her voice.

For the first time since they'd left town, he glanced at her. His gray eyes, flecked with slivers of green, gave nothing away. Firm lips that had once tenderly caressed her own pulled into a straight line.

He studied her face as if seeing her for the first time. She fought down the urge to check for a smudge on her cheek or to tuck back a stray strand of hair.

"Sarah told me to bring you home," he said finally. "She's the one who thought you'd come back. I thought you'd tell me to go to hell."

"I'd never swear."

He raised one arched brow. "What about that time you found your Sunday dress had fallen off the line and was lying in the mud? If I recall, you were very clear about the exact—"

"Luke Hawkins, you hush."

He smiled at her then. A quick flash of humor that exp)sed his white teeth and caused the skin around his eyes to crinkle. The years fell away, leaving behind the friendly young man she had loved for as long as she could remember.

Rachel exhaled suddenly, as if she'd received a blow to the stomach. She could handle his anger, even his scorn—fighting those emotions kept her strong—but dealing with Luke as a friend would be more than she could stand. That last protective barrier might fall away and leave her heart exposed. She'd survived loving and losing him once; a second time would kill her.

"Mama, you got any chicken for me and Thunder?" Mark peeked over the back of the seat.

"Here." She handed him a piece of meat and a napkin. "Don't give Thunder any bones. Do you want a biscuit?"

The boy nodded.

When she had finished serving the men, she began to eat her own meal. Hunger gnawed at her insides, urging her to gulp down the spicy chicken and soft rolls, but she held back. No point in making herself sick. She had to be prepared to start working tomorrow.

"Who feeds the chickens and collects the eggs?" she asked Luke.

He'd braced one heel on the footboard and looped the reins over his left forearm. The horses walked on in the afternoon. "Potter sometimes, or one of the men from the bunkhouse. If everyone is busy, Sarah takes care of it. Why do you ask?"

"I just wondered what my duties would be. Will you want me to cook for the men or—"

"No!"

Rachel glanced at him, surprised by his adamant tone.

He shook his head and swore softly under his breath. "What I meant is that Sarah needs you to help her around the house. The cowboys have their own cook. Once every couple of weeks one of them is assigned to laundry duty. You won't have to deal with them very much at all."

Part of her wanted to believe Luke was bothered by the thought of her coming into contact with the men who worked on his ranch, but she told herself fanciful dreams wouldn't accomplish anything. No doubt he wanted to know where she was to keep her out of trouble.

She should have been irritated by his attitude, but she wasn't. Work was something she was familiar with. She'd been John Steele's unpaid servant since her husband died. There were those back in Kansas who had told her she should have been grateful that her father-in-law had kept her on, that the roof over her head and her son's was more than enough payment. But they didn't know how she'd pleaded with John to allow her to return to her family home. He'd refused and then had threatened to come after her and take Mark, if she left.

A shiver ran through her at the thought of John finding her. He would know where she'd run. He would come after her, but she wasn't worried. Not now. When Luke had offered her the job, the unwritten half of his agreement had been protection. They both knew it. Whatever the future might hold, Mark would be safe.

Luke finished his piece of chicken and took a long swallow of water. They were sharing a jar; he was careful to drink only from his side.

"Do you want another biscuit?" she asked.

He nodded.

She picked one up and handed it to him.

"Thanks." He reached forward and took it, then paused, frowning. "What happened?"

She glanced at her outstretched hand. Her first three fingers were rubbed raw. Blisters marched across her palm; the sore areas looked red and angry. She made a fist and started to draw her arm back, but he reached out and held her fast.

"What happened?" he repeated.

"Nothing."

Luke set his biscuit on the bench between them, then forced her fingers to open. "You've hurt yourself. Did you get burned?"

She shook her head. "It was the reins when I drove in to Horse Creek. I'm not used to driving."

His gaze met hers; concern darkened the gray to slate. "Didn't you use the Steeles' buggy back in Kansas?"

She noticed he said "Kansas" rather than "home." *This* was where he belonged now. She'd do well not to forget that. "No. John didn't like me going anywhere alone."

His eyes continued to search hers, but he knew enough of John Steele to figure out the rest of the story himself. There was no need to tell him she'd been a virtual prisoner, allowed out only to attend church and visit her mother.

"Didn't you wear gloves?"

"Yes." She didn't mention that the leather had worn away to nothing.

"Is your other hand as bad?"

Silently she held it out. Matching sores marred the pale skin. He took both of her hands in his own and looked closely at the injuries. The backs of her hands nestled securely in his palms; long fingers wrapped around her wrists. His thumbs traced the wounds, careful not to touch the tender areas. A feeling of warmth drifted up her arms and settled in her chest.

"I'm sure Sarah has a salve to take care of this," he said. "When we get back, I'll have her give you some."

"I'm fine."

She told herself to pull away from his touch, but she couldn't bring herself to break the spell between them. For the first time since she'd shown up unannounced, Luke was treating her like someone he cared about. He hadn't forgiven her, but maybe he was willing to begin anew.

"Can I have some cake?" Mark asked.

The reminder that they weren't alone caused her to flush slightly. She offered Luke a half smile, then turned to her son. After exchanging the chicken bones for a slice of cake, she licked the crumbs from her fingers. When she glanced across the seat, Luke followed the motion with hungry eyes.

Awareness flared within her. Suddenly the chill of the afternoon disappeared as did the sound of Mark's conversation with his cat. She and Luke were alone; a man and a woman who had recently, very recently, shared a long passionate kiss.

His gaze dropped to her mouth. The look was as physical as that kiss. Her heart fluttered uncertainly. Was that why he'd offered her the job? Did he mean to continue what he had begun that night? Was she prepared to allow Luke Hawkins into her bed?

The wagon lurched suddenly, and he returned his attention to the barely discernible path. Rachel clutched the side of the seat. The discomfort in her hands chased away the last of the tingling. There could be no lovers' games between them. They weren't children anymore; their love had faded along with the memories of what should have been. Besides, he wasn't the sort of man to take advantage of an employee. Despite his anger the night she'd arrived, she'd never feared his advances.

Luke wouldn't take what wasn't freely offered, and she was in no position to offer anything. For all she knew, that part of her had been destroyed.

"Mama, we're done with this." Mark handed her an empty jar.

She smiled. "You two were thirsty."

"Yup. You should have seen how much Thunder drank."

She winced at the thought of sharing her glass with a cat, then placed the container in the basket. "Why don't you try to rest now?"

"Okay." His agreement was followed by a yawn.

After taking up the blanket that had covered the picnic basket, Rachel leaned back and tucked it around her son. The kitten curled up on his shoulder, her back pressed against a sack of flour.

They made quite a picture, the dirty little boy with smudges on his cheeks and crumbs on his chin, and the skinny ball of fur snuggling close to his neck. She brushed the hair from Mark's eyes and tucked the edge of the blanket around his legs.

"I'm not going to fall asleep," he mumbled, closing his eyes.

"Of course not," she agreed.

"I don't want to miss nothin'."

"Anything," she said softly.

"Anything." His reply was followed by another yawn, then steady breathing.

"He'll be out in a second," Luke whispered.

"I think you're right."

She gave Mark one last glance and noted how the bright blanket contrasted with his dull, worn coat. She thought of the bolts of fabric back at the general store. If only she'd bought a few yards, she could have made some decent clothes. But that wasn't possible. Until Luke paid her, all that lay between her and complete poverty was twenty-two dollars. She couldn't risk their nest egg on anything right now. Besides, it would be summer soon. She and Mark would get by. They always had.

"He's a good boy," Luke said, breaking into her thoughts.

"Yes, he is."

"I see a lot of Matthew in him."

Nothing in Luke's voice gave away his feelings, and she didn't have the courage to try to read them on his face. She made a great show of studying the snow in the pitch pine trees.

"Matthew loved the boy," she offered finally.

"And John?"

"John never had time for children. You of all people should know that."

She felt Luke shift on the seat, as though the reminder of the beatings had provided a physical sensation. "I figured Mark being kin might have made a difference."

"It should have. But it didn't."

The wagon bounced over a deep rut. She'd been so busy trying not to notice Luke that she'd stopped holding on to the seat. When the wheels on her side jerked up, she slid along the bench.

As quickly as the motion had begun, it was over. Rachel found herself pressed tightly against Luke. From shoulder to thigh, through the layers of her clothing, she felt the warmth of his body.

She drew in a quick breath. The scent of him—that masculine essence that mingled with the aroma of the leather and the wood and the afternoon to create something irresistible—made her long for that moment by the fire when he'd brushed her hair. She could still feel the gentle tugging of the brush, the strength of his hands when he'd massaged her scalp.

Before she did or said anything foolish, she quickly moved back to her own side of the wagon.

"Sorry," she mumbled.

The tipping of his hat was his only acknowledgment. "Matthew always wanted a son," he said, picking up their conversation.

"So did you." The words were out before she could stop them. "I'm sorry."

"Don't apologize for speaking the truth. I *did* want a son."

This time her study of the snow wasn't a pretense. She was a coward, too frightened to risk seeing the censure on Luke's face. How many times had they talked about having children? How many times had they argued about numbers and names? Two of each, they'd finally agreed upon.

"You never married," she said, voicing the question that had kept her walking the halls of his house.

"That's right." He urged the horses to go faster.

Clutching her hands tightly together, she risked a glance. And wished she hadn't. All the warmth was gone from his eyes, leaving the irises as cold and bleak as a winter storm. But she had to know.

"Was it because I married Matthew?"

"Don't flatter yourself."

"Then why?"

"Never saw the need."

"Don't you get lonely?"

His mouth twisted. "Were you lonely, Rachel? Did Matthew give you everything you wanted? Were you rich enough with him?"

"I told you why I married Matthew. It was because of my father, not because the Steeles had money."

"Of course. But you didn't answer the question."

He wanted to hurt her; she saw it on his face. Whatever truce they'd had was already broken. All her instincts screamed at her to protect herself from him, but she couldn't deny the truth.

"Yes, I was lonely. After you left, I couldn't believe how much I missed you. Even though Matthew and I came to an understanding, I never forgot what had been between you and me. I loved you."

He laughed harshly. "That's where we're different, Mrs. Steele. Your marriage to Matthew taught me I never loved you at all."

They reached the ranch before nightfall. Luke set the brake on the wagon, then stepped down and crossed around to the other side. But Rachel had already lowered herself to the ground. She'd been quiet for the last couple of miles. He thought about asking what was wrong, then shrugged. The girl he'd known hadn't had any trouble speaking what was on her mind. So far, Rachel seemed to have retained that quality. If something was troubling her, she'd mention it soon enough.

"He's asleep," she said, leaning forward to study Mark. "I hate to wake him."

"Then don't."

He lowered the tailgate on the wagon and reached in for several boxes. When he'd stacked them on the porch, he climbed up next to Mark. This close he could see the long lashes that rested against his cheeks, smell the unique scent of dirt and little boy, hear the soft breathing.

He told himself he hadn't missed Mark. The kid had a way of always being underfoot. Yet there was a tightness in his chest as he watched the sleeping boy.

"Here." He picked up the kitten and handed her to Rachel. "You carry Thunder; I'll carry Mark."

"But where should I put her?" Rachel's blue eyes looked no higher than the top button of his jacket.

"Inside. Won't Mark want her in his room?"

"Of course. I just thought . . ." She patted the animal's soft head and turned toward the house. When she reached the porch, she looked back. "Thank you."

There was something in her voice, as if she were in pain. But he couldn't see anything wrong with her stride or expression. Must be those damn ghosts again.

He picked Mark up, careful to leave the blanket around him. When he walked into the kitchen, Sarah was holding Rachel in a tight embrace. His housekeeper looked over at him. Tears filled her pale eyes and traced a path down her cheeks.

"You brought them back," she murmured.

He shifted uncomfortably, adjusting Mark's slight weight. "I said I would." He spoke softly as well, so as not to wake the boy.

"I'll take him." Sarah held out her arms.

Luke shook his head. "Just go turn down the bed."

He followed the older woman through the house. After she'd pulled back the quilt, he set Mark own. Sarah unlaced his shoes, then pulled the covers up over his thin body.

Rachel stepped in between them and placed Thunder on the pillow.

In the twilight Luke could see the conflict of emotions on her face. Gratitude mingled with what looked like stark pain. Before he could question her, she fled the room.

He started to follow her into the hall, but Sarah held him back.

"Let her go," she said, placing a restraining hand on his forearm. "She's tired from the trip. She needs some rest."

"Fine."

By the time Luke and Sarah had unloaded the wagon and stacked the supplies in the pantry, night had fallen.

Sarah glanced at the last pile. "Isn't there another box?"

"No." He sat down in a chair and propped his feet up on the opposite seat. "What were you looking for? Did I forget something?"

"I thought . . ." She closed the door leading into the hallway, then sat next to him at the kitchen table. "Didn't Rachel buy anything?"

He shrugged, then sipped his coffee. "Not that I noticed. Should she have?"

"Haven't you noticed her clothes? They're threadbare. And Mark's, too. All the shirts I washed were patched and made over. Her coat doesn't have a lining anymore. I just don't understand it."

Luke tried to remember what Rachel had worn, but all he could recall was the blush that had stained her cheeks when she'd caught him studying her mouth. In that moment nothing had mattered except his need to possess her.

"Maybe she didn't have a chance," he said. "There wasn't much time to collect the supplies. I wanted to be sure we made it back before dark."

"I think it's more than the fact that you were rushed.

When she left here she only had about twenty-six dollars. That would have been used up quickly in town.''

Unease mingled uncomfortably with the coffee. He glanced over at Sarah. ''But she's Matthew's widow. Why would she want for anything? Maybe she just grabbed the closest things before she ran off.''

''I don't think so.'' Sarah stood up and paced the room. When she reached the far counter, she pulled a plate out of the cupboard and sliced off a large piece of cake. ''It's not just one or two dresses that are threadbare; it's everything they own. You should have made her buy some wool.''

He took the plate and set it on the table. ''How the hell was I supposed to know to tell her that? I don't have time to keep track of nonsense like ruffles and petticoats.''

Sarah turned toward him and placed her hands on her ample hips. ''Luke Hawkins, I will not listen to that kind of talk in my house.''

''It's *my* house,'' he mumbled as he bit into the cake.

A smile tilted up the corner of her mouth, and she patted his shoulder. ''Your house, then. So what are you going to do about it?''

''Me?''

''She's your responsibility now.''

He looked up toward the heavens. ''In less than two weeks I've inherited a dog, a boy, his mother, and a ball of scruff that passes for a cat. The cowboys will be rounding up horses any day now, so I won't have time for this, Sarah. You handle it.''

''I can't take her to town. There's too much work to be done. Besides, you'll need to give her an advance on her wages first.''

Sarah warmed up his coffee, but he refused to be mollified. ''I'll check with Ian and see if he's heading in. If he's not, she'll just have to wait. I'm not having her ride all that distance alone, and you know I can't send her in with one of the hired hands.''

Sarah moved over to the cookstove and began rubbing the already clean top. ''Is Ian coming by to help with the horses?''

If he hadn't glanced up at that moment and caught her blush, he might not have thought her question unusual. ''Yes. Do you want me to give him a message?''

Her shoulders jerked suddenly, as though she'd been caught off guard. ''No. I was just curious.''

She was lying. He could feel it. But why? Had something happened the last time Ian visited the house? Luke frowned, trying to remember exactly when that had been. Before Rachel arrived, certainly. Perhaps as long as six weeks ago. Their neighbor had ridden over to talk about the spring breeding program. After dinner he and Ian had retired to Luke's office. Sarah had brought them coffee and pie and . . .

Had they talked? Damn, he couldn't remember. There was a vague image of the two of them going on about something while Luke worked on the accounts.

He looked up and watched Sarah scrub the counters. Her recent blush had left a pink color on her cheeks. Her hair, while touched by gray, still hung long and thick down her back. Her generous curves would keep a man warm at night. Especially a lonely widower.

''How long since Fiona died?'' he asked, more to test his idea than because he couldn't remember.

''Four years.''

''That's a long time for a man to be alone.''

Sarah spun to face him, her lips forming a perfect O. Then she tossed her rag into the metal sink and quickly untied her plain white apron.

"It's late," she said. "I've got darning to do." With that she fled.

Luke stared after her. So Sarah had feelings for Ian Frasier. His first reaction was that he'd miss her when she was gone. His second, that it was time Sarah had a place of her own. But what were Frasier's intentions?

He sighed heavily and rubbed the back of his neck. That could be determined when the horses returned. Until then, he'd keep a watchful eye on Miss Sarah Green. No telling what other secrets the lady might have in store.

After placing his plate on the counter, he refilled his coffee cup, then located the tin of salve. Although it wasn't much past dark, when he reached Rachel's room, there wasn't any light shining under the door. She must have already turned in. He thought about placing the ointment on her dresser, but when he reached for the door handle, he found he couldn't bring himself to disturb her sanctuary. He backed away quietly, then moved on to his office.

It was close to midnight when he heard soft footsteps in the hallway. Luke dropped his pencil on the desk and walked quickly to the open doorway.

"Rachel?" he called softly.

The light was behind him. The long shadow cast by his body made the areas beyond the room disappear into darkness. A flash of movement by the parlor caught his eye.

"Rachel?" he repeated.

"I didn't mean to disturb you." She took a step toward him, then paused.

Her silhouette was indistinct. The heavy blanket over her shoulders hid the shape of her body from view. Even the features of her face had faded into the night.

"You're not disturbing me. In fact, I have something for you. Come here." When she continued to hesitate, he held out his hand.

Slowly she moved toward him. He was reminded of the time he'd tried to tame a skittish mare. The sorrel horse had approached and retreated, drawn by his offer of an apple, yet fearful of approaching any man. She'd been badly treated by some farmers on their way west. In the end he'd won her over and she'd become a valuable part of his breeding program. He wondered what made Rachel equally cautious.

When she reached the office doorway he felt as if that same mare had kicked him in the belly. Rachel's eyes were red, her mouth swollen. She'd been crying. And he knew with a certainty he couldn't deny that he was the cause of her pain.

Chapter Seven

"What's wrong?" he asked, ushering her inside the office and over to a chair.

"Nothing." But her indelicate sniff belied her words. Why was it that a woman never got to cry in peace? she asked herself as she brushed away the remaining tears. There was always a man lurking around, just waiting for the most inopportune moment to show up. "I'm overly tired. Don't pay me any mind." She sank into the seat and pulled the blanket around her legs. "What did you want to show me?"

He stood in front of her. She could read the indecision in his gray eyes. The urge to find out what troubled her battled with politeness that insisted he follow her lead by ignoring the obvious.

He picked up a tin from the desk. "This."

"What is it?"

"A salve for your hands. It will prevent infection and keep the sores from leaving scars."

She smiled. "We mustn't have scars."

"You know what I mean."

"Yes. And thank you."

She reached out to take the tin, but he shook his head. After kneeling beside the chair, he opened the tin and scooped out a generous portion of the thick white cream.

Then, taking one of her hands in his, he began to massage in the healing ointment. His strokes were slow and sure; he applied enough pressure to ensure absorption but not enough to cause pain.

The glow from the lantern highlighted his rich brown hair, illuminating the reddish tints. A day's worth of stubble darkened the strong lines of his cheeks and jaw. How familiar he was, she thought, fighting the urge to touch his face. And how much a stranger. His mouth tightened as he concentrated on his task. She tried to ignore the weight of his forearms resting on her legs, the scent of his body, the silence of the room.

They seemed to be alone in the world, adrift on a sea of darkness. But what should have been sweet, even sensual, only added to the pain in her chest. Even now she could hear his words, the sound of his voice as he'd told her he'd never loved her.

It was a lie, of course. He had loved as passionately as she. They had pledged themselves to each other with all the idealism and intensity of youth. But having him reject what they'd once had was more than she could comprehend. It wasn't so much that he'd told her a lie; it was that he believed the lie to be true.

He continued to rub in the salve.

"I can do that," she said, watching the way his strong fingers dwarfed her palm.

"No trouble."

No trouble. Of course not. He wouldn't want the hired help unable to work. The bitterness left an acrid taste on her tongue.

In an effort to distract herself from his ministrations, she glanced around the room. Floor-to-ceiling shelves housed dozens of books. A stone fireplace in the corner added warmth and light to an otherwise plain room.

He switched hands and shifted his weight slightly, bringing his chest in contact with her knee. It was like bumping into a warm but solid wall of muscle.

"You have a lot of books," she said to pull herself free of his spell.

"Yes."

"I didn't have a chance to bring any with me. May I borrow a few to continue with Mark's lessons?"

Luke's slow smile caught her off guard. That was twice now he'd looked at her with humor and affection. The rapid pounding of her heart and the sudden heat that flared low in her belly warned her that she'd do well to stay clear of him. He might have convinced himself that there had never been anything between them, but the reaction of her body reminded her otherwise.

"That boy's already a terror. Are you sure you should give him the weapon of knowledge too?"

"He *is* bright, isn't he? And he likes studying. He's better at ciphering than I am." She ducked her head self-consciously. "He's always after me to make up problems for him, but if they're too difficult, I can't tell if the answer's right. The funny thing is, I don't know where he got it from. Matthew and I were both hopeless with figuring. Sometimes I—"

She stopped speaking and squeezed her eyes shut.

Why had she mentioned Matthew's name? Whenever things were going well, she blundered by bringing up the past. It wasn't that she was ashamed of her husband; it was just that she and Luke needed time to adjust to the present.

Instead of the outburst she'd expected, Luke gave her hands a final squeeze, then sat on the floor beside her. She stared in surprise, waiting, but he only rested his wrist on one raised knee.

"You're welcome to any books you'd like," he said,

gazing into the flames. "I'm sure I have a slate and chalk somewhere. I'll leave them on the desk. Between now and summer the ranch will keep me busy, so I'll be gone most of the time. You can conduct your lessons in the office."

"Th-thank you." She, too, looked into the fire as though it held the secrets of the world. "We'll be careful with your belongings."

"Mark mentioned something about a horse. Does he know how to ride?"

"A little. John gave him a pony, but Blackie was very old. He couldn't do more than walk around in the corral." She shifted in her chair. "There's no need to go to any trouble for us, Luke. I don't want to put you out."

Out of the corner of her eye she saw him shrug. "No trouble. Potter's been after me to get the boy up on a horse. He's afraid he'll turn into a nester before long."

She smiled. "Did you tell Potter that *you* used to be a farmer?"

Their eyes met in the shared joke.

"Yes, but I don't think he believed me."

She looked away first. Her thumb traced the path of her blisters, feeling the lingering slickness of the salve, remembering the strength of Luke's touch. "You like it here, don't you?"

"Yeah. It's different from Kansas. More untamed. It would take several days to ride the perimeter of my land, and that doesn't count what I lease from the government and from some folks in town. People here don't care that I'm the bastard son of John Steele's housekeeper."

"Luke, I—"

"No." He glanced up at her, his gray eyes reflecting the light of the fire. "That's the point. Being illegitimate doesn't matter anymore. What I make out of this land is up to me. No one else. I've let go of the past."

She swallowed against the lump in her throat. She was part of the past. That was why he'd let go of her too. "How many cattle do you have?"

He grinned. "Thousands. We won't know for sure until spring roundup. That's usually the last couple of weeks in May. We'll brand the calves and do a head count. I'm also having a small herd driven east."

"East? From where?"

"Oregon. A lot of the settlers took cattle with them when they traveled west. I've bought about three thousand head." He stretched his legs out straight and crossed them at the ankle. "They're Durham blood, more docile than the longhorns, but surefooted and very large. I'm starting a breeding program with Ian Frasier, one of our neighbors. We're buying a blooded Hereford bull together." He paused. "'Blooded' means—"

She cut him off with a laugh. "I know what 'blooded' means. I might be descended from a long line of nesters, but I'm not ignorant. When does this Oregon herd arrive?"

"I'm not sure. Late summer. Maybe September. A few of my men went to Oregon to hire hands to bring them out. I just received notice they're on their way."

He spoke with an excitement and enthusiasm she hadn't heard in years. His hands moved as he described the plans he had for expansion, how he and Ian were going to build up the herd, how they wanted to start selling bulls to other ranchers. In that, he hadn't changed. Luke had always given himself wholly to whatever held his interest, be it a farm, a ranch, or a woman.

Each sentence, each phrase, reinforced his commitment to the land. This land. Kansas had faded into the background, becoming only the name of a place he wanted to forget.

Where did that leave her? In time, when John Steele was

no longer a threat to her or her son, she would have to return to Kansas. Her father's land now belonged to her, and the Steele farm was Mark's birthright. For now Wyoming meant safety and being near Luke, but when the danger was past, she would leave.

A log snapped in the fire. She realized that Luke had fallen silent.

"It's late," she said, starting to rise from her chair.

"Wait." He placed a restraining hand on her leg. The heat burned through to her skin. "I need to ask you something."

"Yes?" She laced her fingers together.

"Why are all your clothes so worn?"

Rachel sprang to her feet. The chair slid along the wooden floor and bounced into the desk. "I can't . . . You wouldn't understand."

"Try me."

He stood in front of her, close enough to keep her in place, but far enough away that they didn't touch. The lamp was behind him, the fireplace behind her. The time had come to tell the truth, she thought.

"There's no money."

He frowned. "That's not possible. The Steele farm is the richest in the county. When I left, there was enough money to cover a dozen bad seasons."

"I know." She stared at the middle of his chest, studying the round button and the weave of the fabric. "John started drinking. Not much at first, or so I thought. After Matthew died . . . I don't know if he'd always drunk that much and no longer felt the need to hide his habit or if the death of his son pushed him over the edge."

"But liquor wouldn't waste the entire fortune."

She paused, unsure if she could be honest. But what did

it matter now? "He gambled. When he drank, he lost. Badly. And he drank a lot."

In a far-off corner of her mind, she noted that her voice sounded steady and calm. Nothing gave away the torture her life had become. Luke wouldn't be able to figure out the torment of living with a drunk. Sober, John Steele had been a man to be wary of, but after he'd consumed a bottle of whiskey, he turned into the devil. No one had been safe from his temper. Not Mark and certainly not Rachel.

"How much of the money is left?" he asked.

"None."

She felt and heard his gasp of disbelief. "*All* of it's gone?"

She nodded. "The Steele farm has been mortgaged for over a year. The bank is threatening to foreclose. John wants me to sell our farm and give him the money." The memories threatened to escape from the box she'd shut them in. Quickly she shook her head and stumbled on. "I refused, of course. Mama doesn't have a head for business, but she's behind me in this. When my father left me the land, I wondered if she'd felt slighted by him, but it's worked out for the best. She doesn't have anything John wants, so he's never troubled her. In the last few weeks before I left, he was after me every day."

"Is that why you ran away?"

If he hadn't touched her, she might have spoken the rest of the truth. But the gentle brush of his finger on her cheek caused her to raise her head and look at him. And when she saw the familiar lines of his face, the compassion in his eyes, the gentle set of his mouth, she found she could not say the words. His disgust would have been more than she could bear.

"Yes," she lied.

"I'm sorry."

"It's not your fault."

"I know. But I should have realized something was wrong. And today we could have bought some clothes for you and Mark."

"We're fine."

"You shouldn't make the trip to town on your own. I'll be tied up for the next few days, but I'll see if one of our neighbors is going to Horse Creek. You can go along and buy what you need."

"I'd rather wait until next month."

"Why?" His fingers traced her cheek, making it difficult to concentrate.

"Because I just would."

His other hand now rested on her shoulder. His thumb rubbed up and down on her bare neck. She realized that the blanket had fallen to the floor, leaving her standing in just her nightgown.

She swallowed thickly and wondered if the flannel was as thin as she remembered. Could he see the shape of her body through the plain fabric? Could he tell that their closeness was making her breasts feel heavy, her nipples hard? Did he know how easy it would be for her to give herself to him, that despite all that had happened, all he'd said and all John Steele had done, she still wanted to be loved by Luke Hawkins?

"I'll pay for the clothes," he said.

"No." She tried to pull away, but he wouldn't let her. His fingers tightened on her shoulder, holding her still.

"I want to. Not only for you but for Matthew. In my position, he would have done the same."

"Oh, Luke. Why did it have to turn out this way?" she asked as she placed her palms on his chest. Through the shirt, she felt the steady beat of his heart.

He cupped her cheeks and tilted her head forward, then kissed her on the brow. "I don't know."

She saw the compassion change to desire. His gaze flickered over her features, lower to her chest, then back to her face. "Rachel, I . . ." One finger touched her right cheekbone and he frowned. "Where did you get this?"

"What?" She reached up to feel for herself, but only encountered his hand.

"There's a scar here. I don't remember it. How did it happen?"

The roaring in her ears sounded like a herd of cattle thundering across the plains. Time bent, then tore, and suddenly she was back in Kansas, in the large kitchen facing John Steele. His black eyes flashed with drunken rage. She could hear him screaming that his supper was late and burned. Matthew hadn't been gone more than a month, and the heavy skirt and petticoats of her mourning dress didn't allow her to move as quickly as usual. When John raised his arm to strike her, she tried to duck, but got tangled in the legs of a chair. The back of his hand cracked across her cheek, his ring tore into her skin. Even now she could feel the pain of the blow and taste the blood.

"Rachel?" Luke's voice came from far away, but it was enough to drag her into the present. "Rachel? Are you all right?"

"Fine," she managed, realizing that she was in Luke's study—and safe. "How did it happen?" She stepped away and touched the scar. "It was just an accident."

The trembling started deep inside her. It was only a matter of moments until it overtook her body. She had to get back to bed before she was unable to walk—before Luke saw the state of her nerves.

"It's late," she said, easing toward the door. "Good night."

"Wait."

She heard him move behind her. She could feel the fear building up inside her, the cold sweat breaking out on her back. She could sense his questions.

"There's more," he said quietly. "You're not telling me everything."

She crossed her arms over her chest. "I have to get up early to help Sarah." Would he ask? she wondered. Part of her recoiled from the shame, but a part longed to share the heavy burden. Would he hold her if he knew? Would he forgive her? Would he love her? The silence continued, counted out in heartbeats.

"Good night, Rachel."

Disappointment flared hotter than the pain. When would she learn? He'd told her face to face that he'd never loved her. It was time to forget the past and get on with her life.

One fact stood out starker than all the others: No matter what had gone on before, Luke Hawkins was lost to her forever.

"A full house." John Steele tossed his cards onto the table and leaned forward to gather up the money.

None of the other men looked at him, but he took their ill humor in stride. No one liked a winner. They didn't like him when he wasn't winning either, but they could go to hell for all he cared. A few more nights like this and he'd have enough to pay off the mortgage.

John poured another shot of whiskey and drank it down in one swallow. He could hardly wait to see the sour expression on Gridley's baby face when he slapped the money on his desk. And when the mortgage was paid off, he'd close his account. Those bastards weren't getting any more of his hard-earned cash.

"Start another game," he said, motioning to the dealer.

"And up the ante." He belched loudly, then poured another shot. "I feel like taking more of your money."

As he reached for the glass, a hand clamped down on his wrist. "I don't think you'll be playing here anymore, my friend. Tonight or ever."

John blinked several times, staring first at the strong fingers holding him still and then at the face of the saloon owner. Cold black eyes bored into his.

He'd heard rumors that Nando had once killed an even dozen Texas Rangers, that his family had been slaughtered during the war with Mexico, that he'd come north with stolen gold and a desire to get even. In the past, Steele had ignored the stories, but now, with the wiry Mexican bending over him, he wondered if they were true.

"Get your Mex hands off me." John tried to tug his arm free. It was like trying to break away from a steel manacle.

"There is a slight problem, my friend."

Before he knew what had happened, Nando pulled him to his feet, then jerked quickly, twisting his arm up and behind his back. Pain shot through John's shoulder. The quick action of the saloon owner caused the others at the table to stand up and start moving back. A hush fell over the crowd. The piano in the corner continued to sound out a song, then faded to silence.

"You're about to lose that hand, Nando," Steele said, glaring over his shoulder. "You've got no right—"

Nando shrugged slightly and tightened his grip on John's arm. "The law gives me the right."

"Damn it all to hell."

The other patrons circled around like vultures. He'd deal with them later, he thought. First he had to get away from the stinking bastard.

His gun was on his right side. He shifted slightly, reaching for it with his left hand.

"Don't even think of it." Nando's breath whistled past his ear. "You have been a loyal customer for many years, so I won't kill you, but never again return to my saloon."

The saloon owner pulled Steele's gun out of the holster. One-handed, Nando snapped open the cylinder. John heard the bullets fall to the wooden floor. Then Nando replaced the empty gun in the holster.

"I know you have trouble," Nando said, pushing him out through the front door of the saloon. John resisted, but the other man shoved hard against his back, forcing him to walk or fall. "Nobody cheats me." With that, Nando pulled up the sleeve on John's free arm and yanked out the three aces he'd tucked into the cuff of his shirt.

Rage filled John. The slimy Mex bastard would pay for this. He'd return and kill Nando. Shoot him in the back.

John stiffened when he heard the ominous click of a hammer being pulled back and felt cold metal pressed against his temple. Shit.

"Walk away," Nando said, standing at the edge of the wooden sidewalk. "Never come back. Not to my saloon or any other in town. Word of your habit will spread."

With that, Nando released his arm. Steele had barely had time to register the fact when a push sent him sprawling into the dirt.

"So much for the rich Steeles," he heard one man say, the words punctuated by a spit of tobacco. "Hell, we ought to shoot him now and put him out of his misery."

"Don't waste a bullet," another said. "Farm'll be up on auction soon enough. Buy it real cheap and get the two widow women in the deal."

Their laughter was muffled when the saloon doors swung shut.

John pushed himself up on his knees, then fell back into the dirt. The last of the drunken haze faded, leaving behind only anger and a desire for revenge. He knew who was responsible for what had happened tonight. It was that bitch Rachel. And Luke. He mustn't forget Luke.

"I should have killed him when he was born," he said, trying again to raise himself into a sitting position. "I should have left him out to die in the cold. Ah, Mary."

"I'll get 'em all for you, Mary," he mumbled, staggering to his feet. "Especially the bastard that killed you. Especially Luke."

He bumped into the first horse tied up front, then leaned against the sturdy shoulder.

Piano music drifted out onto the street. The sound of drunken laughter, the squeals of the whores, made him feel alone. They'd stolen everything, and now they were going to steal his land.

Never, he thought. He'd kill them all first.

Feeling his way along the railing, he found his horse and pulled himself up into the saddle, then urged the animal toward home. The slow gait made his stomach roll. He swallowed long gulps of air.

"I'll find Rachel," he swore to the night. "I'll force her to sell her farm and give me the money. Then I'll take the bitch and make her my own." He grinned at the thought of her young body yielding to him. His son had been dead three years. She'd had plenty of time to mourn. "She needs a man."

He remembered how she'd fought that last time. All he'd wanted was a feel or two of her breasts, then a quick hump. Rachel had attacked him as if she had something worth saving.

His blood quickened at the memory of her taste and smell and the fight in her. Holding his reins with one hand, he moved the other down to stroke himself. It was all her fault. If she hadn't run off to Luke, he wouldn't have had to cheat at cards.

As his horse traversed the familiar road, John Steele began to form a plan. It would be easy, he thought. Kill Luke and bring Rachel back to Kansas. After she sold her farm and gave him the money, he'd use her until he got tired of her whining. Then she could join her lover in hell.

He threw back his head and laughed. The sound drifted across the farmland and echoed long into the night.

"Mama? Mama, wake up."

Rachel opened one eye. "Mark, what are you going on about? It's the middle of the night."

Her son grinned and continued to shake her shoulder. "But they're startin' on the horses today. And you said I could watch."

She rose up on one elbow and squinted toward the window. "It's not even close to light yet. Why aren't you asleep?"

His dark eyes, so like his father's, gleamed with excitement. "I don't want to miss nothin'."

"Anything," she said automatically as she sat up and swung her feet toward the floor. "Is anyone else up yet?"

"Yes."

Rachel glanced up and saw Sarah standing in the doorway. The older woman still had on her nightgown, a thick blue shawl draped over her shoulders.

"Did he wake you?"

Sarah smiled. "It sounded as if the herd had gotten loose inside the house. I'll go start the coffee. You take your time getting dressed. Somehow Luke managed to sleep through the commotion, so I won't bother him yet."

Rachel glanced at her son. "Don't you have something to say to Sarah?"

Mark hung his head and traced the edge of a board with the toe of his worn shoe. "Sorry, Sarah. I didn't mean to make noise this early."

"That's all right. Why don't you come help me fix breakfast? You're going to need a big meal to last all morning. There's a lot of horses in the remuda. Maybe Luke will let you pick out the first one to be broken."

Mark trotted by her side. "You think so? Potter keeps tellin' me that I'm gonna get my own horse, but Mama says I have to wait and see what . . ."

They turned the corner, and Rachel could no longer hear their animated conversation. Sarah was good for Mark, she thought as she stood up and stretched. Her patience and affection had a lot to do with chasing the shadows from his face. In fact, all of the people on the ranch went out of their way to make her son feel at home. A body could get used to this kind of care.

After lighting a lantern, she worked swiftly, making her bed. She'd been gainfully employed for over two weeks now. The days had settled into an easy routine. There was enough work inside to keep both women occupied, but not so much that Rachel didn't have time to spend with Mark. She moved to the dresser and began loosening her braid.

His lessons were going well. And not just the schooling. Potter was teaching him how to care for the motherless calves. A few of the cowboys provided instruction on the fine art of roping, and Luke . . . Luke was showing him how to be a man.

She'd seen the way Mark imitated Luke's way of walking, his style of speech. Only yesterday she'd caught the boy trying on Luke's hat in front of the mirror in the parlor. She still remembered the tightness that had clenched her heart when she'd seen her son wearing that beat-up old Stetson. For a moment Mark had looked like the Luke she used to know—the tilt of the head, the half smile of pride, the set of the shoulders—but then the picture changed and she'd realized she was seeing a young version of Matthew, not Luke. Her eyes had been playing tricks on her.

She picked up the brush and began pulling the stiff bristles through her hair. Still, it was good for the boy to have a man to look up to. Matthew and Luke had both missed out on that.

"I see he woke you as well."

The low masculine voice caused her hand to freeze in place. Turning slowly, she looked up until her eyes met Luke's, then down, away from his amusement. He stood in the hallway, just outside her door. A pair of half-buttoned trousers sat low on his hips. Otherwise he was naked.

She hunched her shoulders to protect herself from view. Not that it did any good. He'd seen this nightgown two weeks before. The only difference between then and now was that the fabric was one wash thinner. How many times had her mother reminded her that a lady pulled on a wrapper as soon as she awoke? You were right, Mama, she thought ruefully.

"He's very excited about today," she said softly, not daring to look up again, but not sure exactly where to set her gaze. At last she clenched the brush in her hands and stared at the wooden handle.

"Wait until spring roundup. The boy won't sleep for a week beforehand."

Rachel smiled. "I hope you're wrong. I have enough trouble getting him to pay attention to his lessons now."

She sensed his nod, then waited for him to go back to his room. Finally, unable to bear the silence, she allowed her gaze to drift to the floor, then travel the length of his body.

His feet, broad and long, with a few dark hairs peeking below the wool of his trousers, made her own naked toes curl under. Long legs supported the weight of his body. The lean strength, more concealed than highlighted by the coarse cloth, made her remember his easy stride when she watched him walk between the house and the barn. He moved with confidence and grace, like a wild animal measuring the length of its territory.

She took in the narrowness of his hips; the pattern of hair, thin at the half-buttoned placket of his trousers, wider at the top of his chest; the muscles bulging and shifting with every breath. Last, she studied his face. Two days' worth of stubble blurred the smooth line of his jaw. His mouth hinted at a smile, but the corners barely tilted up. Gray eyes, the flecks of green brighter in the lamplight, returned her gaze, never dipping lower than her mouth, not giving away a single thought.

"Mark's just a boy," he said at last. "The change in seasons seems like a game to him. Let him enjoy himself."

"I will. But I want to make sure he doesn't get in your way."

Luke shrugged. The slight lifting of his bare right shoulder make her think of how warm his skin had been that night he'd found her by the fire. It made her remember the weight of his body on hers, the taste of his lips.

"I've told the men to watch out for him," he said, never taking his eyes from hers.

She could feel the color staining her face. "I appreciate your kindness."

"I like Mark."

"He likes you, too."

What about me? she wanted to ask, but didn't have the nerve. Instead she broke their visual embrace and turned back to the mirror. "I'd better get ready. Sarah needs help with breakfast."

She sensed more than saw him start down the hall. Then he paused.

"Rachel?"

"Yes?"

"Are you coming to watch the horses?"

She looked over her shoulder and gasped softly. He was facing away from her. There was a faint crisscrossing of scars on his back—mute testimony to the cruelty of John Steele. She hadn't forgotten them, but somehow she'd assumed they would have diminished with time. He'd taken one of those blows for her—the second scar from the bottom. That wound had been deeper than the rest.

She wanted to close the distance between them and trace the pale lines of the scars. They'd faded slightly, but they would never disappear. Her hand went to the small mark on her cheek. The past that bound them together also kept them apart.

"I'd like to," she said. "If you want me there."

He stiffened. The muscles tensed into a solid protective wall. Then they relaxed, and she heard him exhale.

"We'll be in the main corral a little after eight."

"I'll see you then."

Chapter Eight

Sarah flipped the last hotcake and slid it onto a plate. "Here, Mark," she said, handing it to the boy. "Now you eat up. There's plenty of work to be done this morning. Close to a hundred horses will be coming into the ranch."

The boy's dark eyes grew wide as he walked across the room. "A hundred? I can count 'em." He drew in a breath and puffed out his chest. "Do they got names?"

Mark's attention had wandered away from his breakfast. Luke leaned across the kitchen table and grabbed the plate before the contents hit the floor. "Watch what you're doing, Mark. Here." He pulled out a chair. "Sit down and eat." He looked up and winked at Sarah, then turned to the boy. "I'll tell you about the horses. After you're done eating, we'll go find Potter. He's going to keep track of you today. He'll answer all your questions and help you pick out a horse of your own."

"Really?" Mark's grin was so big it looked ready to split his face. "A horse? Of my own? Golly." He tore off a piece of pancake and stuffed it in his mouth. "Wait until I tell my ma."

"Don't speak with your mouth full," Sarah said, ruffling the boy's hair. "And don't forget to drink your milk."

Mark reached out with both hands and grabbed the glass. His arm hit the jug of syrup, but before the sticky liquid could do more than trickle onto the table, Luke grabbed the container and set it upright.

"Children," he muttered, glancing at Sarah.

But she saw the smile lurking in his eyes.

He did well with the boy, she thought, placing the mixing bowl in the metal sink. Mark was so much like Matthew and Rachel, Luke couldn't help but be drawn in. She'd watched him resist Mark's friendly overtures, but the boy was nothing if not persistent. He got that from his mother.

"Am I too late?" Rachel asked as she walked into the kitchen.

"You're just in time to clean up. I left you some biscuits and there's coffee on the stove."

Rachel nodded, then walked over to Mark and kissed his temple. "How's my favorite son?"

Mark mumbled his response, then went on to talk about the horses. Sarah noticed that Rachel never quite managed to meet Luke's eyes. He was equally evasive, glancing everywhere in the room but at the spot where Rachel stood.

So that was how matters stood, she thought as she untied her apron and folded it over a chair. She knew how much Rachel's marrying Matthew had hurt Luke. She'd hoped time had healed that wound along with some others, but so far he'd managed to keep the widow at arm's length. Sometimes her boy could be as stubborn as a mule. Still, she'd seen the way Rachel lingered over his clothes when she did the ironing. Something had lasted through the years. She could only pray it had been enough.

After crossing to the stove, Sarah checked the water heating on the back burner. It was hot enough.

"I'm going to wash my hair," she said as she lifted the heavy pot and started toward her room.

"But you just did it Saturday," Rachel said.

"We've got horses due in any minute." Luke sounded equally incredulous.

Sarah turned slightly and glared at them. "I can wash my hair if I want to and not answer to the likes of you." High color stained her cheeks; she could feel the heat. So what if she wanted to take a little time for herself? It wouldn't hurt anything. Besides, she wanted to look nice for . . .

After reaching her room, she set the pot next to the tub standing in the corner. In a few minutes her clean gray-streaked hair was tucked under a towel. Sarah stood in front of the armoire and studied her clothes. She couldn't wear anything really nice while the men worked with the horses, but she could improve her everyday wool skirt and blouse. There was that navy blue dress she'd made over the winter but never worn.

The light-colored flowers in the fabric brought out her eyes, she thought as she held the garment in front of herself and gazed into the mirror. With two combs in her hair and her pearl earbobs, she'd look pretty without being obvious. A lady was never obvious.

After dressing quickly, Sarah went back into the kitchen. The men had left for the barn and she could hear Rachel working in the parlor. She moved a chair in front of the fire and began to brush out her hair. It would dry quickly; then she'd have Rachel help her put it up in a new style. She glanced at the clock on the wall. He would be here soon. There wasn't much time.

It was almost ten-thirty by the time Rachel made her way to the huge corrals behind the barn. In the past couple of weeks she hadn't had much of a chance to explore the area around the house. Between the barn and the house a couple of men had already cleared and plowed the ground for the vegetable garden. Two bunkhouses stood off to the side, far enough from the main house to allow the cowboys to feel independent but not so far that they could get into trouble on their own.

A dozen or so men stood outside the corrals. Their cheers and shouts warned her of the action before she rounded the corner and was able to see into the big pen. A tall black horse stood between two cowboys. One held on to a rope connected to a halter around the gelding's face; the other attempted to place a saddle on its back.

The animal's coat gleamed with sweat. A blindfold covered his eyes, but he jerked his head up at every sound.

"Ho, boy. Calm down."

Rachel stopped in her tracks. She knew that voice. It belonged to Luke. What was he doing in the ring with that untamed animal?

"Mama, Mama, over here!"

She glanced up and saw Mark perched on the top fence rail. He waved to her and patted the space beside him. On the other side, Potter sat next to the boy. The old man tipped his hat and offered a yellow-toothed grin. Dawg lay on the ground beside the fence and whimpered with excitement. The young dog was growing quickly; his black and white coat gleamed from hours of Mark's careful brushing.

"Howdy, ma'am," Potter said, climbing down. "The little one was wondering if you'd forgotten about the broncbustin'."

"No. I was helping Sarah." She glanced toward the ring. "What's going on?"

"Oh, jes' Luke and Satan."

"Satan?"

"Uh-huh." He took her elbow and steered her toward the fence. "We turn the horses loose every winter, then gather 'em up in spring."

She leaned against the middle railing and smiled up at Mark. "You behaving yourself?"

"Yes, Mama."

She turned back to the old man. Dawg sat up and nosed her hand. She scratched his head and ears. "How do they survive the winter?"

He shrugged. "Same as the cows. Some do fine; others come back hungry and sick. This one"—he motioned to the prancing black horse in the corral—"looks as good when we find him as he did when he was let go. Strong as a bear and jes' as ornery. Luke spent two years breaking 'im. He's one smart fellow. Took to cutting cattle like a babe to mother's milk. But every spring he puts up a hell of a fuss at being ridden, beggin' your pardon. Didn't mean to go airin' my lungs like that." He punctuated the sentence with a well-placed spit of tobacco.

"That's quite all right."

She glanced back into the corral. Luke had set the saddle on Satan's back, but the horse bucked it off before he had a chance to cinch it. Man and beast warily circled each other. Despite the blindfold, the horse seemed to know where the next attack was coming from and whirled to face his opponent.

Dust rose in clouds, drifted across the corral, then disappeared into the clear morning air. The bright sun had chased away most of the night's chill, leaving the temperature several degrees above freezing. But Rachel clutched her arms tightly across her chest.

The smell of horses and earth and leather combined with the odor of the cowboys' unwashed bodies. Across the path came the triumphant squeal of a horse, followed by the thump of a thrown rider.

"Come on, Potter." Mark climbed down. "They're breakin' a new horse in the next ring."

He followed after the boy, then stopped and turned to Rachel. "You want to come watch?"

"No." She offered him a slight smile. "I'll stay here."

The two moved away, an almost comical pair. The wrinkled old man, with his snug-fitting jeans and expensive but worn boots, walked with a rolling gait as though he'd spent most of his life in the saddle. Mark trotted alongside. His patched and baggy clothes didn't conceal his effort to imitate Potter's stride, but he didn't quite have the rhythm. Every second or third step he stumbled and had to skip to catch up. Dawg trailed behind, his nose never more than a few inches from Mark's knee. They stepped into a crowd of cowboys. She lost sight of them and turned back to the corral.

"Hey, Luke. You're not going to let that old mule get the best of you, are you?"

Luke grinned at his detractor. His gaze swept over the crowd at the railing. He seemed to pause when he saw her standing there, but the hesitation was so brief, she couldn't be sure.

Once again Luke raised the saddle to Satan's back. Once again, the gelding shied away. But this time Luke was quicker. Before the animal could do more than dance away a few feet, the heavy leather seat settled onto his back and Luke secured the cinch.

"That's showin' him." The crowd at the fence cheered its approval.

Luke motioned for the other man to hand him the rope attached to the halter. The cowboy did so, then pulled off the blindfold.

Satan immediately lunged at the man, trying to take a bite out of his arm.

"Don't let him get you, Pete," the cowboy next to Rachel yelled out. "Come on, show him who's boss."

Pete ducked out of harm's way and used a white handkerchief to distract the horse. While Satan continued to watch for his opportunity to punish Pete, Luke stuck his left foot in the stirrup and swung himself astride.

Satan reared up suddenly; his long front legs pawed at the air. The crowd around the corral grew silent. For several seconds the beast stood on two legs. Then he dropped to all four and began to buck.

Rachel clutched the railing in front of her and held her breath. Beside her, the cowboys cheered and called out advice, but her world had been reduced to the wild horse and the man who sought to tame him.

One small portion of her mind acknowledged they were well matched. Powerful muscles bunched and released with each kick. The black horse gleamed in the morning light. Luke sat easily in the saddle. Unlike the other men, he didn't use a quirt to beat the horse. Instead he held on to the horn and leaned into the rocking motions. She saw him speaking to Satan, but couldn't hear the words.

"He could sweet-talk that horse into jumping through fire."

Rachel glanced at the tall man who'd moved next to her. Tanned skin provided a handsome background for strong, regular features. "Does this happen every year?"

"Yes, ma'am. In a couple of minutes Satan will go all sweet on him, trotting around like a regular show pony." A Texas twang added flavor to his speech. Black eyes captured hers. "I don't believe we've met. I'm Jake Evans, Luke's foreman."

"I'm Rachel—"

"I know who you are." His bold glance quickly took in her dress and worn shoes, then returned to her face. "We don't get many pretty ladies out here. Especially widows."

She took the hand he offered, noticing how his long,

callused fingers and wide palm dwarfed her own hand. She was sure he'd broken hearts from here south to the Mexican border.

But behind the good looks, there was an edge to Jake Evans that told her he'd lived hard. The twist of his full mouth hinted at cynicism, the set of his shoulders, pride. Yet he held her hand with the gentleness of a mother tending a babe.

When he released her, she felt a blush climb her face, and she quickly turned her attention back to the corral. As Jake had predicted, Satan loped docilely around the ring, his head held high, his black tail flying out behind him like a banner.

She watched as Luke worked the horse, urging him to canter, then gallop, and running him to the far fence before bringing him to a stop. They moved as one, without any visible means of communication. Rachel thought she saw Luke's hands tighten on the reins, his knees press against Satan's powerful shoulders, his body lean slightly with each turn, but she wasn't sure. Neither tried to dominate; they worked with mutual cooperation.

A flash of envy caught her unaware. Foolishly, she wanted Luke to take as much time with her as he had with the shiny black gelding. She wanted him to speak to her and coax her and touch her with velvet-gloved strength. She wanted him to look at her with respect and admiration. And love. Most of all she wanted him to care about her the way he had all those years ago in Kansas.

"Luke was sure surprised when you showed up," Jake said, leaning against the top railing. "Never seen the man so riled." Before she had a chance to wonder if he'd read her thoughts, he offered a wink. "If you ask me, he needed shaking out a bit. Does a man good to look at things in a new way."

She wondered how much Luke had told his foreman

about the past, but she didn't want to ask. Instead, she watched the work inside the corral. "How long does it take to break all the horses?"

"About two weeks. There's only a dozen or so young 'uns that need a professional. That's why we hire Pete. He comes through every spring and gets 'em started. After that, each cowboy works with his own string. I make sure we've got enough of each."

"Each horse?"

"Each duty. We need quick horses for cutting steers from the herd, calm ones for the night watch, and smart ones for roping." He took off his hat and slapped it against his thigh before setting it back on his head. "Ain't nothing worse than roping with a stupid horse. Might as well call it a day and get drunk."

Even over the cheers of the cowboys in the next corral, Luke heard the gentle sound of Rachel's laughter. There was no need to glance over and see who she was with. He'd known it was just a matter of time until Jake made his move. The man was slicker than a greased stirrup and couldn't resist a woman, especially an attractive one. No doubt he was over there telling her lies about his past and making promises designed to get her into his bed.

White-hot anger flared, but he pushed it away. First of all, he'd told Jake hands-off around Rachel, and his foreman would respect that order. Second, it wasn't his business who she made time with. She was just his employee. It wasn't as if they had an understanding.

Something of his agitation and its source was communicated to Satan. The gelding reared suddenly, forcing Luke to hold on with his thighs; then the animal struck out for the far side of the ring. A half-dozen long strides covered the center of the circle and brought them directly to Rachel. The horse skidded to a stop, sending a cloud of dirt into the air.

Luke looked down, expecting to see her cowering from the large beast and Jake playing protector. Instead, Rachel was offering a slice of apple on her palm. Satan sniffed a couple of times, pretending indifference, then used his lips to daintily take the treat.

"There, boy," she said, patting his head as if he were Dawg. Her hair, pulled back in a simple knot, shone like pale gold. A few strands had pulled free and lingered against her cheek. "Is that good? It's just dried apple, but I soaked it all night. Soon we'll have fresh from town, and then I'll bring you a whole one."

Satan flattened his ears as if he didn't want to believe the promise, then stuck his head over the railing and blew noisily on her hair.

Rachel and Jake laughed. Luke steeled himself against the intimate glance they would no doubt exchange. But instead of turning to his handsome foreman, she looked up at him. Her blue eyes offered shy appreciation of the morning's activities.

"How many more horses will you break?" she asked.

"About eight. Just my string." He swung down from the saddle. "I ride Red around the ranch, but when I go out on the range I need the others."

Jake stepped between the rails and grabbed the lead. "I'll walk him out, boss, so you can show Mrs. Steele around."

She favored him with a smile. "Please call me Rachel."

"That I will. Rachel." He tipped his hat, then led Satan away.

The anger threatened again, but the hard truth took care of the problem. Luke had no claim on her, now or ever, and he didn't want one. He'd seen how little a woman's promise meant. He'd never trust again. There was no room for soft words or sweet lies. The whores in town were the most honest women he knew. They told a man up front what he was expected to pay, and their price was only in coin.

"You must be busy," Rachel said, twisting her hands together. "I'll go find Mark, and you can get back to"—she gestured toward the other corrals—"whatever else you have to do."

In the bright light of day he could clearly see the patches on her woolen skirt. The cuffs of her blouse looked as if they'd been made over two or three times. Even her shoes were coming apart. There was a hole in the leather on one, and the sole was loose on the other. He swore under his breath.

"I'm sorry," she said, cautiously moving backwards. "I didn't mean . . . I'm sorry."

"It's not your fault," he said, peeling off his gloves and stuffing them into his back pocket. "It's just—" He exhaled and took her arm. "It's not you."

She fell into step beside him. "How long have you had Satan?"

"Six years. We rounded him up the first year I was here, but I couldn't get a saddle on him till the following spring." He grinned at the memory. "I still have his teeth marks on my arm."

"I hadn't noticed." She glanced up at him then, her eyes wide with horror. Bright red patches blossomed on her cheeks. "Oh, my."

He chuckled and looked around them. "Don't worry. Nobody heard your confession. Your reputation is still intact."

They stopped in the middle of the yard, halfway between the two corrals, and faced each other. Despite the people and noise all around them, he felt as if they were alone.

"I want you to go to town and buy some clothes as soon as I can arrange an escort."

She opened her mouth to protest, but he silenced her with the shake of his head. "I won't let you go alone. It isn't safe."

"Why? I got here without any help or trouble."

"Agreed." He placed his hand on her arm, more to feel her warmth than to keep her from moving away. It didn't matter that he didn't trust her. It didn't matter that he refused to let go of his anger and bitterness. It didn't matter that she'd betrayed him. There was a fire inside him. The flames had always burned only for her, and until he had her, there wasn't a prayer of ever moving on. "But we weren't that close to spring roundup when you arrived. Now there are plenty of cowboys riding around looking for work. A woman on her own would be considered fair game by all comers."

The color fled her face as quickly as it had arrived. The haunted expression returned to her eyes, and again he wondered what other secrets she kept from him. Even with the security of her job and his tacit offer of protection, she continued to pace the halls at night.

He felt her tremble.

"I understand." She looked away. "There's no rush. Mark and I can get by."

"You deserve better. I'll be speaking with Ian Frasier later today. He's our nearest neighbor. If he's not going in, I'll send a message to the Valois family. They live on the other side of us. One way or the other, we'll get you into town."

Before she could answer, he heard Mark calling out.

"Mama! Luke! Look. Potter found me a horse."

Rachel's son ran as quickly as the horse he was pulling let him. The bay gelding, slightly smaller than most of the other cow ponies, had a black mane and tail and three white feet. Despite the winter spent foraging for food, the horse seemed sleek rather than starved. When the boy reached them, he came to a halt and grinned.

''Potter says he's too small to carry the cowboys but that he's just right for me. Potter says he's smart and already broke and don't need more than cleaning up. Potter says—''

''Hold on.'' Rachel brushed the hair out of Mark's eyes. ''Not so fast, young man. It's not for Potter to say whether or not you can have a horse. Luke might have plans for this one. Besides, we can't afford to board him.''

The light in Mark's eyes died, and he dropped his chin to his chest. ''But, Mama . . .''

Luke glanced from the boy to the animal. It bobbed its head a couple of times, then leaned forward to smell the boy. Beside the pair, Dawg circled closer and closer, trying to herd the unmoving horse. By the corral, Potter anxiously watched the proceedings. Luke sighed. It would take a stronger man than him to stand up to the lot of them.

''You're going to be responsible for him,'' he said sternly. ''That means feeding him twice a day and grooming him and making sure he gets enough exercise. You can't just—''

But the rest of what he was going to say got cut off when Mark dropped the lead rope and threw his arms around Luke's waist.

''Thank you, Luke,'' he whispered. ''Thank you more than anything in the world. I'll take good care of him. I promise. Me and Dawg.'' He looked up with tears in his eyes. ''Does he have a name? Can I give him one?''

''Call him anything you want.'' Luke felt a tightness in his throat as he bent down and returned the boy's embrace.

''Socks.'' Mark grinned and wiped his cheeks.

''Socks?''

'' 'Cause of the white feet.'' Mark grabbed the lead rope and tugged. ''Come on, Socks. Potter is gonna teach me how to take care of you." He motioned to the puppy yapping at his heels. "This is Dawg. You gotta listen to him 'cause he was here first. Dawg, this is Socks. He's my new horse."

Luke turned back to Rachel and caught her watching him. Now it was his turn to feel the heat of a blush on his face. "A boy needs a horse. It'll teach him responsibility."

"You're a good man." She looked at him a little longer, then stepped closer. He could smell the fresh scent of soap and the subtle fragrance of her skin. "Thank you."

She rose up on tiptoe. He obligingly turned his face. But instead of kissing his cheek, she placed one hand on his chest and planted her lips firmly on his.

The contact lasted all of three seconds. With the people all around them, Luke had little opportunity to enjoy her sudden boldness. But when she squeezed his hand and flashed him that shy smile before moving toward the house, he found himself thinking of other ways to make her thank him again.

"There's only three pies. Is that enough? Maybe I should have made four. And the apples are dried. Even though we soaked them, it's not the same as fresh. I wish we had fresh. Do you think he'll notice? I just don't think it's the same." Sarah bunched her apron into a ball, then smoothed it over her stomach and thighs.

"Sarah, calm down." Rachel grinned. "You're acting like a chicken without its head. Three pies will be fine. There'll only be one extra person for dinner. That's almost a pie each. Do you want me to check the stew?"

"No!" Sarah raced to the stove and lifted the lid off the heavy pot. "I'll do it." She tasted the mixture and grimaced. "Not enough salt." She tasted again. "Maybe not. What do you think?"

"Come here." Rachel took the spoon from her hand and set it on the counter. After leading Sarah to the kitchen table, she pushed her into one of the chairs. "Sit down. I don't want you to move until it's time to serve the meal."

"But I have to—"

"Just be still. I'll take care of the food. The state you're in, you'll end up destroying everything. What are you so nervous about?"

"Nervous?" Sarah reached into the mending basket and pulled out a pair of Luke's trousers. "I'm sure I don't know what you're talking about. I'm fine." She studied the fabric, turning it over and over in her hands. "Where's the tear in these? I can't find it."

Rachel shook her head, then picked up a heart-shaped piece of buckskin from the floor. "They're not torn. They need to be foxed."

"Oh. Of course." Sarah pinned the buckskin over the seat of the pants and down the inseam, then threaded a three-sided needle. But before making her first stitch, she set the garment on the table and sighed. "All right. Maybe I am a little . . . out of sorts. It's just that we don't have company very often, and I want things to go well."

"I see." And so she did. There were splashes of color on the housekeeper's cheeks, and excitement had added a gleam to her pale blue eyes. "So who is this company?"

"No one special." Sarah rose from the table and stared out the window. "Ian Frasier is one of our neighbors. He and Luke have been working together on a breeding program."

"Yes, the blooded bull. Luke mentioned something about that to me."

"So then you know." Sarah untied her apron and folded it. Then she patted her braid and adjusted the few curls around her face.

"And you and he have an understanding?"

"Understanding?" Sarah's mouth dropped open. She pulled it closed and swallowed before she was able to speak. "I can't imagine what ever gave you that idea. He's just a rancher. Nothing else. Now if you'll excuse me, I want to check on the table. We'll be eating in the dining room today. Ring the bell when the stew is ready."

Rachel dutifully checked the entrée in question, all the while chuckling to herself. So Sarah had a beau, did she? Rachel could hardly wait to meet the man who had reduced the ever-confident Sarah Green to a quivering young maiden. How far had the budding romance gone? she wondered. And more importantly, did Luke know he was in danger of losing a housekeeper?

She slowed her stirring. What would happen if Sarah and Ian did decide to marry? Could she continue to stay here with Luke? There would just be the two of them . . . alone in the house. Mark wouldn't count as a chaperon. What would happen to her reputation?

This time her laugh was more terror than humor. It was a little late to be worrying about that, she told herself firmly. Besides, her time here was limited. As soon as John ceased to be a threat, she would return to Kansas. There wasn't any reason to stay on the ranch. Luke had gone out of his way to make that very clear.

A shout from outside pulled her out of her reverie. She covered the stew, then bent down to check on the biscuits. How handsome Luke had looked on his horse, his tall, strong body moving gracefully with the animal. It was both sad and ironic, she thought, walking to the window to gaze at the men hovering by the outbuildings. Six years and several hundred miles had passed between them. They'd grown older, wiser, and apart.

She heard Sarah enter the kitchen.

"Is everything done?" the older woman asked.

"Yes. I'll go ring the bell." She walked out through the pantry and onto the back porch. The thick cord attached to the clapper had been recently replaced. Luke always took care of the little things. It was his way of showing pride in his land.

If only, she thought, then pushed the melancholy away. It was too late for if-onlys. The past was over; it was time to get on with the present. She had made her choices and now she needed to accept and live with the consequences. Besides, it wasn't all bad. She had her son. He was worth any price. And she had her memories. No one could take them away. And she had hope. Despite all that had happened, despite Matthew and Mark, despite John's threats and rage, despite the pain, she'd never stopped loving Luke.

She grabbed the rope and rang the bell three times, then brushed her palms on her skirt and turned to wait for him.

Chapter Nine

"I'd be obliged if you'd pass me some more of those fine biscuits," Ian Frasier said as he smiled at Rachel. "I'd walk from here to Mexico for a taste of Sarah's cooking. Although I hear tell, lass, your cakes are as light as angel wings."

Luke rolled his eyes. Ian was in rare form. Usually, he ignored the other man's compliments, but today, after watching Rachel with Jake, Luke felt on edge. "Lay it on any thicker, Frasier, we'll be needing hip boots to get around."

"I'm just being an appreciative guest, you ungrateful pup. An old man like me doesn't have much opportunity to spend time in the company of ladies. You must have made a pact with the devil himself to have two such fine specimens living under your roof."

Mark's eyes grew round as he gazed up at Luke. "You know the devil?"

Luke smiled. "Ian's just making a joke, Mark. It doesn't mean anything."

"Oh." The boy looked reassured. He chewed thoughtfully, then frowned. "You talk funny, Mr. Frasier. How come?"

"Mark, that's not polite." Rachel frowned at her son.

"I didn't mean nothing by it, I just wondered—"

144

"I know what you meant, lad. I'm from a far-off land called Scotland. Do you know where that is?"

Mark shook his head. "Is it by Kansas? I been to Kansas."

The adults laughed. Luke easily picked out Rachel's sweet tone. He hated the way the sound made his groin thicken uncomfortably. As soon as they finished with the roundup, he was going to have to make a much-needed trip into town. A night or two with an accommodating woman would ease his ache. Dear God, it had better, or he'd do something both he and Rachel would regret.

"Scotland is across the ocean, thousands of miles away. It's a bonny land with high mountains and honest hardworking people." Ian paused.

"Do ya miss it?" Mark asked.

"Sometimes."

"You got any kids?"

Ian set his fork down and wiped his mouth with his napkin. "I had a boy, a few years older than you, but he and his mother died some years ago."

Mark nodded. "My pa died, too, and so did Luke's. It hurts sometimes, don't it?"

"Aye, laddie, it does."

Luke watched his friend's gaze drift from the boy to Sarah. His housekeeper had hardly touched her meal. He was about to comment on the fact when he noticed the couple seemed to have forgotten there were other people at the table. They were staring at each other. Sarah's pale eyes glowed with an inner light, and Ian's looked the same.

"Sometimes it helps to make new friends," Mark said, oblivious to the undercurrents at the table.

"That it does," Ian said, never breaking the connection. "Sometimes new friends can mean as much."

Sarah blushed, then tossed her napkin on the table and

rose to her feet. She looked everywhere but at Ian. "Who wants pie?"

"You really think the Oregon herd will make a difference?" Ian asked as he settled down in the chair across from Luke's desk.

"You're just jealous, old man, because you didn't act quick enough."

Ian made a rude gesture, then sipped his coffee. "Will you earn back your investment?"

"Should double it, at least. Yearlings are going for twelve dollars a head in Oregon, two-year-olds and cows for eighteen. And the unbranded calves come with their mothers. Last year they sold for about thirty-six a head in Cheyenne. If I sell enough, we can buy two more bulls next spring."

"Aye. That'll help. There's a couple of your horses over at my place. One of my men will bring 'em tomorrow."

"No rush." Luke leaned back and set his feet on the table. He studied the Scot, trying to see him through Sarah's eyes.

Ian Frasier was handsome, in a rugged, unkempt sort of way. His hair and beard had once been carrot red, but now streaks of gray toned down the bright color. Craggy features hinted at a stern but kind nature. In their dealings, Ian had always been fair; he was a hard worker and honest.

Luke shifted uncomfortably in his seat. What the hell was he supposed to say? Sarah was like a mother to him. While part of him wanted to ask about Ian's intentions, another part reminded him that it was none of his damn business. Ian wouldn't play fast and loose with Sarah; she wasn't foolish enough to fall for a cheap line. The truth was, their relationship was not his concern.

"You wouldn't be planning a trip to town anytime soon, would you?" Luke asked.

"Not me, but a couple of my men will be going for a few supplies. What do you need?"

"Rachel and the boy didn't bring enough clothes with them. She needs some wool and cotton to make a few things, but I wouldn't want to send her in with the cowboys."

"No. A lass that pretty would be taking a risk with my lot. I've kept them busy for the last few weeks. They'll be wanting to visit Milly's place for an hour or two." Ian frowned. "You could have Rachel write out a note. The cowboys can drop it off at the general store with my supply list and pick up the fabric after they've had their fun. What do you think?"

"Good idea. Thanks." He took some gold coins from the desk.

"Put your money away. We'll settle next time I'm here." Ian stood up. "If you'll excuse me, I'll pay my respects to the cook and be on my way. The cloth will be here by the end of the week."

"I appreciate that." Luke rose, and the two men shook hands.

After Ian left the room, Luke shuffled through the papers on his desk. Among the supply lists were rosters of the cowboys and suggested assignments of duties. Spring roundup was only a couple of weeks away. By then the horses had to be broken and ready to begin work. Every year Luke and his men struggled to be prepared on time, and every year they made it . . . barely. Still, it beat hoeing beans.

The last sheet contained the list of cows Luke was considering for breeding with the new bull. Damn. He'd meant to discuss that with Ian. Still holding the paper, he hurried down the hall and out through the kitchen. But when he reached the edge of the porch, he paused.

Ian and Sarah stood together next to Ian's horse. Although they weren't touching, something about their posture spoke of a closeness. She handed Ian a carefully wrapped pie. He smiled his thanks, then raised a hand and touched her cheek.

There was nothing especially intimate in the gesture, yet Luke felt like a child spying on his parents in bed.

Conflicting emotions rose within him: happiness for Sarah, selfish regret at losing her, envy for the family he'd been promised but never had. Silently he turned and made his way inside. He'd talk with Ian later.

"What do you think? I thought I might make Mark a pair of trousers and a shirt in both wool and cotton. How hot is it during the summer?"

Sarah leaned over Rachel's shoulder and studied the length of cloth. "Very. But not for long. Sometimes the nights are cool. You're right to make both. Here." She took the scissors. "I'll start cutting. We need to get this done before the spring roundup. Once they start bringing in the calves for branding, we'll spend all our time cooking for the men."

"Luke told me the cowboys have their own cook."

"That's true most of the time, but during roundup we have cowboys from all over."

"You mean from Horse Creek."

Sarah grinned. "Farther than that. Some years the territory covered is over four thousand square miles. The Stock Growers Association gets all the cattle ranchers together and they travel from ranch to ranch."

Rachel couldn't imagine covering that much land. "How long does the roundup take?"

"Five, maybe six weeks. Luke will know when we're expecting the cowboys. Then you and I will start preparing."

"I hope my cooking is up to the task."

Sarah patted her arm. "Don't worry none. You'll do just fine. Besides, at the end of the day they'll be more interested in quantity than in how fluffy your biscuits are."

Maybe she'd get lucky and all the calves would be branded in a day, Rachel thought. Yet she had to admit the roundup sounded exciting. She and Sarah continued to work together, using patterns made from Mark's old clothes. Conversation drifted from cattle to sewing to old friends.

A knock at the back door interrupted them.

"Sarah?" Jake Evans walked in through the pantry. "I wanted you to know the rest of the vegetable garden is ready for planting. Now, I know exactly how Luke is going to take this, so don't you dare mention my name." The tall, handsome foreman grinned.

"Don't you fret," Sarah said, winking. "I'm sure he'll believe me when I tell him Rachel and I plowed the land ourselves."

"Yeah. Fortunately the man who did the work suddenly has some important business on the east eighty. And I think I'm going to take a well-deserved ride into town." He tipped his hat toward Rachel. "Anything I can bring you, ma'am?"

"Thank you, no."

"Then I'll be on my way before the boss shows up."

With that he left, his easy stride carrying him out of the house, toward his waiting horse.

"Why will Luke care that the garden's bigger this year?" Rachel asked.

Sarah measured coffee into the pot, then filled it with

water. "You've seen those wagons on the road, haven't you?"

She nodded.

"Farmers coming by to try their luck. The ranchers don't want the land parceled out or fenced in, so they've spent years telling people crops won't grow."

"But vegetables grow fine. The season's a little short, but that just means you have to plan ahead."

"You know that, and I know that, but Luke doesn't want some farmer to see our garden and get the idea of buying some land around here."

Rachel grinned. "That's why we plowed behind the barn."

"Exactly." Sarah sat back down at the table and continued cutting out the pattern. "I refuse to buy canned vegetables if I don't have to. Having you to help means I can put up twice as much."

Rachel pinned down the next pattern piece and nibbled on her bottom lip. "How mad is he going to be?"

"Nothing that a quarter acre of gooseberry plants won't take care of."

"You're going to bribe him with the promise of pies?"

Sarah winked. "There's little enough a man won't do with the right encouragement."

When the coffee was ready, Rachel poured them each a cup and returned to sit at the table. Sunlight filtered through the lace curtains and marked the passing hours. Luke would be back soon. As usual, her heart pounded a little faster at the thought of seeing his face. As the days grew longer and his work multiplied, she found herself missing the sound of his voice, the feel of his presence in the room.

She'd taken to saving the ironing for when he was gone overnight with the herd. Then, after she'd finished the pressing, she had an excuse to creep into his room.

Touching his clothes, running her fingers over the smooth pillowcase and the well-used quilt, was almost like being with him. Sometimes, when it got dark, she imagined that they were alone together, loving each other long into the night. Sometimes she recalled all the dreams that they'd once had, and she pretended they'd come true. Sometimes she'd place her hand against her stomach and pray for a miracle, that if he couldn't love her, he could at least give her a child. A part of the man was better than nothing at all.

"There. I think that takes care of the cotton." Sarah folded the remaining fabric and reached for the wool. "I know you want to make up clothes for Mark first, but don't forget about some things for yourself. I have a couple of petticoats you can cut down and a lovely length of lawn for a camisole and pantalets."

"Oh, I couldn't take your things."

"Of course you could. I have more than I need."

The other woman's offer caused Rachel to blink back tears. "Thank you," she murmured. "You're being more than generous." How she'd love to have something pretty to wear for Luke.

"Pshaw. It's no more than I'd do for any neighbor. Besides, your mother isn't here to look after you, and I feel responsible."

Rachel leaned back in the kitchen chair and sighed. "Do you think she's all right?"

"Your mother?"

She nodded. "We agreed that it wouldn't be safe for me to write. I sent a note to one of her friends when I was last in Horse Creek and told her I'd arrived." She glanced at Sarah and then away. "I didn't say where I'd arrived, of course, but I'm sure she knew. I understand that this is all for the best, but I still miss her."

"Will you ever go back?"

Rachel glanced at her friend, but Sarah was busy laying out the wool and smoothing the patterns. "I don't know. I can't return while John Steele is alive, but eventually, yes, I'll have to. My family is there." Except, of course, for Sarah and Luke. But if the glances Sarah and Ian Frasier had exchanged were anything to go by, the housekeeper might soon have a home of her own. As for Luke, he'd made it very clear how he felt about having Rachel around.

"Mark likes it here," Sarah said, pinning the patterns in place.

"So do I." She spoke the words softly, without daring to look up from her work.

Luke was late for the evening meal. Rachel had just finished settling Mark in bed when she heard a familiar voice in the kitchen. Drawn by a power she could not resist, she made her way toward the sound.

It was already the middle of May. While the days seemed warmer, the nights retained enough nip to bring gooseflesh to her skin. But instead of returning to her room for a shawl, she rubbed her hands up and down her arms and hurried toward the light. There'd been an ease between them. Since the shared moment after he'd broken Satan, Luke had lost some of his reserve.

Tonight he sat at the table, an untouched plate of food in front of him. Sarah stood next to the sink. When Rachel entered the room, both glanced up at her. Sarah's expression was suspiciously guilty, but Luke's, as usual, gave nothing away.

There was an awkward pause.

"Good evening," Rachel said finally, still hovering in the doorway. "Am I interrupting?"

Although her question was directed at Luke, it was Sarah who answered. "Not at all. I was just going to my room.

Good night.'' She walked over to the table and rested a hand on Luke's shoulder. Then she smiled at Rachel and quietly left the room.

''Can I get you some coffee?'' Rachel moved over to the stove and reached for the pot.

''I'm fine.''

''Oh. All right.'' She poured herself a cup and set it across the table from him. ''You're not eating. Don't you like the chicken?''

''It's perfect.''

This time the chill that raced over her had nothing to do with the weather. His clipped voice and continued avoidance of her eyes told her something wasn't right. Fear tasted bitter in her mouth.

''What's wrong?''

He leaned back in his chair. The shift in position put most of his face in shadow. The contours of his strong features blended into something harsh and unfamiliar. Broad shoulders strained the seams of his faded wool shirt. He had rolled up the cuffs, exposing broad wrists and muscled forearms.

She wanted to reach forward and touch the sprinkling of hair covering his tanned skin. She wanted to ask him to tell her what was wrong, beg him not to be angry, promise to make everything right again. She wanted him to hold and comfort her.

''Sarah tells me you're still thinking of leaving,'' he said. ''Why did you bother to take the job?''

''Leaving? I'm not. I mean, I will eventually, but not for a while.''

''And how long are we to be blessed with your presence?'' The words, heavy with sarcasm and anger, seemed to hit her directly in the chest. The long fingers she'd so admired in the past now clenched into a tight fist.

"It's not like that."

"So how is it?"

"She told you we were talking today?"

He nodded, moving his head the barest fraction.

"Sarah asked me if I'd ever go back to Kansas and I said yes. That was all."

"I see." He reached for his cup and sipped the coffee. The white of his knuckles belied the casual action. "You still haven't answered my question. How long?"

"I don't know." She rose and began to pace the small room. "You of all people should understand. I remember what it was like growing up, even if you don't. Every day John Steele told you that you were nothing. A child with no name, no prospects, no family. He was right. You *were* alone." Her voice shook with emotion. She took a breath to steady herself. "Each harsh word, every blow, hurt me, too. I loved you and I hated what he was doing."

"Not enough to keep you from marrying Matthew."

"I did what I did then for my father. In the future I'll do whatever I have to for my son, anything to keep him from suffering that same torment. I'm all he has."

He turned away, but she refused to be ignored. She leaned forward and placed her hands on the table. "You made a place for yourself here. I admire that. Don't deny Mark the same opportunity. I own my father's farm in Kansas. Mark will inherit the Steeles' land. I won't turn my back on his inheritance or mine. Our lives are tied up with the soil. We're farmers."

"Then go back now," he said. "Leave and work your land."

Her arms formed a protective barrier over her chest. "I can't."

"Why?"

"I—I just can't go back. Not now."

"When?"

"When John Steele is dead."

With a swift catlike motion, he rose and stood in front of her. "What aren't you telling me?" he asked, his gray eyes blazing with anger as he stared into hers. "Why do you fear him so?"

"I've already said."

"No." His low voice matched her own, but while hers exposed her fear, his more than hinted at menace. "You haven't told me anything. So he drinks. He always drank. And the gambling isn't new. Did you run from him because there wasn't any money? Did you think I'd be rich by now and you could take from me as well?"

Unshed tears burned, but she willed them away. She crossed her arms tighter. "You don't understand. I never wanted to hurt you. I came here because I had nowhere else to go and because of what we had shared."

He cupped her chin in his hand and turned her face toward the lantern, as if to judge her expression. "How easily you tell your lies. Are you hoping I'll marry you and take care of all your problems?"

"Luke, don't. Please."

"Go ahead. Beg, sweet Rachel. I like the sound of my name on your lips. I always have." He traced her mouth with his thumb. "Call it a weakness of mine."

There was no gentleness in his touch, no punishment, either. Just the cold contact of betrayal.

"I loved you," she whispered. *And I still do.* But that thought was better left unspoken.

He reached behind her and pulled the pins from her hair. The long strands tumbled down her back and into his waiting hands.

"It's too late," he said, raking his fingers through her hair. He eased forward, using his body to force her to move.

Slowly she inched away until the counter pressed into her back. Through the layers of her dress and petticoats she felt the hard wood on one side and the unyielding strength of Luke on the other.

"It's too late," he repeated. "Someone's cast-off bastard was never good enough for you."

"No! No! You're wrong. It was never like that." She placed her hands on his chest. "I never cared about who your parents were."

He ignored her words. After smoothing her hair down her back, he separated it into two sections and pulled them over her shoulders and the front of her dress. She glanced down. The pale gold tresses contrasted with the tanned strength of his hands. She felt as well as saw the gentle tugs as he pulled the strands through his fingers.

"Why didn't you come to me after Matthew died?"

She caught her breath in an audible gasp. It would be easy to lie and say that John had prevented her, but Luke deserved better than that. It was true she'd tried to leave the Steele farm, but she'd wanted to go to her mother, not to Luke.

"Because of Mark. I wanted him to grow up near his inheritance. Near the land."

She felt the pounding of his heart beneath her palm; the slow rhythmic beat seemed as constant as eternity itself. His scent surrounded her, making her remember, hope, and want. Heat from his body warmed the iciness inside her.

"It was better to live in Steele's hell than risk your precious inheritance. I should have realized that earlier. It makes sense. You wanted the best."

"Luke, that's not the way it was."

He silenced her with a glance. "You married Matthew to help your father. You stayed because of Mark."

"Yes."

He lowered his mouth closer to hers. But instead of a kiss, she felt the breath from his words. "You've always chosen duty over me. Your family over your promise. Money over love."

"It's not about money," she said, appalled by what he was saying. "Mark is my son. I'd die for him. If he were your son, you'd do exactly the same. I had no choice. There are things you don't know. John made me—"

"I don't care." Moving his hands to her neck, he caressed her throat. "You'll do well to remember that. I may want you"—he captured her wrist and pulled her hand down to cup the length of his arousal—"but that's all."

The burning in her eyes grew too great to contain. She pulled free of him and ran toward her room.

Luke waited until he heard her door shut. Only then did he exhale the breath he'd been holding. Swearing loudly in the still evening, he wished for a bottle of whiskey to deaden the pain. Once again his own rule forbidding liquor on the ranch came back to taunt him. There would be no liquid oblivion, no escape from the ghosts.

How much more real they'd become now that Rachel filled his days as well as his nights. Perhaps his words had been enough to scare her off. It would be better for everyone if she left for good.

But wishing her gone didn't ease the ache in his chest or his groin. After walking out the back door, he stripped off his clothes and stood naked in the rapidly cooling night air. Clouds hovered overhead, blotting out the moon. He raised his face toward the night and waited for the elements to ease his need.

Luke looked over the list of cows. There were several possibilities for breeding with the new bull. If he was able to buy two new bulls next year, his whole plan would change. But he wouldn't know whether or not he'd have the money until the herd from Oregon arrived. And that wouldn't be until September.

"Ah, hell." He pulled a gold coin out of his pocket and flipped it.

"Whatcha doin'?" Mark stood in the doorway to his office. Thunder, slightly larger now and a whole lot less mangy, dangled from his arms while Dawg sat patiently at his side.

"Working."

"Mama says I'm not to disturb you when you're busy." Mark grinned. "But when you're in the office, I can't have no lessons, so I wanted to tell you that you can work as long as you'd like."

Luke smiled in spite of himself. Like Thunder, Mark looked much better than he had when he arrived. The new clothes fit him, although he needed new shoes. His face had lost its pinched look and his sandy hair, while still hanging into his eyes, gleamed with good health.

"I appreciate that," he said.

Mark moved farther into the room. Dawg whimpered, but stayed in the hall.

Somehow the rules about the dog had relaxed enough to allow him inside, but Luke wouldn't go so far as to let the flea-bitten critter into his domain.

"Can I help?" Mark asked.

Luke's refusal got lost in Mark's pleading look. The boy liked nothing better than to work around the ranch. It didn't matter if it was milking cows, grooming the horses, or mending a fence. Once lessons were over, he was somewhere underfoot, always asking questions, always trying to help.

"This is just paperwork," he said finally, not wanting to disappoint the boy. "But if you wait about a half hour, I'm going to be working with the last of my horses. You can watch me break him.''

"Really? Golly!'' His dark eyes widened. ''I been helpin' with Socks every day. Potter says he's the smartest horse ever.''

"Glad to hear that.''

Mark leaned against the desk. Thunder squirmed out of his embrace and began to investigate the surface. The tapping of Luke's pen caught the cat's attention, and she swatted it with her paw. He tried to pull the pen away, but that only interested her more. She followed the movement, her body crouched low against the desk top, her tail trembling with excitement. When he dropped it, the soft clatter startled her. She hissed and arched her back, then sprang onto her prey. Calico cat and pen tumbled together, then fell neatly into Luke's lap.

Thunder landed on her back. She quickly righted herself and settled onto her haunches and began to wash her face. Mark laughed. Luke picked up the pen and tossed it on the desk.

"I better get goin','' Mark said, ''so you can come outside with me.''

"It shouldn't be very long.'' He smiled at the boy.

"Luke?''

"Yes?''

"When's the roundup? Potter told me it starts in May, but when I asked Mama this morning, she said it was the second of June. Did I miss it?''

"No. It takes a while to work all the ranches. They'll be getting here in about two weeks.''

The boy nodded. When he reached the doorway, he leaned over and patted Dawg, then glanced back. ''What if they find our cows on someone else's land?''

"Some of our cowboys are with the roundup to make sure they get back home."

"Oh. Good." Mark pushed his hair out of his eyes and grinned. "I'll be waitin' in the barn."

"Fine." He picked up his pen.

"Luke?"

"Yes, Mark."

"Do ya think . . ." The boy glanced down and shuffled his feet. "Potter says I'm getting to be a good rider. You think maybe I could ride . . . you know, outside the corral?"

Mark's thin shoulders hunched forward as if he expected his request to be met with a blow. Damn John Steele for his violent temper, and damn Rachel for subjecting the boy to it.

"Tell you what," Luke said, trying to keep the anger from his voice. "I'll take you riding at the end of the week."

Mark's grin was almost blinding. "Thanks, Luke. Can I bring Dawg? He likes to follow when I'm ridin'. He won't be no trouble."

Luke sighed. "Sure." With his luck, Mark would want to buy some sheep to give the dog something to do. But the boy's next request was worse. Much worse.

"You think Mama could come with us, too? She ain't been riding in a long time. My grandpa wouldn't let her none, but I know she likes horses."

Luke flinched. It had been three weeks since he and Rachel had been alone. Three weeks of an uneasy truce. Three weeks of avoided glances and mumbled greetings. Could they manage a whole day together without angry words?

But even while he was thinking of a polite way to tell the boy no, he realized that he and Rachel had to come to some sort of understanding. As much as he wanted her gone, he couldn't stand the thought of forcing her to return to John Steele. She was here until it was safe to return to Kansas.

Maybe a day together was the answer. Things certainly couldn't get more uncomfortable between them. Besides, he'd missed seeing her smile.

"Go ahead and ask her," he said.

Mark let out a whoop and ran down the hall calling for his mother.

Luke patted the sleeping kitten in his lap and smiled grimly. He'd leave it up to Rachel. Let's see if she was brave enough to risk a day out with him.

Chapter Ten

"I thought you and Luke were going riding."

Rachel glanced up guiltily. "We were—I mean are. I just have a few things to take care of." She sat on the floor in Mark's bedroom, sorting through the boy's clothes. "I want to straighten his drawers."

"Uh-huh." Sarah folded her arms over her chest. "You wouldn't be avoiding Luke, would you? Or is it the ride you're afraid of?"

Rachel tilted up her chin. "I'm not afraid."

The older woman looked unconvinced as she stepped into the room. "It's not like you to hide."

"I don't have anything to wear."

"I found an old split skirt of mine. I took in the waist and let out the hem. Should fit you just about right."

Rachel swallowed and tried again. "I'd need boots and—"

"Don't even bother. Luke found an old pair. They might be a tad large, but you can stuff a sock in the toe. What else?" Sarah sat on the edge of Mark's bed. "You want to tell me the real reason you and Luke have been avoiding each other for the past couple of weeks?"

Rachel stared down at the shirt she held, then smoothed the material and folded it. "He hasn't forgiven me for choosing duty and my family over him. I explained about

162

Mark having only me, but that didn't help. He doesn't care about me anymore.''

''Have you given him reason to?''

''What?''

Sarah shook her head. ''All those years ago you promised to wait and didn't. Now I understand you had trouble with your daddy, and I respect your decision to marry Matthew. But all this time you've had a family to take care of. You've had Mark. And Luke''—she looked out the window—''he's had only me. And I'm no blood kin to the boy.''

''Sarah, you know he thinks of you as his mother.''

''That he does. And I think of him as my son. But you're the woman he built all this for.'' She motioned to include the house and the ranch. ''You're what kept him going through the winters. That first year it was the love; after that, it was the hate that kept him alive.''

Rachel felt as if she'd been slapped, but Sarah wasn't finished.

''It's been over six years,'' the older woman continued, staring directly into her eyes. ''And you showed up on the doorstep with no warning. I'm not saying I wasn't happy to see you and the boy, because I was. You've been a real help to me, and Mark is a joy, but at the first sign of trouble you came running north, expecting Luke to have spent all this time waiting for you. He's not the same man, Rachel. And part of the change is because of you.''

''I wrote,'' she said softly, too ashamed to protest more.

''I know. I'm not implying what you did was wrong. But you've got to see how he feels. As soon as you can, you'll be heading back to Kansas without a single thought about what you're leaving behind.''

''That's not true. I love Luke.'' The pain filled her chest until she thought her heart might be crushed. The way Sarah

talked about what she'd done made it sound so selfish, as if
she'd wanted to take advantage of Luke. It hadn't been that
way at all. She swallowed thickly. "Not a day's gone by
that I didn't think of him, remember the past, miss him.
Even when I was married to Matthew, I didn't forget."

Sarah rose from the bed, walked over, and touched her
shoulder. "Then, child, you've wronged both men. Maybe
it's time to think about making amends."

Rachel sat on the floor and stared at the clothing in her
hand. Sarah's words echoed over and over in her mind. Had
she really expected Luke to spend the last six years waiting
for her? She wanted to protest that she hadn't, that she'd
thought he would marry and go on with his plans for the
future. But a corner of her mind reminded her that in all her
dreams about being reunited with Luke, she'd assumed he
would be alone. Never had there been the specter of a wife
and children lingering in the background.

At first his anger over her determination to return to
Kansas had surprised her. Of course she had to go back and
claim her land, not for herself, but for her son. But now,
looking at the same conversation through Luke's eyes, she
could see that he must have thought she was here to use him.
To take the job he offered and his money, to accept his
protection. And in exchange for what? What, outside of a
few chores, had she done to deserve his hospitality? To
thank him, she promised to run off the first chance she got.

Burying her face in her hands, she tried to cool the shame
heating her cheeks. The color refused to recede. All this
time she'd been walking around feeling noble and superior,
flaunting her choice of duty over love like a talisman against
past sins, when in truth she was a selfish, thoughtless child.

And what would her plans mean to Mark? The boy grew
to love the ranch more and more each day. It wasn't just the
land he'd miss, either. If she took him home—no, if she

took him back to Kansas—he'd grow up without Luke to guide him. Her son needed the influence of a man in his life. He needed to be shown the narrow path of truth and strength, how to face the world with dignity and honor. How to keep his promises.

The hollow feeling inside her was darker than pain. A lethal combination of shame and guilt swirled in her belly like an evil serpent.

What had she done? How could she have been so thoughtless and self-centered?

She'd leave. First thing in the morning she would pack up her clothes, take Mark, and . . .

She touched the shirt she held. The soft wool, all new and clean, had been paid for by Luke, pinned and cut by Sarah. Even the sewing had been done by both women. Nothing in the shirt was wholly hers.

Would running away make things better? Would running ease Luke's pain? Make him feel more cared about, less used? Would running keep Mark safe?

Moving stiffly, as if she'd suddenly grown old, Rachel rose to her knees and put Mark's clothes away. Then she made her way to her bedroom.

As Sarah had promised, the split skirt and boots were waiting for her. She dressed as quickly as she could; clumsy fingers stumbled with tasks that seemed unfamiliar. After buttoning the skirt, she went to put on the blouse she'd worn that morning, then bunched it in her hand. Again, Sarah's words rippled through her mind.

The other woman was right. She'd thought of no one but herself and Mark. She remembered how Luke had driven to Horse Creek to bring her back. How he'd offered her an outrageous salary so that she would have some funds of her own. How he'd found a horse for Mark, then paid for the upkeep of the animal.

It was time to stop running. To make her stand here—in Wyoming. Sarah would be gone soon, taking her opportunity for happiness with Ian Frasier. And when she left, Rachel would step in and fill the gap. If she began this moment, there were still not enough days in her lifetime to repay what she owed Luke.

The fact that she loved him only made the burden of debt worse. How carefully she'd protected her heart, forcing him to take all the chances. For the first time, she would risk everything for the man. At last honor and love had the same meaning.

She opened the door of the armoire and pulled out a cotton blouse she had made recently. The crisp blue fabric was three shades lighter than her eyes. Luke had always liked her to wear blue. After fastening the buttons, she tucked the hem into her skirt and smoothed the cuffs in place. Then she pulled the pins from her hair and wound it into a simple braid. Finally she reached for the hat Luke had brought her last week. At the time she'd thought he was mocking her, but now, with her clearer vision, she recalled how, as he'd set it on her dresser, he'd warned her about the dangers of sunburn during the Wyoming summer.

The light beaver felt seemed heavier than her straw and flower hats, but the brim would provide shade from the sun. Taking a deep breath for courage, she walked to the door and out into the hall.

Outside, she heard Mark before she saw him.

"Get 'em, Luke. You can do it."

As she rounded the barn, she saw her son perched on the top of the corral railing. In the center stood Luke, twirling a rope, and a black and white spotted horse was trying to stay out of reach.

"What's going on?" she asked as she neared the fence.

Mark looked over his shoulder. "Mama! You're coming

with us. Look, Luke. It's Ma. Hey, is that a new hat? It looks like a cowboy hat. Can girls wear 'em, Luke? Don't you have to be a cowboy?''

"No. I tried to get one for you, Mark, but I couldn't find one small enough. We'll check next time we go into town." Luke tossed the rope. The horse shook its head and ducked to the left, but the lasso fell cleanly over its neck.

Mark applauded. "I'm going to get Socks saddled. Don't go without me."

"We won't," Rachel promised, not daring to glance at Luke. She watched her son climb down from the railing and race into the barn. She sensed more than saw Luke lead the horse toward her. Heat flared on her cheeks, and she felt as awkward and shy as a schoolgirl. What must he think of her? She'd been selfish and thoughtless and stupid and—

"Hey. You're looking mighty fierce about something."

She looked up and met his eyes. They both stood close to the fence. In the bright spring morning, the flecks of green in his irises seemed more pronounced. She'd expected censure and resentment, but never carefully controlled amusement.

"I was just thinking about something Sarah said," she admitted at last. "Is this the horse I'll be riding?"

"Yes. His name is Paint."

She held out her palm and let the horse take her scent. "He doesn't look familiar. Whose string is he from?"

Luke grinned. "No one's. We prefer straight-colored horses out here. Sarah's ridden him a couple of times. He's broke and everything, but . . ." He shrugged.

"Oh, I understand. When you say 'we prefer straight-colored horses,' you mean that *men* prefer them. Pintos are all right for women and children."

He shifted uncomfortably and handed her the rope. "Something like that. Hold on to him while I go get the saddle.'' He walked two paces, then turned back. ''You're going to have to ride astride.''

She wrinkled her nose. ''It's fine with me, if you don't mind me walking a little funny in the morning. At least no one will be able to see the bruises.''

He arched a single brow. ''You treat me real nice today and I might offer you a rubdown.''

It was just that easy, she thought as he disappeared into the barn. A few kind words, a shared moment of humor and it was as if the betrayal had never happened. But if she looked hard enough, she could still see the hurt lurking behind Luke's easy smile. He was a good man. Strong and honorable. The best she'd ever known. She didn't deserve his kindness.

When Paint was saddled, Luke swung up onto his back. The animal reared once or twice, then circled the ring at a comfortable trot. As with Satan, he and the horse became one. Luke moved with an easy swaying motion. Well-worn trousers clung to the muscles of his thighs, then disappeared into fine leather boots. His ivory cotton shirt was open at the neck; a bright red bandanna circled his throat.

Nervous weakness invaded her limbs, but it wasn't fear of riding that made her tremble. It was the knowledge that even if she wasn't worthy, she still loved him. And wanted him. The raging fire had only grown hotter in the last six years.

Socks and Mark trotted out of the barn. ''Are you ready? Can we go?'' Dawg barked playfully from the horse's side.

''Almost.'' Luke brought Paint to the edge of the ring and dismounted. After unlatching the gate, he led the horse out. ''He's all calmed down. You sure about this?''

Rachel reached up and settled her hat more securely on her head. It had been a long time since she'd been on a horse. Apprehension and excitement tightened in her stomach.

She nodded.

He handed her the reins. She clasped the leather in her left hand. When he bent over and made a step by lacing his fingers together, she stuck one foot in the stirrup and allowed him to boost her up. Paint side-stepped when she shifted on his back, then flicked his ears and exhaled with a noisy blow. Luke watched to make sure she was settled, then headed for the barn to get his own horse.

Mark laughed. "Look, Mama. You're really riding."

"Did you doubt me?" she asked, adjusting the reins in her hands and urging the animal to walk.

"I just don't think I seen you on a horse before." Mark watched her from under his straw hat. "Sarah said she was packin' a lunch. Do you got saddlebags, too?"

"Have," she said automatically, before glancing over her shoulder. "Yup. Two of them. Looks as if we've got plenty of food."

Paint continued to walk around in a large circle. When they neared the barn, Luke appeared leading Satan.

"Everybody set?" he asked, springing effortlessly into the saddle.

"Head 'em out," Mark cried, kicking his horse with more enthusiasm than strength. Socks endured patiently, already well used to the boy's energy. When Luke urged Satan forward, Socks struck out as well, staying in front of the other two.

Rachel took a deep breath, pleased she'd loosened her corset and would be able to ride in comfort. Bits of her conversation with Sarah continued to haunt her, but she pushed them away. Tonight when she was alone, she'd take out the words and examine them one by one. For this moment she would think only of the day, the boy, and the man. Each deserved her full attention.

"You and Sarah have been busy," Luke said as he rode next to her.

Had he already heard of their conversation that morning? "What do you mean?"

"Lots of things. Sewing new clothes for one."

"Oh, that. Yes, we have been. Thank you again for the fabric. I'll pay you back as soon as—"

"I'm not interested in your money." He dismissed her with a curt flick of his hand. "The boy deserves better than being dressed like a waif. He won't want for anything."

"While you're here" was the unspoken completion of the sentence. Rachel shifted slightly in the saddle as much to find a more comfortable position as from guilt.

"Luke, I don't want you to think—"

"I like that blouse you're wearing. Is it new?"

She glanced down at the pale blue cotton, the tiny buttons, and the lace trimming the cuffs. "Yes." Her voice was soft, the words forced to fight their way past the tightness in her throat.

"It's pretty."

He stared straight ahead. They might have been discussing the weather. For all she knew, it mattered as much—or as little—to him. Fierce emotion welled up inside her. She wanted him to notice her, to talk to her, and to love her as he had all those years ago.

"Thank you."

Once again she glanced at him out of the corner of her eye. He continued to look directly in front of him. She shifted again on her saddle. The warmth of the sun felt pleasant after the cool nights. The air was heavy with the scent of spring.

"And you've done a fine job ironing my clothes."

"Ah, I'm glad you're pleased."

"But the garden is another matter."

"Garden?"

"Sarah knew how I felt about it last year. But she's gone too far this time. The garden's twice as big. What am I supposed to say if some farmer and his family come rolling along the road? It's going to be pretty hard to convince them that nothing grows around here when you and Sarah are sitting on the front porch shelling peas."

She smiled. "We'll sit in back."

He glared at her. "It's not funny."

"No? Would it help if I told you she's planting gooseberries?"

He fought a grin, then flashed her a wink. "It might."

A movement up ahead caught her attention. Socks shied to the right as Dawg took off into the underbrush.

"What the . . . ? Mark, are you all right?" she called.

The boy turned the horse around and trotted back to meet them.

"Did ya see it? There was a jackrabbit. Dawg's gonna try and catch it, but I don't think he's fast enough."

"Be careful," Rachel said, checking to make sure he was still securely seated in the saddle. "I don't want you falling off."

"Oh, Ma. I'm a good horseman. Potter told me." With that, he urged Socks back up the path. A few seconds later Dawg tumbled out behind them and ran to catch up with Mark.

"I guess the rabbit got away," she said.

"Are you surprised? How good a sheepherding dog could he have been if someone was trying to drown him?"

She smiled. "I'm glad Potter saved him."

Luke shook his head as if he doubted the old man's sanity. "There's a watering hole about an hour or so up the road. I thought we'd head there. Mark can play, maybe even swim if it gets warm enough. I don't want to tire him out on his first ride.''

She glanced up and saw her son practically bouncing in the saddle. ''Tiring him out isn't such a bad idea. He's so excited about the roundup, seeing the cattle and the cowboys, I can barely get him to bed each night.''

''He's a good boy.''

Rachel smiled and ducked her head. ''You've had a lot to do with that.''

''Me?'' Luke glanced at her, his brows drawn together. ''You've only been here a few weeks. If anyone is responsible for Mark, it's you.''

''What I mean—'' She swallowed against the lump in her throat. Why was it so hard to speak the truth? Had she been hiding it for so long that she felt awkward saying the words? ''You've spent a lot of time with him, and I want you to know I'm grateful. We descended upon you with no warning. Someone less kind would have turned us away.''

Luke must have tightened his hold on the reins, because Satan suddenly tossed his black head and snorted restively.

''I'm a lot of things, Rachel, and none of them are kind. And I sure as hell don't want your gratitude.'' The friendliness fled his expression, leaving behind a mask of indifference. With a swift kick of his heels, he urged his horse into a trot, then a canter, and quickly left her in the dust.

By the time they reached the watering hole, Rachel was hot and irritated. Although the hat protected her face from the sun, rivulets of perspiration trickled down her back. Mark and Luke had stayed in front, racing from tree to tree, laughing and talking.

She'd wanted to join them, but hadn't been sure of her welcome. She'd had her first chance to express her feelings, and she'd handled it badly. But if Luke didn't want her gratitude or her affection, what did he want?

A blush crept up her cheeks as she remembered how he'd placed her hand against his arousal. Even now she could feel the hard ridge pressing into her palm. The restrained need left a hollow tingling in her breasts and at the top of her thighs. He'd always been able to make her tremble with just a kiss. What would it be like if they actually joined together?

Her nights with Matthew had been pleasant, if occasionally painful. But her husband hadn't wanted to play and talk, lingering over kisses, as she had with Luke all those years ago. The quick couplings in the marriage bed hadn't been what she'd expected. Had it been her fault? Was Sarah right? Had she wronged her husband by continuing to mourn her loss of Luke? Had he sensed that and held back his affection?

"You planning to spend all day up on that horse?"

She glanced down and saw Luke standing beside Paint, holding the reins.

"Oh. Are we here?" She glanced around the clearing. Pitch pine trees formed an uneven half-circle. Socks and Satan were already hobbled and eating grass. In the distance she heard Mark's high-pitched shouts as he and Dawg chased some real or imagined prey.

"You've been here for several minutes." After tying the reins to a nearby tree, he held out his arms.

She kicked free of the stirrups and swung her right leg over the saddle, then slid down. He caught her before she touched the ground; he wrapped his arms firmly around her waist. Somehow her hands came to rest on his shoulders.

Perhaps it was her recent recollections of the passion they had shared, perhaps it was the nearness of the man she loved, but suddenly she could feel the heat from his body.

Her breasts were crushed flat against his chest. Their heartbeats thundered in a matching rhythm.

With him holding her so close, her feet still dangling free, their breath mingled as they stared at each other. She could count the individual lashes surrounding his gray-green eyes. He'd shaved that morning. The line of his jaw was clean and well defined. Firm masculine lips teased her with a grin, then straightened as desire flared.

Yes, she thought, held fast in his embrace, unable to move forward or back, constrained simply to wait.

"Your son is down at the watering hole," Luke said, never taking his gaze from her face. "He'll be back in about a minute. This would be awkward to explain, don't you think?"

"Yes," she whispered, then slowly licked her bottom lip.

She felt more than heard his groan.

"I'm still mad as hell at you," he ground out, as he lowered her to the ground. Their bodies slid together in exquisite contact. "But that doesn't seem to matter a damn. Guess you've always been my weakness, Rachel Steele."

She kept her hands on his shoulders. Raising herself up on tiptoe, she rested her breasts against him. When their mouths were a scant breath apart, she spoke. "I'll never hurt you again, Luke. I swear on my life."

Hope blossomed briefly, then withered and died. The mask returned, and she could no longer see into his soul. He grabbed her wrists and lowered her hands to her sides. "See to your son."

The late morning faded quickly into afternoon. By the time they'd eaten their picnic lunch, even Mark's boundless energy had been expended. The boy flopped down on a blanket close to the watering hole. Dawg curled up protectively beside him, and soon the two were fast asleep.

Luke stretched out against a tree and stared at the pair. There was something so innocent and trusting about the sleeping child. Mark assumed that his world was safe and secure. Whatever pain he'd suffered had been left back in Kansas. If only it were that easy for the rest of them.

He glanced over at Rachel. She, too, leaned against a tree. Her skirt, secondhand but less patched than her regular clothing, was spread out over the blanket. The light blue of her blouse made her eyes look like a midsummer sky. A long braid hung over one shoulder; the ribbon at the end teased the full curve of her left breast.

Pulling his hat down slightly, he continued to observe her while appearing to doze. He hadn't known it was possible to want and hate in equal measures. A deep breath filled his lungs. No, "hate" wasn't the right word. He didn't hate her. That was the problem.

A string of curses fell silently from his lips. Some men found solace in the bottle, others in cards or easy women. Some men had weak characters, lied, or beat their children. He supposed he had as many flaws as the next man, but his only weakness was Rachel.

For six years he'd worked like the devil to exorcise her from his mind. But the ghosts were too strong. And then, without warning, she'd strolled back into his world. Still as beautiful as ever. And still able to make him mad with wanting.

He could have taken her that night by the fire. Dear God, he should have. Even now it would have been easy for him to give in to the need. But she would leave. John Steele might live for another twenty years, but when he died, she'd return to Kansas and claim her precious inheritance. Once again she would choose duty over love, family over him.

The hell with her, he thought, sitting up straight and pushing his hat back on his head. He didn't need her. He didn't need anybody. She could come and go as she pleased. If Sarah left to marry Ian, he'd need someone to tend the house. Rachel would be a hired hand, like Potter or Jake, nothing more. The fact that he wanted her in his bed didn't change anything. He clenched his fist tightly and closed his eyes. . . .

"Luke?"

"Huh?"

He started at the sound of her voice.

"Wake up."

She'd moved silently to his side. Kneeling beside him, she glanced anxiously into his face. "You were mumbling something. I think you were having a bad dream."

He didn't remember falling asleep, but the sun had moved across the sky and his anger seemed to have evaporated, leaving behind only passion.

A man could drown in her eyes, he thought, staring at her. He'd heard tell the oceans went on forever, but they couldn't be any bluer, any deeper than this. He should be punishing her, he told himself, and yet the exact nature of her crime became lost in the sweet smell of her perfume. Or was that scent simply Rachel herself?

She leaned forward and tentatively brushed back a lock of his hair. "I've been thinking, and I want you to know that—"

With one swift movement he reached for her shoulders and eased her into a sitting position beside him. Her hands settled on his arms, pressing and kneading the hard muscles. His palms made circles on her back, feeling the laces of her corset, the warmth of her skin.

"Don't," he murmured as he reached for her. "Don't say a damn thing."

Like a morning fire on a chilly day, it began with a spark. The pressure, softer than he remembered, coaxed the flame.

His lips covered hers; light kisses chased away any lingering secrets, broke through the lies until all that remained was the need. For this heartbeat, want overpowered anger. The past was forgotten, and there was only this woman. Despite the sunlight, the horses, the sleeping boy and dog, they were completely alone.

He cupped her jaw and tilted her face to bring her closer. Fuel was added to the fire.

She clutched at him, pressing her full breasts flat against his chest. Fingers drew him, begged him, but still he kept their kisses fleeting, as if to punish them both.

He could hear the increase in her breathing; it matched his own. He nibbled her lower lip. Each tiny bite drew a soft moan from her; sparks flew out to land on his body and singe his skin. The hottest, most potent, settled on his groin. Already swollen flesh strained for release.

When she parted her lips to draw in more air, his tongue pushed past to delicately trace the sensitive moistness within. First he stroked the inside of her lip, back and forth, feeling the smoothness, savoring the taste. Only when he had supped his fill did he reach past for her tongue.

They met in quiet hesitation, afraid of the power, unable to resist the passion. As she touched him in return—point to point, side to side, all swirling and plunging, niceties forgotten in the quest for sensation—the fire became a raging storm, engulfing them both in a sensual smoke of desire. Flames lapped through his body. Wanting, fed by heat, grew until it had a life of its own.

He stroked and tasted her mouth as if he could consume her. Her breasts burned against his chest; only the feel of her naked skin against his would begin to heal the wound.

His hand moved slowly up her side; one thumb rested against the underside of her full breast. And still he held her close, as if to keep her from pulling away. She leaned forward, urging him on, silently begging for his touch. As if to encourage more, she thrust her tongue past his and into his mouth. There they again began the dance.

Fiery desire tore through him, pulsating embers surrounded his groin. He closed his hand fully over her breast, capturing her moan of delight with his kiss. Through the layers of cloth he felt the weight and curves and hardness of her nipple. Toying with the puckered nub, he trailed kisses from her ear to the high neckline of her blouse. A row of buttons blazed a trail to the flesh he sought.

"Luke," she moaned softly.

In the background he heard the soft nicker of one of the horses. Behind them, Dawg or Mark stirred restlessly. This was neither the time nor the place.

He pulled back and swore out loud.

Rachel glanced down at the hand that cupped her breast. Placing her palm on top, she squeezed, then moaned softly. Their eyes met in silent understanding.

"I'm going to take a swim in the watering hole," he whispered.

"But it's runoff from melting snow. You'll freeze."

He planted one last kiss on her lips. "I know."

The stage arrived in Horse Creek early in the afternoon. John Steele waited until the other passengers alighted; then he slipped the flask out of his coat pocket and took a long swallow.

He was closer now; he could feel it. Excitement joined the whiskey in his belly.

The stage driver stuck his head in the window. "You gonna git out or do you want to head back to Cheyenne?"

John smiled slowly. "I've got business to take care of here." He pushed open the door and stepped down. "Where can a man find a clean bed and a friendly game of poker?"

The driver, a short man with dirty clothes and three days' growth, pointed up the street. "There's several saloons for the poker. Some even have rooms to let. The Cattle Run offers beds an' women to fill 'em."

"Much obliged," John said, reaching for his single bag. The heat in his belly dropped lower. Maybe they had a blonde like the whore who'd left him. He'd like taking her hard. Maybe he'd even pay a little extra and make her act like she was afraid. "And where might I find a little information?"

"About?"

"A ranch nearby."

The driver's eyes gleamed. A slow smile split his dirty face, exposing yellow teeth and a gap where two were missing. "I kin help you with anything you want to know. My brother-in-law owns the Cattle Run. If'n you make it worth my while, I might even talk him into givin' you a discount on one of his little ladies."

"You don't say."

Chapter Eleven

"They should be back from their outing soon." Ian Frasier pushed up from the kitchen table and smiled. "My thanks for the meal, Sarah. You have a way of making a man resent his own cooking."

"It wasn't anything special," Sarah said, wiping her hands on her apron. "I'm glad you stopped by."

Ian picked up his hat and turned it over and over in his hands. "You'll give Luke the message?"

"Of course. I have a list of supplies I need, and I know Rachel wants to get a few things in town. Not that she didn't appreciate the cloth your man brought."

"No trouble at all."

The soft burr became more pronounced, or maybe she was simply a foolish old woman. She continued to wipe her palms on her apron until Ian set his hat on the table and reached forward to still her movements. Big work-roughened hands held her own. Somehow they looked right together.

"Are you sure you wouldn't like to join Rachel tomorrow? I wouldn't object to your company."

Dear God, she was almost forty, yet she felt as nervous as a schoolgirl. Slowly Sarah raised her head and gazed into Ian's face. Lines from both weather and time added kindness to his craggy features. He was a good man—honest. She couldn't find one better.

"I'd like that," she said quietly, her fingers returning the pressure of his. "But I have baking to do. Perhaps you could join us for the evening meal next week."

"Aye. I'd be honored." He studied her for a moment. "A man grows tired of his own company after a time."

Her heart fluttered against her ribs. Did that mean . . . ? Did she dare . . . ? "S-so does a woman." She could feel the flush of her cheeks. Would he scold her for her boldness?

But instead of scolding, Ian chuckled. "You're a beautiful woman, Sarah."

When she started to protest the compliment, he leaned forward and kissed her lips. His mustache and beard provided a tickling contrast to the smooth firmness of his mouth. Hard, strong hands pulled her close.

Before she could catch her breath, he'd released her.

"Ah, lass, you make a man forget his place."

He gave her a last lingering look, then picked up his hat and walked out of the room. Sarah stood where he left her and raised a hand to touch her trembling lips.

Rachel glanced again at the list in her hand and the huge pile of supplies stacked beside the store counter.

"It's all here," the saleswoman said. "But you're welcome to go over it again."

Rachel laughed. "I wouldn't know where to begin. How much do I owe you?"

"Sixteen dollars and seventy-one cents. That includes the shoes for your boy and the length of material." The woman smiled. "I got some hats over there in the corner. There's one with a blue feather that would look mighty pretty with your blouse."

Rachel glanced over her shoulder. She could see the

wispy confections of lace and felt. What might it be like to buy something simply because it would look nice?

She stared at the two ten-dollar gold pieces in her hand. Luke had told her to purchase supplies and spend the change on whatever she wanted. The hat was tempting, but not tempting enough. After six years of John Steele expecting her to account for every cent she spent, buying shoes for her son and an additional length of cloth was about as much indulgence as she could manage.

"Just what's here," she said, handing the woman the coins. When she'd received the change, she dropped it into her reticule and went looking for Ian. The stocky Scotsman was studying the rifle display. "I've finished my shopping, Mr. Frasier. Whenever you'd like to leave, I'm ready."

"Call me Ian, lass. We're neighbors. Here in the territory, that makes us practically blood kin. I'll get the boys to load us up." He winked at her, the action lowering, then raising one of his bushy brows. "If we time the trip right, we'll arrive back in time for supper. I admit I wouldn't turn down another of Sarah's home-cooked meals."

Rachel smiled. "And I know she wouldn't object to your company at the table."

"You think so?"

Their eyes met. "I'm quite sure."

"That's good to know." He smiled and nodded with satisfaction.

She stood back and allowed Ian to precede her from the store. While the shopkeeper's sons loaded the wagon, she walked back to look at the hats. There had been a time when she'd had pretty clothes and a nice home. After she'd married, Matthew had taken the time to buy her fancy hats and yards of silk and velvet. But after his death, everything had changed. What little cloth John had consented to give her she'd made into clothes for Mark. When the drinking got bad, there might be months between trips to the general store. John had left every night for the saloons, but she was forced to stay on the farm. If she never saw that man again, it would be fine with her.

Smiling her thanks to the woman behind the counter, Rachel pulled on her gloves and made her way to the wagon. Two adolescent boys tightened the last rope over the supplies, then touched their hats and went inside. Ian came around to help her into the seat. But just as he took her arm, she glanced across the street.

A saloon—the Cattle Run, the sign said—took up most of the block. Several men loitered around in front. A man pushed through the swinging doors and scanned the wooden sidewalk, as if searching for someone.

An uneasy feeling drifted over Rachel. Her heart pounded high and hard in her chest. All the blood seemed to drain from her head.

The man removed his hat and wiped his forearm across his brow. She gasped. Dear God, it was as if her thoughts had conjured him out of nothing.

John Steele. Here. In Horse Creek.

That could mean only one thing: He'd come after her.

She jerked her arm from Ian's protective hold and spun to face him.

"That man!" she gasped.

"What? Lass, you've gone as white as a sheet. Are you ill?"

"Hush." She crouched down, hidden by the wagon seat and the large wooden wheel. "There's a man across the street. He mustn't see me."

She was afraid Ian might argue, but he held her gaze for a moment, then nodded.

"Stay here. I'll get in on the other side; then you climb on. As soon as you're settled, pull the blanket up around your shoulders and head. I'll whip up the team, and you'll be home in no time.''

Rachel bit hard on her lower lip. The taste of blood mingled with fear. She'd known he would find her eventually. But not so soon. There hadn't been enough time.

Mark! Oh, please, let her son be safe.

A sob rose in her throat. What if he'd already gone for the boy? She almost screamed out her pain. But then the quiet voice of reason reminded her that Mark had been fine this morning. There was no way John could have made his way out to the ranch and back already. If John was in Horse Creek, then Mark was safe with Luke.

''Now, lass. Climb on.''

Rachel lifted her skirts with one hand, more concerned with speed than with propriety. Ian leaned to the side and helped pull her onto the seat. As soon as she sat down, he tossed the blanket around her, then released the brake and snapped the reins to urge the horses forward. Rachel turned slightly, daring a single glance over her shoulder.

John stood where she'd last seen him. But his attention was focused on something at the other end of town. She breathed a sigh of relief. He hadn't seen her. They'd escaped for now. But it wouldn't be long before John showed up at the ranch.

Luke heard the wagon pull up in front of the house. He left Red with Potter and walked out of the barn. Rachel didn't bother to wait for Ian to come around and help her down. She grabbed up her skirts and stepped down.

He grinned at the flash of petticoat and leg exposed by her action, but the smile faded when he caught sight of her face. All the color had faded, leaving behind ashen skin and a haunted, hunted look in her eyes.

''Rachel?''

She spun at the sound of his voice. Relief chased away the fear, and she hurried toward him as quickly as her heavy skirts would let her.

He met her halfway across the yard.

"What's wrong?" he asked as she threw herself into his arms. Automatically his hands moved comfortingly over her back.

"Luke. Oh, Luke. He's here. I saw him. Oh, God, he's here."

"What are you talking about?" He grabbed her upper arms and held her so he could see her expression. "Who is here?" But he already knew the answer to his questions. Knew the name even before she spoke it.

"John Steele. I saw him in town."

Her words hit him like a sucker punch. The air rushed out of his lungs. As he stood there holding her, smelling the sweetness of her skin, feeling the warmth of her body, he realized how easily all this could be lost. John Steele had delighted in making Luke's life hell. The older man would enjoy taking Rachel away from him now.

"Did he see you?"

"No. The men had just finished loading the supplies. I walked outside to get in the wagon, and I saw him across the street. At the Cattle Run Saloon." Her gaze drifted past him toward the barn. "Where's Mark? Is he all right? I have to see him."

She tried to wrench free of his grasp, but he held her tight. "Mark is fine. He's with Potter, grooming Red. You can't let the boy see you like this. He'll know something is wrong."

"No. You don't understand. I must *see* him." She tugged one more time, then seemed to collapse against him. "Oh, Luke, why now? Why did he have to come now?"

There wasn't an answer to her question. He held her

tight, murmuring soothing words and waiting for the sobs. But although she shook as if fighting a fever, there were no tears.

Looking over her head, he saw Ian talking with Sarah. The older woman glanced anxiously toward Rachel. A fierceness rose up inside Luke. Rachel and Mark were his responsibility. John Steele wasn't going to get his hands on either one. Luke would see him dead first.

"But does this mean I don't get to go ridin'? Luke, you promised I could see the herd."

"And you will, Mark, but not today. Your mother wants you to stay close to the house. You're not to go outside by yourself. Not even to the barn. Someone will take you there and leave you with Potter."

The boy's mouth turned down, and he slumped in his chair at the kitchen table. "But I don't need nobody lookin' after me like that. I'm not a baby. Mama . . ." He looked up at her, his large dark eyes pleading.

Rachel sighed and folded her hands on her lap. She felt old and tired. Night hadn't provided any respite from her fear. The shadows had seemed menacing, ready to pounce and carry her away. She and Luke had talked about the danger and had decided that Mark needed the best possible protection. But they'd been foolish to think her son would quietly accept the required changes. In the harsh light of morning she wanted to think she was overreacting, that John wouldn't come for her. But she could still see the controlled rage in his eyes, taste her own blood after he'd hit her, feel the weight of his body against hers, ripping, seeking, probing.

She wrenched herself back into the present and tried to smile at Mark. "Do you remember when we lived with Grandpa?" she asked.

Mark slowly nodded his head.

"Do you remember how he got so angry with you all the time?"

"Yes, Mama." The boy's voice was subdued. "You said if we ran away together, we could hide from him and he'd never hurt us again." He turned to Luke. "He used to hit us all the time. Mama more than me."

Rachel felt Luke stiffen in his seat and heard Sarah's gasp of disbelief, but she never looked away from her child.

"I saw Grandpa in town yesterday. He might come here. That's why Luke and I want you to stay close to the house and always be with an adult."

Mark's eyes grew wide and fearful. "I won't go no-where. I promise."

Luke rose from his seat and walked around the table. When he reached the boy, he crouched down by the chair. "No one's trying to scare you. But I want you to be careful."

"I will."

He cupped Mark's face. "If you see your grandpa, I want you to get on Socks and ride to the clearing where we had the picnic. Do you remember where it is?"

"Uh-huh. North to that grove of trees, then I go this way." He raised his right hand.

"That's right. There's some cowboys camped out there. They'll look after you till one of us can come to get you. Potter has already saddled Socks. He's in the stall by the back entry. All you have to do is climb on and go. Can you do that?"

Mark looked from Luke to his mother, then nodded slowly. "Are you going to protect my ma?"

"No one is going to get hurt."

"Promise?"

Rachel reached out and touched Mark's shoulder. Luke took her other hand and completed the circle. "I promise."

For nearly a week nothing happened. Rachel wondered if she'd simply imagined seeing John Steele in town. All the cowboys had been given his description, but no one reported seeing a stranger on the land. The roundup was only days away. She and Sarah spent most of their free time cooking. But no matter what she did, Rachel couldn't escape the fear that followed her like a shadow.

She tipped the last of the rinse water off the back porch and straightened up. Pressing her hands into the small of her back, she tried to ease the washday ache. At least they'd finished with the sheets. Sarah was hanging them out in the warm afternoon sun.

Rachel shaded her eyes and stared toward the barn. Mark and Dawg were playing with one of the cowboys—Billy, she thought his name was. Every day one of the men had stayed behind. It had been Luke those first two days, but when John Steele hadn't arrived, he'd gone out to help with the cattle. The peaceful scene, the sound of her child's laughter, the excited barking of Dawg, made her feel safe . . . almost. If it hadn't been for the glint of the gun strapped to Billy's thigh, she could have convinced herself nothing was wrong.

As if sensing her attention, Mark looked up and waved. Then the boy pointed at something behind the barn and ran off. Billy followed close behind.

Rachel stretched again and returned to the kitchen. There were biscuits to be started for tonight's dinner. And potatoes that needed scrubbing. As she bent down to scoop up some flour, a cold shiver racked her body. Instinctively she stiffened and spun around.

He stood silhouetted in the doorway to the dining

room—a tall, broad man with enough strength to crush her to dust. All his features were indistinct except the unholy gleam in his eyes.

"Well, missy, looks like I found you after all."

John Steele's low voice unlocked her frozen limbs. She screamed and ran for the pantry and back door. In two steps he'd overtaken her. A powerful arm tightened around her. One hand covered her mouth.

Drawing in air through her nose, she tried to fill her lungs. She could taste his sweat and her own fear. The scent of his body, unwashed and feral, made bile rise in her throat.

Luke! she screamed against his palm, but little sound escaped.

John laughed, his warm breath fanning her ear like a fetid wind. "Fight me, Rachel. Go on. You know I like that."

He tightened his grip, momentarily cutting off her breathing. When she struggled, trying to kick him, he knocked her off-balance with a single sweep of his legs. She fell hard against the kitchen counter, then slipped to the floor and landed on her rear. In the second it took him to grab her again, she drew in a breath and screamed for Luke.

"Bitch." John hit her across the face. The room lurched as pain exploded in her cheek. "Don't do that again."

He sat on her thighs, his crotch nestling against hers. After capturing her wrists, he held them together with one hand. She turned away and opened her mouth to scream. Then she saw it: He was holding a knife.

"You make one more sound," he whispered, leaning closer, "and I'll carve you up so bad your own son won't recognize you." Hot breath stirred the loose strands of hair around her face.

"What do you want?"

"You know exactly why I'm here. You're coming back.

You're going to sign your farm over to me, and then we're getting married.''

Strangely, all the fear disappeared, chased away by her will to survive. The throbbing in her face eased to a tolerable ache. Eventually someone would come into the house. She could only pray it wouldn't be Mark or Sarah. If she could just keep John talking long enough.

"I'd rather die than go anywhere with you."

His thin lips pulled into a straight line. "Don't tempt me, sweet Rachel." He placed the point of the knife against her throat.

Cold metal pricked her skin. She felt the sting and a wet trickle that disappeared into her collar.

"I'm not afraid," she whispered, staring into his black eyes. A lock of hair tumbled onto his forehead. She hated the fact that it reminded her of Mark.

"Maybe not for yourself. But what about the boy? Once you're gone, who will take care of him?"

"Leave him out of this." Panic made her careless, fatally exposing her greatest weakness.

"Don't give *me* orders." He ran the point of the knife over her chest to her right breast, then circled the tip. Even through the layers of clothing she felt the pressure of the blade.

"Beg me," he taunted.

Gathering up her courage like a tattered cloak, she leaned close and spit into his face. It hit his cheek and dripped down to his chin.

"Bitch." He drew his hand back to hit her again when the sound of a bell cut through the room. "What the hell—"

"You'd better run, John," she said, narrowing her eyes. "Someone knows you're here. That's the supper bell. In about two minutes, twenty hungry cowboys are going to be heading this way."

He glanced around nervously. "It's not suppertime. You're lying."

"Am I? Do you want to take that chance?"

A surreptitious movement caught her attention, but she didn't dare look away from John. Sweat broke out on his forehead and upper lip. She could see his apprehension and growing concern.

He rose to his feet, then roughly pulled her up after him. "There's horses out front. Are you going to come quietly or do I have to knock you senseless and tie you to the saddle?"

Someone raced across the kitchen, a flash of color and flapping skirt that could only have been Sarah.

"Wait!" Rachel screamed, trying to twist free of John's grip on her arm. "He's got a knife."

Sarah launched herself at the man's back. John cursed and dropped the knife. Rachel fell to the floor and searched for the weapon. As she clasped the handle, she glanced up and saw Sarah go sliding across the floor. The older woman came to a stop in a heap by the window.

"Sarah." Rachel started to crawl toward her. She'd covered half the distance when John reached down and grabbed her foot.

"No!" She twisted around and raised the knife. "Let go of me."

"What the hell is going on here?" Luke ran into the kitchen. "Steele!"

Luke lowered his head like a charging bull. His shoulder crashed into John's midsection. Rachel heard the whoosh of air as John hit the wall. Before he could collapse, Luke grabbed his shirtfront and pulled him back to his feet. A right hook connected with Steele's jaw, a left with his ribs.

John bared his teeth and tried to charge the younger man. Luke sidestepped. John tumbled to the floor and lay on his side. Blood ran out of his mouth. He looked over at Rachel and saw the knife in her hand.

He rose to his feet and lunged. She scrambled back and kicked a chair between her and John. Luke pulled her up, then pushed her behind him and into the dining room. When she was out of harm's way, he turned back to face his opponent.

The two men circled each other. They were similar in height and build, but while Luke had youth on his side, John had cunning and wouldn't fight fair.

Rachel glanced toward the pantry and back door. Please God, keep Mark outside with Billy and safe.

"Luke, be careful," she cautioned.

"Don't worry," he said, never taking his eyes off John.

"She keep you warm in bed?" John asked with a low chuckle, wiping the blood off his mouth with his sleeve. "Did you finally get what you mooned after all those years? Must have stuck in your craw to know Matthew had her first."

She saw Luke tense, his hands balling into fists. Under the window, Sarah began to move toward the doorway. Rachel leaned into the room and pulled the other woman to safety.

"There's a gun in Luke's study," Sarah whispered as she climbed to her feet. "I'll be right back."

"She's a hellcat," John said. "But sure worth the trouble. She's the only thing that got me through those long, cold winters."

The older man's ploy worked. Luke glanced toward Rachel. John moved in and landed a solid punch to his face. Luke staggered back a step, then lunged and began pummeling John with body blows. By the time Sarah returned with the gun, John lay on the floor, knees drawn up to his chest, breathing hard.

Luke took the gun Sarah held out and pointed it at the man. The cocking of the hammer echoed in the still room.

"I could kill you."

John closed his eyes and breathed heavily. "But you won't."

Luke glanced over at Sarah, then at Rachel. He urged her closer and touched the blood on her neck. She could see the rage in his eyes, the need for revenge.

He glanced back at Steele. "Give me one reason not to."

"Luke." She touched his arm. "He's not worth it. Let the law take care of him. I can't let you kill for me."

"I want to shoot him."

Their eyes met briefly. "No. You don't."

Footsteps sounded loud on the back porch. "Did someone ring the bell?" Billy walked into the kitchen. "Holy— What's going on, boss? We were in the bunkhouse and weren't sure we heard the bell. Is this the guy?"

Mark came in behind him. The boy took one look at John and screamed. Rachel grabbed her son's arm to pull him from the room, but he twisted free and ducked behind Luke. Mark stared at John.

"You gonna kill him?" he asked, pointing at the gun. "Ma, is Luke gonna kill my grandpa?" Mark looked confused.

Rachel felt Luke's anger, his indecision. She took Mark's hand and moved toward the dining room.

John Steele chuckled. "Yeah, you bastard. You going to kill the boy's grandpa?"

She looked over her shoulder and saw Luke lower his gun.

"Get him out of here."

Billy pulled John to his feet. The older man swayed slightly to maintain his balance. One arm cradled his ribs.

Already his eyes were swelling shut, and his nose looked broken.

"She ain't worth it," he said as Billy led him from the room.

Luke followed him to the door. "If he tries anything, Billy, shoot to kill."

"You shouldn't be taking time away from the cattle. I'm perfectly able to walk." Sarah glared at Luke over her bowl of stew.

"The cattle can get along without me," he said, smoothing her hair away from her face. "And it's not that often I get to take care of you. Maybe you should try to be grateful for the attention."

His teasing was rewarded with a smile. "I just don't enjoy being treated like an invalid. I have a bruise on my shoulder and that's all."

"It could have been worse." He shifted uneasily as he sat on the side of her bed.

"But it wasn't. I'm fine. Don't fret anymore." She swallowed some more broth. "How's Rachel?"

"I don't know. She's in the kitchen, taking another bath."

Sarah's eyes darkened. "That's the third one since they took him away this afternoon. She's trying to wash away a lot more than dirt."

"I know." He stood and paced to the window. It was already night. The lantern light caused the glass to reflect the contents of the room. "I've tried to talk with her, but she won't come out of the kitchen."

"Do you want me to see what I can do?" She set the bowl on the nightstand and started to pull back the covers.

"No. I'll go. You rest."

She settled back against the pillow. "How's Mark?"

Luke smiled for the first time since he'd found John Steele attacking Rachel. "He was scared for a while, but now he's happy as a pig in mud. He knows his grandfather won't ever bother him again. Potter made a cot for him in the barn. Thunder and Dawg are fighting for a place next to him." He tugged the curtains closed.

"Is Billy back yet?"

"He rode in an hour ago. John Steele is in Horse Creek, behind bars. You try to sleep now."

"I keep telling you, I'm fine. See to Rachel."

"I will. Good night." He bent over and kissed her brow.

Sarah placed her hand against his cheek. "I'm glad you didn't kill him," she said.

He nodded, then stepped back. He couldn't say the same.

After turning down the lantern, he moved into the hall. The walk to the kitchen seemed both too long and too short. In truth, he was afraid of what he'd find there. Something in Rachel's eyes had hinted that she'd gone to the point beyond pain.

When he reached the kitchen, he hesitated. Light shone from under the door.

"Rachel," he called softly as he tapped on the wood.

"Yes?"

"It's Luke."

"Go away."

Her voice was clipped and obviously frightened, but there was an edge to her tone. It didn't reassure him.

"Rachel, I'm coming in."

"No! Go away."

"I won't hurt you. I just want to make sure you're all right."

"Leave me alone, I'm fine."

He drew in a deep breath and pushed open the door. Two lanterns—one on the counter, the other on the table—threw her slender body into silhouette. The tub sat in the middle of the room. Rachel knelt in the water. A chemise and pantalets clung to her body, the light cotton made translucent by the moisture. Her hair was piled high on her head.

He'd expected her to be scared, even to cower from him. But instead, she ignored him as she scrubbed frantically at her wrists. Even from a distance he could see her skin was red and raw.

"What are you doing?"

She glanced up. Unfocused pain, almost like madness, reflected in her eyes. She held out her arms. "I can't make it go away. Help me. Make it disappear."

When he didn't move forward, she bit her lower lip and began to scrub again. "I'll do it myself, then. I'll rub and rub until it's gone. *He* did this. He hurt me." Her words took on a singsong quality.

Luke crossed the room in three quick strides and knelt beside her. Grabbing one hand, he forced her to stop. "What do you want gone?"

"The mark. Here." She showed him the bruise on her wrist. The raw skin, almost bleeding in patches, had darkened with the imprint of a man's hand.

His anger was as tangible as her distress, but he hid it as best he could.

Tenderly he touched the injured skin. "You can't wash the bruises away. Only time can do that."

Her blue eyes, dark and wild with unshed tears, met his. The wildness faded slowly, leaving only pain.

"He hurt me," she said again.

"I know. I'm sorry, Rachel."

She leaned forward, and he held her next to him. She trembled in his embrace, but didn't cry. As he murmured soothing words, he felt her relax. Her heartbeat slowed.

Gradually her chemise dampened his shirt and he became aware of the chill in her body.

"You're freezing," he said, then stood and pulled her to her feet. "Take off these wet things. I'll go turn down your bed."

"No." She crossed her arms over her chest. "Don't leave me."

He glanced quickly at her near-naked body and swallowed. "I'll turn my back, then."

"All right."

He circled away and listened to her remove her clothes. Then there was silence.

"L-Luke, could you get my towel?"

He grabbed the length of cloth on the table. Despite his best intentions, he couldn't resist looking at her.

The marks of Steele's attack were clearly visible. One bruised cheek distorted her face. The prick on her neck no longer bled, but he remembered the trail of blood he'd wiped away. Dark splotches marred her delicate wrists and forearms.

In between the remnants of violence lay perfect beauty. Full breasts, heavy and gleaming in the half-light, swayed as she breathed. A tiny waist flowed into hips broadened slightly by childbirth. He liked the womanly shape of her, the pale triangle of hair that pointed toward her secret places.

He felt the beginnings of an arousal drift through his body, but tonight the ache was easily manageable. He'd skin himself alive rather than frighten Rachel in any way. He'd lived with the wanting for so long it had ceased to matter. In a way, seeing her naked made it easier to bear.

The vulnerability of her body reflected her raw, exposed spirit. John had done more than prick her skin; he'd reached inside and damaged some unique part of her soul. He should have killed him when he had the chance.

"I know why you hate me," she said, taking the towel he offered and beginning to dry her skin.

"I don't."

Any pleasure he might have gleaned from looking at her body shriveled when he saw an ugly bruise on her thigh. Anger rose up and threatened to engulf him.

He reached for the nightgown draped over the chair. Only when the delicate lawn had settled over her curves did he feel in control enough to look at her face.

Whatever demons had forced her to bathe three times seemed to have disappeared into the night, but her pain was almost worse.

"It hurts so much," she whispered, blinking frantically. "I feel that I can't bear it another second."

He reached up and touched the bruise on her face. "I'm here."

"I know."

The time had come to have his questions answered. "What really happened in Kansas? Why did you run?"

She closed her eyes and drew in a deep breath. A single tear escaped to roll down her cheek.

"He tried to rape me."

Chapter Twelve

Rage. A powerful black beast entered the room and stole the air from his lungs. Muscles tensed, fists clenched. He cursed himself for not killing John Steele. Only that lone tear kept him from giving in to his emotions.

Acting more from instinct than sense, he drew her next to him. When she melted bonelessly into his embrace, he lifted her into his arms, then left the room.

"I'm so tired," she murmured against his neck. "But I'm afraid to sleep."

He kicked open her door and sat her on the bed. "I'll be right back."

"No." She clung to him, her arms around his neck in a death grip. "Don't leave me. I can still hear him, feel him."

He loosened his grip and forced her to look at him. "I'm just going to close up the house. I'll only be a minute. Do you want to come with me?"

She bit her lower lip. "I'm being foolish. Go on." She gave him a gentle push toward the door.

After dumping the bathwater, Luke doused all the lanterns but one and made a quick tour to check that the locks were secured. The memory of Rachel's panic made him work quickly. One thing was clear: He couldn't leave her alone tonight. He finished and returned to her room.

She sat on one side of the mattress, the spread pulled up

to her waist, her knees pulled toward her chest. Long hair, now released from securing pins, tumbled around her shoulders like a mantle of pale silk. Large eyes, dark and sad, followed his every move.

"You don't have to sit with me or anything," she said, wiping her face with the back of her hand. "I'll be fine."

He glanced at the neatly pulled-back spread, the plump pillow resting next to hers, the slight quiver of her mouth. The contradiction between her words and her actions almost made him smile. She needed him and was telling him so in every way but words.

"I think we'll both sleep better if we can keep an eye on each other, don't you?"

"Wh-what do you mean?"

"I'm spending the night here"—he pointed to the bed—"with you."

She relaxed against the pillow supporting her back. "Thank you, Luke. I'm sorry to be—"

He leaned over and placed one finger on her mouth. "Stop apologizing. You didn't do anything wrong."

He sat down and pulled off his boots. When he started to pull off his shirt, he glanced at her. "Do you mind? I'll keep my trousers on."

"You can undress," she said, avoiding his eyes. "I mean, I know you won't— That is, I'm not afraid of you."

He hesitated, then quickly stripped off his shirt. After lowering the light, he climbed in beside her.

The mattress had been made for a couple who were prepared to be intimate. His shoulder brushed her hips as he stretched out. He had a bad feeling it was only going to get worse.

The sound of their breathing echoed in the room. The lantern cracked as it cooled. Outside, night creatures played their tuneful symphony.

"I'm sorry," she said at last.

"Stop saying that."

"I meant I should never have come here. I put you and Sarah and everyone in danger."

"We're all fine. Everything worked out. When the circuit judge comes through town, John will be tried and sent to prison for a long time. I'll go into Horse Creek and make a statement. With any luck, you won't even have to be at the trial."

He felt her shudder.

Turning so that he supported his head on his hand, he tried to see her through the darkness. But the moon only provided enough glow to highlight shapes, not expressions.

"Do you want to talk about it?" he asked.

"No." She sniffed. "Yes. I don't know." She took a breath. "Yes. It would be better."

She straightened her legs. The hand closer to him began to pick at the covers.

"It started a long time ago. Maybe while we were growing up, I'm not sure. He used to watch me. When I first married Matthew, I thought I was imagining things, but after a while I knew I wasn't. I never worried much about it, though. Until Matthew was dead."

Her voice sounded strong, as if she were telling a story about someone else. He wondered how much the control cost her.

"I told you before that John started drinking after the funeral."

"Yes."

"That's was also when he started . . . hitting. He hadn't done that since you and Matthew were boys."

Luke's stomach tightened into a knot. He recalled the bruise on her cheek, the same cheek that . . . "Is that how you got that half-moon scar? Did he hit you?"

"Yes."

The picking on the spread grew worse. He captured her hand and held it still.

"I tried to leave, to go back to my mother's, but he wouldn't let me. He said I'd have to leave Mark behind. You know how he was with children."

He thought of the scars on his own back. "Yes, I know."

"About a year after Matthew died, John came after me in the kitchen. He said all he wanted was a k-kiss. I tried to stop him, but he was so much bigger and stronger. One kiss." She laughed, a soft, choking sound. "'What could it hurt?' he said. But it did hurt. Sometimes he'd go for months without touching me, but I could always feel him watching."

Luke laced his fingers with hers as if holding her tight enough would chase away the past.

"Then one day he wanted more. He tore my dress and touched—" She swallowed.

He put his hands on her hips and eased her down next to him. The sheet tangled at his waist. After he turned onto his back, he pulled her close until her head rested on his shoulder. He could feel the satin of her hair on his bare chest, the weight of her arm. Once again he took her hand in his and laced their fingers together.

"You don't have to tell me any more," he said.

"I want to." Her breath danced upon his skin. "My corset made him angry. He cut it open and then touched my breasts. He'd been drinking at the saloon. It was very late. I was afraid to scream because I didn't want Mark to find us." She raised her head as if to look at him. "He didn't put it inside me, but he hurt me all the same. And then he passed out."

Luke resisted the urge to pull her closer. Her words painted an image of horror and degradation no woman should ever have to endure. "I'm sorry," he whispered. "Dear God, Rachel, I've been a selfish bastard."

"You? Why?"

"Because I knew John Steele. I should have realized."

"You're wrong. None of us knew him. There's an evil in him we only guessed at." She rested her head on his shoulder. The moisture of her tears burned through to his soul.

"I swear by all that is holy," he whispered fiercely, "he'll never hurt you again." As if to seal the promise, he raised her hand to his lips and kissed her palm.

"Wake up, sleepyhead. It's already ten, and there's lots to be done."

"What?" Rachel pushed her hair out of her face. Why had she gone to bed without braiding it, and what was Luke doing in her bedroom?

Then, like a clap of thunder, the memories of the previous day crashed in on her. John, the knife, Luke, their fight, and finally the recollection of him holding her long into the night. Panic from the horror battled with gratitude.

"Oh, my," she said, pressing her hands to her cheeks. "Oh, my."

"I assume by that pink glow on your face you're feeling better."

"Ah, yes." She grabbed the covers and pulled them up to her throat. Only then did she dare to look at his face.

He took her breath away. This morning his eyes were clear gray, with no hint of green. Thick brown hair curled around his ears, with a single lock falling onto his forehead. His blue work shirt and snug-fitting trousers reminded her he was all male—and that they'd shared a bed last night.

"Sit up," he said.

She complied, then smiled when he set a breakfast tray

on her lap. A small bunch of flowers poked out of a glass.

"How sweet," she said, sniffing their fragrance.

"Mark picked them. He was worried because you slept late, so I told him we'd stayed up playing cards."

She glared at him. "You'd better not have told him that. Playing cards indeed. I've made it very clear to him that gambling isn't something gentlemen indulge in. I can't believe—"

His smile erupted into laughter.

"Oh. You're teasing me." Suddenly feeling shy, she glanced down at the tray.

He sat next to her, his thigh pressing intimately against her own. It hadn't seemed wrong last night. In the darkness their closeness had been her anchor in the storm. She'd expected John Steele to find her in her dreams, but there had been no nightmares.

She remembered waking once and feeling Luke's arm around her waist, his leg thrust intimately between hers. The rhythmic sound of his breathing had lulled her back to sleep. But now, in the light of day, the memory of what they had shared embarrassed her.

What must he think of her weakness? She recalled how he'd come into the kitchen while she was bathing. At the time, she'd felt caught up in the grip of some madness. His warm words and tender touch had brought her back from the edge.

But later . . . She'd stood idly by while he watched her dress. Then she'd practically begged him to join her in bed!

"Luke, I want to explain about—"

He picked up a piece of toast and shoved it into her mouth. "Eat. I'll do the talking for the next few minutes. All right?"

She nodded and chewed.

"When you're done here, I want you to pack enough

clothes for yourself and Mark for about a week. The roundup is due to start, and I'd feel better if the two of you were with me. Sarah's coming, too.'' He held up a hand to stop her questions. ''Don't panic. I'm leaving a couple of men to keep watch on the place. I don't expect trouble. It's just a precaution.''

The veiled reference to John Steele dampened her spirits. She wouldn't put anything past him, but Luke knew him as well as she did.

She sipped her coffee. ''I've never been to a roundup. Mark will love it.'' She remembered the waking nightmare that had haunted her just a few short hours before and how Luke had held her close until the trembling stopped. ''Do we all camp out together?''

He touched her cheek, traced the outline of the bruise. ''No. We'll set up a site away from the others. Someone will be with you all the time.''

''Don't do this, Luke,'' she said, holding his hand firmly against her face. ''Don't treat me like some maiden aunt with delicate sensibilities. I'm strong. You know that. I'm grateful for what you did. I'm not saying I've forgotten what happened''—a shudder raced through her—''either yesterday or before. I'll always remember. But sometimes it's better to just keep going.''

He studied her thoughtfully. They were close enough for her to inhale the scent of his skin, feel the heat from his body. She wanted to draw him close, have him lie with her again, only this time it wouldn't be a restful escape; this time they would complete the dance they had begun a lifetime ago. If he held her tight enough, she could forget everything else.

''If that's how you want it,'' he said.

''It is.''

''Fine.'' He rose to his feet and shoved his hands into his

trousers pockets. "I need to ride into town and make a statement for the sheriff. I was going to put it off, but it's better if I go now."

A sudden coldness gathered in her belly and swiftly moved outward into her arms and legs. He meant to leave her? Alone? He couldn't! But her brave words still echoed in her mind. The future had to be faced. It might as well be now.

"I agree," she said, gazing down at the tray on her lap. How pretty the flowers looked against the white linen underneath. "Do we leave for the roundup when you return?"

"No." He paced to the window. "You'll go as soon as you're ready. Jake Evans will stick close until I can join you tonight." She glanced up and caught his grin. "I know what you said about not being coddled, but humor me on this, please. I trust him to keep you and the boy safe."

"I don't mind being with Jake." The speed with which Luke's grin faded almost made her laugh out loud. The gray of his eyes darkened like a coming summer storm. "Don't frown at me like that, Luke Hawkins. I like Jake, and all the bad temper in the world won't change that, so get used to it."

"Jake's real popular with the women in town, but he's not used to ladies," he growled in warning. "You're playing with fire."

She pushed the tray aside and rose from the bed. Sunlight streamed in through the window. A quick glance down showed her the lawn of her gown became almost transparent in the brightness of day, but she didn't reach for her robe. After last night there were no more barriers between them. Let him see her as she was.

When she was standing directly in front of him, she

reached out and placed her hands on his chest. Her palms rested over the steady beating of his heart.

"I like Jake Evans the same as I like Potter and Ian. He's honest and good with my son." She took a deep breath and stared into his eyes. The gray had lightened some, but the mask was firmly in place; she couldn't read his emotions at all. "I'm grateful to you."

"I don't want your gratitude." He started to turn away.

"No. Listen to me." She grabbed the cotton of his shirt and held him in place. "I *am* grateful. Why shouldn't I be? You've stood by me when you had no reason to. But it's more than that, Luke. It's always been more. I . . ." At the last minute her courage deserted her. She couldn't say the words that had been filling her heart for so long. "I've never forgotten what we meant to each other," she offered instead.

For a moment he searched her face as if looking for an answer to a question. When she smiled slowly, she wondered what he'd found.

"I've never forgotten either," he said softly.

John Steele sopped up the last of the stew with his biscuit. When he'd devoured the final bite, he leaned back on his cot and belched. He hated to admit it, but the food in jail was a damn sight better than his own cooking. Servings came hot and plentiful, and the coffee was made fresh every morning. If it wasn't for the problems with the farm and that bitch Rachel, he'd almost be content to stay.

The setting sun shadowed the patterns of his bars on the far wall. It had been almost a month since Luke's men had ridden him into Horse Creek. From what the sheriff had told him, the circuit judge wouldn't be by any time soon.

That was fine with him. The more time he spent in this backwater town, the better. Once he was sent to a federal prison, he'd be stuck. But here—he glanced through the cell bars at the old man sitting at the front desk in the main office—he had a good chance of escaping. It was all a matter of timing.

Sipping on the hot coffee, he stifled a sigh of contentment. Amazing how much clearer a man's thinking became when he wasn't drinking. John couldn't remember the last time he'd been sober for more than an hour or two. Probably back before Rachel had come to live in his house. Seeing her every day had put a strain on his self-control. While his son was alive, he'd clamped down on his urges, taking them out at the local brothels or easing the ache with his own hand. But after Matthew died, he'd seen no reason to hold back. The bitch resisted because she was afraid of what a real man would be like. If he hadn't passed out that one time, he would have had her already.

The memory of her pale blond hair and soft skin quickened his blood. He wished he'd had time to rape her there in Luke's kitchen. He would have liked to tie her hands and feet until she was all helpless and pleading. He could simply have pushed her skirt up. After taking his fill, he could have left her there for Luke to find. His finger toyed with the buttons on his trousers.

Luke! Anger curled in his belly. How many times had he told himself to kill the boy? Now he was paying for his generous spirit. Luke had Rachel, and he wasn't going to let her go without a fight.

John smiled. That didn't really matter. He'd had nothing to do for the past weeks but think up a plan. And he had. All he needed now was a cool head and a little luck. After what had happened recently, he was due for some luck.

"What do you think, Mary?" he asked softly.

There was no answer, but he could feel her close by. How many times had her sweet spirit kept him company through the long winter? If he didn't remember how she'd left him, if he only recalled the times before, when they'd had each other and nothing else mattered, he could see her smile. But when he thought about those last days, when she'd chosen someone else over him, her perfect face disappeared from view and there was only the cold, violent rage and the promise of death.

He'd made a vow this time: Luke would die. John would force Rachel to return with him to Kansas. Once the farm mortgage was paid off, he'd take her again and again until he grew tired of her. It would all be so easy.

"And then we'll be alone again, Mary. And you'll love me again, just like you used to."

The sound of the front door opening broke into his thoughts. John sat up on the bunk and smiled when he saw his visitor. Right on time. Everything was falling into place.

"Hey, Steele. You're lookin' fine. Guess they're treatin' you right." The man tipped his ragged hat at the sheriff, then hurried toward the cell.

John shrugged. "Can't complain." Making friends with the stage driver had been smart, he told himself. Vern was his ticket out. He'd been playing the man like a fish on a line; he was only days away from being lured in.

"I brung you some tobacco, like you asked."

"Fine." John reached into his pocket and pulled out a gold piece. "I appreciate the trouble."

Vern grabbed the coin in his grubby hand, then gleefully held it tight. "Do ya need anything else?"

John motioned for him to pull over a chair. The sheriff glanced up at the scraping sound, then went back to his reports. John picked up his own stool and moved it closer to the bars.

"I could do with a woman, but I don't guess you'd be able to fit one of those in your pocket."

Vern guffawed, his mouth opening wide to expose rotting teeth. "I heard about what you did to Annie up at the Cattle Run. My brother-in-law weren't too happy."

"I paid him for the inconvenience."

"I knows, but howdy, when I saw her . . ." Vern shook his head and took a quick sip from the hip flask that was never far out of reach. After slipping the container back in his jacket pocket, he wiped his mouth on the back of his hand. "She couldn't walk none for almost a week. What all did you do to her?"

John smiled at the memory. The young whore had pleased him well. He'd made her dress up like a lady; her brown hair was the exact color of Mary's. After he'd taken her tenderly, he'd had her put on a blond wig. Then he'd treated her like the slut she was.

"Just beat her up some. What does it matter? I paid for my time."

Vern whistled in appreciation. "I had me a whore once." His beady eyes skittered around the cell. "Didn't like payin' for it none."

More than likely the whore had laughed at him, John thought derisively. Vern wasn't anything but useless vermin. When he'd served his purpose, he'd die as well. But until then . . .

John pulled out another gold piece. "Next time, bring me some more tobacco. And a bottle of whiskey."

Vern took the coin, then looked over his shoulder. "The sheriff don't let prisoners have whiskey."

"It's not for me." John winked.

Vern chuckled uneasily, as if he didn't get the joke but didn't dare not join in.

"I sure wish I could get to my money," John said, baiting the hook.

"Yeah. Too bad." Vern licked his lips greedily. "Are

you sure you couldn't tell me where it's buried? I could dig it up for you and bring it in.''

"I would if I could remember, but it was almost dark when I set out. I'd have to find the place myself. If I could only get out of here." He glanced at the cell as if seeing it for the first time. "But that sheriff . . ." He looked at the older man on the other side of the room. Morgan might be a stickler for enforcing the law, but he was hard of hearing, so John knew he could speak freely. "He's a real pain in the ass. If I only knew when he was going to be gone, I might be able to work something out with one of the deputies." He looked hard at Vern. ''Then I could go get my money.''

Vern nervously sipped again from his flask. Greasy hair fell into his eyes. The coat he wore, despite the warm summer day, was several sizes too large and smelled like a pack of badgers had taken up residence.

"Maybe I could help ya. You know, find out if there was something he had to go do in Cheyenne. If you was lookin' for a partner, that is.''

John held back the urge to tell the other man he'd see him in hell before he gave him another cent of his money. But it didn't matter. There wasn't any fortune buried outside of town. And the gold he'd been giving Vern was what he'd won at poker in the Cattle Run. They hadn't been as quick out here to catch on to his cheating. But none of that mattered. He only needed to break out of jail. The rest would take care of itself. His plan was simple. Rachel would help him, or he'd kill her. Luke was as good as dead.

''Why, Vern,'' John said, leaning forward and placing his hand on the other man's arm, ''can't think of anyone I'd rather work with. Partners it is.''

Chapter
Thirteen

"I suppose we should call it a draw," Rachel said as she stared at the dam of wood and mud. "The harvesting is almost done. You're welcome to the rest of the water."

There was no flash of movement, no flap of a beaver tail against the stream, but she knew the family was in there. Listening to her. Probably laughing.

For almost three months she'd fought to keep the irrigation ditch open. For the same amount of time, the beavers had been building a dam. Nothing had dissuaded them, not traps, not Dawg's loud barking when he tried to herd them, not even Potter and Jake's attempts to move the babies. That particular afternoon had earned both men deep scratches and bites. In the end, Rachel had been forced to break through the wood construction every morning to water the garden, while the beavers had spent every night building it back up. Did they ever sleep?

"Next year," she said as she glared at the dam, "I'll have two irrigation ditches dug and you can have one all to yourselves." With that, she turned and started back to the house.

The summer had passed quickly, she thought as she ambled along the path. The flowers of spring had long since faded. The motherless calves that had once seemed so lost and helpless now played on a range close by. The rest were well on their way to being weaned. The days had grown short, the nights cool again. John Steele still waited in jail.

At the top of a rise, Rachel paused to stare down at the ranch. The house stood on her left; smoke rising in the clear late-summer afternoon announced that Sarah had already started dinner. It would be a special meal. Ian would be joining them tonight. She wondered if he and Sarah were at last ready to make an announcement. For three months they'd exchanged significant glances, and once Rachel had seen them kissing behind the corral. But so far, nothing had been said.

Several feet beyond the house was the barn. Most of the animals were outside, grazing. Mark's horse had somehow opened the gate to the garden and was feasting on what was left of the carrots. The boy was nowhere to be seen, but if this day was like any other, he was inside, helping Potter.

Mark was the most changed by the passing time. He'd grown out of his clothes. But good food and a world filled with people who cared about him had done more than increase his size. He was well on his way to being a man. He'd turned six that summer and was taking responsibilities more suited to a boy several years older. She was proud of him. Proud and sad. In the course of growing, he'd ceased to be her little boy in a lot of ways. Now there were some things he'd talk about only with Luke. Man talk, he called it. No girls allowed. Not even moms.

She wasn't jealous; but sometimes she felt like the only one who was out of step with the rest of the world. Everyone else had a purpose, a place to be and a reason for being there. She seemed to be waiting for . . . something.

A slight rumbling shook the ground. Rachel stared west, shading her eyes against the sun. A dust cloud quickly settled into a group of men riding for the ranch. They'd been gone almost a week. The man in front, seated easily on a large black gelding, made her heart flutter against her chest.

Luke was home!

She picked up her skirt in her hands and ran toward the house. This was foolish, she told herself, as she hurried up the back porch steps. He wouldn't even notice.

But the words of common sense didn't stop her from racing to her room and quickly unbuttoning her blouse. Thunder reclined on her bed. The cat stretched and offered her chin to be scratched. Rachel gave her a quick pat. When Thunder meowed in protest, she smiled. "Later I'll give you a thorough scratching. I promise."

The cat yawned.

After washing up as well as she could, Rachel slipped on a clean blouse, then quickly brushed out her hair and secured it in a neat braid.

She remembered how, on the roundup, the breeze and constant riding had prevented her from wearing her hair up. When she'd despaired of ever looking tidy again, Luke had admitted he liked her hair down, either tied back or in a braid. Since then, whenever she'd had the chance without being obvious, she'd bowed to his preference. It was a small enough thing to do for the man she loved.

Pulling the thick braid over her shoulder, she secured a ribbon around the end, then flicked it back out of her way. She could hear the sound of the men in the barn as she hurried toward the kitchen. Sarah had spent the afternoon in the bunkhouse making a list of supplies to get the cowboys through the winter. Lengths of cloth had to be ordered for towels and linens, along with new trousers, shirts, and boots. They needed lanterns, rope, food, tobacco, even a saddle. Their requirements were endless.

Rachel added more wood to the stove, then pumped water into a bucket. After a week on the trail, Luke would want a bath tonight. She'd better heat plenty of water.

Before she could lift the heavy bucket, she heard footsteps behind her; then a large masculine hand reached out and clasped the handle.

"I'll do that."

"Luke!"

She spun to face him. As her gaze hungrily devoured him, she resisted the urge to step into his embrace. He wouldn't appreciate that. Although the summer was moving on to make room for fall, her relationship with Luke seemed to be stuck in one place. Despite the encouragement she'd given him the morning after John Steele had attacked her, despite the fact that Luke had placed his bedroll next to hers during the roundup, despite the fact that he was always around when she was fighting the memories, he'd never once kissed her or touched her in a way that suggested anything but comfort.

Either he was as thick as a stump or she didn't interest him anymore.

But as she took in the lines of weariness in his face, the sweat stains and dust on his clothes, she couldn't help but notice how his attention seemed to linger on the tight bodice of her new blouse. Then what was he waiting for? she wondered. Did he still worry that she carried scars, compliments of John Steele? They were as much a part of her as the marks Luke had on his own back. She was healing and ready to put the past in its place, if he'd let her.

"How did it go?" she asked as he poured the water into the waiting pot.

"Good. We've fixed most of the fencing. The bulls are being rounded up to be kept closer to the ranch. We've got enough hay if the winter turns bad."

He set the empty bucket on the floor and stretched his back. "I can't wait to spend the night in my own bed. I'm getting too old to sleep on the ground."

"Don't let Mark hear you say that. He's still trying to persuade me to let him go with you to the fall roundup."

Luke grimaced. "That's no place for the boy. We collect the steers that are going to market, then head 'em for Cheyenne and the railroad. There'll be too much going on for someone to keep track of him."

She held up her hand. "*I* understand the problems. I guess I'm just warning you that he's planning to start in on it again at dinner. I've threatened him with a whipping if he continues to be a bother, but I'm sure he knows I'd never hit him."

Luke reached forward and cupped her face in his hand. She could smell the sweat and the horse, but the odor wasn't unpleasant. It was all male, reminding her of how many nights she'd lain awake, wanting this man.

"He's a good boy, Rachel. Let him feel his oats. If he goes too far, I don't share your reluctance to tan his hide."

She smiled, enjoying the rough calluses against her smooth skin, the affectionate smile tugging at his lips. "Big talk, cowboy, but you're worse than I am where Mark's concerned."

"I'll take care of it," he repeated.

He hadn't shaved while he'd been gone. A week's worth of growth shadowed the clean line of his jaw and gave him a dangerous air. The room became charged with heavy expectancy, like a humid afternoon before a thunderstorm. Only this time the skies were clear and the lightning flashed in Luke's eyes.

Desire and love gave her the courage of twenty warriors.

"I've missed you," she said softly, never taking her gaze from his.

She felt more than saw him tense. One arm circled her shoulders. Long fingers tugged on her braid, forcing her head back, her chin up toward him.

But instead of their mouths melting in glorious heat, he ran the tip of his tongue across her lower lip. The unexpected moist contact caused her to gasp. Her eyes flew open. ''What do you—''

He chuckled and released her. ''I'll admit you're tempting, but I smell like the cows I was chasing and your son is about ten feet from the house. Hand me that cloth.''

''What for?'' She reached for the towel.

''I don't want Mark asking questions about my state.''

She followed his gaze and saw the outline of his arousal clearly visible through his trousers. Luke collapsed in a chair and dropped the cloth on his lap. By the time the boy flew through the door, Luke was sipping water and answering questions about the trip.

''Luke! Luke! You're back.'' Mark skidded to a stop in front of the table. ''Did you finish the fences? Me and Dawg have been workin' with Potter. All them calves are weaned now. Potter says they'll be goin' out with the herd this winter. Can I help you take 'em out? Potter says I'm real good on Socks now, and Dawg keeps the calves in one place.''

''Hold on.'' Luke pulled off the boy's hat and set it on the table. Then he hooked a chair with his boot and pushed it out. ''Sit, young man.''

Mark sat.

''Say hello to your mother.''

Mark glanced up. ''Oh, hi, Ma. I didn't see you there.''

''So I noticed. We're eating in a couple of hours, but you can have a piece of cake if you're hungry.''

''Starvin'. Dawg, too.'' The animal in question thumped its black and white tail on the floor.

''Dawg can wait for his supper,'' she said hastily, noticing the glare Luke shot the animal. No doubt he'd had ample time to regret his decision to let Potter keep the dog, but it was too late. Dawg and Mark were inseparable, but there was no need to remind Luke of that fact.

After cutting two slices of cake, she set them on the table. "Jake was by earlier today, Luke. Said he hadn't heard anything about the Oregon cattle. He expects them to arrive any time."

"Whatcha gonna do with 'em when they get here?" Mark asked, brushing the crumbs from his face.

"We've got to go through the herd, pull out the sick ones and the ones we're going to sell, then put the rest out on the range."

"You gonna let me help with takin' the cows to Cheyenne?" Mark's young face lit up with anticipation.

Luke looked over the boy's head and met Rachel's gaze. He seemed to be asking for an easy way to tell the boy no.

"Mark, we've talked about this. Luke won't have time to always be watching you," she said, moving up behind the boy. "There'll be too much activity."

"But I went to the spring roundup," he said, his voice suspiciously thick.

"That was different, son." Luke sighed, then continued. "During spring roundup we put the calves in pens. It's more controlled. Here, everything is on the range. You could get hurt or left behind. Your ma would be real mad if that happened."

Rachel touched Mark's shoulder. "I know you want to go. Maybe next year, when you're bigger."

"That's not fair." He slid out of his chair and ran toward the hall. Dawg trotted after him. "You're treating me like a baby, but I'm not. Potter says I can help and everything." Fat tears tumbling down his face and the trembling of his lower lip belied his statement. He sniffed once. "I don't want no supper."

With that, he ran to his room. Dawg's nails could be

heard clicking along behind him. The door slammed shut; then there was silence.

Luke stared after the boy. "I've known him only a short time. Tell me. Is it getting easier or harder to handle him?"

She thought for a minute, then laughed. "Both, I think."

He shook his head. "At least there's just the one."

Instinctively Rachel touched her stomach. A wave of longing threatened to overwhelm her. She'd sell her soul for Luke's child, she thought. Even as the image formed, she looked up and caught him staring at her. It was too late to hide her feelings; he knew what she was thinking.

His gaze dropped to her fingers tightening protectively over her womb. Without a word he rose, grabbed the bucket of warm water from the stove, and headed down the hall.

The evening meal was half over when someone knocked on the back door.

"I'll get it," Mark said, already out of his chair.

"Sit!"

Rachel and Luke spoke together. Mark sank back in his seat. While they smiled at each other over the boy's head, Jake walked in from the pantry.

"Evening, folks," he said, removing his hat.

"You eat yet?" Luke pulled out a chair. "There's plenty."

"Yes, Jake." Sarah rose. "I made a roast. There's fresh corn and—"

"Nothing for me." The cowboy shook his head. "We've already had our meal." He glanced at Luke and grinned. "They're here. I just talked to one of the cowboys. He rode ahead. The herd'll be here in about two, maybe three days."

"Well, I'll be—" Luke stood up and tossed his napkin on the table. He grinned at Ian. "What do you have to say about that, you cheap old Scotsman? I'm going to sell those cattle for twice what I paid. Maybe more.''

Ian sipped his coffee, then winked. ''I think you'll buy the next bull, Luke.''

''How many made it?'' Luke asked.

''About twenty-eight hundred head. And, according to Andy, they're all in good health.''

''Hot damn! This calls for a celebration.''

''Yeah,'' Jake drawled. ''Too bad you don't allow whiskey on the place.''

Mark jumped up. ''Can we see 'em, Luke? Can we go look at the cattle all the way from Oregon?''

''You bet, son.'' He scooped up the child in his arms. ''Tell you what. We'll pack up some food and bedrolls and go camp out till the herd arrives. How would you like that?''

''Hot damn!'' Mark crowed.

Rachel glared at Luke. ''Thank you so much for introducing that expression into his vocabulary.'' She took her son from his arms and set the boy on the floor, then crouched next to him. ''You will not swear, young man. Do you understand?''

Mark did his best to look chastised, but she could see he was squirming with excitement. ''Yes, ma'am. I won't say it no more.''

''Anymore.''

''Anymore,'' he agreed.

''Good.'' She brushed the hair from his eyes. ''If you're finished eating, why don't you go tell Potter about the camp-out? He'll need to get the supplies ready.''

The boy flew from the room. Luke offered her a hand up.

''It's not the fall roundup, but it's close,'' he said quietly. Besides them, Ian, Jake, and Sarah were discussing the virtues of the Oregon-bred cattle.

''You're good to him. Thank you.''

Gray eyes held her own. "You're welcome to join us. We'll stay for about three nights, maybe more. Winter comes early to the territory. This might be your last chance until spring."

She remembered the easy intimacy of the spring roundup when, despite the hard, long hours of work, there had been time to be with the man she loved. She remembered the comfort of his bedroll so close to hers each night.

"I wouldn't miss it," she said, longing to reach out and touch him but unwilling to risk rejection.

"We'll leave in the morning."

"That soon? Sarah and I will need to do some cooking tonight. How many of us will there be?"

"Just Mark, you, and me. A couple of cowboys will come along, but they'll take care of themselves."

Just the three of them? Almost like a family. For a moment she allowed herself to acknowledge that Mark always fell asleep shortly after dark. That there would be several long evenings with her and Luke, alone.

"Boss?" Jake broke into their intimacy. "You want me to come with you?"

"No," Luke said, never taking his eyes away from hers. "You take care of the ranch. I'm taking Rachel with me."

They rode out shortly before noon the next day. Mark urged his horse to the front, blazing a path for the others to follow. Luke and Rachel followed at a more sedate pace; the wagon brought up the rear.

As they passed the last of the pens, she looked over at him and laughed. "Do you mean to tell me that these mean old bulls are kept close to the ranch so that they can be fed and sheltered, but you let the cows and calves forage all winter on their own?"

"The bulls are expensive. That one"—he pointed to a

far corral holding a single bull—"cost almost five hundred dollars. I don't want my investment starving to death."

"But he's so big. Why would he have any trouble finding food?"

"Sometimes their size works against them. It would be easy for him to get caught in a snowdrift or slip on ice. Bulls might be large, but they aren't very smart."

"Kind of like Dawg?"

He glanced at the black and white dog trotting along at Socks's side, then back at Rachel. Excitement shone out from her face, and her smile was contagious. "Exactly like Dawg," he said.

The riding outfit she wore was new. A deep navy split skirt, more fitted and suited to riding than Sarah's old hand-me-down, outlined the long lines of her legs. The short jacket, discarded in the midday warmth, brought out the color in her eyes.

When she'd first walked out of the house, he felt as if one of his bulls had gored him in the chest. Sometimes he forgot she was beautiful. The light gold of her hair, the startling blue of her eyes, the creamy skin, still pale and unlined by time. As he'd stared at her with all the intensity of a starving man facing a meal, he'd realized he was twenty-eight, almost twenty-nine years old and he'd only ever loved one woman.

The realization hadn't helped his equilibrium, but he'd managed to get the wagon loaded and everyone up on the horses without anyone noticing something was wrong. Six years of hating her didn't matter anymore. In the space of a summer she'd made him see that there was no escaping his destiny. He was a part of Rachel, and she was a part of him. It would be easier to cut out his heart than try to forget her.

So what was he supposed to do about their relationship?

He looked over at her, sitting straight and secure in her saddle. The horse's slow gait made her sway slightly, as if performing some erotic dance. Every step caused her full breasts to move slightly against the pale white blouse. He knew exactly what she looked like naked; he remembered the taste of her mouth, the scent of her body, the heat of her desire.

She wanted him; he'd read that in her eyes. And she wondered why he hadn't responded to her subtle invitations. Another man would have jumped at the chance to ease his ache deep within her willing body. And yet he held back.

There was a part of him that still didn't trust her. The last six years had been a living hell. John Steele was in jail. Rachel could safely return to Kansas anytime. Yet she hadn't said a word about leaving. Was he waiting for her to promise to stay forever? Did he trust her? Did he believe she was willing to let the bank foreclose on her farm? Was this ranch enough for her, or did she want more? Would he believe the promises if she made them?

So many questions filled his mind. There weren't any answers, especially to the most important ones of all: Could he bear the pain of losing her again? Was anything worth that? This time it would take more than anger and pride to sustain him through the long winter; hell, through the rest of his life.

"Luke?" Rachel's soft voice broke into his thoughts.

"Yes?"

"What are they doing over there?" She pointed toward a field where several men were working.

"They're harvesting the last of the hay. We grow our own."

"For those prize bulls of yours?" Her smile was teasing.

"Uh-huh. If there's a bad storm, we try to get the extra hay out to the rest of the herd." He shrugged. "We aren't always in time. Fortunately the winters have been pretty mild the last few years, but it pays to be prepared."

"You've done a good job here."

"I worked hard."

"It shows."

Their eyes met. He could see she half expected him to blame her for the long hours. But for the first time since her arrival, he couldn't seem to find the anger. It had been fading fast since her confession all those months ago. They'd both paid a high price for their choices in the last few years, perhaps it was time to move on.

"Thank you," he said at last. "I'm very proud of the ranch."

He looked past her to the endless acres and the cows dotting the landscape. For better or worse, he was committed to the land. Whatever decisions were made about the future, wherever Rachel chose to live the rest of her days, his life was here. He'd made his stand in the Wyoming Territory, and he would stay until he died.

Mark turned Socks and rode back to them. "How much longer are we gonna keep going?" he asked, circling the horse until it faced front again.

"We'll ride till about three. There's a fine place to camp due west of here. There's a stream. We can try fishing for our supper."

"Golly." Mark adjusted the small cowboy hat he wore. "Are the cattle comin'? Today? Will it be today?"

"Not until late tomorrow or the following morning." Luke grinned. "Believe me, you'll know."

Rachel glanced at him out of the corner of her eye. "How?"

He laughed. "Twenty-eight hundred head of cattle make a lot of noise and stir up a storm of dust."

She smiled gamely. "I can't wait."

"Me either." Mark slammed his heels into Socks's sides, urging the horse to trot up front again.

"Good thing you refused to give him those gut hooks. Socks would be a mass of sores by now."

Luke stared at her. "Gut hooks? Who on earth taught you that term?"

She tipped her head down and blinked flirtatiously. "Why, sir, a lady must never divulge the source of her information."

"Rachel," he growled, fighting a sudden wave of jealousy, "I don't want you spending time with the cowboys. They don't know how to act around decent women, and I—"

Her teasing laughter halted his speech. "If you could see your face, Luke Hawkins. It was Potter. He told me Mark had asked you for spurs, then explained what cowboys called them." She urged Paint closer, then reached out and patted his arm. "But I do appreciate your concern."

Feeling as callow as a schoolboy caught kissing his girl behind the barn, he pointed up the path to a pitch pine several hundred feet away. "Last one to that tree has to search for firewood." With a slight pressure of his knees, he urged Satan to break into a trot, then a canter.

"I'll get you, Luke," she called out behind him. "And when I do . . ."

John Steele paced his cell from end to end. It didn't take more than three steps before he had to turn around. Where the hell was Vern? It was past time.

He glanced at the clock mounted on the wall opposite the sheriff's desk. Seven-fifteen. Vern had sworn to be here no later than seven. If he ever got his hands on that weasel, he'd sure—

"Hey, Steele, you're mighty restless tonight. You know there's a moon for you to howl at."

"Go to hell, Nate," John said as he forced himself to sit down on the bunk.

The deputy laughed. "If you're real nice to me, Steele, I'll play poker with you when your friend shows up. Who knows? You might win this time."

John chuckled, too, not letting the older man see his clenched fists. Hurry, Vern, he thought grimly.

The plan had fallen perfectly into place. Sheriff Morgan, being an organized and careful man, had made reservations on the stage three days before. Vern had come running with the information as soon as he'd found out.

Yesterday Morgan had left for Cheyenne and wasn't due back till the end of the week. He'd left Nate in charge.

The deputy was young and easily bored. A deadly combination, but he didn't know that yet. All John needed was a bottle of whiskey and a deck of cards. And that fool Vern.

"Steele!" Vern burst through the door and practically ran to the cell. "Sorry I'm late. My brother-in-law wanted me to do some work at the Cattle Run, and I didn't want to say—"

John shook his head to silence the man, then pointed toward the desk in the corner.

"Oh. Howdy, Nate. Sheriff still gone?"

Nate rolled his eyes. "You're sure stupid, Vern, aren't you? Of course he's still gone. You took him into Cheyenne on the stage. He'll stay gone until you bring him back." The tall, lanky man rose to his feet and sauntered over to the cell door. "What you got in that smelly coat of yours?"

"Me?" Vern's beady eyes darted back and forth between the deputy and John. "Just a bottle of whiskey."

Nate puffed up as if to prove his authority. John groaned silently and wondered why God was punishing him by surrounding him with morons.

"Vern, you shouldn't have brought whiskey in here," John said, struggling to save the situation. "It's against the rules. Morgan's just an old man. Not much of a sheriff at all. But Nate here's young. He wants to do the job right. You've insulted him. Now apologize."

"But . . ." Vern looked at him as if he'd lost his mind. "But you told me—"

"Apologize," John thundered.

Vern cowered back. "Gee, Nate, I didn't mean nothin' by it." He held out the bottle. "I guess you'd better take this, then."

Nate looked at Vern. John held his breath. Come on, he thought. Take the damn bottle. You want to. Drink it.

As if reading his mind, Nate pulled the cork out of the bottle and took a long swallow of the whiskey. "Good stuff, Steele. You always go for the best. I admire that in a man." Pulling up a chair, he drank again. "Go on and drag the table up to the bars. You got the cards, Vern?"

By the time they started on the second bottle, John was almost out of money. Not that it mattered. He'd kept a close eye on Vern's drinking, hadn't taken more than a sip himself, so Nate had consumed most of the alcohol. The tidy young deputy now sat with his shirt half open and the whiskey bottle cradled between his thighs.

"Got me two ladies," Nate said, blinking quickly as if to bring them in focus.

John glanced down at his cards. Nothing. Again. He tried not to mind. All his luck had to go into the escape. "I'm out."

Vern squinted. "Three twos. Beats your ladies, Nate."

"Ah." The deputy groaned and reached for the bottle.

While he was swallowing, John gave Vern a quick kick. The other man jumped in his chair and swallowed.

"Now," John commanded quietly.

"Now what?" Nate set the bottle down on the floor.

Vern leaned forward as if to grab the cards, but instead plucked the key ring from the deputy's waistband, and pulled Nate's pistol free from his holster.

"Hold on one damn minute."

Nate tried to grab his weapon back, but Vern threw the key at John and kept the gun pointed at the deputy. Instantly John was on his feet and fumbling with the lock.

"What the hell are you doing, Steele? You can't leave that cell. Gimme my gun, Vern." Nate tried to stand. His feet supported him for about two seconds; then he collapsed in a heap. "Damn, that was fine whiskey. Steele! I command you to halt."

But John was already free. Excitement coursed through him. He made his way across the small office to the collection of weapons secured on the opposite wall. There were only three keys on the ring. He searched until he found the right one, then unlocked the case and pulled out two rifles. Ammunition was in the drawer below. He scooped all of it out and dumped it on the desk.

"John, you think you should take that stuff?" Vern asked, still standing by the open cell. "Sheriff might get mad."

John laughed, and continued to open drawers. "No madder than he's going to be when he finds out I'm gone." In the bottom drawer, two knives gleamed in the lamplight. He pulled out the larger of the two and slid it into a sheath on the inside of his boot. After picking up the smaller knife, he tested its weight and balance on his palm.

Nate struggled to his feet. "Steele, I'm going to have to ask you to get back in your cell."

"Shut up."

Nate took a couple of steps forward. John looked up and saw another pistol sticking out of one of the desk drawers. He pulled it out and tucked it into his waistband.

Vern fumbled with the firearm that he held. "I ain't never had me a gun. We don't get trouble on the stage, and when there's gold or somethin' they gimme a guard."

John groaned. Why wasn't he surprised? They were all fools. "I'll teach you how to use it. Did you bring the bag?"

Vern pulled a wad of cloth out of his coat pocket. "Yup. Jes' like you said."

"Put the ammunition in it." He walked over to Nate. "Sorry to do this, old friend."

"What?" The deputy paled suddenly, his bravado fading as he saw the knife in John's hand. "You can't hurt me. I'm a deputy."

"Don't worry," John said, moving him toward the cell. "No one's going to get hurt. I'll just lock you up so you can't go for help."

"Oh. Fine." Nate staggered the last few steps into the cell, then collapsed onto the chair John had been using. "Someone will come by in the morning with your breakfast. They'll let me out and— Hey, what—"

John stepped behind the man and grabbed his hair, then pulled his head up with a swift jerk and slit his throat with the knife. Blood spurted across the room and poured down Nate's body.

"Jesus Christ, John. Why'd you do that?"

John turned and saw Vern standing by the desk. "I had to, Vern. He made me angry."

Vern swallowed and held out the bag. "I packed the bullets, like you said. We gonna get the gold now?"

John wiped the knife on the back of Nate's shirt, then dropped it on the floor. "Not yet. I've got some other business to take care of first. Did you bring those two horses like I asked?"

"They're waiting out back."

John took the ammunition and headed for the door. "You know anything about cattle, Vern?"

Chapter Fourteen

"I know Luke has his rules, but I didn't think a wee drop would hurt." Ian held out a flask and winked at Sarah.

"I won't say a word," she promised.

After pouring them each a half inch of amber liquid, he handed her a glass. She took it, sighing deeply when she saw her hands trembled slightly.

It was just Ian, she told herself firmly. But reminding herself didn't seem to help. Why was she so nervous tonight?

Because Luke and Rachel are gone and you're alone with him, a voice in her head responded.

Sarah glanced around the parlor. Everything was in place; the wing chairs and horsehair sofa stood exactly where they belonged. A fire roared away, chasing the slight chill from the room. Dinner had been an unqualified success, the biscuits fluffy, the meat tender. Even the pie, Ian's favorite, had been perfect. She should have felt happy, or at least content, but instead, there was a fluttering just under her rib cage and she couldn't make it go away.

"To a lovely lass," Ian said, raising his glass to hers.

"And a f-fine gentleman." She almost groaned when her voice cracked. He must think her a dolt. Taking a gulp of the drink for courage, she almost passed out when the fiery liquid hit the back of her throat.

"Wh-what is this?" she gasped, between coughs. "Not whiskey."

"Not whiskey," he agreed, taking the glass from her hand and setting it on the table. A large hand firmly patted her back. "'Tis fine brandy. You need to treat it with more respect. Otherwise it'll bite you back."

She wiped the tears from her eyes and frowned at his smile. "I'm so pleased I could be the source of your amusement."

"I would have warned you if I'd known you were set on drinking it down all at once. Now . . ." He put the glass back in her hand. "Sip it. Savor the flavor, the body. Fine things are meant to be enjoyed slowly."

There was something about his eyes, she thought. Something beyond the kind expression and laughter-induced wrinkles crinkling when he looked at her like that. She wished she had more experience with men. She'd been around them her whole life, but always as a sister or mother or employee. Never as a woman.

Ian reached for his own drink, then leaned back on the sofa, one arm stretched out across the back, his hand resting inches from her shoulder. She sensed he was waiting for something, as he stared into the fire. An admission of her feelings perhaps. A sign that she . . .

That she what? Cared for him? That much was true. That she wanted him to show her how it was between a man and a woman? A heated blush stole up her cheeks. She was forty years old. Maybe it was too late. Maybe her time was past.

The ticking of the wall clock sounded loud in the room, and still they sat side by side.

"What do you think?" he asked, indicating his glass.

She took a tiny sip. "It's lovely. From Scotland?"

"No." He chuckled. "France. But don't be telling

anyone. I wouldn't want the neighbors to know my weakness.''

In the firelight his red hair and beard glowed like fire. Her fingers clenched. Would he be shocked if she reached up and stroked . . .

"Dammit." Ian set his drink down and turned to face her. "Lass, your eyes are showing me things I've got no business seeing." He leaned forward and touched her face. "You're a fine woman, Sarah Green. And it's late. I don't want to overstay my welcome." He started to rise from the sofa.

"Wait." She placed a hand on his arm. "Don't go. I mean, I don't want . . ." She could feel the strength of him through the wool of his shirt. His muscles tightened and relaxed. She wasn't sure if his reaction was good or bad, but she didn't let go.

"Sarah. Sarah, look at me."

Slowly she raised her head until she could see his face. Firelight reflected in his eyes, causing them to burn with a flame she'd never seen before.

"I'm not a young buck anymore, but I'm still a man. I canna continue to sit with you like this. I dinna mean to be rude, but there are things a man wants." His burr thickened with each word. Warm hands reached out to cup her face. "Do ye understand what I'm tryin' to say, lass?"

He wanted her. She understood that much. Ian Frasier wanted *her*. There hadn't been many miracles in her life, and she wasn't about to let this one escape. She set her glass on the table.

"I understand." She swallowed, never taking her gaze from his. "Luke and Rachel won't be back for three or four days. I think"—her voice grew faint and she cleared her throat—"it would be all right if you stayed a little longer."

He chuckled softly, a warm masculine sound that sent

shivers rippling down her spine. "I'll stay until morning, if I stay at all."

"Yes," she murmured. "That's what I meant."

With a groan, he leaned forward and gathered her against him. He took possession of her mouth as confidently as he wrapped his arms around her shoulders and back. Firm lips pressed against hers, his tongue sought entry. She felt as if she'd been thrown into the fire.

"Oh, Ian," she murmured as he nibbled a path across her jaw and down to the collar of her dress. He felt strong and solid, and he wanted her!

"I think," he said, gently squeezing her shoulders, "that we might want to continue this in your bed."

She nodded, then rose and held out her hand. When their fingers laced together, he picked up the lantern and followed her down the hall. They reached her room, and she stepped aside to let him pull back the spread. One by one she removed the pins from her hair. The long chestnut tresses tumbled around her shoulders as she stepped forward.

He met her in the middle of the room and began unbuttoning the front of her dress.

"Ian?"

"Aye?"

"I've never been with a man before."

All motion stopped. He studied her face as if confirming the truth of her statement. Then he kissed her gently. "Are you afraid?"

"No. I just wanted to tell you."

"Do you want me to stop?"

She pressed his hands against her breasts. "Show me, Ian. Show me what happens when the lantern goes out. Touch me as a man touches a woman. I want to know why I feel on fire."

"I will, lass." He kissed her mouth. "But we'll be leaving the lantern on."

Rachel clutched the blanket around her shoulders and poked at the embers from their fire. The ashes were as cold and damp as the morning.

"Damn," she said softly, then went searching for the matches.

"Don't tell me I heard Rachel Steele *swear*?"

She looked up and saw Luke standing in the clearing by their camp. He'd been down to the creek. Damp hair was slicked back from his face. In one hand he carried his razor and a towel; the other hand rested on one hip.

"Did you actually wash in the creek?" she asked. "It must be freezing."

"No worse than that bucket you used. And don't change the subject. You swore." He grinned. "How far the mighty have fallen."

"I'm sure I don't know what you're talking about. I didn't swear. Aha!" She held up a box of matches. "Found them. Could you please hand me some kindling?"

"You swore and now you're lying about it." Luke picked up a handful of wood chips, then crouched beside her. "Hardly a sterling example for that son of yours."

"He's asleep," she said, trying not to get lost in his gray eyes. The laughter and affection were as potent as his passion, and twice as dangerous. This Luke tempted her into confessing her feelings. "It's your word against mine. I'm not worried."

"Oh, so that's how it is." He reached out and pushed a strand of hair off her face. "Perhaps I should demand a forfeit for keeping silent about your transgression."

"You sound like a traveling preacher."

"So speaks the sinner."

"I didn't sin—"

"You lied."

"About?"

"Swearing."

He was moving closer and closer as they spoke. Now their faces were inches apart, their breath mingling in the morning mist.

"All right," she whispered, falling into his gaze. "I did swear. I confess."

"And what of your other sins?"

"I confess to them as well." His lips had just touched hers when she felt something warm and wet on her ear. "What the— Dawg!"

Luke growled something much harsher than "damn" and rose to his feet. "I should have made Potter shoot the mutt when I had the chance."

Dawg, sensing they were talking about him, swiped Rachel's face with his tongue, then whined for his breakfast.

"You'd rather raise sheep than admit you like him," she said, moving to stand next to him.

"That dog? He's stupid and useless and—"

"And you think he's cute."

Luke muttered something vulgar under his breath.

Rachel smiled. "Now who's lying? I saw you patting him last night."

He glared at her. "There was a burr in his coat. I didn't want him lying down next to Mark and scratching the boy."

"Sure."

His mock anger evaporated. "Well, maybe I don't think about drowning him all the time. I'll go get the firewood."

She pulled the blanket tighter around her shoulders. This new Luke, the one who teased her and freely offered affection, was impossible to resist. Not that she wanted to.

If only she had the courage to say the words, to tell him that she loved him.

But she was afraid. Only three months ago he'd been a cold, uncaring stranger. She hadn't begrudged his attitude when she'd shown up unannounced, but how much of it lingered, hidden behind his easy smile? What if she offered her heart only to have him turn away? What if she offered her body only to have him use her and then reject her?

Dawg whined again. She leaned down and patted his soft fur, then turned toward the makeshift dressing area. Two sheets, strung up between trees, offered some privacy. After changing her blouse and straightening up her hair, she went to prepare breakfast.

They rode out due west shortly after ten. One of the cowboys accompanying them had ridden ahead. Around eleven-thirty, they saw him galloping back toward camp.

"They're here," he said, pulling his heaving horse to a stop. "About an hour or two away. Guess they made better time than Jake thought they would."

Luke thanked the young man, then turned to Mark. "Ready to see some Oregon cattle?"

"Golly, yeah!" The boy adjusted his hat, then kicked Socks. "Come on, boy. Let's go meet the herd."

"You up to this?" Luke asked.

She glanced at her son, trotting in front of them. Low clouds hung like cotton batting against a sky of deep clear blue. The taste and nip of fall filled the air. Soon the snow would come, producing long winter days with no relief from the endless falling white.

Shifting slightly in the saddle, she glanced at Luke and nodded. "Let's go," she said, wondering what he'd think if she admitted she'd follow him anywhere.

At the top of the next rise, they paused to watch the cattle pour onto the grassy plain. Underneath them, the ground shook slightly from the pounding of so many hoofed feet. Dust hung around them like an ever-present cloud, and low moans echoed in the morning. The scent of dirt and cattle drifted in the air.

And still they came. Mark counted out loud, giving up when he reached two hundred. With shorter legs and horns, these animals looked less rangy than the Texas longhorns that made up most of Luke's stock.

A creek snaked through the range. The cattle gathered on the banks of the stream to drink their fill; some splashed through to the other side. A dozen or so cowboys kept the herd in check, always circling to make sure no cow got left behind.

"Did you keep this range open for them?" she asked.

"Yes. They'll stay in the area for a week or so to fatten up. Then we'll split the herd into manageable groups and turn them out into the winter pasture."

"You must be very proud."

He looked straight ahead, staring at his new wealth. "It was a gamble. I'm glad it paid off."

Mark urged Socks closer to her side, then handed her the reins. "Dawg and me are gonna investigate."

"Don't go near the cattle," she warned.

The boy rolled his eyes and dismounted. "Ma, I'm a cowboy now. I know what to do." With that, he ran toward a grove of trees, Dawg following, nipping at his heels.

"Sarah told me that when you first arrived, there weren't many head of cattle at all."

"There were some. The man who owned the place before hadn't paid much attention to his breeding stock. He pretty much let them do what they wanted. I rounded them all up, culled out the weak and the sick, then sold off everything mangy. That didn't leave me with much of a herd, but there were plenty of mavericks on the range."

"Mavericks?"

He swung down from his horse and tied Socks and Satan to a tree. Then he held out his arms. She slipped down into his embrace and stepped back quickly when he didn't seem inclined to linger.

"Mavericks are unbranded cattle," he explained. "Whoever finds them keeps them. There are several dozen strong head out there."

After untying the blanket behind his saddle, he shook it out, then laid it on the ground. Rachel sat down and leaned back against a tree.

"You love it here." She wasn't asking a question.

"That I do."

He offered her a lazy smile. The hat shaded his eyes, but she had a feeling they'd be focused on something she could only imagine: all his dreams for the future. Did they include her?

"There's changes coming, though," he said. "We had more nesters coming through this summer than all the last six years past. And there's been talk of fencing in the range."

"What would that mean to you?"

"Cattle need room to feed. You fence them in, you limit the size of the herd." He picked a blade of grass and studied the stalk. "The land won't always be free. Eventually the government is going to force the ranchers to buy or at least rent grazing land. That will up the price of cattle."

"How much land do you actually own?"

He shrugged. "My acreage is about four times the size of your farm. I lease several hundred acres from a woman in town."

Rachel stiffened. "What woman?"

He leaned back until he was resting on his side, his head supported by one hand. "A real pretty one. She owns a saloon in town. Didn't always. Used to be some society lady from back east.''

''How nice for you,'' she managed between clenched teeth. So he had someone in town, did he? Well, it didn't matter to *her*, she thought, ignoring the desire to slap his face and rip his precious lady friend's eyes out.

''Yup. About seven months after she got here, she married the gambler she'd been working with. They've got two kids now, and a third on the way.''

Rachel glared at him. ''You did that on purpose.''

He smiled. ''You bet.''

''Scoundrel.'' She sighed and settled back against the tree. ''Did you ever find out which relative left you the land?'' She remembered Luke's excitement when he'd received a letter from a lawyer telling him he was the long lost heir to a Wyoming Territory ranch.

Luke pushed back his hat and frowned. ''No. I had the lawyer do some investigating, but he couldn't come up with anything. He'd been contacted by a law firm in New York City, but they couldn't help, either. Near as I can tell, it was someone related to my mother.''

''I guess it doesn't matter anymore,'' she said. ''It's yours now.''

Luke reached out and captured her hand in his. ''What about the Steele farm, Rachel? What are you going to do about that?''

She'd been dreading the question for weeks. What was there to do? She didn't have the money to pay off the mortgage, and she wasn't about to sell her land and her mother's to cover John's gambling debts.

''I don't know. I sent a letter to my mother, telling her that John is in jail. The bank is holding off on the foreclosure, for now at least.''

He looked at her, asking silently for a promise that

neither of them put into words. Say it, her heart commanded. Tell him you'll stay for as long as he wants. But he didn't ask, and she couldn't find the courage to offer. Instead he mentioned something about a harvest social in town, and she told him about the preserves she and Sarah had put up.

Sarah pushed her long hair over her shoulder and measured out the coffee. She hummed quietly as she completed the familiar task. But it wasn't familiar at all. For one thing, it was after nine in the morning. Guilt rose up inside her, but she pushed it away. So what if she hadn't risen with the sun? She and Ian had stayed awake long into the night. Then, even before the roosters announced the dawning light of day, he'd again led her to the edge of the world and shown her how to soar.

Even the thought of their intimate joining brought a heated rush to her cheeks. How nimbly his fingers had danced across her skin; how easily she'd made his breath quicken in return. Even if he left the house never to return again, she'd be grateful for all eternity for that single night of love.

"There you are, lass."

She turned at the sound of his gruff voice. He was neatly dressed, making her aware of her bare feet and wrapper-clad body. Self-consciously she brushed her hair off her forehead and tried to speak.

"Ian" was all she managed.

He glanced at the pot on the stove. "I see you've started the coffee. I hate to be ungrateful, but I've got a herd to attend to and must be off." He stepped forward and kissed her cheek. "My horse has been in the barn all night, so Potter has an idea of what went on. I'll speak to the man. No one else needs to know."

"Thank you." She clung to him for a moment before releasing him. "Be on your way."

He walked to the pantry doorway, then turned back. "I want you to know—" He cleared his throat. His normally tanned complexion darkened with a reddish hue. "That is to say, last night was very special."

"For me, too." She clutched the wrapper more firmly around her throat. When he hesitated, she gave him a push. "Go. Get to work. I have things to attend to as well."

"I'll be by at the end of the week." His long stride carried him quickly out of the house.

Sarah moved to the window and watched him walk to the barn. A feeling of contentment stole over her. She would never forget last night. Ian had given her a wonderful gift. In return she would be sure to make him feel welcome but not obligated. Perhaps in time he'd see that she loved him. If not, they'd go on as before. She had her miracle. One couldn't ask for more. Still humming, she poured the coffee, then went to her bedroom to dress.

It was almost four in the afternoon when she heard the commotion in the front yard. At first she thought John Steele had returned. Before she could go for Luke's gun, she heard a pounding on the front door and a familiar voice calling out her name.

"Open up, Sarah. It's Ian."

"Ian!" She swung the door open. "What are you doing here?"

He pushed past her and began pacing the room. "I haven't had a moment's peace since I left here. All I can think about is you." He paused, then grabbed her and held her tightly against him. "I love you, Sarah Green, and you'd make me the happiest man in the territory if you'd agree to be my wife."

She thought she might faint from the shock. "Marry? Me?"

"You dinna think I took last night lightly, did ye?" His callused hand traced her face. "I wanted to say something this morning, but we slept late and I had the herd to manage. I thought I'd go into town in a day or so to buy the ring, but I decided not to wait."

She silenced him with a smile. "Yes, Ian. I'll marry you."

"You won't regret this," he promised, then kissed her thoroughly. Even as their tongues mated, his fingers started on the buttons of her blouse.

"Ian! What are you doing?"

"What do you think, lass?"

"But it's the middle of the afternoon."

"I canna be waiting for nightfall." He pressed himself fully against her.

"But we're in the parlor."

"Aye. And that sofa looks mighty comfy."

Lightning ripped across the night sky. The bright light, followed by a crash of thunder, jerked Rachel awake. She sat up, then cringed when the boom shook the air.

"Luke?" Her voice sounded weak and shaky.

"Hush, love. I'm right here."

Warm arms reached out of the darkness and held her close. She could feel his strength, hear the steady beat of his heart.

"Is Mark awake?"

Luke leaned over her and studied the still bundle on her other side. "Surprisingly, no. I guess he can sleep through anything."

"Is it going to rain?"

Another bolt of lightning split the heavens. He gazed

upward. "I'm not sure. It could just be an electrical storm, but it feels damp. There's a couple of tarps in the wagon. I'll go get them."

Rachel huddled under her blankets while he was gone. Again and again the flashes of light and crashes of thunder reverberated overhead. Dawg whimpered, moving around Mark until he was between her and her son.

"Hush," she murmured soothingly, patting the animal's head. "We'll be fine." Dawg licked her palm in appreciation.

Finally, when she was beginning to debate going to find Luke, he returned.

"Here." He handed her a square of canvas. "I felt some drops on the way back. Keep yourself and Mark covered." He began rolling up his blankets.

"Where are you going?" she asked. The glow from the dying fire didn't illuminate his face, but she sensed something was wrong. "Luke, tell me."

"The new herd is restless. It could just be the storm, but I don't want to take any chances. The last thing we need now is a stampede."

"Stampede! Should Mark and I move to higher ground?"

He hesitated. "I'd really like you to head back to the ranch."

"Now? But it's the middle of the night and there's a storm."

"The lightning is moving east. In another fifteen or twenty minutes it'll be safe. Staying or going, you'll get wet. I'd just—" He shrugged. "I can't explain it. I'd feel better knowing you were safe at home."

Home. That was where she wanted to be as well. "I'll start packing right away. What about the wagon?"

"Leave it behind. Just take the horses. Three of the cowboys will go with you to lead the way."

"But aren't you coming with us?"

"No. I need to stay with the herd."

Something cold and ugly grew in her chest, a tight knot that signaled a premonition. "Luke . . . Come with us."

The first drops of rain began to fall. She felt several in her hair, and one splashed onto her cheek. He brushed the moisture away. "You think I don't feel it, too? I'll be careful. But I have to stay here. I'm counting on you to keep Mark and yourself in one piece. Come on."

He pulled her to her feet, then began packing up their belongings. Rachel draped the canvas over Mark until she was ready to wake him. As she and Luke worked together, three cowboys appeared, leading their horses behind them.

"There's something out there," the tallest one said, addressing Luke.

"Maybe it's just some coyotes looking for calves."

Rachel saw another man start to speak, but Luke warned him off with a shake of his head. She fought down the panic. Losing control now wouldn't help anyone. Her first concern was for Mark. After that she could only pray for Luke's safety.

At last the saddlebags were full. Rachel awakened Mark, then settled him on his horse. The tarp covered his small body and most of the horse as well. Luke boosted Rachel up, then spread his bedroll over her lap.

"What's this for?" she asked.

"You're going to have to carry Dawg. He'd never go with one of the other men and I'm afraid he'll get lost or trampled in the dark. See that you keep your legs covered. I don't want you getting scratched."

She held out her arms and took the animal. Dawg

scrambled for balance, then settled into a reclining position, his side leaning against her chest.

"You'll go back on a different path," he said, tucking the tarp around her. "It's a little longer, but you won't be in danger from the herd."

Lightning again cut through the night; this time the flash seemed farther off. But instead of a single clap of noise, two sharp sounds echoed in the night. She saw the cowboys glance uneasily at one another.

"Get them the hell out of here," Luke said, hitting Paint on the rump.

"Luke!" Rachel pulled up on the reins. "Ho, Paint. Luke, was that a rifle shot?"

He looked up at her. One hand rested on her leg. "Be careful, Rachel. No matter what happens, head directly for the ranch."

The rain fell harder, making it difficult to see. She brushed the drops away, not sure if they were rain or tears. "Luke, come back with us."

"I can't."

"We've got to head out, ma'am," one of the cowboys said.

"I know." She glanced down at Luke one last time. "I love you," she whispered.

Another boom of thunder drowned out his reply. And then they were moving away from the camp. She stared over her shoulder, but couldn't see anything through the rain. Then came the call, splitting the night.

"Stampede!"

Chapter
Fifteen

The cowboy rode into the camp and stopped in front of Luke. "Stampede, boss," he said, breathing heavily.

"I heard you the first time. Let's go get 'em."

He spared Rachel one last glance, but she and the others had already disappeared into a grove of trees. He could only pray that they'd find their way home safely. There was something very wrong tonight. The herd should have been too tired to be bothered by the storm. Something else had upset them. He didn't know what it was, but he could almost taste the danger.

He and the cowboy rode quickly back to the range where the cattle had been grazing. In the wet night Luke could get no clear picture of what was happening; he just heard the pounding of hooves and the lowing of three thousand spooked head.

"Where are the point riders?" Luke asked the man riding next to him.

"They was asleep, but I think they're out in front now."

The trick was to get ahead of the herd and gradually turn it back into itself. After running in a circle, the animals usually came to a stop.

"Send a dozen men up to join them. Once they're calmed down, I want everyone on patrol. Something set these cattle off, and it wasn't just the storm."

Luke rode down the side of the rise toward the thundering mass of animals. Across the range was a hill and west of that, mountains. There might be all kinds of critters up there to bother the herd. Or it might not be something on four legs at all.

Easing Satan forward, he circled the rapidly slowing cattle. There was something out there. The rain began to let up slightly. When he reached the foot of the hills, he stared up. Heavy clouds blocked the moon. Rough terrain threatened Satan's footing. There was no way to find whatever it was in the darkness. He might take chances, but he wasn't a fool. In the morning he could—

Satan shifted and nickered softly. Luke looked up and, as a bolt of lightning cut across the night, caught a glint of something metal. A gun.

Instinctively he ducked. For the second time that night, a shot echoed with the thunder. Satan reared back. Luke clung to the gelding with his hands and legs. The rifle sounded again, and the night exploded into darkness.

After settling Mark into bed, Rachel went back to the kitchen. There was no point in trying to sleep. She couldn't. Not until she knew Luke was safe.

Tremors raced through her. She could still feel the terror that had gripped her when she'd heard that gunshot. Please God, she prayed, let him have survived.

Sarah poured her a cup of coffee, then pulled out a chair. "Sit down, child. Pacing like that won't bring him back any faster."

"Aye." Ian took the chair across from hers and reached out for her hand. "Luke's a strong lad. He'll be home in no time."

Rachel smiled with a confidence she didn't feel. Something *was* wrong. She could sense it. The moment she'd heard the gunshot, she'd known Luke was in danger. Again she prayed.

Staring into cups of rapidly cooling coffee, the three waited in silence. At one point she looked up and saw Ian standing with his arms around Sarah. Rachel focused long enough to wonder what the Scotsman had been doing at the house in the middle of the night, but then she dismissed the question. Nothing mattered now but Luke.

The clock in the parlor had just chimed five when they heard the sound of horses by the barn. Rachel slammed her cup on the table and ran out the back door. A dozen cowboys had crowded into the area beside the corral. She scanned the group, searching for a beloved face. Then she saw a body draped over an unfamiliar horse. The scream inside her built up until it burst forth with a high, keening wail.

Rachel leaned against the bedroom wall. She didn't make a sound, barely breathed as the doctor completed his examination. The older man fussed about, clucked his tongue from time to time, and shook his head. After binding the bullet wound on Luke's arm, he'd done little more than poke and probe. She felt her grip on sanity slipping slowly away. If he didn't tell her something, and soon, she was going to completely lose control.

Just when she was sure he was being deliberately slow, the doctor motioned for her to come forward. Rachel pushed away from the wall and walked toward the bed, hands squeezed tightly together, fingers laced in an attempt to still the trembling.

"Will he live?" She was surprised her voice sounded so calm.

The little man, with spectacles perched on his nose, gave her a kindly smile. "I wish I could say. There's no problem with the arm. Change the bandage once a day and sprinkle the wound with the powder I'll leave. That will help to prevent infection. As for the rest . . .'' He frowned and tucked his hands into his trousers pockets. ''I'm not sure why he's still unconscious. I don't feel any internal injuries, but I can't be sure. There's still some swelling on the right leg. It could be broken. The men say he was thrown or fell from his horse. He might have hit his head. There's a bump low on the back, but it doesn't seem that big. The best thing now is to let him rest and wait. I'll be by in the morning to check on him again.''

Rachel knew politeness demanded that she thank the doctor for his care, but she didn't have the strength. She still didn't know if Luke was going to die.

When the other man had left the room, she sank down at Luke's side and clutched his hand. Let Sarah take care of the social niceties.

His color was good, she thought as she brushed the hair from his forehead; his breathing was steady and deep. Maybe he was just sleeping.

She studied the lines of his face, the strength inherent in his bare chest and shoulders, then smoothed the covers pulled up to his waist. He was naked below the white sheet.

''Luke,'' she whispered. ''Luke, can you hear me?''

There was no reply. His fingers, warm against her own, remained limp within her grasp.

''I love you. Please don't leave me. Not now, when we've finally found each other.''

Tears began again, flowing down her cheeks and dripping onto their joined hands. For a second she thought she felt a stirring against her thumb, the slight tensing of muscles. When she glanced at his face, his eyes remained closed. Still, the flutter of movement had given her hope.

''We'll get through this together,'' she promised. ''I

didn't come all this way just to lose you now. You're going to get well. Do you hear me?''

And so began Rachel's vigil. Aside from an hour or two with her son, she spent all her waking hours and most of her nights at Luke's side. The doctor returned every morning for three days. With his last examination, he'd announced there were no broken bones. The body could heal on its own, or not; it was out of his hands. They could only wait.

Rachel talked with Luke, begged, pleaded, and swore at him, and demanded he wake up and speak with her. It was all in vain. He thrashed about several times, often in a fever and calling her name and asking for water. After drinking, he'd drifted back into his place of darkness, never having truly awakened.

Her greatest enemy wasn't exhaustion; it was fear. Fear that Luke would die. Fear that John Steele would come for her.

Her hand felt for the pistol tucked in her skirt pocket. The sheriff had come back two days after Luke had been injured. The kindly old man had explained how John had broken out of jail and killed a deputy in the process. They thought he'd accomplished the escape on his own, but he had made friends with a man in town. The two of them could be together. Ten men were out looking for both of them, but there had been no sign. The sheriff thought John had headed back for Kansas.

The sheriff was wrong, she thought. John was nearby. Waiting. He'd already tried to kill Luke; next he would come after her. This time she wasn't going to make it easy for him. This time she planned to put up a fight. She stroked the barrel of the gun lightly. A dozen cowboys kept watch on the ranch house, and still she couldn't feel safe. But she pushed the fear away. Luke was all that mattered.

''Mama?''

Rachel looked up and smiled. She rose from her chair and walked over to Mark. "Yes?"

Her son stood in the doorway, a book in his hands. "I thought maybe I could read to Luke. I always like it when you do that for me when I'm sick."

Brown eyes, so much like Matthew's, stared up at her. She wasn't the only one suffering. She saw the pain on Sarah's face, and it was reflected in Mark's.

"That's a good idea," she said, stepping back to let him in the room. "What book did you bring?"

"One on cattle. He likes the ranch. I thought it would be better than a story." Mark perched on the chair and stared solemnly at the unconscious man on the bed. "Howdy, Luke. It's me. Mark. I'm gonna read something to you. Maybe, when I'm done, you could wake up and talk to me some. Ma and me miss you. Dawg, too. He wanted to come with me, but I know you don't like him in your room."

With that, the boy opened the book and began to read about cattle bloodlines and breeding stock. Rachel listened to his young voice as he stumbled over unfamiliar words. The ache in her heart was eased by love. Somehow Mark's spirit had survived despite the horror in his young life. John Steele might have beaten his body, but he'd never touched the spark inside. She'd been blessed with her son; if only God would see fit to grant her one more boon.

While Mark watched Luke, she went to get some of the rich broth Sarah had prepared. They hoped the smell of food would help Luke return to consciousness. The housekeeper stood at the counter kneading bread. In the last three days she'd suddenly aged. The gray in her hair no longer blended with the chestnut; lines deepened around her eyes and mouth.

"How is he?" Sarah asked when Rachel walked into the kitchen.

She shrugged. "The same. The fever hasn't come back today. Mark's with him now. I thought I'd take him some broth."

"That's a good idea." Sarah brushed her hands against her apron and took a cup down from the shelf. "He looked better this morning, don't you think?" The older woman's hand shook as she ladled the liquid into the cup.

Rachel gave her arm a comforting squeeze. "Luke will pull through. I feel it."

"I hope you're right. He's my boy. Not by blood maybe, but mine nonetheless. I couldn't bear it if something happened to him."

"It won't, Sarah." She took the cup and carried it back into the bedroom.

After a half hour, Rachel had Mark close the book and told him to take Dawg outside to play. The men there would keep him safe.

"Do you think I helped?" he asked, that same lock of hair tumbling down his forehead.

"I'm sure you did." She bent down and kissed his cheek. "But Luke is still resting. Why don't you go on now? Maybe we'll have some news by suppertime."

Her son looked at the still form on the bed. "Is he gonna die, like Papa did?"

He seemed so grown up most of the time, handling his horse with practiced ease, getting underfoot in the barn. Even at his lessons he moved quickly, grasping concepts, reading new words, easily learning his numbers. At times she forgot he was only six years old and still very much a child.

"I hope not. We have to pray very hard."

"I am, but—" Tears fell from his brown eyes.

Rachel dropped to her knees and held out her arms. Mark

flung himself into her embrace, clutching at her neck, burying his face in her shoulders.

"I'm scared. I don't remember Papa much," he said, his voice muffled by tears. "I got that picture we brung with us, but I can't see him inside my head when I close my eyes. And when I try real hard to see him, I see Luke instead. I don't want to forget Luke like I forgot Papa." He raised his head and looked at her. "Am I bad?"

"Oh, Mark." She hugged him tighter, holding on to his warmth and love. "No. You're not bad. Papa knows that you can't remember what he looked like. And he's happy that Luke is helping you grow up. He and Luke were friends. The best of friends. There isn't anyone else he'd trust with you."

Mark sniffed and wiped his nose on his shirtsleeve. "What about you, Mama? Does Papa trust Luke with you?"

Who else but a child could seek out the core of the matter? Would Matthew have wanted her to be with Luke?

She remembered Sarah's statement that she had, by loving Luke but marrying Matthew, wronged both men. At the time she'd thought the older woman hard and judgmental. Yet now, with Luke lying close to death, just as Matthew had a few years ago, she wasn't sure. She could recall, with painful clarity, her wedding day. The small clapboard church had been filled with people who'd come to see the heir to the Steele fortune marry the girl who had once loved another. After they had spoken their vows, when the minister asked if anyone knew a reason why the marriage should not take place, Matthew had looked at her.

"Are you sure?" he'd asked, his brown eyes, so much like Mark's, delving into her soul.

She hadn't been sure. All she'd wanted, prayed for, was Luke's return. In those few seconds, when time had been counted in heartbeats, she'd waited for him to walk through the door. Had imagined him striding up the aisle, gathering her in his arms, and saying, "I know a reason. Rachel Thompson belongs to me."

But he hadn't arrived. The minister continued with the ceremony. After he pronounced them man and wife, she'd looked at Matthew. "I'm sure," she'd said, speaking the first lie of her marriage. How many others had there been?

Mark stirred in her arms. She smiled at him and brushed the tears from his cheeks. "Yes, Papa would want me to be with Luke. He loved us both, and he knew we loved each other."

Mark nodded solemnly, then called for Dawg and headed toward the barn.

She watched him go, her boy-man. The world was a simple place for him; right and wrong were easily defined. If only that were true for her as well.

Rachel took her place next to Luke. She stirred the broth in the cup. "Sarah thought you might be hungry. It's been three days, Luke. Please wake up."

He didn't respond. She set the spoon down and took his hand in hers. She wasn't sure if he could hear her, but something compelled her to continue speaking with him. At first she'd felt self-conscious, but now conversation flowed easily. She talked about everything but John Steele's escape.

"Mark is worried about you." She smiled. "He's a good boy. I see your influence in him. He asked if it was all right to care about you. He's having trouble remembering Matthew. I am too, sometimes. I can remember us growing up together. That much is very clear. But later, when we were married, I just can't recall many specifics."

She leaned forward and touched his face. Four days' worth of beard scratched her fingers. "It was a mistake to marry him. I was trying to save my family, but all I ended up doing was hurting you and Matthew. Sarah was right. I wronged both of you. Foolishly, I thought I could take care of everything myself without anyone getting hurt. Instead, we've all suffered. I'm so sorry, Luke. When I think of all the years we've lost . . . Can you ever forgive me?''

She leaned back and cradled his hand against her stomach. Closing her eyes, she continued her quiet talking. ''I swear I'll never leave. I don't care what happens to John Steele or his farm. I hope he starves out there on the range. I'm going to stay here with you. For as long as you'll have me.''

She was silent for a moment. ''They've started the fall roundup. Ian's been helping Jake get everything done. You know, I think there's something going on between Ian and Sarah. He was here the night of the storm. I didn't think about it until later, but it was very late when Mark and I arrived back. And since you've been sick, he's been here almost every night. You don't suppose . . .'' She grinned. ''Well, why not? Sarah is still a lovely woman, and she deserves someone special in her life. I suspect we're going to have a wedding before Christmas.''

''Did you bring me soup to look at, or do I get to taste it as well?''

Rachel froze. That raspy voice sounded familiar. Was it really Luke or was her mind playing tricks on her? She opened her eyes.

''Well?'' Luke raised his head off the pillow, then groaned. ''My head hurts.''

''Luke! You're awake.''

''Damn right I'm awake. And hungry.'' He tried to sit up. The movement put pressure on his injured arm. He winced and glanced down, than sank back against the bed. ''What the hell happened? I feel as if I've had a run-in with a two-ton bull. The last thing I remember is . . .'' He looked at her. ''Why are you crying?''

''Am I?'' She touched her face and was surprised when she felt tears. ''I guess I'm happy you woke up.''

''What do you mean?'' He stirred again. ''Why wouldn't I wake up?''

''Hush.'' She leaned over him. ''Don't get yourself worked up. You've been unconscious for three days.''

She thought about running to tell Sarah that Luke was going to be fine, but she couldn't tear herself away just yet.

''Three days?'' He glared at her. ''That's not possible.''

''Do you remember the stampede?''

He nodded, then rubbed his hand over his jaw. As he felt the thickness of his beard, his eyes widened. ''That's about all I do remember.''

''One of the cowboys found you lying on the ground. You'd been shot.''

He glanced at the bandage on his upper arm. ''Anyone else hurt?''

She hesitated.

''Tell me,'' he insisted.

''All of the men are safe, but Satan was killed. I'm sorry, Luke.''

He swore. ''How?''

''He broke his leg. Jake had to shoot him.''

''What else has been happening while I was sleeping? You said something about Sarah leaving?'' He glared at her as if it were all her fault.

''You heard what I told you?''

He shrugged, then gingerly touched his arm. ''Most of it, I think. I'm not sure. There were some strange dreams. I kept trying to go away, but you kept talking and talking. Finally it just seemed easier to wake up.''

She picked up the cup of broth and stirred it. ''If I'd

known you were going to be so bad-tempered, I wouldn't have prayed so hard for your recovery.''

''Help me sit up,'' he commanded.

''No. You're going to drink this; then you're going to rest. No sitting up until tomorrow.''

''I will not be treated like some weak pup.''

''If you're so strong, sit up yourself.''

When he opened his mouth to protest, she shoved in a spoonful of hot liquid. He swallowed and glared at her, but continued to drink until the cup was empty.

''Now, isn't that better?''

He grumbled something about bossy women.

She laughed. His eyes were bright and clear, and if his temper was anything to go by, there was nothing wrong with his head.

''I'll go get some water to freshen you up and tell Sarah you're back among the living.''

As she started to rise from her chair, Luke reached out and grabbed her arm.

''Rachel, I—'' His gray eyes glowed with flecks of green, and his lips pulled into a reluctant smile. ''I could feel you with me. It made a difference.''

''I'm glad.'' A wave of shyness swept over her. How much of her ramblings did he remember? Had he heard her ask for forgiveness? Tell him she loved him?

Suddenly unable to face him, she pulled free of his grasp and hurried out of the room. ''I'll be right back.''

The jackrabbit broke through the clump of bushes, then zigzagged across the path. John Steele aimed and pulled the trigger. The gunshot echoed in the still afternoon.

He lowered the rifle and laughed. ''Three for three. That should hold us for a couple more days.''

He and Vern had stolen enough supplies from a store in

town to last them a few weeks. Despite their need to stay out of sight, he refused to give up his fresh meat. Vern had gone out hunting a couple of times. Once the fool had spent the whole day shooting, the sound of bullets filling the air for hours. And all he'd come back with was a graying old squirrel too tough to chew. After a week John wasn't sure he could stand much more of the other man's company.

Only a little longer, John reminded himself. He needed Vern until he had Rachel in his hands. Then the mangy stage driver would cease to be useful. He'd kill him and take pleasure in his dying.

John picked the rabbit up by its hind legs and dropped it into the bag with the others. What he needed now was some information about that bastard Luke. Was he dead or not? At the last minute the coward had ducked. Steele knew he'd at least nicked him, but was it enough?

It was damned frustrating, John thought as he walked back toward his camp. But if Luke wasn't dead now, he soon would be. Three sticks of dynamite would take care of that. And then he'd return to Kansas.

John wondered about the farm. Who had brought in the crops this year? Had they been left to die? He closed his eyes and thought about the long fields, the smooth plowed earth. God, he missed the farm. He'd had some men working for him, but they wouldn't have bothered to hang around. Without his firm hand, they were all lazy and useless. Hell, they'd probably run off months ago. That was something else Rachel owed him for.

Tomorrow he'd ride out to the ranch and see if the guards were still in place. As far as he knew, there hadn't been a funeral for Luke Hawkins, but he could always hope.

As John neared the camp, Vern thrashed through the bushes to meet him.

"Whatcha get, John?" He took the bag and peered

inside. "Oh, rabbit. Great. I'll make that stew again. You liked it, didn't you?"

"Yes, Vern. I liked the stew." He glanced down at the man's waist and stiffened. "What the hell are you doing with that?"

Vern patted the dynamite tucked in his belt and grinned. "Protection. I don't shoot my gun good. If that posse comes lookin' for me, I'll just light up a stick an' toss it at 'em."

"You ass, you'll hurt yourself." Before I'm done with you, John added silently. "Or worse, kill us both. Give me the dynamite."

Vern stepped back and held the bag protectively in front of him. "No. It's mine."

John resisted the urge to put a bullet in the other man's face and be done with it. "Keep it, then. Just don't go too near the fire."

Tonight, while Vern was sleeping, he'd get the dynamite back and hide it. The last thing he needed was an unexpected explosion. He walked toward his saddle.

Vern followed behind. "Do ya think we could go get the gold soon?"

"Maybe." He pulled a bottle of whiskey out of his saddlebag and took a long drink. After almost three months of being sober, it sure seemed good to feel the fire roaring in his belly. But he was careful to limit himself. His plan required perfect timing, and that meant a steady hand. He glanced over at Vern.

If there was a weak link, Vern was it. Still, he needed another pair of eyes, and he couldn't be picky about who they belonged to. In a few days he'd have his answer. If Luke was dead, there was a bottle of whiskey to help with the celebration. If he wasn't . . . John smiled and gulped another mouthful. Then it was just a matter of time.

*   *   *

"What do you think?" Luke stood by the window, letting the sun warm his bare chest. He rotated his shoulder. When the joint felt loose and relaxed, he tensed his arm. Pain ripped through the healing gunshot wound.

"I think I've seen you look better, boss." Jake lay sprawled on the bed.

"Ain't that the truth." Luke clenched and unclenched his fist, ignoring the waves of fire racing through the muscle. "But it takes more than a kick in the face to do me in."

"Thank God." His foreman placed his hands behind his head. "Cattle have already left for market. Should be in Cheyenne this time tomorrow."

"You always wanted to cull the herd. Guess we'll find out come spring if you know as much as you think you do."

"Worse that can happen is I'll get fired."

Luke grinned. "Nope. The worst that can happen is I'll tell that dancing girl you're interested."

Jake flinched. "I'd rather lose my job." The lanky Texan looked him over, starting at his head and scanning down to his bare feet. "That's a nasty bruise on your ribs. Don't recall seeing that color of purple before. Must hurt like hell."

Luke shrugged. "It's not that bad. There's a matching one on my right knee." He motioned down to his trouser-clad leg. He'd managed to hold on to his pants, but that was all. Rachel and Sarah were adamant about keeping him inside. To that end, they'd taken away his boots and jacket. There would have been a fight about the matter, except that he was still as weak as a kitten. It would be at least another week before he was fully recovered.

He crossed his arms over his bare chest. "I think this is where Satan fell on me."

"You're lucky you didn't snap in two. He was a big horse."

"Yeah." Luke stared out the window. From his bedroom he looked out onto the range and not much else. The barn and corrals were on the other side of the house. "Did he go easy?"

"The leg was broken in two places. I took care of him myself, boss. One shot to the head. I'm sure he didn't know what happened."

"I appreciate that, Jake."

He'd always scoffed at cowboys who mourned the passing of their mounts. In the future he wouldn't be so callous with his words. Satan was the first horse he'd tried to break. There'd been a bond between them, something he couldn't explain to anyone.

He turned back and glanced at his foreman. "What else is going on?"

Jake's gaze shifted away, and his body stiffened. "Same old routine. I'm deciding which cowboys to keep on for the winter and which to let go."

"And?" Luke limped to the straight-back chair, then sat down straddling the seat. He folded his arms over the back. "There's something wrong. Rachel and Sarah are jumpier than a mare in heat. Every time I go down to a meal, Ian is at the table and several of the men are hanging around outside. And you're carrying a loaded gun."

Jake exhaled, then sat up and leaned against the headboard. "You've only been back among the living for three days, boss. We didn't want you to worry."

"I'm fine. The doctor says there's nothing wrong with me a little rest won't cure, although I might go crazy if I'm cooped up in this house much longer. So what don't you want me to worry about?"

"John Steele broke out of jail."

Luke was glad he was sitting down. An icy cold raced over him, and the room began to spin. Just when he was convinced he was about to topple over, everything cleared. Anger chased away the weakness. Anger at himself. He should have killed the bastard when he had the chance. Now Rachel's life was in danger and it was all his fault. His hands tightened into fists, and he cursed his injuries.

"When?"

"Right around the time you got shot. The sheriff came by and told us. Steele killed one of his deputies. There's a posse out looking for him. He thinks Steele hightailed it back to Kansas after trying to kill you. Rachel disagrees, and I think she's right. I've armed all the cowboys. Rachel and Sarah are carrying guns. There's a dozen men guarding the property at all times. Ian's here because of Sarah."

Luke focused on the last alarming statement. "Because of Sarah? I remember Rachel saying something about her leaving, but I didn't pay it any mind. Sarah hasn't said anything when she's been mollycoddling me."

"Seems that she's been keeping company with Ian."

Luke chuckled. "I thought they were up to something."

"Ian wants to marry her right away and take her out to his place. That way there'll be one less person for us to watch."

"He's right. John wouldn't care about who he hurt, as long as he got Rachel. Do we have patrols out looking for him?"

Jake nodded. "Now that you're better, I want to head one up. There's too many places for a man to hide out there. We may never find him. But I know the land better than almost anyone."

"I'm going with you."

"Don't be a fool. You couldn't ride more than a mile or two without passing out. You'd only get in the way."

Luke hated having to admit that he was right. "You go on ahead, then, but as soon as I'm better, I'll head out."

"Don't do that. Let us take care of him."

"Why?" Luke frowned at him. "I'm not staying here and waiting for Steele to come after my family. I had him at the business end of a gun once, and I let him go. This is all my fault. I'll see this thing finished."

"By killing Steele?"

Luke thought about the pain in Rachel's eyes, the way she'd tried to scrub away the bruises, the trembling when she'd told him about the attempted rape. "Yes. I want to kill him."

Jake rose to his feet. "I'd think about that, boss, if I was you. Killing a man isn't something you can ever take back. Once it's done, it's done, and you have to live with it for the rest of your life."

He stared at his friend. Jake's expression gave nothing away, but Luke could see past the mask. "Did the man you kill deserve to die?"

"It was him or me," Jake said. "I didn't give it much thought at the time. Still, it wears on me."

"I understand. But there isn't any other way out. I owe Rachel that. Hell, I owe myself."

Jake picked up his hat from the dresser and put it on. "I'll take some men out and look for Steele. If we don't find anything, we'll be back in four days. Think you'll be fit to join us by then?"

"Fit or not, I'm going with you."

Chapter Sixteen

"I want to go after the gold now." Vern's beady eyes darted from left to right. "I been out with you all this time and ain't seen none. You promised."

John stared at the other man's throat. His fingers itched to wrap themselves around Vern's skinny neck and squeeze tight, blocking the air. He thought about how Vern would struggle, his legs thrashing, his eyes wide and popping out of his head.

A smile tugged on the corners of John's mouth. First Vern would fight hard, clawing at the death grip on his throat. Then gradually he'd relax as life flowed away. The powerful vision gave John a jolt of awareness that was almost as good as sticking it to some whore.

"John." Vern stepped closer. "What about the gold?"

"Stop it!" John shouted, jumping to his feet and tossing the last of his coffee into the fire. Another day like this one and he wouldn't just imagine killing Vern, he'd do it. "I'll take you to the gold when I'm damn good and ready." He stepped toward the smaller man. "You got a problem with that, you're welcome to leave."

Vern shrank against the tree trunk and nervously stroked the dynamite stuck in his belt. "No, John, I don't want to leave. I'll wait. I just thought"—he licked his lips—"that you might want to get some gold now. It don't matter none."

John swore. There wasn't any gold. But Vern would be dead soon and he'd stop harping on it. He glanced away from the other man. It stuck in his craw that Vern still hung on to the explosives. There hadn't been a good time to take them away. Every time John tried, Vern put up a fuss. Still, in a couple of days it wouldn't matter.

"I'm going to ride to the ranch," John said. "I'll see once and for all what's going on. Then we'll get the woman. Once I have her, you can take all the gold you want and we'll part ways."

Vern grinned. "I like that, John. It's a good plan. I'll make supper while you're gone."

"Do that."

He quickly saddled his mount, then turned the animal east. The morning was fading fast, but there was still time to get to the ranch and back. Maybe he'd get lucky.

"John! John! Help me!"

Vern's wild shrieking caused him to shift around in his saddle. The other man was dancing wildly by the campfire. The fuses from the sticks of dynamite hanging from his belt had somehow caught fire.

"What do I do?"

"Throw 'em, you stupid bastard. Throw 'em hard."

Vern yanked the sticks free and tossed them about ten feet. They rolled slightly and came to rest next to the keg of gunpowder.

"Holy shit." John kicked his horse into a trot, then urged it to a gallop. "The whole mountain's going to blow."

"John, wait for me," Vern called, running behind.

There was no way the other man would escape the blast, John thought as his horse jumped over a stream, then continued to run down the path.

An explosion thundered through the air. The ground below shook violently. Rocks and loose earth began to roll free. John knew then, in a split second of certainty, that the whole mountainside was going to go and there wasn't a damn thing he could do about it.

As had happened that first night she had arrived at his ranch, Luke awakened to the grandfather clock chiming the hour of two. He rolled over and wondered what had disturbed his sleep. The dreams were so much a part of the darkness that he no longer expected them to leave him alone, but this time it hadn't been a ghost that woke him.

Slipping off the edge of the bed, he pulled on his trousers. The loaded pistol, never far from his side, fit snugly in his hand. If John had come calling . . .

Stepping quietly into the hall, he felt the stillness of the night. The house stood silent, a sentinel protecting those within. He could smell the lingering odor of the evening meal, the rising bread, waiting for morning.

Dawg stirred in the doorway to Mark's room, raised his head and whimpered, then lay back down to sleep. Luke relaxed, knowing there could be no stranger inside. The animal might be stupid, but he'd protect Mark to the death if he had to.

Luke eased the gun into his waistband and moved toward the parlor. He knew now what had awakened him. Past and present blurred together in the night until he wasn't sure he hadn't lived this moment once before.

As he had once before, he sensed more than saw her standing by the window. The lantern on the table by the sofa didn't provide enough light to reveal her face; only the shape of her body and the liquid satin of her hair were clear to him. He stepped into the room, but didn't approach her.

He remembered his anger when she arrived, his pain at touching her, the agony of her confession, the contentment at her expression of love, the rightness of having her by him when he was unconscious.

"I didn't mean to wake you," she said, repeating the words of that first night.

"You didn't."

A light wrapper covered her, dropping in a straight line from her shoulders. One hand pulled back the drapes. "It's been three days and your men aren't back yet. John will come for me, won't he?"

She deserved the truth, no matter how much it cost both of them. He took a step closer. "Yes."

"I won't let him take me," she said fiercely. "I'd rather die."

"Rachel—"

"No." She looked at him. Her face, half in shadow, half illuminated by the lantern, reflected her conviction. "I need to say this. If something happens to me . . ." She paused and stared out into the night.

Her words pierced him like a dagger. "Nothing will happen to you. I'll never let John Steele hurt you again." He couldn't bear to be without her.

"I know you mean that," she said quietly. "And I believe you. But just in case, I need you to promise you'll take care of Mark for me. That you'll love him and raise him as your own."

"I already love him like a son."

"Promise me you'll never punish him for my mistakes."

"Rachel." He moved closer still, until he could reach out and touch the tears on her cheeks. But he did not.

"Promise me—" She swallowed. "Promise me that you won't let him forget Matthew. Ever."

The dagger plunged deeper into his heart, and he felt his lifeblood flow away. She could ask no greater sacrifice. He hated her for giving Matthew that which he had been denied. She might as well have asked for his soul.

"Promise me."

He gazed into her eyes. He saw she expected her payment for her request to be high. What she couldn't possibly know was that if he was forced to fulfill her promise, he would have lost her. If she was gone, he would have no use for his soul. And Mark would be the only part of her to remain.

"I promise."

She sighed, her relief as visible as her fear had been. "Thank you. I wish I could do something in return, but I know that's not possible. For what it's worth, I'd like to stay with you for as long as you'll have me. I won't go back to Kansas, no matter what. I love you, Luke Hawkins. I've always loved you. I was wrong to marry Matthew. And both of you paid the price for my folly."

He leaned forward and touched her tears. "I'm not interested in your apologies. There was a time when I wanted to hurt you, make you suffer as I had, but that doesn't matter anymore. Nothing matters except this."

Rachel felt his hands move away from her face and down her neck, then tug gently on her hair. She raised her face toward his. The fire burned out of control, and she could only pray to be consumed.

His kiss was gentle, a soft pressure that soothed and healed as much as it aroused. His fingers tangled in her long tresses, bunching them up in his hands, then letting them slide free.

She leaned closer, longing to become lost in his strength and passion. Her palms traced broad shoulders, warm skin. Beneath her touch, the muscles of his arms clenched and relaxed, rippling as though the contact burned as it pleasured. She was careful to avoid the bandage as she urged him on. But still he held back some part of his passion, touching his lips to her cheeks, her ears, her jaw, but not drawing her nearer in his embrace.

She arched her head back, exposing her neck to exploration. He trailed tiny bites to the collar of her wrapper. When she would have reached up to untie the ribbon, he lifted his head and gazed at her.

"Tell me you love me."

"I love you," she said solemnly.

"Tell me you'll never leave."

"I'll never leave."

"Promise."

Now it was her turn to swear. She took his hand and pressed it over her rapidly beating heart. "I promise."

With that, he laced his fingers with hers and picked up the lantern. They crept silently down the hall, pausing only to reassure Dawg, then made their way into Luke's room.

He shut the door and shot the lock home with an audible click. Rachel stood silent. She wasn't sure what he expected. It was true her marriage had taught her what a man wanted from a woman, but Luke wasn't Matthew. If their roles had been reversed, she knew that her late husband would have taken her in the parlor; their quick mating, accomplished on the floor, would have been over almost before it had begun.

She remembered the pain of Matthew's thrusts. The memory of John tearing at her clothes also joined them in the room. She wanted to be all things to Luke. Was that possible?

Her love for him swelled inside her until there was no room for doubt. If pleasuring him meant suffering discomfort and facing her demons, she would endure gladly.

Luke smoothed the bed, then pulled the quilt up and over the mattress. The sight of the familiar print, lovingly sewn by Sarah's hand, caused a lump in her throat. She and Luke would join now, as fate had prevented them from doing in the past.

She walked to his side. The lantern sat on the dresser, the glow reaching to the edge of the bed, but not beyond. She stood in the pool of light and reached for the bow at the neck of her wrapper.

One by one, she released the ribbons. Luke watched, his eyes devoid of color, his expression unreadable. Only the rapid rise and fall of his bare chest and the ridge pressing against the buttons of his trousers indicated he was affected by her at all.

When the robe fell to the floor, he reached out and cupped her chin. "Are you afraid?"

"No," she lied quickly.

"The truth."

"A little, but it doesn't matter. I want to please you."

"I will never hurt you." He swallowed. "Tell me to stop and I will." His grin flashed white in the dim room. "Even if it kills me."

She nodded.

He pulled up her gown until it bunched around her waist, then started to lift it over her head.

She crossed her arms over her chest. "What are you doing?"

He frowned. "Taking off your clothes."

"Why?"

He instantly released her and stepped back. "Rachel, I thought we were going to pleasure each other in bed. Did I misunderstand?"

"No. Of course not."

A sudden blush raced up her face. She remembered those afternoons in the barn years ago, when he'd bared her to the waist and lavished attention on her straining breasts. The memory sent ribbons of sensation racing over her skin. Perhaps she would do well to forget her experiences in the marriage bed and let Luke do what he would.

"I didn't realize," she said, feeling foolish. "I . . . Never mind." With one quick motion, she yanked the gown up and over her head.

He inhaled suddenly, the gasp sounding loud in the room. She fought the urge to cover herself, but he gazed at her with reverence, as though she were something wonderful to behold. The attention embarrassed her and made her proud.

Gently, with cautious hands touching nothing untoward, he lowered her onto the bed. She rested on her back, he on his side, facing her, one hand toying with her hair.

"In this light, it's almost silver."

"Are you saying I'm getting old?"

"I see changes. The girl became a woman." He traced the curve of her hip. "I prefer the woman."

Her legs stirred restlessly and brushed against the wool of his trousers. Part of her wanted him to undress—she felt vulnerable in her nudity—but part of her felt safe with the barrier of his clothing between them.

"I've dreamed of you," he murmured, continuing his caress, his fingers tracing the length of her thigh, then the narrowness of her waist.

"Nightmares is more like it."

He propped himself up on his elbow and glared at her. "I'm trying to be gentle here, Rachel. You're not helping."

"Oh." She giggled. "Sorry. I guess I'm nervous."

"What have you got to be nervous about? I'm the one doing all the work."

"Work!" Playfully she pushed on his shoulder until he rolled onto his back. "If this is too much trouble we don't have to be here at all. I'll just collect my clothes and return to my own room.'' She leaned over his chest and glared at him with mock anger.

"God, you're beautiful."

With that, he pulled her close. Their mouths met in a fury. Lips parted, tongues swirled. His hands moved from her shoulders to her buttocks. Long sweeping strokes left hot fire dancing on her skin. Her breasts flattened against his chest; his warm patch of hair teased her sensitized nipples into hardened points. Legs tangled together; the weave of his trousers provided a scratchy counterpoint to the gentle rocking of his hips.

She felt the hard ridge of his erection pressing against the top of her thighs. While she brushed her tongue against his and ran her fingers through his hair, she waited for him to fumble with the buttons on his pants, and then thrust himself inside her. Gradually, tension invaded her legs and back, and she stiffened.

"I told you," he whispered in her ear, then nibbled on the lobe. "I won't do anything you don't want me to do. Relax."

His tongue darted into her ear, and she jumped. "Luke, that tickles."

He did it again slowly, running the tip around the top of the curve, then sucking the lobe. Her breasts grew heavy and ached. Fire shot into her belly, and she melted against him.

"That's more like it. I won't hurt you."

With a quick twist of muscles, he turned her onto her back. A strand of hair got caught on her mouth and he tenderly brushed it away. He leaned toward her. She pursed her lips, but instead of kissing her, he traced a path from her chin to the base of her rib cage. Then he blew gently on the thin, moist line.

She shivered, but not from the cold. In the lantern glow,

he looked like a statue, some fine work of art, far greater than any mortal man. She knew this form, the shape and planes of his face, the width of his chest, the feel of his hands on her face. She knew the sound of his voice, his laughter, the light in his heart, the darkness in his soul. Only she had the power to hurt him; only she had the power to heal.

"Love me," she whispered.

He knelt, one leg between hers, the other pressing against her thigh. When his hands spanned her waist, then moved slowly upward, she arched her torso toward him. He stopped just below her breasts, close enough for her to feel the warmth, but nothing more.

For the last time she thought of Matthew's untutored coupling. Then she locked the memory away in a place where it couldn't disturb her anymore. She belonged only to Luke now.

She looked at his face, saw the desire tightening the lines around his mouth, and still he hesitated. His promise came back to her: He would do nothing she didn't want.

Slowly, cautiously, afraid she'd misunderstood, she sat up slightly, forcing his palms to cup her breasts. She moaned softly, her eyes meeting his.

"Yes," she whispered. "Touch me."

It was as if she'd released the floodgates. His mouth again closed over hers. Long masculine fingers traced random patterns over her curves, drawing closer and closer to her nipples. When at last his thumbs flickered over the tips, she sucked deeply, drawing his tongue into her mouth.

Again he began to rock his pelvis gently, his hardness brushing against her hip. Her hands pressed on his back as if to urge him closer. He broke the kiss and swore.

She froze.

"No," he said with a chuckle. "I like it."

Boldly she lifted her chest toward him. He leaned down
and nuzzled one breast. His tongue repeated the dance his
fingers had played, moving closer to the peak, loving it
gently. Each moist flick caused hot pressure deep inside her,
as though a line of pleasure ran through her belly to the
secret place between her legs. He caressed each breast
equally, his hands raising her to meet him, then leaving
trails of fire across her skin.

A pressure began. Something uncomfortably urgent. A
pounding that increased her heartbeat and thundered in her
ears. As if of their own accord, her hips moved in time with
his, seeking a rhythm that increased rather than relieved her
sense of urgency.

Luke half sat up and brushed the hair from her face. His
fingers trailed gently down her ribs and across her stomach.
She knew their destination. A few minutes ago that thought
would have terrified her, but now she was willing to allow
him his way. The ache made her arch toward his touch as his
palm smoothed the tight curls. He pressed slightly harder.
The need inside her increased, yet eased, all at the same
time.

''Luke,'' she murmured, not sure what to ask for.

''Hush.'' He kissed her lips tenderly. As his hand slipped
between her legs, his tongue moved past her lips. As a
finger sought, then found a point of sensation so intense she
thought she might explode, his tongue began to slowly
stroke and caress her own, mimicking above, the magic
created below.

Questions formed, but she could not ask for answers.
Colors blurred, but she could not identify them. Heat flared
and did not burn. She yearned for something impossible, yet
instinctively she reached for that end.

He moved faster. When she required more breath than
the kiss would allow, he applied his wiles to her nipples,

tormenting them until she felt herself begin to lose control. There was a moment of fear; then she reached out and touched his broad chest, rubbing her fingers against the hair and skin, trying to express with her touch that which she did not understand.

She strained for release. And when it came, she was so startled she almost forgot to breathe. His fingers moved in time with the endless ripples, prolonging the sensation until every inch of her body had been filled and drained.

When the last of the light faded, leaving behind a pleasurable drowsiness, she turned toward him for an explanation. Instead of speaking, he pulled her close, his tight embrace healing the last of her wounds.

They held each other. Her heart slowly returned to normal, but she felt his thundering rapidly. Gradually she became aware of his erection pressing against her stomach. At last she understood the urgency of his need.

Communicating without words, she shifted against him. His eyes met hers. The gray fire burned brighter than ever. She pushed at his shoulder until he relaxed onto his back. Following his lead, she traced a moist line from the hollow of his throat, through the mat of springy hair, down to the waistband of his trousers. Raising herself to her knees, she massaged his chest, used her thumb and forefinger to tease his flat nipples, and nibbled slowly across his jaw. His rapid breathing and low moans collected inside her, and she wondered if the magic would be possible again.

Then, as he had, she kissed him deeply, plunging past his lips to mate with his tongue. And her hand reached down to cup him.

He pulled her down on top of him, trapping her palm between them, then rocked quickly back and forth.

She could deny him nothing.

"Take your clothes off," she said.

He stood and quickly dropped his trousers. She stared at his nakedness, some of her boldness fading in the face of reality. Then she smiled and held out her arms.

He joined her again, but not between her legs. Instead, he knelt beside her.

"Touch me," he urged.

He was hard. Her fingers traced the length and breadth of his satin heat. He groaned at her tentative caress.

"Do it this way."

His hand covered hers and he molded her fingers until they encircled him. Then he showed her how to move up and down the shaft. She stroked with the speed he dictated. When she had mastered the motion, he released her and placed his hands on his hips.

"Exactly like that," he urged, then closed his eyes.

She watched him, seeing the pleasure chase across his face, the tensing of his muscles as he strained toward his end.

She slowed, then stopped.

He looked at her. "What's wrong?"

"I want to please you." She felt the blush starting at her toes and prayed the room was dim enough that he couldn't tell. "And I'm happy to do this. But I don't understand."

He touched her cheek. "Why I don't want to be inside you?"

"Yes."

"I do. But I think this is easier for you." He smiled. "For now."

"You think I'm afraid?"

"Aren't you?"

She searched her soul. "Not anymore. Not of you. I like this." She rubbed his silky length. "Does it feel the same?"

"You keep that up and we won't need to have this conversation."

"Luke. Be with me. In me."

Moving with liquid grace, he knelt between her thighs. Carefully he pressed himself against her, filling her until she wondered how she'd survived without him. Arms around each other, face to face, they moved together. His thrusts were slow and sure, deep and thorough. The pressure began again. It built up, climbing with each plunge.

She looked up at him, the way his mouth tightened with concentration, the lock of brown hair that fell forward, the straining and trembling of his muscles. The magic would return. Not this time—she felt him tense toward his completion—but soon.

The pace quickened. He rocked quickly twice, then stiffened. Their eyes met and locked. The mask was gone. He was raw and exposed; she drank in the sight of his release, the ecstasy rippling through his frame. His lips parted as if in prayer.

The only word he spoke was her name.

Luke propped his head up on one arm and studied Rachel as she slept. It was just after dawn. Fingers of light crept across the bed, illuminating a bare leg and the carelessly exposed curve of her right breast.

Long hair streamed out on the pillow. Picking up a strand, he inhaled the sweet scent, then rubbed the pale gold silk against his lips.

After years of dreaming, wondering about lying with her, he had at last tasted her passion. Blood rushed to his groin as he recalled the wondrous light in her face when he'd touched the softness of her body, then moved to caress the moistness between her legs. Although a mother and a widow, she'd come to him as much a virgin as the day he'd left Kansas. Never before had she experienced the heights of passion. He was pleased he'd been the one to hear those first cries of discovery, to see the sheen of need glistening on her skin, to feel the aftermath of pleasure rippling through her body. For reasons known only to him, Matthew had chosen not to teach her the pleasures between a man and a woman.

Luke rolled onto his back, frowning slightly when pain ripped through his arm. He wasn't completely healed, but that hadn't stopped him earlier.

He grinned, remembering how he'd woken up a couple of hours before dawn and caught Rachel leaving to return to her own bed. Their whispered good mornings had become long and passionate. She'd learned her lessons well, offering herself eagerly to his touch, spreading her legs and urging his hand to find the appropriate rhythm. After pleasing each other, they'd fallen back into an exhausted sleep.

Outside, a rooster crowed loudly. Jake would return today, Luke thought. And together they'd go out and find John Steele. When the old man was dead, Luke would return to the ranch and tell Rachel she was safe forever. And then . . .

The future grew less clear after that. All he knew was that he couldn't lose her again. His life had come full circle. She loved him and had promised to never leave. They would be married.

Plans of when and how many to invite were suddenly pushed aside when he heard a scraping sound in the hall. Instantly he tensed, then quietly slid out of bed. His gun was where he'd left it, on the floor beside his trousers. After silently cocking the hammer, he stepped behind the door.

The footsteps grew louder, then paused. Luke eased back the lock. The doorknob turned. He raised his gun.

A tall man took one step into the room. ''I see you're still in bed, you lazy old—''

Luke jabbed the barrel into his neck. "Freeze," he commanded in a low voice.

"What the hell is going on here?" the man asked, keeping his voice equally quiet.

"Jake?" Luke lowered the gun. "You should know better than to sneak into a man's bedroom."

His foreman turned to face him, taking in his nakedness, then glanced back at the bed. "I guess you're right, boss."

Luke frowned. "It's not what you think."

Jake laughed.

Rachel jerked awake at the sound and started to sit up. The sheet pooled around her waist as long hair tumbled over her shoulders, exposing more than concealing her bare breasts. "What on earth— Oh!" She yanked the covers up to her shoulders.

Jake tipped his hat. "Morning, ma'am." Then he looked at Luke. "I'll wait in the kitchen."

"You've got news?"

"Yeah."

"I'll be right there."

Luke quickly pulled on his trousers, then hurried down the hall. When he walked into the kitchen, Jake had already started coffee.

"So. What did you find?"

His foreman offered him a grin. "Half a mountain blown away. Two dead horses and pieces of what used to be John Steele."

Chapter Seventeen

"Dead? Are you sure?" Rachel stared at Luke, unable to take in what he was saying.

He nodded. "Near as Jake and the other men could tell, there was some sort of explosive in the camp. Probably dynamite. The whole side of a mountain has been blown away. No way anyone could survive that."

"Dead. I can't even imagine." A heavy cloak of fear slid from her shoulders and disappeared. Dead. John Steele was dead.

Even repeating the words to herself didn't make it seem more real. After all the years of torture and punishment, he could never hurt her again. She was free. Free to live her life without worrying about Mark's safety or her own. Free to come and go as she pleased without carrying a gun. Free to finally let go of the past.

She rose from her seat at the table, then crossed the kitchen to stand in front of him. When he held open his arms, she stepped into his embrace.

"I can't believe he's gone," she said, resting her cheek against his chest. "That it was all so simple."

"Simple? Hardly. After all that's happened . . ." His arms tightened briefly; then he reached down and touched her chin, forcing her to look at him. "Do you want me to tell Mark?"

His clear gray eyes contained only a hint of green this morning. She remembered how they'd darkened with fire during the night. His body felt warm next to hers, and familiar. She now knew, with a lover's intimacy, the exact shape and texture of every part of him. He had shown her how much he cared. That gave her all the strength she'd need.

"I'll tell him. And I want to telegraph my mother. Could we go into town or—"

He cut her off with a quick shake of his head. "You're not going anywhere today. You've spent the last week caring for me and worrying about John. Write up what you want the message to say. I'll have one of the men take it in. He can wait for a reply, even spend the night in town if he has to."

"Fine." Slowly she disentangled herself from his embrace. "I'd better go write the message and then tell Mark that his grandfather is dead."

"Rachel?"

"Yes?"

"Are you all right?"

She smiled and patted his arm. "It's a lot to take in. I'll be fine." She felt his gaze on her back as she left the room.

"So Grandpa will never come back?"

"No." Rachel sat crosswise on the narrow bed, leaned back against the wall, and tucked Mark more firmly under her arm. His short legs didn't even reach past the edge of his bed. "He's gone forever. He'll never hurt us again."

Mark nodded, then twisted around to look up at her. "Is he with Pa in heaven?"

How could she explain that God had no doubt prepared some special brand of hell for the likes of John Steele? Better for the boy to grow up believing in the goodness of the world. He'd seen too much of the bad already in his young life. "I don't know," she admitted at last.

"I don't think Pa would want to be with Grandpa, do you?"

She smiled at his wisdom. "If they are in the same place, God won't let Grandpa hurt anyone ever again."

"Do you promise?"

"Yes."

Thunder jumped on the bed. Her calico coat gleamed from her rich diet of table scraps and mice from the barn. She crossed the spread, walked across Mark's legs, and settled onto Rachel's lap. She patted the cat with her free hand.

"Are we gonna stay here, Mama?"

Thunder raised her head slightly, urging Rachel to scratch under her chin.

"Would that make you happy?" Rachel asked, rubbing the cat's jaw, then smiling as a raspy pink tongue swept across her fingertips.

"I like it here. I like Sarah and Potter and Socks and Dawg and mostly Luke. I don't want to go away."

Rachel leaned down and kissed the top of his head. She and Luke hadn't had a chance to talk about last night, but the warm glow in her belly told her that everything would work itself out.

"I think we'll be staying," she said quietly. "This is a good place to raise a family. But"—she glanced down at her son—"we have to wait and see what Luke says. He hasn't asked us to stay. So don't you go talking about this to anyone yet."

Mark laughed with the confidence of youth. "Luke won't want us to go back to Kansas. He loves us."

*   *   *

The day passed quietly. After Mark finished his lessons and ran outside to play in the barn, Rachel went to help Sarah in the kitchen.

"That's the last of the berries," Sarah said, motioning to the bowl of fruit resting on the counter. "Thought I'd make a pie for tonight."

"Seems odd to be celebrating a man's death."

Sarah clucked her tongue. "We're not celebrating anything to do with John Steele. In fact, if I never heard or even thought his name again, it would be too soon for me." She wiped her hands on her apron and began to measure out the flour. "Maybe it's a sin, but I can't mourn his passing. He was evil and deserved to die. I'm only sorry he took those horses and that stage driver with him."

The sheriff and his posse had been out to the site of the explosion. They thought two men had been camped there. Now both were dead.

"I won't miss him," Rachel said, sorting through the berries. "I just can't believe it's over. It seems too easy somehow. I guess it will take time."

"You've got as much of that as you need." Sarah added the ingredients to a bowl and began to make the crust. She cleared her throat. "Ian and I are thinking of getting married at the end of the month. We don't want anything fancy. Just the two of us at the church in Horse Creek. And you and Luke, if you're willing to stand up with us."

Rachel leaned over and hugged her friend. "I'd be honored to stand up with you, Sarah Green. You've been like a second mother to me my whole life. I'm glad that you and Ian are going to tie the knot."

The older woman winked. "Could be that we'll make it a double wedding?"

Rachel blushed. "Now, whatever gave you that idea? Luke and I haven't really talked about anything specific."

"That's not what Jake Evans said this morning."

"Oh!" She covered her cheeks with her hands. "He didn't . . . That is, I never planned . . . Oh, my!"

"Don't worry, child." Sarah's smile was kindly. "No one needs to know. Jake's closemouthed enough for that. I happened to catch him at a weak moment, when he was backing out of Luke's room. Seems he got an eyeful and was almost overcome by your womanly charms."

In spite of her chagrin, Rachel laughed. The look on Jake's face had been a strange combination of admiration and shock.

"I can't imagine how I'll face him again."

"Don't worry. He's comfortable enough with the painted women in town, but has always steered clear of ladies. He'll be more embarrassed than you. No doubt he'll avoid the house till sometime next spring."

"You'd better be right." Rachel finished with the berries, then walked to the window. "I hope I get an answer to my telegram soon."

"You sound worried."

"I am. It's silly, I know." She turned back and tried to smile. She had a feeling it wasn't very convincing. "I'll rest easier when I know everything is fine back in Kansas."

The cowboy returned shortly after sundown. Luke heard him in the yard behind the house and went out to meet him.

"Any trouble in town?" he asked as the man dismounted.

"Nope. But this is the longest telegram I ever seen. Took fifteen minutes to git it all down. Here." He handed it over. "I'll be turnin' in now, boss. Unless there's something else?"

Luke studied the sealed envelope. Telegrams were expensive. What could Rachel's mother have had to say that would take so long? "No. Thanks for taking care of this. See you in the morning."

He thought about opening and reading the message before he took it in to her, but that wasn't his way. The telegram was for Rachel. She'd tell him about it soon enough.

She had just come from putting Mark to bed. They met in the hall.

"Is that it?" she asked.

"Yes. Why don't we go into my office?"

She took the slim envelope and followed him. When they reached the room, she sank into a chair in front of his desk. The crinkle of paper sounded loud in the still room as she smoothed the sheet flat. He glanced at her, but she was engrossed in her reading. Squatting in front of the fireplace, he stacked several logs onto a handful of kindling, more for something to do than because the night was cool.

It was September. Summer's grip loosened as autumn drifted over the land. The room might be warm, but all of a sudden he could feel winter's chill sweeping across his soul.

The silence continued. At last he looked up and saw her staring straight ahead, the telegram crushed in her hands.

"What does she say?"

Rachel glanced at him, then away, but not before he saw the concern and determination in her eyes. Something inside him knotted up tight and cold.

"There's trouble with the farms. The bank wants its money or it's going to foreclose. Mr. Gridley has been pressuring Mama to take out a mortgage on our farm to cover the debt, then pay it off with next year's crop. The foreman quit." She sighed. "Mama never had a head for business. I was always the one who took care of things."

"And?"

"And she wants to know what to do. I can't advise her on the loan without looking at the books and seeing what the crops are expected to bring in."

He rose to his feet. The bitter taste on his tongue was unfamiliar. Then he knew: It was fear. "Dammit, Rachel. What are you trying to say?"

"I have to go back."

The cold knot grew and grew until he felt it pressing against his ribs. He swore. The long string of curses filled the room.

"Luke, don't. It's not like that. It will only be for a few weeks. I'll straighten everything out, and then I'll come back."

"Let it go."

"Let what go?"

She moved behind him. He turned swiftly and grabbed her arms. His fingers sank into her tender flesh. The contact had to hurt, but she didn't pull away. She faced him fearlessly, as she always had.

"Let the goddamn farm go," he said. "Let the bank take it. That's what you said you were going to do. What's changed?"

"John's dead."

"So?"

"The Steele farm belongs to Mark now. It's his birthright. I can't let that be lost. Not if there's a chance to save it. Don't you see? And when I've straightened everything out, I'll come back."

He released her and paced to the window. The walls began to close in on him. It was happening again. Despite all that had been between them, despite the night of passion, her words of love, and her promise to stay, it was happening again. His fragile dreams exploded into a thousand tiny slivers of glass. Each embedded itself in his chest and sliced away at his flesh until he knew he'd bleed to death.

"What happened between us meant nothing," he said, gripping the window frame. "None of it."

"No, Luke. You're wrong. I love you. I'm not leaving for good."

He laughed harshly. "That's what it looks like from here, Mrs. Steele. Your mother can't handle the farm? How can you fix that in a few weeks?"

"I'll hire a new foreman, then talk to one of the neighbors. I'm sure someone would keep an eye on things, for a share of the profit."

"It's always about money. You're running back hoping to save your rich farmland. Why? Suddenly this ranch doesn't look so grand anymore?"

"Listen to me." She walked to his side and clutched his arm. "I meant it when I told you I loved you. I want to be with you forever. Why can't I go home for a few weeks?"

"Home. Yeah. Right. Home has always been Kansas, hasn't it?"

She bit her lip. "I didn't mean home."

"Sure."

He jerked his arm free of her touch. The quick movement caused her to flinch and step back. The flash of sheer terror filled him with such anguish that the pain of her leaving seemed insignificant. He clenched his fists at his sides.

"I'd never hit you."

"I know." Her terror faded, leaving behind confusion. "I'm sorry. I just reacted. It doesn't mean anything."

"Just like calling Kansas 'home' didn't mean anything? My God, I've been a complete fool. You played me like a fish on a line. Inch by inch you've reeled me in. And I didn't see it coming."

"No. Never like that." Tears filled her blue eyes, but he

knew now they meant nothing. ''Why can't I make you understand?''

''Because I already do. The point you're missing, Rachel, is that you've made your choice and I lost. Once again duty and loyalty to your family have won out over your feelings for me.''

''You *are* my family. And so is Mark. But you can take care of yourself. He's just a boy; he depends on me to look out for him. I keep remembering how hard it was for you growing up on the Steele farm. You had nothing. And every day John Steele reminded you of that. Don't ask me to put Mark in that position. You of all people should understand that. I want better for him.''

Her words produced memories he refused to acknowledge. ''He could have this.'' He swept out his arm to include the whole ranch. ''Isn't it good enough? Why does he have to have that damned Kansas land?''

''Because it's been in his family for years. Because you might want to leave this ranch to your own sons.''

He looked down at his chest and half expected to see a large gaping hole. That was how it felt. She was betraying him again. ''Not a whole hell of a lot of chance of that happening now, don't you think? Tough for you to get pregnant when we're hundreds of miles apart.'' He turned and walked to the doorway, then glanced back at her. ''Or was that your way of telling me that I'd better think about taking up with someone else?''

The color drained from her face. ''I don't deserve this from you. I'm not saying I'm not to blame for the past. I am. But despite what you think, nothing has changed. I'm going to return to Kansas, take care of the farms, then come back.''

He shook his head. ''Don't bother. You're not welcome here anymore. Ever.''

* * *

"But I don't want to go. Mama, you said we could stay here on the ranch. You promised."

"Mark, stop it." Rachel served his oatmeal. "I didn't promise. I know you don't want to leave, but it's only for a short time. Not even two months. And don't you want to see Grandma again?"

"Maybe." He took a spoonful of the cereal and shoved it in his mouth. "But what about Socks and Dawg and Thunder?"

"I'm sure they'll be taken care of." Although she suspected Dawg would be relegated to the barn.

"What if they forget me?"

"They won't forget you." She heard the edge of temper in her voice and took a deep breath to control herself. Twenty-four hours ago her life had been perfect. Now everything was spinning rapidly out of control

Sarah removed the cinnamon rolls from the oven. "Animals don't forget, Mark. They'll be waiting. Like the rest of us."

"I don't want to go." Mark pushed back his chair, flew across the room, and wrapped his arms around Sarah's legs. "Don't let her take me. I want to stay with you and Luke."

Rachel saw that her friend shared the boy's feelings. Why didn't anyone understand? She wasn't leaving; she was trying to set things right. As soon as that was done, she'd come back.

Rachel left the kitchen and walked toward her room. After yesterday evening she wasn't sure about her welcome when she did return. She knew he had spoken in anger. With time he would come to understand. And forgive. He had to; he was her only love. Luke's door had been locked. But while the first time had been to provide privacy for their loving, the second had been to shut her out. If he'd tried to hurt her, he'd succeeded. If he'd hoped to change her mind, he'd failed.

Was she wrong? Mother didn't need any farmland. She owned the house and had a steady income. Rachel sighed. Should she simply let the bank take over the Steele farm? Would Mark, years from now, understand her decision? And what about Luke? Why couldn't he trust her to return?

She sat on the bed and closed her eyes. She'd thought their love could withstand anything. She'd been wrong.

"When will you leave?"

She glanced up and saw Sarah standing in the hallway. "Tomorrow. There's an afternoon stage to Cheyenne. I'll spend the night there, then catch the train the following morning." She shook her head. "Am I making a mistake, Sarah? Are Luke and Mark right?"

"Only you can answer that. I understand your tie to the land. It's how you were raised." The older woman lowered her head. "As for me, all I've ever had was Luke and now Ian. Nothing in the world seems more important than the two of them."

Rachel sat alone long after Sarah returned to the kitchen. She could see the past so clearly. She'd been wrong to marry Matthew, wrong to betray Luke. Was she making the same mistake again? Was there any way to prove to him that her love was sincere and freely given? Was there something she could do to convince him she planned to return?

Luke worked until past ten. Rachel sat in the kitchen and waited, the ticking of the clock marking the passing hours. Just when she'd given up hope, she heard his step on the back porch. He walked through the pantry and into the kitchen.

"You're late," she said. "I was worried."

He ignored her. There was water warming on the stove. He poured it into a basin, then stripped off his shirt and washed his face and torso. She watched the play of muscles rippling in the lantern light, the puckering of the scars across his back, scars that John Steele had created with strokes of the lash.

When Luke had dried his skin, he tossed the towel onto the counter, then dumped the water outside. On his return trip, he started to walk past the table without saying a word.

"Are you just going to ignore me?" she asked, rising to her feet.

He paused, but said nothing.

"Luke, I love you. I'm coming back."

"I told you before. You won't be welcome here. You've made your choice. Live with it."

"No. You can't mean that. How can you ignore all that's been between us?"

He spun to face her. "What's the matter, Rachel? Having second thoughts? Are you afraid one of your landed farm boys won't know how to please you? Are you afraid of marrying another Matthew? Someone who won't even bother to remove your nightgown before he takes you?"

She didn't know this cold, angry stranger. She'd seen him when she first arrived, but it hadn't mattered as much. Then there had been only a past and an assortment of dreams between them. She'd had only the memory of loving the boy. Now she understood the joy of loving the man, both body and soul. He couldn't turn his back on her—on them.

"My decision to stay or go had nothing to do with us or that night. It's all about Mark."

His gray eyes flashed fire, but not from any heated passion. These flames were cold, and the burns they caused would not heal. "It has everything to do with that night.

You lied your way into my bed. You made me promise to look after your son, made me promise never to let him forget precious Matthew. And now you're leaving.'' He bunched up his shirt in his hand and walked away. ''I don't even want to look at you.''

''Luke, don't.'' She ran to his side, her hands clutching his arm. ''Please. I must go. I've thought and I've thought, and it's the only choice I have. I'm doing this for Mark. He's my son.''

He stopped and looked down at her. ''I never knew my mother or my father. I was just some bastard kid that John Steele raised. He made my life hell for twenty-two years. You go ahead and do what you think is right. I don't care. As for me, my debt to him and that farm is paid. I never want to see the place or hear about it again. This ranch is *mine*. It's the only thing I've ever had that wasn't tainted by John Steele, and that includes you.''

She felt as if she'd been slapped. Her head jerked, and she dropped her hand from his arm. He walked away without another word, without even looking back. Slowly she sank to the floor and pulled her knees up against her chest.

She'd lost him. For a few hours they'd been in love and now it was gone. Had the mistake been hers? Was her desire to save the farm for Mark misplaced? Or did Luke not trust her enough? Was he too caught up in the past to understand that they had grown up and become people with obligations? That caring for her son didn't make her love Luke less.

When the cold from the night seeped into her bones, she rose slowly and made her way down the hall. The door to Luke's room stood closed.

Quietly she tried the handle. It opened.

She moved inside and stood staring at the bed. There

wasn't enough light from the moon to see if he was awake or not.

"Luke?"

He said nothing.

"Mark and I are leaving in the morning. I'm doing what has to be done. And when everything has settled down on the farm, I'm coming back. I don't care if you make me sleep outside in the snow; nothing will keep me from you. I love you. I'll always love you. And if you turn your back on what we have together, then you're a fool."

John Steele moved out from behind the corral and limped closer to the house. The wound in his leg had started to bleed again. He could feel the warm blood dripping into his boot. Damn. That old doctor outside of town hadn't done much of a job fixing him up. Maybe another shot of whiskey would make the pain bearable.

He pulled the bottle out of his coat pocket and took a long swallow. His fingers hurt as he tightened the cap. A couple were broken; that he knew for sure. And he had enough cuts and bruises to make him look like the sole survivor of a shipwreck. He welcomed the pain. It meant he wasn't dead. Somehow, when all hell broke loose, he'd been tossed behind a tree. The wide trunk and sturdy branches had protected him from most of the rockslide. He'd seen part of Vern's arm go rolling by.

John checked the bullets in his gun. There were only six. Not enough if Luke caught him before he got Rachel. Thank God the guards were gone. No doubt everyone thought he'd died in the explosion. Damn Vern and his stupidity.

He limped closer to the house. It was only a couple hours past midnight. He had to get inside before the moon came up and—

The back door opened suddenly. John ducked behind the

barn. When he looked around the corner, he saw that brat kid sneaking outside carrying a lantern. His dog came after him.

"No," Mark said, his voice easily audible in the still night. "You have to stay inside. If they come after us, you'll bark and they'll find me. Besides, you won't be able to keep up with Socks for long. Now, git." With that, he pushed the dog into the house.

John grinned. When he least expected her cooperation, Lady Luck smiled down on him. All this time he'd been worried about how to get Rachel away without anyone knowing. The boy would do just as well. Better, in fact. The drugs he'd stolen from the doctor would last longer in Mark's small body. He'd be easier to tote, too, once the sedative took effect.

Mark slung a sack over his shoulder and headed for the barn. When he reached the door, John stepped out from the darkness. "How you doing, son?"

Rachel stirred restlessly, pushing away the moistness pressing against her hand. It nudged her again.

"What?" she asked sleepily, rolling onto her back.

Dawg whimpered and pawed the quilt on her bed. She opened her eyes and struggled to a sitting position. It was barely light. She'd fallen asleep in her dress without bothering to pull back the covers. What would have made her forget to—

Memories of the previous day and night crashed in on her. She buried her head in her hands and groaned softly. Today she was leaving Luke's ranch. And if he had his way, she would never come back.

Dawg nosed her arm.

"What's the matter? Did Mark forget to let you out?"

She swung her legs over the side and stood up. "Come on, boy."

The dog followed her to the back door, but when she pushed it open, he just stood beside her, whining.

"What? Are you hungry?"

Dawg barked, then butted her leg with his head.

The last bit of sleepiness fled as vague unease slipped over her. Something was wrong.

She picked up her skirt and ran through the kitchen and down the hall. Mark's door stood ajar. She burst into the room. It was empty. The carpetbag containing his clothes stood where she'd left it last night, but the boy was nowhere in sight and neither was the small bag he'd planned to carry himself.

"Mark?" she called softly. "Where are you?"

There was no reply. Dawg nosed her hand and whimpered anxiously.

She dropped to her knees and clutched the animal's face. "What do you know, boy? Have you seen Mark? Can you find him?"

Dawg barked softly and shook himself impatiently.

She checked the parlor and dining room, then tapped on Sarah's door.

"What's going on?" The older woman clutched her wrapper tightly around her body.

"Mark. He's not in his room. Is he with you?"

"No." She frowned. "Maybe he went out to the barn to say good-bye to Socks."

"Oh. I didn't think of that. He never leaves without telling someone where he is, but I'm sure you're right." Rachel glanced down at the animal by her side. "Let's go check the barn, Dawg."

But her small son was nowhere to be found. Potter was already up and brewing his coffee. "Ain't seen the lad, ma'am. I sleep right by the door. No way he could get by without waking me up."

"I see." She clutched her arms to her chest. "Thanks. Maybe he went for a walk or something."

"I could help you look," Potter offered.

She shook her head. "I'll let you know if I don't find him."

She left the barn. Where could Mark be? Was he hiding on purpose so that they couldn't leave? But that wasn't like her son. He might be angry at her, but he'd tell her straight on. Could he have run away? That *was* a possibility. But he would have taken Socks. Mark didn't like walking when he could ride.

She was deep in thought as she approached the house. Dawg ran ahead of her, then darted to the right and started barking. She walked to his side.

A small cloth bag lay on the ground. Mark's bag. She picked it up, then frowned. It was empty. That didn't make sense. Why would he leave an empty—

She felt something small in the bottom. Small and hard and circular. Her breath caught in her throat. No. Dear God, anything but that.

Slowly she reached inside and closed her fingers around the object. There was a piece of paper in the bag as well, but all she could bring herself to do was clutch the small circlet of cold metal. She pulled it out and stared at it.

Then she screamed long and loud, stopping only to draw breath and scream again.

"No! Mark! Nooooo!"

Luke flung open the back door and ran out, Sarah close behind him. Potter appeared from the barn.

Luke reached her first.

"Rachel, what is it?"

Tears ran down her face as she held out her hand.

He took the ring and studied the dark and intricate design. "Where did you find this?"

"In here." She showed him the bag. "Mark. He's got Mark."

"Whose got Mark?" Sarah asked.

Rachel felt the earth lurch. "John Steele. John Steele has my son."

Chapter Eighteen

"Near as anybody can tell, he came through Horse Creek in the night. Two horses were stolen. Probably he was headin' for the train in Cheyenne." The sheriff pulled out his pocket watch and checked the time. "It would have left about four hours ago."

Luke swore out loud, as he paced the sheriff's office. "We never had a chance to stop him. But how can we be sure that he got on the train? He might have ridden south."

The conversation continued to flow around Rachel with an almost unintelligible rushing sound. Since she'd found Mark gone and read the ransom note, she'd been unable to think about anything except that her son was in danger and she couldn't help him. The ride to town had passed in a blur.

All this suffering because John needed money to pay off his debts. If only she'd mortgaged her farm as he'd demanded all those months ago, she thought, Mark would be—

Please God, let my boy be safe.

Her thoughts swirled together, overlapping and blending until nothing made sense. Rachel clutched the edge of the desk in front of her. This was real, this hard cool wood. As was the pain.

Behind her was the jail cell where John Steele had spent three months of his life waiting for trial. That same cell floor held the stains from the blood of the deputy he'd killed the night he escaped. She had known he was evil. Now she knew he was mad as well. And he had her son.

"I've sent a telegram on to the Cheyenne station," the sheriff said. "If anyone saw Steele and the boy, we'll find out. You might want to head down to Cheyenne this afternoon and take the train tomorrow."

Luke nodded. "I'd also like to send a message to the sheriff in Kansas. He can be waiting for John when he arrives and—"

For the first time since they'd ridden into Horse Creek, Rachel spoke. "No!" She looked up at him and shook her head. "Don't do that. If John feels threatened, he'll kill Mark, if for no other reason than to punish me. Let him get to the farm. Mark knows the house. If there's trouble, he'll have a better chance there."

Luke started to protest, but she held her ground. "I know John Steele better than all of you. The only thing he cares about is that farm. He wants the money for the mortgage, and I'm the only one who can get it. As long as Mark is safe, nothing else matters. He can have everything."

Luke's jaw tightened. "And I'm supposed to let him have you as well?"

The sheriff cleared his throat. "Why don't we go to the telegraph office and see if they've heard from Cheyenne? Couldn't be too many men alone with a boy gettin' on that train this morning."

Rachel nodded and allowed Luke to help her out of the chair. Everything seemed out of focus. Her whole body ached, and she felt that she'd never be warm again.

She thought about Luke's question. The answer was yes. If the price for Mark's life was hers, she was willing to pay. Tenfold, if necessary. She'd do the same for Luke. Too bad he wouldn't believe that.

The telegraph office was in the front of the post office and newspaper building. As they walked in, the operator tapped three times on the key, then rose to meet them.

"Sheriff, I got your answer." The young man thrust out a sheet of paper.

"Much obliged, Samuel." The sheriff read, then looked up, his kindly, wrinkled face pursed in thought. "Yup. John Steele was seen with a boy. They got on the train."

Rachel felt her heart pounding against her ribs. "Did Mark look all right? Do they mention that? Was he hurt?"

"They don't say, ma'am."

Luke touched her arm. "John won't hurt Mark. He needs him to get what he wants."

The burning began behind her eyes. "You don't know that. No one knows for sure. Mark won't take well to being kidnapped. John might get tired of keeping him quiet and kill him on the train, then throw him out the window." Luke tried to put his arm around her, but she pulled away. "I'm fine."

"Why don't you let the sheriff telegraph ahead for some men to watch the train? Not to approach him," Luke added when she started to protest, "but to make sure he doesn't injure Mark."

"No. Don't." She twisted her hands together. "We don't know them. Someone could try to be a hero and take on John Steele alone. He's already proved he doesn't mind killing people. The most likely person to suffer if something went wrong is Mark. I won't take a chance with his life."

"You're right." He touched her face, brushing away tears she hadn't felt fall. "I just feel so damned helpless. This is my fault, Rachel. I should have killed him when I had the chance."

"No. I'm the one who stopped you. If anyone is to blame, it's me. I just w-want—" Her voice cracked. She drew in a deep breath and stood taller. "I want my son back."

"Then we'd better head for Cheyenne."

John swallowed from the bottle, gulping until he'd poured the last of the whiskey down his throat. The wound in his leg had started to fester. He could feel the heat of infection moving up his thigh.

This was all Vern's fault. John cursed the other man's stupidity and his easy death. He felt cheated. *He* was supposed to have killed Vern. He'd wanted to do it slowly, making him suffer. Still, there was nothing he could do about it now. In a few hours he'd be back in Kansas. Then it was a short ride to the farm.

He glanced over at the sleeping boy leaning against the window of the train. Mark hadn't been much inconvenience at all. He'd come to once, but the medicine made him drowsy enough to be manageable. If he decided not to kill Rachel right off, he might keep her drugged as well. Then she'd be less troublesome.

He grinned and sank lower in his seat, wincing when he moved his leg.

"I'm almost home, Mary," he murmured into his chest as he tipped his hat over his face. "You seem closer on the farm. I'd forgotten that. All this will be behind us. It'll just be you, me, and Rachel." Mary didn't mind about the other woman. Rachel would serve her purpose, but he didn't care about her. Mary knew that.

He wondered briefly if Rachel would come alone as he'd instructed. If that damn bastard was still alive, he'd come with her. Didn't matter either way. He'd kill Luke. And he'd kill her son. Just to teach her a lesson.

He raised his hat slightly and glanced again at the sleeping boy. Not right away, though, he thought with a grin. He'd let her give him the money and think everything was going to be fine.

He imagined the look on her face as he watched her lover and then her son die in her arms. He laughed softly and closed his eyes to sleep.

Luke fought the rage and the guilt. Despite what Rachel said, this was all his fault. He could feel the weight of the gun in his hand, see John Steele crouched on the kitchen floor at the ranch, feel the other man's contempt. He should have shot him when he had the chance.

Then he remembered the sound of Mark's voice asking if he was going to shoot his grandpa. No, he couldn't have killed Steele in front of his grandson, no matter how much the man deserved to die.

The train moved through the night; the clicking of the wheels on the rails had lulled most of the passengers to sleep. Rachel sat upright beside him. Her pale face only hinted at what she must have been suffering. She wouldn't eat, barely sipped any water, and didn't attempt to rest.

Her fingers were laced together on her lap, the white knuckles visible in the dimly lit car. She'd withdrawn from him. Now, when he'd had time to think about and regret his harsh words, she didn't want to listen to his apologies.

Luke touched the loaded pistol tucked into his coat. There was another in the carpetbag they'd brought. One way or another he'd make sure John Steele didn't get out of this alive.

"Do you think Mama will have time to get the money?" Rachel asked softly.

"She said she would. Your mother has always been stronger than you thought. That's where your strength comes from."

She tried to smile and failed. "I don't feel very strong."

She stared straight ahead. "All I can hang onto is how much John loves his farm. That, if nothing else, will keep Mark alive. I'm trying to think like him, imagine what his next step will be, but I can't get past the fear."

Luke covered her hands with his. "I'm here for you, Rachel. I won't let anything happen to you or the boy."

"You're going to kill him, aren't you?"

He looked at her, but she continued to stare forward.

"Yes."

"It's right. I shouldn't have tried to stop you before. I see that now." Her hands moved until his rested between her palms. "I do love you, Luke Hawkins. Whatever happens to us, I wanted you to know."

He started to speak, to say what was in his heart, but she silenced him with a shake of her head.

"No. Don't say anything. I couldn't let myself believe it now. Tell me when this is over. After John is gone, show me what you feel. Take Mark and me back to Wyoming and help us forget this ever happened."

"I will," he promised.

Rachel's mother and the local sheriff met them at the train station in Kansas. After picking up the ransom money from the bank, the four of them took a wagon out to the Thompson farm.

"Stay with me," Rachel's mother urged her.

"No. I have to be the one to take the money to John. Otherwise he might hurt Mark."

"I just don't like you being in danger."

"Nothing's going to happen," Luke said, stepping out of the wagon and helping the older woman down. "You have my word that I'll keep Rachel safe."

David Brown, the new sheriff, offered Mrs. Thompson a

smile. "Don't worry, ma'am. Before nightfall, John Steele will be behind bars."

Luke glanced at the other man. Someone might go to jail this day, but it sure wouldn't be Steele. He climbed back into the wagon and picked up the reins.

Rachel sat next to him. He could feel her trembling, but it wasn't from fear. When she'd stepped off the train and seen her mother standing next to the sheriff, he'd thought she might explode. He understood her concern. John Steele was as stable as a lit stick of dynamite. The last thing they needed was to get him spooked. Only David Brown's promise to keep out of the way until Mark was safe kept her from throwing him out of the wagon.

"Mark'll be fine," Luke said.

"Two of my deputies are out at the Steele farm right now." The sheriff stuck a pinch of snuff inside his cheek.

"They'd better stay out of sight," she said, glaring at the older man. "I've tried to tell you he's very dangerous. If anything happens to my son—"

"Rachel, it will be all right," Luke said.

"They're good men. They won't make a mistake. Now"—Sheriff Brown reached behind him and pulled out the bag containing the money—"let's go over the plan one more time."

Luke ducked behind the tree. It had been seven years since he'd last seen this godforsaken place. But he'd never managed to forget it. Every building, every blade of grass, was firmly embedded in his memory. If he was destined for hell, the devil could make it easy on himself by sending Luke back to the Steele farm.

He looked up and saw David Brown creeping around to the side of the house. The deputies were concealed some-where in the brush. After checking the gun tucked in his coat pocket, Luke pulled the second weapon out of the bag and made sure it was loaded.

Six bullets in each. Twelve all together. He was a crack shot out on the ranch. He could only pray the skill wouldn't desert him if John tried to use Mark or Rachel as a shield.

The sound of a wagon turning up the path caught his attention. This was the part of the plan he hated most. Rachel sat tall and alone on the seat, the reins loose in her hand. In the midafternoon sun her hair glowed like corn silk; a long braid hung down her back. She looked determined. He knew she didn't have a gun; she hadn't wanted one. All he could think of was how easy it would be for John to take her out with one shot.

When she pulled up in front of the house, she picked up the bag containing the money and climbed slowly down. Luke cocked the hammer and waited.

As she walked toward the front steps, Rachel could hear her heart pounding in her ears. It sounded so loud, she wondered if she'd even have to announce herself. Around her, hidden from sight, four men watched. She could feel their presence even though she couldn't see them.

The house was exactly as she remembered it. Two stories tall, it stood white and gleaming against a perfect Kansas sky. The wide porch looked as it always had. An old couch sat on one side of the door, two chairs on the other.

How many times had she stood on those steps and stared into the sunset, wondering if she would ever escape from John Steele's grasp? In the distance, the fields stretched on forever. They were bare now, empty and forgotten. Would crops ever grow there again?

The front door stood open. The interior of the house was in shadow. She held the small bag in front of her stomach and called out.

"I'm here, John. I brought the money."

Something moved. John Steele stepped onto the porch, a bottle of whiskey in one hand, a pistol in the other. She was close enough to see his dark eyes, the lock of black hair that tumbled onto his forehead. Close enough to see the sweat coating his face.

"'Bout time you got here."

She recognized the slow, careful speech. He was drunk. Not drunk enough to black out, but drunk enough to be as mean as a wounded bear.

"I have the money," she repeated, holding out the bag.

"Bring it here."

"Where's Mark?"

John took a long drink, then belched. "Boy's right here."

"I want to see him."

"Show me the money."

Rachel took a breath. "Show me the boy."

John smiled slowly. "Oh, bitch, I've missed you. The way you fought me all the time. It was never easy. That makes it better. Before this day is out I'm going to spread your legs and fuck you."

She fought the shudder that raced through her. Bile rose in her throat. As the sun beat down on her bare head, she wondered if she'd live to see the night.

"Show me Mark."

John shrugged, then reached down and pulled up something from behind the couch. It was Mark and he looked unconscious. Panic threatened.

"What have you done to him?"

"Nothing." John let him fall back to the floor. "Just gave him something to keep him quiet. He'll come out of it in a couple of hours. Now show me the money."

She opened the bag and tilted it so he could see the bills. When he motioned for her to come forward, she walked slowly. Mounting the steps, one at a time, she wished she'd listened to Luke and taken the gun he'd offered. It would be so easy to shoot John Steele. So easy.

"Gimme it."

She shoved the bag at him, then ducked around to the back of the couch and dropped to her knees. As John had said, Mark appeared to be sleeping. His chest rose and fell with each steady breath. His small body was dirty but cool to the touch, and his color was good.

John pawed through the money and laughed. "It's all here. I'll give you credit for being thorough, Rachel. You always took care of details."

She glanced up and saw him toss the bag onto the couch. Then he drank from the bottle again. If only Mark wasn't unconscious, they could make a break for it. But there was not way she could carry her son and move quickly. If only—

"Is he dead?" John asked.

"No. He's sleeping. Just as you said."

"Not him. I mean Luke. Is Luke dead?"

She could smell the alcohol on his stale breath. The question caught her off guard. Dead? She remembered the stampede. John had started it with a rifle shot. She'd suspected it was an attempt to kill Luke. Her father-in-law wanted to know if he'd been successful.

"Yes. He was shot in the chest."

But she'd taken too long to answer. John's eyes flashed black fire. "So he survived, did he? Too bad. Still, it gives me a chance to watch him die slow. I'll like that."

She glanced toward the wagon, but from her place behind the couch, she couldn't see anything. John leaned against the door frame and grinned.

"I know you're out there, Hawkins. Step into the clearing or the bitch dies."

Before she could react, he grabbed her arm and forced

her to her feet. One arm held her against his chest, the bottle of whiskey dangling between her breasts. The other hand held the gun to her head.

"Now, Hawkins!"

He cocked the gun.

She saw Luke move out from behind a large tree.

"No, Luke. Don't!" she called.

"Shut up," John mumbled. "Or I'll hurt the boy."

Every breath he took forced his chest against her back. The heat from his body, the smell of unwashed skin, made her want to retch.

Luke walked forward until he stood between the wagon and the steps to the porch. The sun cast his long shadow over the flower garden on the east side of the porch.

"Let her go," Luke said, aiming his gun at them. "Let her go or I'll shoot."

"No. Drop it, Hawkins. Drop it now." John jabbed the barrel into her cheek. "I mean it."

Luke slowly lowered his weapon to the ground, then stood, his hands hanging loose at his sides.

"That's more like it," John said. "I'm finally going to kill you, boy. I thought about doing you first, but I've changed my mind. I'm going to shoot you in the belly so you'll hurt real bad. Then I'm going to make you watch while I shoot the boy and this one." He jabbed the gun into Rachel's face again.

Rachel never took her eyes off Luke. He watched John. She could feel the sheriff and his men moving closer, but was afraid to look for them.

"You know why you're going to die last, Hawkins?"

"Because you're a sick bastard."

John laughed. "Because you owe me." He lifted his arm and drank from the bottle. The pressure against her neck almost cut off her breathing. She gasped. Then he lowered his arm. "You ever wonder why I hate you so much?"

Luke shrugged. "You're nothing to me."

"That's where you're wrong."

John moved forward slightly, forcing Rachel to walk with him. She stared at Luke. He never once glanced at her, instead concentrating on John Steele. But she could feel Luke's love, and it made her strong. When he gave her the signal, she would duck out of the way. She only hoped the deputies wouldn't be too late.

"You killed her," John said.

"Who?"

"Mary. My wife. My first wife. The doctor told her, but she wouldn't listen. Said it didn't matter."

"You're rambling, old man. The whiskey finally pickled your brain."

Rachel could feel John's rapid breathing. Every breath whistled past her ear. She tried to twist away, but he held her fast.

"No so quick, missy. You'll have your turn next." He drank again from the bottle. "Mary wanted a baby. She had one. But it killed her. *You* killed her."

What? *No!* Rachel screamed silently. No! That couldn't be true.

Luke stiffened. His hands formed tight fists. "You're lying."

John laughed. "That's right, Luke Hawkins. Mary Hawkins Steele was your mother. That makes you my son. With her last breath she made me promise to raise you to be a man." He moved the gun away from Rachel's head and held it out in front of him. "I did that. Now you die."

"Get down!"

Rachel dropped to the porch. She heard gunshots ring out, then the thump of John Steele's body hitting the floor.

Fearfully she glanced up. Luke stood where she'd last seen him; a pistol dangled from his hand.

"Are you hurt?" she asked.

He shook his head.

She scrambled to her feet and ran to check on Mark. The boy stirred slightly, then opened his eyes. "Mama? Where am I? I heard this loud noise."

"Oh, Mark." She held him close and breathed a prayer of thanks.

"How's the boy, ma'am?" Sheriff Brown stood over her. His deputies hovered around the body.

"Seems fine. Thank you." She looked up, expecting to see Luke. But when the sheriff moved back, she saw that the front yard was deserted and he was nowhere to be seen.

Chapter
Nineteen

Two days later they buried John Steele in an unmarked grave on the far side of the churchyard.

Rachel stood with her mother. As the preacher spoke of redemption and forgiveness, she fought the urge to rage at a God who would allow such injustice. John Steele might be gone from this world, but his legacy of abuse and torment would live on to disrupt all their lives.

Words about heaven and eternity floated on the crisp September air. She could bear it no more. Bending down, she picked up a handful of dirt. After squeezing it into a ball, she leaned forward and let it fall.

The thud of the clod hitting the coffin made her sigh with satisfaction. She patted her mother on the arm, then walked away from the cemetery.

So many lives tangled together. Even after two days, she had trouble absorbing the truth of John's claims. Luke, his son? Not possible. And yet it was true.

At last so many little things made sense. Now she knew why Matthew and Luke had walked with the same easy, confident stride. Why, in a certain light, Mark looked much like Luke. Why that same lock of hair tumbled down over their foreheads, why they were both so good at ciphering. The same blood ran in their veins, uncle and nephew.

But to have John Steele as a father. She shuddered and

pulled her shawl tighter around her body. What would that knowledge do to Luke? Why hadn't John Steele taken his terrible secret to his grave?

Rachel climbed into the wagon, then urged the horse forward. In the last two days Luke had spent most of his time at the Steele farm. From dawn till dusk, he'd walked the land. He'd returned for the evening meal silent and haunted, barely eaten, then left to sleep in the barn. He spoke to no one. Not to Mark, not to her mother, not to her.

As she turned down the road that led to the Steele farm, she shook her head. All the time they'd spent arguing over Mark's birthright had been for nothing. Luke was John's older son. The land belonged to him. He'd raged at her for wanting to save something that, in fact, belonged to him.

When she reached the house, she tied the horse to a tree, then walked toward the porch. She hadn't been back since the shooting. Everything was as she remembered, right down to the bloodstain on the wooden floor of the porch.

She stepped over the dark circle and went inside. The house was deserted. A quick tour showed no one had picked up or cleaned in several months. Apparently Luke hadn't disturbed anything either.

From the back door, she could see out over the land. The bean field lay dying in the sun. The stalks, heavy and bent with their rotting crop, barely moved in the breeze.

Shading her eyes, she scanned the horizon. There he was, walking toward the house. She would wait. They had to talk about the future, their future.

After priming the pump in the kitchen, she worked the handle. Water sputtered out, first muddy and dark, then gradually lightening, turning clear and cold. Dishes sat on the counter; remnants of meals had dried into an unidentifiable crust. Maybe she should just throw everything out and start over. But that wasn't her decision. Everything in the house belonged to Luke now.

Rachel leaned against the counter and fought against her tears. A knot of worry inside her refused to go away. What if he still wouldn't talk to her? How could they plan a future together in the face of this new past?

Clasping her hands together, she waited until she heard footsteps on the back porch.

Luke walked into the kitchen. He stopped when he saw her.

"Is it done?" he asked. His gray eyes, so cold and blank, never looked at her.

"Yes. He's buried."

"Good."

He stood in the entrance to the room, his body stiff, his face expressionless, but that wasn't what made him look different. There was a detached air about him, as though part of him was gone.

"Some people have been calling at my mother's," she said. "They came to pay their respects."

"Like hell. This county's always been interested in what was happening with the Steeles. They just want to gawk at the only surviving Steele son."

He practically spat out the last word.

"Luke, don't. It doesn't matter who your father was. You've made your own way. You've always been your own man."

"You know what I found?"

"What?"

"This." He pulled a letter out of his jacket pocket and waved it. "It's addressed to John— It was sent to my *father* by an attorney in New York. It seems that seven years ago he bought an old run-down ranch in Wyoming Territory, then arranged to give it to me and make it look like an inheritance.''

Rachel hoped she looked calmer than she felt. The ranch was from John? "Then he must have cared about you."

He laughed harshly. "You don't get it, Rachel. He bought the ranch to get *rid* of me. There were some other notes and letters. I read them. Matthew was in love with you. John bought the ranch so his son—his other son—could marry you."

"No." She shook her head. "That's not true."

"He arranged everything." Luke walked across the room. "He cared only about Mary. The rest of us were nothing to him."

She followed him into the parlor. "Luke, I . . ."

He stopped and looked at her. The pain and horror revealed in his face made her freeze in her tracks. She wanted to go to him and offer comfort, but like a wounded animal, he would attack all who approached.

"I hated him," he said quietly, almost without feeling. "Every night, while I lived here, I prayed he would die. Every day I planned on leaving. He kept me around for all those years by talking about how my mother had been sick. He said I owed him and had to pay back her debts. He made me feel *grateful* to have a roof over my head and his generosity." He shook his head. "Yeah, he was real generous. I stayed here twenty-two years." He crushed the letter and dropped it to the floor. "And then I escaped to something far away. Something John Steele had never touched. Something that was mine."

She moved closer to him, but he didn't see her. He was looking past her to a pain she could only imagine.

"And I built up that ranch with nothing but determination and hard work. I was so damned proud of it. I'd made my mark." He turned to the window. "But it's not mine.

Nothing's mine. It's all his. I can't get away from it now."
He held out his hand. "The blood of that perverted old
bastard runs in my veins."

"Luke." She reached out to hold him.

"Don't." He pulled away. "Don't touch me. It's all
changed. I'm not the kind of man you should be around."

"I love you. None of this matters."

"You're wrong. It matters most of all. How can you stay
in the room with me? Aren't you afraid I'll hurt you? Hit
you, maybe? Get drunk and kill your son?"

"No. Never. I trust you."

He shook his head. "I think about it. That's all I can
think about. Will I wake up one morning and be John
Steele? Can I escape my destiny?"

"Luke, don't do this to yourself."

He walked to John's desk at the far end of the parlor.
There was a key in a cup on top of this desk that unlocked
a drawer below. "Matthew knew."

"Knew what?" She went with him, but didn't try to
touch him or offer comfort.

"About me. Who named Mark?"

"What?"

"Who decided what to name the boy?"

"I don't remember." She thought about the day
she'd given birth. "We talked and . . ." Matthew had
stood beside her bed and stared down at his son. She'd said
something about her father and Matthew had . . . "He
did. He told me he wanted our son to be named Mark."

"It's here." Luke unlocked the drawer, then pulled out
the family Bible. He flipped to the New Testament and
pointed to the Gospels: Matthew, Mark, Luke, and John.
"He was telling me all the time, and I never listened."

She stared, disbelieving. "No. It's a coincidence." But

she sensed, with a cold feeling of certainty that made her skin crawl, that Matthew *had* known. "How?"

"By this."

The front of the book contained the list of marriages, births, and deaths. Rachel leaned closer. There was her marriage to Matthew and, below it, the entry of Mark's birth. Above . . . Her breath caught in her throat: "June 1852, John Steele and Mary Hawkins united in marriage. November 1854, born Luke Hawkins Steele."

But the mention of Luke's birth had been crossed out. And below it, was the line showing Mary's death.

"There are letters," he said. "A few relatives sending their condolences on the death of his wife and child. He told them I'd died. Apparently no one ever found out the truth. When Sarah arrived, he told her I was the bastard son of his former housekeeper. He told me the same thing." His eyes, so empty and cold, briefly met hers. "I preferred his lies."

"I still love you."

"It's too late."

Luke turned and walked out of the room.

"Where are you going?" she asked, following him to the front door.

"To Wyoming."

"But what about this farm? It's yours now."

He stopped on the top step. "Keep it. Sell it. Give it to Mark. I don't care what you do with it." He stepped down.

"What about me?"

He took a deep breath, but didn't turn around. "You were right. You have a duty to your son, to see that he's raised knowing he has something in his future that will be his. You belong here, Rachel. Kansas is your home."

"No!" He couldn't leave her! "I love you, Luke. You can't do this. I want to be with you." Never had she expected him to leave. It was like stepping onto a rotting board and falling into a bottomless pit. "I want to come back to the ranch and marry you."

"How can you? I'm John Steele's son."

He never came back. She waited all that day and the next. And for a week. But he never returned. Mark asked every morning if Luke would be coming by, but eventually even the boy gave up.

Rachel sat in her mother's kitchen and stared at the books in front of her. The Steele farm could be saved, but only at the price of her own. Even with a mild, wet spring, they couldn't bring in a big enough crop to cover the debt. Farmland was selling at a premium in the state. She could sell one to save the other, but she couldn't keep both.

At one time the decision would have been easy. Her own farm had been her father's; she'd been raised there. The Steele farm held only unhappy memories. But so much had changed. Now the land belonged to Luke.

She clutched her shawl more tightly around her shoulders and stared out the window. It was already November. Snow threatened from a heavy gray sky. The winter would be especially cold this year, for she would spend it alone.

Come spring she would travel to Wyoming and try to persuade Luke they belonged together. But until then she could only hope.

"Rachel?"

She turned and smiled. "Yes, Mama?"

"Are we destined for the poorhouse?"

"Hardly. But we'll have to sell one of the farms. There'll be enough money left over to keep you in style, so you'll still be able to buy hats."

"I couldn't bear to be without them." Mrs. Thompson

smiled as she put her arm around her daughter. "You want to save Luke's land, don't you?"

"Yes."

"Then sell what must be sold to do that."

"Are you sure? We can keep the house. It's on a separate deed." She searched the blue eyes that were so much like her own. "And you'll still have your income."

Her mother patted her cheek. "You're my daughter. I want what will make you happy. I've never had anything to do with the farm. It doesn't matter to me. Besides, your father left the land to you."

"I know. But I didn't want to make the decision without your consent."

"I appreciate that." The older woman looked out the window. "I think we'll have snow soon."

"Yes."

"Will you go to Luke?"

"In the spring."

Her mother glanced at her. "And if he won't have you?"

Rachel drew in a steadying breath. How many times had she asked herself that exact question? "Then I'll live in the barn and follow him onto the range until he grows sick of me. But I'm not giving up. We've lost too much time already."

There was snow for Christmas. Luke urged Red through the bank to the last watering hole. Ice was forming around the edges. He chopped it away, then mounted his horse and headed back to the barn.

Ian and Sarah were expecting him for dinner. All his favorite foods, she'd promised. He'd go, more because she'd be hurt if he didn't than because he wanted to. He hadn't had much of an appetite lately.

After leaving Red with Potter, Luke walked toward the

house, then in through the back door. Only silence greeted him. For a time, Dawg had stayed in the house, but now the animal slept in the barn. Luke couldn't bear to watch Mark's pet mourn the loss of his owner.

He looked around the kitchen. It was time to hire a housekeeper to take Sarah's place now that she'd married Ian, but he just didn't care enough. His clothes got washed with the men's. And he used only the kitchen and his bedroom. Even he could manage to keep two rooms reasonably clean. Besides, having someone else in the house would force him to deal with Mark's and Rachel's rooms—and the past.

There were days when he could make himself go for hours without thinking of anything, when he could blot out the past and present and ignore his need. Other times he felt he was drowning in quicksand. Suffocating slowly, inch by inch, dying without her.

Nearly seven years ago, when he left Kansas, he'd felt, for the first time in his life, that there was hope. Rachel had promised to wait for him; he had promised to return for her. When he went back and found she'd married Matthew, he knew nothing could ever be the same.

But loving then, and losing, hadn't prepared him for losing her now. Then there had been hopes and dreams, whispered promises for the future. Now he knew the sound of her voice as she soothed her child to sleep, the feel of her body, soft and supple, reaching out to welcome his. He knew how she looked when she was tired, happy, sad, aroused. He'd seen her capacity to love those in her world, her ability to love *him*.

No, nothing had prepared him for being forced to leave her. Seven years ago she'd been the one to walk away from the vows of love; this time the break was his. That didn't make it any easier to bear.

He walked down the hall, his footsteps echoing in the stillness. He'd sent most of their belongings to Kansas, but a broken whistle and a torn shirt still lay on Mark's dresser. He didn't think the boy would miss them. He'd also kept a few things of Rachel's—a comb, a bar of scented soap, one of her nightgowns. When the days grew endless, he would stare at his meager treasures and remember what could have been, back before he knew the truth.

After changing his shirt and trousers, he went into his office. There was still time before he had to leave for Ian and Sarah's place. As always, paperwork waited. There were decisions to be made about the coming season. Ian was buying a herd in Oregon. Luke wondered if he should try that again or settle for the cattle he had. Were they going to buy one bull or two?

The large envelope still lay on his desk. The day it had arrived, he'd felt a flash of hope followed by resignation. He didn't recognize the small, even writing; it wasn't from Rachel. But it was from Kansas.

Every day he promised himself he'd open it tomorrow. And the next day he did the same. Three weeks of promises had passed, and still the envelope remained sealed.

"Hell. What's the worst it could be?" With that, he slit the flap and pulled out the papers inside.

The empty ache in his chest had been such a constant companion that at times he almost forgot about it. But sometimes, like now, it flared up to burn hot and bright, ripping through his gut with searing intensity.

A deed. Some damn lawyer had sent him a deed to the Steele farm. That meant the debt to the bank had been paid. Rachel didn't have any money of her own. How had she . . .

He remembered the bag containing the ransom money.

She had mortgaged her own family farm to raise that cash. Now what had she done?

He stared at the document and swore. She was trying to prove something to him. She'd proved it all right: She was crazy. By paying off the Steele mortgage, she'd put her own property in danger. The crop next year wouldn't bring in enough to cover what she owed the bank. He swore. Unless she'd sold her land outright.

Why? After all her talk about Mark's birthright, why would she risk everything?

He didn't even have to close his eyes to see her standing in front of him. Without trying, he could hear her voice, feel her touch, smell the delicate scent of her skin.

It was killing him. Day by day he was dying from wanting her. It didn't matter that he wasn't worthy of her anymore, that tainted blood flowed in his veins. It didn't matter that he'd inherited the legacy of a madman. He couldn't forget her and he couldn't move on.

All she'd asked was a chance to love him. He'd taken her devotion to her child and twisted it until he made her ashamed of her own protective instincts. He'd ignored her pleas for understanding, her confession of uncertainty. He'd lost the only woman he'd ever loved. And now, when he knew he could never forget her or let go of what should have been, she was out of reach. The barrier between them was as insignificant as a grain of wheat, as vast as the wilderness. What stood between them was the truth. A bit of information that had changed the nature of his whole world.

Slowly, almost without conscious thought, he opened the desk drawer and reached for the secret compartment. With a quick press, the panel popped open, exposing the contents. There was the deed to his ranch and the stack of letters. Each letter had a singed corner, a scar from his attempt to destroy her words.

The oldest letter was over six years old, the newest barely three. For the first time he picked them up and opened the envelopes. Then he began to read.

Rachel stared at the papered walls of the dining room and frowned. If it had been her decision to make, she would have ordered new wallpaper from the general store. But it wasn't up to her; the Steele house now belonged to Luke.

Rubbing her hands up and down her arms, she shivered slightly in the cold February afternoon. Snow covered the farmland, the white blanket stretching as far as the eye could see. Come spring she'd return to Wyoming and persuade Luke they belonged together. She'd already hired a new foreman. Together they'd planned the crops and discussed hiring a crew. Nothing was keeping her in Kansas except the weather. As soon as it was safe to travel, she'd be on her way.

"Mama, Mama, there's someone coming." Mark flew in from the parlor and grinned at her.

"Well, go see who it is."

She smiled as he tore across the room and out the front door. At last the sadness had left his eyes. She didn't tell him about her plan to return to Luke. Time enough when they were ready to go.

She heard voices out in front of the house. Oh, no, not callers! She'd moved back into the Steele house to make peace with the ghosts. It had taken several months, but she could finally sleep through the night without being disturbed by memories of the violence of the past. However, living here alone with Mark made her fair game for the neighborhood gossips. Several women had taken to dropping by to check on her. Their concern was kind, but . . .

She glanced down at the stained apron, then felt for the cloth protecting her hair. Too late to change. They'd have to see her as she was. It was their own fault for showing up unannounced.

"Mama!" Mark ran into the room. His dark eyes glowed.

"What is it?"

"Here. He said to give you this."

She took the piece of paper and glanced at it. A deed. She looked up, but Mark had run back outside. "What is this?" She read the print. It was for *her* farm? No one knew she'd sold it to the bank and what she'd done with the money except . . .

"Luke?" She pulled the cloth from her head, unmindful of the hair that tumbled around her shoulders, then ran out onto the porch. "Luke?"

A man sat on a chestnut horse. Instantly she recognized Red, then the height and breadth of the rider. Her heart pounded in her chest; her breathing grew rapid. She stepped forward, barely registering the cold of the air, the dampness of the snow piled up on the porch. Could he be real or was this some wonderful dream that would float away forever?

The man urged the horse closer. She blinked several times, but he remained in front of her.

"Luke," she whispered, clutching the paper in her hand, barely able to believe. Thank you, God. "You came back."

He nodded. The brim of his hat shaded his eyes; his expression gave nothing away. "I got your letters."

"I didn't write."

"The old letters you sent all those years ago. And the deed. You sold what you had for me."

Did she dare hope? "I wanted to save your farm."

"I know. And I saved yours. I bought it from the bank. Why are you crying?"

"Am I?" She touched her face. "I'm so happy to see you." She took a step closer. "How did you get here?"

"The train runs in winter. Maybe it's not as reliable, but it gets through."

"Does this mean you're staying?"

"If you'll have me."

The front of his jacket bulged suddenly. He undid the top three buttons, and a calico cat climbed out and yowled.

"Golly, Thunder!" Mark held out his arms. The cat jumped into his embrace, then rubbed her face against his chin.

"Socks and Dawg are at your mother's house." Luke swung down from the horse.

Her chest ached with the joy.

He walked forward two steps and stopped, then pulled off his hat. Gray eyes searched her own. "I'll always be John Steele's son. I can't make that go away."

"I know. It doesn't matter. I love you, Luke Hawkins. But I don't want you here."

"What?"

She glanced at the deed in her hand. "How did you pay for the farm?"

"I let Jake buy into the ranch. I've been thinking about taking on a partner for some time now."

She stared at the handsome face before her. Each line, each plane and hollow, was as familiar as her own. She would grow old with this man, be at his side, bear his children. They would live together in a house filled with love and promise. But not this house.

"I want to go back to the ranch," she said.

He turned the hat over in his hands. "Are you sure? I'm willing to stay here, if that's what you think is best."

"Thank you for that. But we've both suffered here. There are too many bad memories. I want to go back to where we were happy together. I want to help you raise cattle. I want to argue with you about the size of the garden and . . .''

He took the steps in one long stride, then gathered her close. His hands moved up and down her back. "I love you, Rachel. Always. Not a day went by that I didn't miss you and love you during all those years we were apart and these last months. I'll never let you go again."

He stiffened suddenly and stepped back. His gaze dropped down to her stomach. "What the—"

She rested her hand on the bulge barely concealed by her skirt and petticoats. "I'm pregnant."

His mouth dropped open. "When?"

She raised one eyebrow. "As I recall, it was at the beginning of September."

"No. I meant when are you having the baby?"

"The last of May."

"Are you all right? Have you seen a doctor? Is there anything I can—"

She took his hand and placed it on her belly. "You're here. Everything is going to be fine."

The baby stirred. Luke grinned and tossed his hat in the air. "Hot damn!"

"Hot damn," Mark echoed, climbing up to join them.

"You're going to have a brother or sister." He picked the boy up and held him close.

"A brother. I already told Mama no girls."

Rachel laughed.

"I wouldn't mind a girl if she looked just like her mother," Luke said.

He wrapped his free arm around her. She held on to the two men in her life. It was as it should have been all those years ago. Their love had survived the trial of fire; now it would last them a lifetime.